Masters Of The Broken Watches

RAZI IMAM

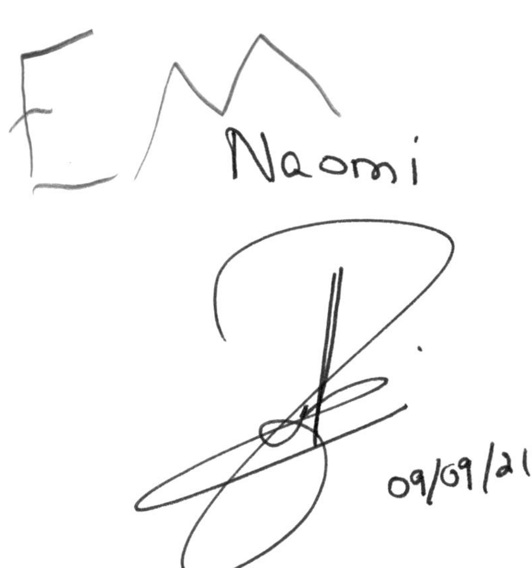

Masters Of The Broken Watches
by Razi Imam

This book is a work of fiction. Names, characters, locations and events are either a product of the author's imagination, fictitious or used fictitiously. Any resemblance to any event, locale or person, living or dead, is purely coincidental.

Cover Designer: Maegan Beaumont - MW Designs
Cover photograph provided by: Depositphoto
Interior Design and Formatting: Deborah J Ledford - IOF Productions Ltd

Issued in Print and Electronic Formats
Trade Paperback ISBN: 979-8616971159

Manufactured in the United States of America

Masters Of
The Broken Watches

RAZI IMAM

Praise For
MASTERS OF THE BROKEN WATCHES

"*Masters of the Broken Watches* is an incredibly self-aware 21st century global science fiction thriller. Its profoundly universal themes of family, love, determination and discovery are woven within an accessible yet fast-paced plot with incredibly relatable and captivating characters." - Farhad Asghar

"This book is jam-packed with action, adventure and magic! It takes you on a fantastical journey filled with descriptive imagery from start to finish. One of my favorite lines from the book is: "Gleaming beauty of the illogical moment."–which to me, perfectly surmises much of what the very real characters experience. A page turner for sure!" - Hina Khan

"*Masters of the Broken Watches* envelopes the reader in a world of adventure, science, mystery, and heart! It perfectly intertwines proven science with imagination that leaves you wishing the world in *MOTBW* could be a reality. An absolute page turner that is so vividly written that it feels like you are pausing a movie when putting the book down." - Zoha Imam

"*MOTBW* is one of those books that is hard to put down and once you have finished it, it makes you desperate for the sequels. It has a theme that touches upon the deepest mysteries of the universe that have mystified humankind since the beginning." - Sobia Ahmad

"Fast paced, gripping and entirely plausible. The length and depth of scientific research is commendable. Looking forward to the next episode, the twists and turns and the direction the story takes." - Arif Hasan

Praise For
MASTERS OF THE BROKEN WATCHES

"I found the story quite compelling and the book was difficult to put down. The science fiction was extremely imaginative and the characters believable." - Arnold Shoulder

"*Masters Of The Broken Watches* is one of those books that completely drags you in, and makes you fall in love with its characters. This is a novel with a thrilling concept at its core. I love the way the author mixed adventure, action and commonplace everyday life occurrences. Like the wonderful mouth watering recipes from around the world, which tempt you into the kitchen to try them out for yourself! In newspeak 'Double Plus good' can't wait for the sequel!" - Atiya Hasan

"A fascinating read that will make you question how we think and perceive time. Written in a pacy and punchy style, the broad arch of the story will leave you thinking about the possibilities for the future. The core concept is a unique take that combines an action thriller with science and philosophy."
- Kashif Hasan

"I was absorbed from the first page and couldn't put it down! Such colorful & vivid writing of a great action story interwoven with scientific facts and theory. I thoroughly enjoyed getting to know the characters and look forward to their further adventures!" - Lynne Zapadka

Praise For
MASTERS OF THE BROKEN WATCHES

"As an avid reader, finding a book that is wondrously unique is like finding a rare gem. Masters of the Broken Watches is such a book! This science fiction thriller is an action-packed paged turner featuring exceptional and well-developed characters (some you'll love; some you'll love to hate!) and a plot that's unlike any I've come across before. It's comprised of all the things that make up a masterful story. The level of research the author had to perform in order to write this book is impressive to say the least. You will not want to put *MOTBW* down, and you'll be left aching for a sequel. I highly, excitedly recommend!" - Ruth Netanel

"A rousing adventure. I finished *MOTBW* last night and thought it was excellent! I found it to be filled with so many clever, creative ideas and interesting characters who were constantly thrust into difficult situations I didn't know how they were going to escape. For all the grandness of the story, it was the details included (the food, the technology, the settings) that really grabbed me and pulled me in. It's a truly impressive work." - Shad Connely

"The author has masterfully created a fantastic adventure while weaving in details predicated on scientific principles. The reader is empowered to vicariously experience this stimulating journey through the eyes of the protagonists. This novel is a captivating page-turner that is hard to put down." - Andy Mecs

DEDICATION

Wave:
A wave brings energy, motion and power.
It shapes the shores, carves rocks and creates structures.
It brings balance, and rejuvenation.
It brings life.

This book is dedicated to my wife Saman, the wave of my life.

"Your reality is not what you see, feel or live.
It is what you think, wonder and dream."

~ Razi Imam

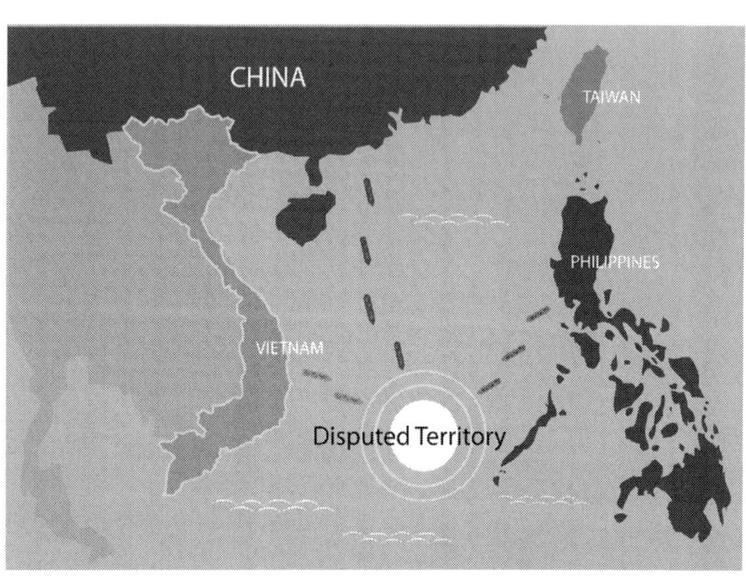
CHINA
TAIWAN
PHILIPPINES
VIETNAM
Disputed Territory

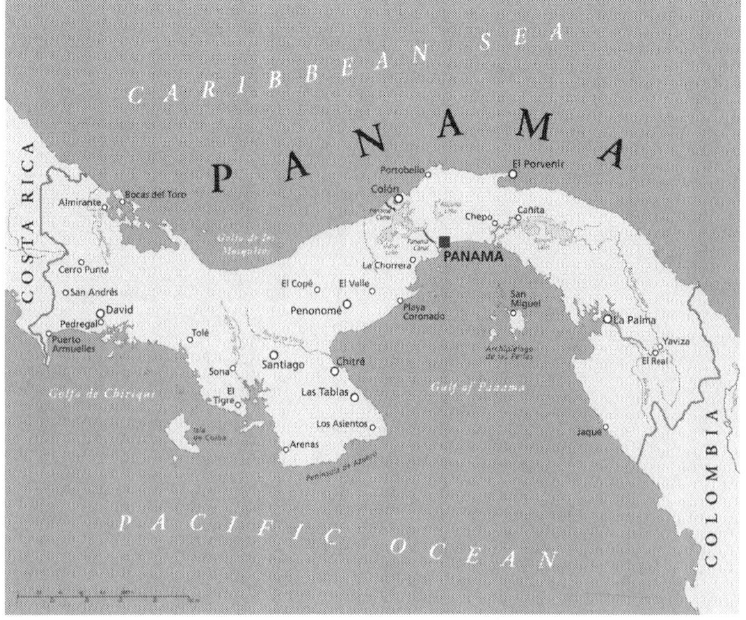
CARIBBEAN SEA
PANAMA
COSTA RICA
Portobello
El Porvenir
Colón
Almirante
Bocas del Toro
Chepo
Cañita
PANAMA
La Chorrera
Cerro Punta
San Andrés
El Copé
El Valle
David
Penonomé
Playa Coronado
San Miguel
Pedregal
La Palma
Puerto Armuelles
Tolé
Yaviza
El Real
Santiago
Chitré
Soná
Golfo de Chiriquí
Gulf of Panama
El Tigre
Las Tablas
Los Asientos
Jaqué
Arenas
PACIFIC OCEAN
COLOMBIA

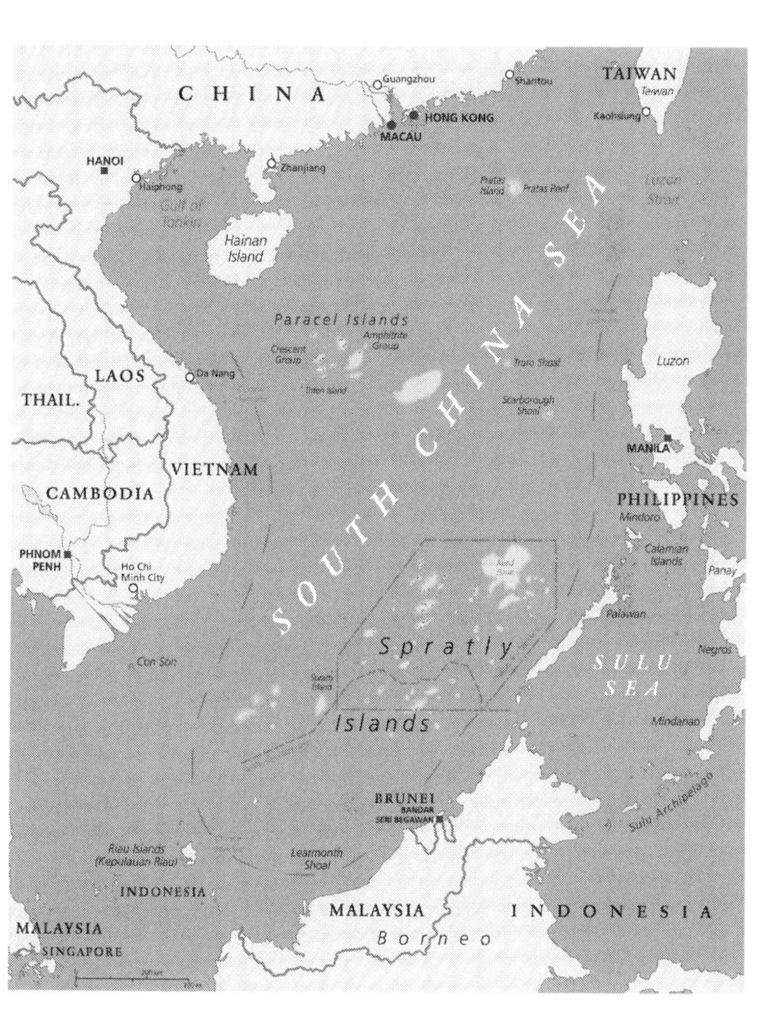

CHINA
TAIWAN
Taiwan
Guangzhou
Shantou
Kaohsiung
HONG KONG
MACAU
HANOI
Haiphong
Zhanjiang
Gulf of Tonkin
Hainan Island
Pratas Island
Pratas Reef
Luzon Strait
SOUTH CHINA SEA
Paracel Islands
Amphitrite Group
Crescent Group
Triton Island
Truro Shoal
Scarborough Shoal
Luzon
MANILA
LAOS
THAIL.
Da Nang
VIETNAM
CAMBODIA
PHNOM PENH
Ho Chi Minh City
PHILIPPINES
Mindoro
Calamian Islands
Panay
Palawan
Negros
Spratly Islands
Con Son
SULU SEA
Mindanao
Sulu Archipelago
BRUNEI
BANDAR SERI BEGAWAN
Riau Islands (Kepulauan Riau)
Learmonth Shoal
INDONESIA
MALAYSIA
Borneo
SINGAPORE

PROLOGUE
The Red Mist

Yucatán Peninsula - 300 A.D.

"THEY ARE TAKING my child away!" Itzel cried, looking out of her hut at two approaching military guards. The red mist behind them blurred through her tears.

"Itzel, Quiche law is clear," her husband Sachihiro answered softly. "When the war chief summons for a family's baby, he must be handed over." Tears flowed down his cheeks as he held their ten-month-old boy in his lap. The baby reached his hands up to his father's face, cooing.

"They are taking him into the red mist!" Itzel shouted. "I will miss his entire childhood." She gazed at her child, stroking his forehead.

One of the guards barged in and took the child from Sachihiro's arms. Itzel followed him out, crying and pleading, "Don't take my child! Please, please, don't take my child!" Other villagers stood outside their huts, watching the traumatic separation.

Itzel and Sachihiro hung close to the guard as he approached the mist. A second guard pointed his obsidian spear, warning them not to follow. They collapsed to the ground in despair as the guard and their baby disappeared into the wall of glowing red particles.

Three days later, a young man approached their hut. Itzel stepped outside and smiled as the man bowed. She traced her hands across his face. "Sachihiro," she called, her voice trembling, "our son has returned."

CHAPTER ONE
The Su Vang Fish

PHAM KAI STEPPED into his front yard. His house was tiny, a single room with a small area for a kitchen. The walls were made of coarse cement with a thin corrugated sheet of tin for a roof. The floor was a packed mixture of mud and red clay that gave off an earthy scent when water was sprinkled on it. It was a clean house. His front yard was a small piece of land no bigger than a dinner table. An old wooden bench sat under a blue tarp stretching out from the house, supported by two bamboo sticks. He sat down, admiring the changing shades of the dusky sea.

There were dozens of boats anchored in the water, including his modest twenty-five-foot schooner. It had a deep hull to store fish and a small cabin to protect him from rain and storm. A ninety-horsepower engine allowed him to head deep into the South China Sea, where there were strong fishing lanes. The top of the cabin had two spotlights that helped him navigate treacherous reefs at night. His boat was painted deep blue, with an orange and yellow accent stripe running its full length. On the beach were scattered several round, traditional blue bamboo basket boats. They were quite sturdy, used to transport fish from the boats to the shore.

Pham Kai was a third-generation fisherman. As a young man, he remembered the long debates he had with his father about not wanting to go into the family business. Pham Kai wanted to become an engineer. It was such a big world, he'd thought, with so many experiences to be had. But he had been anchored to fishing by birth. While sitting on his bench, he often wondered what it would have been like if he had followed his dream. Now, at fifty-three, it was too late for him.

Every evening, his wife Minh would join him on the bench, and they would look out to sea. She would chat about her day and he would smile and nod from time to time. Soon after, they would walk down a gravel pathway and reach their usual spot, a village sports bar—no more than a tiny shop with a cooler full of local beer. There were two foosball tables placed outside under the same kind of tarp, they had at home, accompanied by a few tables and benches.

They would find a spot with a view of the sea and order two cold beers. Often, other fishermen and their wives would join them, and they would spend hours talking about their day, which to Pham Kai was the same old routine—leave at two in the morning to catch fish, be back home four hours later to clean them with the help of his wife, then take them to market to sell to local stores and restaurants, and return home by noon. He would earn 700,000 Vietnamese dong a day, equivalent to thirty American dollars. Life was hard yet honorable in this tiny Vietnamese fishing village of Nhon Ly.

Each time, after the third beer, the stories would shift to fantasy. Tales would be told of fishermen in other villages who had caught the famous su vang fish. Su vang was a rare delicacy, and it was believed they held unique medicinal properties. A fully-grown specimen could fetch as much as $25,000. This was the dream of all fishermen—to one day find a su vang in their nets. Such a catch would change their lives, allowing them to move inland to a better home, educate their kids, and maybe even travel.

Tonight was no different. Stories were flying and so was the beer. Pham Kai remained quiet and listened. The loudest and most boisterous fishermen had peculiar marks on their hands and necks, like two puncture holes. Out of courtesy, he didn't ask about them.

On their walk home, Minh did not say much. Often, she would be discussing local village politics or bigger economic issues related to fishing, like pollution. Pham Kai was always impressed with her knowledge–she would have made an amazing leader or businesswoman, had she been given a chance. She was the one reason his long years as a fisherman didn't seem so hard. She was his best friend and his life.

"Why so quiet?" he asked.

Minh hesitated, sighing. "Pham Kai, I found a lump on my left breast last week. I got it checked at the local health clinic. They took an X-ray, and the doctor said I need to get to a hospital in Qui Nhon City for further tests."

Pham Kai stared at her. "Why didn't you tell me all this before?" he asked.

Minh smiled. "Look at you. I knew you would get too worried. I wanted to make sure before I said anything."

Pham Kai shook his head in frustration. He remained silent for the rest of the walk, all the while holding her hand. As they reached their house, he turned to her. "Tomorrow, we'll go to the hospital in Qui Nhon. We'll meet the doctors and see what they have to say."

The next day, they took the early morning bus, arriving in the city two hours later. Pham Kai had never visited such a large hospital in his life. They waited eight hours before the doctor could see them.

After looking at the X-ray, the doctor ordered an immediate biopsy. While Minh rested for the night in one of the wards, Pham Kai found a wooden pallet in one of the corridors. He laid out a small towel to protect himself from splinters, and slept.

The next morning, they both waited for the doctor in an examining room with bare white walls, every minute felt longer than usual.

She appeared, holding a file with Minh's test results. Placing herself on a rotating stool, she opened the file and leafed through it. "There is no easy what to say this," she said. "Minh, you have an aggressive form of cancer. You need immediate surgery, then chemotherapy." She paused to see if the simple couple understood the significance of what she was saying.

Minh started tearing up. Pham Kai held her close and asked, "What does this mean? Can she be cured? When do we start the treatment?"

The doctor nodded and said, "Here's the problem—if we wait to get you treated under the government program, it'll take a year-and-a-half before your turn comes up. And that may be too late. I recommend you take the private treatment route."

She paused again. The doctor knew that this humble couple might not have the funds for private treatment. She bowed and left the two of them in the cold lifeless room.

On the bus ride home, they were able to find seats next to one another. He held her hands and kept hugging her. Minh knew this was killing Pham Kai inside. He was such a strong man. He'd faced extreme danger so many times while out fishing—getting caught in storms and surviving sixty-foot waves. But this was different. This was her storm.

"Minh, we will sell our boat and our house to start your treatment."

She smiled. "I'm sure we'll be able to work something out, but I don't think we should sell our boat. It provides our income. And selling our house will mean we'll have to rent. Let's just get home. We can discuss this later." She squeezed his hands and put her head on his shoulder.

Once they got home, they ate their dinner in silence, and afterward they walked to the same bar. This time, Pham Kai paid closer attention to the boisterous fishermen. A few of them regaled stories of a fisherman who had caught a su vang near the ominous Bombay Reef, a particularly nasty member of the Paracel archipelago. It was dangerous to fish in that area, as most of the islands didn't have well-documented reef maps. Even worse, there was the threat of being caught by the Chinese Navy. There were stories about them torturing Vietnamese fishermen for days and then releasing them.

On their walk home, Pham Kai held his hands behind his back and Minh knew he was deep in thought.

"What are you thinking, Pham Kai?" Minh asked.

Pham Kai stopped. He could see the lights of the fishing boats on the bay and hear the waves breaking on the beach. "Minh," Pham Kai said, "I'm going to catch a su vang."

CHAPTER TWO
Bombay Reef

IN HIS THIRTY-plus years as a fisherman, Pham Kai had on several occasions ventured close to the Paracel Islands, where the quality and quantity of catch was always strong. But for the last ten years or so, he had avoided them. The danger of fishing in these waters was too high.

Bombay Reef was ten miles long, located near the south-eastern zone of the Paracel Islands. A rock-strewn lagoon sat at its center. Visibility approached zero when squalls rose up. The surrounding sea was greenish-blue in color, with clarity that allowed one to see the ocean floor at twenty to thirty feet. The area was known for sunken wrecks, so the reef wasn't the only thing that could cause problems—wrecked ships could sink fishing boats, too.

Pham Kai reached underneath their bed and dragged out an old metal trunk. Pulling a tiny set of keys from the inside pocket of his kurta, he opened the padlock. Tucked inside sat a bundle of papers wrapped in a faded plastic sheet, held together with a rubber band. He began to lay them out on the jute floor mat.

Minh watched him sort the papers under the soft lantern light. The pages were old, with a light brown tint, their ink faded with age. They were nautical maps of the Paracel Islands, hand-drawn and annotated by his father and grandfather. They were more accurate than any modern map, and the notes detailed wind speeds, current changes by time of day and month, every last detail of the reefs and sunken wrecks. If he had any chance of helping his wife, these papers were the key.

Pham Kai started to sketch out a plan to reach the reef. It was about a hundred nautical miles from his beach. He could get there in about three to four hours, give or take wind speed and current. He was glad it wasn't monsoon season, which would have further complicated his mission. The trunk also contained his grandfather's wristwatch, an old Tissot, complete with a metal strap, in addition to a small compass and an old-style lantern.

Minh saw the wristwatch. "What are you planning?" she asked.

"I need an extra set of nylon nets to increase our odds of catching the fish," he explained. "I'll pawn Baba's things to buy the materials."

"Please," Minh pleaded, "I don't want you to do this."

"What would I do without you?" Pham Kai asked her, helpless. "I must find a way to get your treatment started, and this plan is the only chance we have." Minh lowered her eyes toward the jute mat, knowing he wouldn't change his mind.

THE NEXT MORNING, Pham Kai got to the village pawnshop and met with the owner, who had run the place for over forty-five years. He recognized Pham Kai's grandfather's watch. "Did you know your grandfather was one of three people in the entire village to have a wristwatch at the time?" He regarded Pham Kai with sad eyes. "Life must have thrown you a real test."

Pham Kai nodded, determined.

"Tell you what," the owner said. "I'll hold the wristwatch

for you. One day you may want it back. You can keep the compass and lantern." He then loaned Pham Kai the funds needed for his plan.

Pham Kai went straight to the local store and bought the necessary items for his fishing net. He spent the afternoon building it, then went to bed after an early dinner. At 9:00 p.m., Minh woke him and gave him a large mug of chai. She made it how he liked it—piping hot, sweetened with cane sugar and milk. Pham Kai took the mug and sat on the bench, looking out at the sea. After finishing the chai, he got ready in his standard fisherman gear—a loose-fitting hooded shirt, heavy trousers, rubber boots, and his favorite khaki cap. There was nothing special about the cap, except that it fit well and he thought it was lucky.

He embraced his wife. "Go to sleep. I'll be back when you wake up, and if the sea favors us, I'll have a su vang."

He walked over to the beach, dragged his small blue basket boat into the water. With a few rapid to and fro motions of the paddle, he headed to his fishing boat. He climbed aboard a few minutes later, and stowed away his gear and basket boat.

At a quarter to two in the morning, he reached the coordinates highlighted in his notes. The ocean was pitch dark—he couldn't even see the far distant lights of container ships heading to Vietnam. As he shut down the motor and dropped anchor, he could hear the water splashing against the reefs and rocks of Bombay Reef. He kept a keen eye out for Chinese patrol boats—if they were to come, he would need to shut down all movement and hope they didn't notice him in the dark.

He grabbed the net, walked over to the starboard side, and switched on the spotlight attached to the top of the cabin. The surrounding area lit up, showing the reef and a nearby school of fish. He folded the net over his left shoulder, opening it and flipping the weights over his right hand. He then walked over to the edge of the boat and in one smooth, practiced motion, swung the net out over the water.

The net made a subtle splash and sank. Using the drawstring attached to the Braille lines, he began to haul the net back in. He caught about a dozen fish in his first cast, and it took a bit more strength than usual to pull the net onto the boat—the hauls were larger out here. One by one, he placed each fish in a large galvanized tin bucket full of seawater. He cast three more times on the starboard side before switching to port.

The port side yielded little—the fish had moved. He decided he needed to take the boat maybe half a mile north, alongside the reef. Five minutes later, he anchored again. As he shut off his motor, he caught a glimpse of a spotlight in the water about a mile away. He wasn't sure if he had been seen—his cabin lights and spotlights were off, and the water hitting the reef was loud, so they couldn't have heard his motor running. He rushed and tied one end of a thirty-foot rope to the bow of his vessel and the other end to his basket boat. He then lowered the basket boat into the water, and without making a sound stepped into it with his anchor. He rowed deeper into the heart of the reef, dropped anchor to secure his position, and then pulled the fishing boat closer to him.

The patrol boat approached, chugging to a stop about two hundred feet away. He could see the captain in the cabin. He was shouting at his crew in Chinese. They started sweeping the surface of the sea with their spotlights in a consistent figure eight pattern. The spotlight kept missing Pham Kai each time by a few feet. Holding his breath, the only noise he made was the water lapping against the sides of his basket boat. Just as he thought they were going to spot him, the boat swung away and sped to the southern tip of Bombay Reef.

Pham Kai pulled the anchor and climbed back onto his

fishing boat, pulling the basket boat up behind him. He noted the patrol boat's movements—they remained in sight for over an hour, then moved around the reef behind the lagoon and out of sight.

He cast his nets for another hour, catching several dozen more fish. At six in the morning, he headed back. An hour later, after confirming he was safe, he shut off the motor and anchored. He inspected his catch as the sun rose. He'd caught a good number of the standard fish found in these waters, but a su vang wasn't among them.

A little after ten in the morning, he anchored near his beach and paddled ashore. Minh greeted him with two plastic buckets to transfer the fish, but she had to run for two more, as the catch was twice as large. Exhausted, Pham Kai went inside to change. He emerged a few minutes later to find Minh staring at the buckets. "Minh, I'll try again tonight," he said, sitting next to her.

By mid-afternoon, they had sold all four buckets and returned home. This was a good earning day—twice as much as usual.

That evening, Pham Kai studied his grandfather's maps. Based on last night's experience, he should be fishing on the north side of Bombay Reef. It was far more treacherous, but if there was any chance of finding a su vang, he thought it would be in that area. He'd have to take his basket boat in order to get close, maybe even float on top of the reef, and cast his nets there. That was where the rare, exotic fish bred and lived.

Planning in his mind, he lay down and slept, only to be awakened by Minh. She had dinner ready, and Pham Kai realized how hungry he was. She had made her specialty, a fish curry with mint, ginger, and coconut milk. She had added basil and cumin seeds for extra flavoring and red ground chili for spice. She had squeezed a full, fresh lemon into the curry base, and then cooked the fish in the curry for twenty minutes, adding noodles at the end. The key to her recipe was fried onion, with fresh cut cilantro and ginger as garnish on top. It was Pham Kai's absolute favorite meal, and he devoured two healthy bowlfuls.

CHAPTER THREE
The Catch

WANG LI, THE captain of the Chinese patrol boat, was getting ready for another night shift, shaving over the sink in the tiny quarters furnished by the government. It was more of a naval hostel for sailors and cadets, not for officers—they had better quarters than what he'd been given. The mirror he peered into was small, flecked with toothpaste and shaving cream. No one ever wiped it clean. It had a crack in the corner, and he was convinced cleaning it would cause it to break, bringing him bad luck.

His starched uniform was laid out wrinkleless on his bed. He was the only captain who used starch, and the other officers made fun of him for it. It prevented the fabric from breathing—no small thing in the muggy heat of the South China Sea. But Wang Li was determined to look sharp. It inspired respect from his crew, or so he thought.

He mused about the previous night. He hated Vietnamese fishermen with a passion—they were a low class of people who had no respect for Chinese sovereignty. He wished he had the authority to sink their boats on sight. He knew he'd caught a glimpse of a Vietnamese fishing boat. His crew felt he'd imagined it, but Wang Li was sure of it. He wanted to catch the bastard. He knew he was lurking near Bombay reef, trying to outsmart him.

* * *

PHAM KAI PULLED up about a mile from Bombay Reef, shut off the motor and the cabin light, and waited. Instead of casting his nets from his boat, he decided to go deeper into the reef using his basket boat.

He lowered it into the water, along with his gear, and stepped aboard. He then rowed toward the edge of the reef, where the waves were strong and violent. He had to time his forward motion with the incoming waves so that his basket boat would glide over the reef. It took him three tries, and the forward motion of the waves and volume of water lifted him over the reef. As soon as he reached the other side, the water was calm. It was still pitch dark, and all he could see of his fishing boat was the orange and yellow stripe on its side. He could see it despite the non-reflective paint, but one had to know what to look for to make it out.

Standing and balancing himself, he got started, the lantern giving off just enough light for him to work. He began casting both nets, one after the other. For the next few hours, he worked nonstop. His breathing grew heavy, and sweat poured off him. His hands grew sore from all the pulling, and his lower back started to cramp. His bucket overflowed with fish, and the floor of his boat was strewn with them. He checked his watch, a Casio replica, and it was 4:00 a.m. He had lost track of time.

As he started to navigate back, he realized that he couldn't return the way he'd come—the force of the waves hitting the edge of the reef was too strong. He needed to go south and cross over the reef into the sea where the water was calmer. It took him forty-five minutes to get back to his boat. He hauled everything aboard, emptying the fish into the tin buckets.

At almost five in the morning, Pham Kai started his motor

and navigated toward Vietnam. Safe in Vietnamese waters an hour later, he once again inspected his catch in the light of the rising sun. There were several dozen fish of all colors and sizes, but again, there were no su vang among them.

PHAM KAI'S NIGHTTIME adventures continued for three weeks. Minh grew worried that his strategies for eluding the patrol boat were getting bolder. The catches he brought home were large, with some excellent variety that fetched them good money, but he was putting himself in extreme danger.

Pham Kai knew he had figured out the patrol's routine, and using his grandfather's notes, he had discovered a key natural channel in the reef, allowing him to take his boat deep inside where he was invisible amongst the waves and mist. Every night, he started his fishing from the north end of the reef, then used the hidden channel to move toward the center. Transferring onto his basket boat, he would fish right on top of the reef.

Tonight was no different. Paddling his basket boat, he could make out the outline of the lagoon, and it didn't look friendly. It had an old feel to it, as if time had stopped. Pham Kai shrugged off his misgivings and started casting his nets. Once in a while, he would notice a beautiful luminescent light in the water, but it wasn't fluorescent plankton—this was quite different, and moved in a distinct pattern.

After several casts, Pham Kai decided to cast both nets one more time before heading back to his boat. As soon as he cast his second net, his basket boat started to spin in a strange way—the current was changing and gaining strength. An undertow had formed, and he was caught in it. This sudden movement of current occurred when a massive underwater cavern formed and water rushed in to fill the void. It created a negative pressure, pulling at the surface water and forming a massive whirlpool—once someone was caught in it, the likelihood of survival was low at best. But the water wasn't behaving like a typical whirlpool–it was moving slow. Puzzled, Pham Kai had no time to ponder it further. He had to escape.

He had to get to the part of the whirlpool that would slingshot him out. His nets were pulled in a circular motion too, more fish were getting caught in them. He held the rim of his basket boat and jumped into the water, stretching himself out. He needed the combined momentum of the boat, the nets, and his body weight in order to escape.

Swirling around and around, focusing not to lose his frame of reference, his speed increased. This was the moment he'd been waiting for. He held his breath as he was flung from the whirlpool, hanging on to his basket boat for dear life until he was clear. He lifted himself back into it and collapsed with exhaustion. His head was spinning, water had invaded his lungs, and his hands felt like mush.

He sat up holding the sides of his little boat. His tin bucket was still inside–most of the fish had spilled from it, flopping on the floor. His lantern was gone. Using his last bit of strength, he hauled in his nets, heavy with fish. He searched for his fishing boat and paddled toward it, thankful the current hadn't pulled it onto the rocks.

Back aboard, he retrieved another lantern from the cabin to inspect his haul, most of it still trapped in the nets. Untangling them, bringing the lantern close, he froze. He stared at his catch–in front of him lay two adult su vang fish. The first was beautiful, over a foot long, silver with tan scales. The second was also as impressive. He knew they both were worth enough for Minh's treatment and then some.

For generations, the sea had provided for his family. Today, it had been beyond generous. Pham Kai wasn't religious, but he did believe in the miracle of the sea. How else could he explain the forming of the whirlpool? He would never have caught the su vang without it. He brought out a cooler from the cabin and placed the first one inside.

He lifted the second su vang and it was bright, as if it were under a spotlight. Pham Kai paused as the realization hit him. His heart sank.

In his excitement, and with the noise of the waves hitting the reef, Pham Kai hadn't heard the patrol boat approach. They had discovered his secret channel.

Wang Li smiled as he turned to his crew. "You're all idiots. You should be court-martialed for taking so long to find this lowlife." The crew stared at the tired, feeble-looking Pham Kai in disbelief.

There was still some distance between the two boats. Pham Kai dropped the su vang in the net, ran into the cabin, and started the motor. Maybe he could go deeper into the reef where the patrol boat couldn't follow. A cannon-like explosion splintered the cabin wall and a harpoon, lodged deep into the side of the steering wheel housing. Pham Kai wasn't going anywhere.

Wang Li jumped aboard with two of his officers, who pulled Pham Kai out of the cabin. They attached a six-foot wooden plank to his outstretched arms, its length running across his back at hip level. His hands were tied to the plank with nylon ropes around his wrists. The restraints exposed his shoulders, making them protrude outward at a painful angle. The officers forced him to his knees and stood behind him on each side. Wang Li gazed down at him, not saying a word. He smiled at him, exposing his yellow teeth.

A metal rod with two tiny prongs on one end hung from Wang Li's gun belt.

Wang Li barked at him, "You scum of the earth. You're fishing in the sovereign territory of the People's Republic of China. You're breaking our military laws by even being here. Today, you'll wish you were never born. When I'm done with you, you'll never be able to use your hands to fish again."

The two officers grabbed Pham Kai's arms on each side. Wang Li unclipped the metal rod and pressed a button on its side. A spark leaped between the two prongs.

Before Pham Kai could register what was happening, Wang Li brought the sparking rod down and pressed it against Pham Kai's neck.

Pham Kai had endured pain in his life, but he had never experienced anything like this. He convulsed as the voltage surged through his body. Flopping to the floor of the deck, his whole body twitched. He could hear them laugh as they lifted him back to his knees. Wang Li brought the rod close to the other side of his neck and held it there. The anticipation of getting shocked again was agony for Pham Kai.

Instead of touching his neck with the electric rod, Wang Li barked, "Rip his shirt off."

They ripped Pham Kai's shirt down to his waist. Wang Li brought the rod down and placed it on his right shoulder joint. He then pressed the button and 1200 volts moved from the rod straight into Pham Kai's right shoulder, and he fell to the floor again. This time, however, he didn't black out. It felt as if his arm had been ripped from its socket. He checked it in a panic—it was intact, but the entire length of it was shaking.

The officers were laughing at how his arm was no longer in his control. They once again lifted Pham Kai upright. Tears flowed down his face, and his stomach convulsed. His heart pounded hard. He knew he had lost—they weren't going to let him go. They were going to shock him to the point of no return. He would never be able to move his hands again.

As Wang Li brought the electric rod close to his left shoulder, Pham Kai somehow summoned his deep fisherman strength. He sprang up and rammed his head into Wang Li's nose. Before the officers could react, Pham Kai rushed toward the port side of the boat and jumped into the water.

Underwater he tucked his legs, flipping them over the

plank like a reverse skip, and brought the plank in front of him to use it as a floating buoy. Kicking his legs, he swam deeper into the reef where the patrol boat couldn't follow. He wasn't just swimming for his own life—he was swimming for Minh's.

The water of the channel was rough, and the rocks were sharp and dangerous. His knee hit the reef, and he could feel it bleeding. Far behind him, he could hear a commotion. Wang Li was shouting orders at the top of his lungs. They switched on both spotlights and swung them everywhere, searching for him.

Pham Kai managed to find a rock protruding from the reef about a hundred yards away from the boats. He swam to the other side of it and started to wade. Two additional crew members had jumped aboard his boat and were smashing his equipment. He saw flashlights moving on deck—they were going through his catch. After more shouting, they jumped back onto their patrol boat, pulled out the harpoon with a tremendous splintering sound, and navigated away into the darkness. Pham Kai wondered if they'd ripped out the entire cabin wall.

He stayed behind the rock for half an hour, making sure the patrol boat was out of the reef. He started scraping his left hand over the protruding rock, as his right hand was still hurting from the shock to his shoulder. Soon, the rope split and his left hand was free. He then used his free hand to open the knot on his right.

He moved the wooden plank in front of him and started to swim toward his boat, dreading the inevitable, yet thankful they hadn't sunk it. It must have been the steady worsening of the current that caused them to abandon him to his fate.

Exhausted, flinching with pain, Pham Kai pulled himself aboard and collapsed onto the deck. He dragged himself to the basket boat and, using one hand, started searching the net. "No. Oh, no."

He kept searching, desperation setting in with every passing moment. Finally, kneeling next to the nets and the cooler, he sobbed. The su vang fish were gone.

They had taken both fish, and any hope of saving Minh with them.

CHAPTER FOUR

Cerro Tacarcuna

DR. SEBASTIAN MILES arrived at *Ultimo Rufugio* around noon, a popular restaurant in the coastal town of Bocas del Toro, Panama. It was a colorful establishment run by a loving gay couple that prided themselves in serving healthy cuisine prepared with ingredients sourced from local farms. The wooden dining tables were painted light blue, and the ceiling had equidistant beams running the length of the restaurant with old surfboards placed over them. Instead of walls, the restaurant opened onto the ocean, giving the feeling of dining outside while enjoying cover from the sun.

Sitting down at a small table for two, Sebastian realized that one of the legs was shorter than the others, making the table wobble. Tucking a folded napkin under the leg, something caught his eye—a large mural of the Panamanian jungle on the back wall. He sat up and studied it, fascinated by the hidden animals throughout. A big green frog peeked through the leaves in the foreground, a bird-like creature blended in with the tree branch on which it perched, and a monkey-like animal sat hidden at the base of the tree.

Maria Rodriguez walked in. She was a professional explorer who had to sign off on Sebastian's project before his boss at the Bocas del Toro Marine Research Center would even consider funding it. *A Junoesque mountain climber*, he thought tapping his fingers on the table.

Maria was tall and slender with sharp features, yet a particular softness to her face. She had a golden complexion—a natural tan of some sort—and her black shoulder-length hair had reddish-brown streaks from frequent swimming in seawater. She walked over and sat across him in one smooth elegant motion. She crossed her legs, revealing toned muscle.

They ordered two Soberanas and sparkling water. After a few introductory exchanges, Maria jumped in. "So, tell me about your adventure."

Sebastian cleared his throat, took a sip of his beer. "I need your help in searching for a unique marine life that I believe lives deep in the Panamanian jungle."

Maria pulled her hair back, tying them with a beaded band that initially served as a bracelet. "Marine life in the middle of the jungle?"

Sebastian nodded. "It's a specimen that in my opinion is related to an evolutionary mystery belonging to the *Cerithideopsis Californica* and *Cerithideopsis Pliculosa* family."

Maria smiled. "*Cerithideopsis*? You want to go into the Panamanian jungle to find snails?"

Sebastian laughed rubbing the back of his right hand with his left thumb. He'd hoped that by using scientific names, she wouldn't catch that fact. "Not just any snails—*the* snails that would solve one of the most powerful questions of evolution: how did humans evolve?"

He pressed on. "I've been researching this field for over five years and based my doctoral thesis on the subject at the Scripps Oceanography Institute. You see, there's a big problem with the current evolutionary theory. It doesn't explain how humans evolved. Scientists have yet to find a clear connection between apes, monkeys, and humans based on Darwin's theory. Around twenty million years ago, humans separated from primates, and some of us believe they evolved based on a theory by renowned evolutionary biologist Stephen Jay Gould called "Step Evolution"—the process by which a species takes a genetic leap forward to adapt to their changing environment. We know Step Evolution exists among many other species, but we still lack conclusive evidence, living or fossilized."

Maria leaned forward, propping her chin on her hand. "Interesting. So, these snails may be able to prove Step Evolution?"

"Yes!" Sebastian confirmed. "This discovery would be as significant in the field of genetic engineering as gravitational waves were for astrophysics."

"Why do you think these snails can be found in the Panamanian jungle?" Maria asked.

"Maria," Sebastian said, taking a technical tone. "Evolutionary scientists believe that the Isthmus of Panama, where we are sitting today, is the perfect location for such finds.

The formation of this tiny strip of land connecting North and South America parted the ocean three million years ago, forever separating entire families of marine life. As a result, these families each evolved in their own way, in two separate oceans that became different from each other in terms of temperature, depth, and currents. Many of us believe there may be a marine life that has survived this massive geological movement using Step Evolution. However, we have yet to find such a specimen in any of the inland waters of Panama." Sebastian paused to check if he still had Maria's interest.

"Go on," she said, leaning closer.

"As part of my PhD at Scripps, I researched a French explorer, Jean-René Gustav. Among his many expeditions, the one that caught my eye was in 1920 when he went deep into the Panamanian jungle. In his journal, he mentions that he climbed through a crevice into the heart of a mountain, discovering a body of water with bioluminescent snails. The entry then ended with that information. According to the known facts of *Cerithideopsis Californica* and *Cerithideopsis Pliculosa* his find of these bioluminescent snails is a powerful indication of Step Evolution. I've been searching for the mountain ever since, and I think I've found it."

"What makes you so sure?" Maria asked.

"Do you believe in being at the right place at the right time?" Sebastian said. Maria kept staring at him with her big eyes, and then blinked once. He took it as a yes and continued. "Last weekend, I was heading home after yet another failed expedition—adding to the grand total of thirty such attempts over the last ten months. Frustrated, I was at a traffic light in my car, when across the road I noticed a woman selling mangoes at a meager fruit stand—a wooden cart on four wheels." Sebastian's stared at his beer bottle, lost in the memory. "The strangest feeling came over me. I can't explain it. So, I pulled over.

"Maria, you should have seen this lady. She was a glorious woman. She had a bright red shirt with a triangle-shape pattern, and some kind of wrap for a skirt—bright orange, with prints of animals. Her face was so distinct, even powerful, with a long, tattooed line running from the center of her eyes to the base of her nose, and this large nose ring. It turns out she belonged to a remote indigenous tribe called the Kuna. While buying some mangoes, I asked her if she knew of a mountain that had water inside it. At first, she looked surprised to hear such a question. Then she started speaking fast in Spanish. My Spanish isn't great, but I was able to catch the following details." Sebastian's voice dropped to a conspiratorial hush.

"She explained that her people knew of a mountain deep in the jungle, just like the one I described. She said the gods had possessed it when the Earth was born, and inside it lived an ancient animal. After I promised her that I'd respect the mountain and the creatures that dwelt there, she agreed to tell me its location. The mountain is *Cerro Tacarcuna*, in the Darien Province. I couldn't believe my luck."

Maria smiled. "You're going off the word of a, as you said, 'glorious fruit stand lady.'"

Sebastian returned her smile. "Sometimes the answer lies in stories that have been handed down through generations," Sebastian said, leaning in. "How she described the mountain and the animals inside leads me to believe she was talking about Jean-René Gustav's mountain. I've analyzed detailed charts of the terrain and studied the pathways of underground streams—and they too support the story. If the charts and journal are correct, we need to climb approximately 2,500 feet up the mountain, where we'll find a unique geological formation—a small ledge with a granite table. Somewhere around that table is a crevice that will lead us into the heart of the mountain, and to the snails."

"*Cerro Tacarcuna* is a formidable mountain, deep in the jungle. And we would need an extremely skilled river boat captain to even get us close to the base," Maria said, considering the challenge.

"That's why it's so important that you help me," Sebastian replied.

Maria focused on a slow-moving ceiling fan, thinking about Sebastian's proposal. She found herself considering his looks for the first time as well—he was a handsome man, in an unconventional sense. Athletic, with dark curly hair and a square jaw sporting a shadow of a beard. His ocean-blue eyes had a unique quality to them—it wasn't the color, but something more mysterious. She felt there was something different about him, something powerful. Ignoring those thoughts, she asked, "Ever gone mountain climbing?"

Sebastian smiled. "I've climbed a few mountains. I'm no

expert like you, though."

Maria laughed. "Okay, Sebastian. Let's go get your snails."

* * *

TWO WEEKS LATER, and after a vicious hunt, they found a riverboat captain. He was a grungy chain-smoker who made his living ferrying tribes deep into the jungle. In a harsh, raspy voice, he explained, "I'll only wait twelve hours for you at the drop-off point. You're fools to go so deep into the jungle." Ignoring his comment, they paid his advance.

After getting final sign-off from Keira, Sebastian and Maria began the five-hour river journey toward Cerro Tacarcuna before dawn. Landing on the shore as light was breaking, Sebastian was taken aback by the natural beauty of the place. The plants were so green they were almost radiant, and flowers abounded in deep reds, yellows, and violets. Wild fruit trees grew everywhere—mango, coconut, and guava. He spotted some toucans with their bright yellow beaks, perched high on a flowering Saman tree. The fragrances, too, were mesmerizing, from vanilla flowers to sandalwood trees.

"Did you know that Christopher Columbus landed at Bocas Del Toro on one of his later voyages?" Sebastian said. "He found it so beautiful, he named it Puerto Bello."

Maria smiled. Sebastian's passion was contagious. She pulled out her satellite map of the area one final time to confirm her calculations. It would take them three hours to cut through the jungle and reach the base of the mountain, two hours to climb to 2,500 feet, two more hours to descend into the crevice, and maybe longer to get back out—that was if all went according to plan. If they were lucky, they would be back just in time to catch the boat before it left.

She extracted a machete from her backpack. It was a well-worn blade with a strong wooden handle. She wrapped her fingers firmly around the handle and began slicing and hacking a path toward the mountain base. Surrounded by thick vegetation, this part of the jungle wasn't so beautiful. The air was muggy, almost suffocating.

A short while into their foray, Maria looked back and warned Sebastian of the sandbox trees in the area, which had sharp thorns. Maria snaked her way through the unblemished foliage. Sebastian, on the other hand, was starting to get cuts and bruises.

Noticing Sebastian's condition, Maria stopped at a tree. Plucking a few leaves, she crushed them in her hand and gave him the paste to apply to his cuts. "I have cortisone cream in my backpack," she said, "but these leaves will act faster. They're from the Guembe tree. It works miracles on cuts and bruises."

At various points, Maria would take her can of spray paint and mark a tree or a rock—breadcrumbs for their journey back. The sounds of the jungle were distinct and foreboding—a combination of rustling trees, screaming insects, and the occasional howls and calls of various animals. Panama's rainforests weren't for the faint of heart.

Three hours later, they reached the base of *Cerro Tacarcuna* and got ready to climb.

"Ready? If I'm going too fast, stop me," Maria said while strapping on her climbing gear.

"I'll keep up," Sebastian said, not one to back down. Yet privately he hoped she would slow down.

Just like her ability to snake the jungle, Maria was a rock climber without parallel. Watching her was like watching a ballet—she knew where to place hooks, where to hammer spikes, where to swing over, where to grapple. She bent in impossible curves and contractions, moving from one rock to the next in a knowing, deliberate effort to discover the easiest path for Sebastian to follow. Sebastian watched in awe, wondering if she practiced Capoeira, the beautiful Brazilian martial art that combined dance and acrobatics. He followed her path, slipping and sliding more than he would have liked.

Around noon—which felt like a lifetime to Sebastian, but in reality was only about two hours—they reached the landing, laying eyes on the granite table for the first time. It was no bigger than five feet by four feet, jutting out of a vertical wall of rock that continued up to the summit. Several boulders that must have fallen during the last earthquake, situated at random around the table. He couldn't, at first glance, see an opening or a crevice. Maria began pulling out their rappelling gear so she could anchor their rappels once they found the crevice.

Precious time passed as Sebastian traced each and every granite line. Compounding matters, they heard thunder in the distance. The forecast hadn't predicted rain. A more troubling thought crossed Sebastian's mind—what if the fruit vendor was wrong? What if Cerro Tacarcuna wasn't the mountain he'd been seeking all this time?

Just as he was about to share his concern with Maria, he realized that one of the boulders sitting at the wall of the table had a different pebble formation around it than the others. He pulled out a sledgehammer and chisel from his backpack and began chipping into the rock. Sebastian removed his shirt, which was tattered from the journey, and wrapped his hands to protect them from the debris as he continued to work.

Maria paused her prepping of the gear and observed Sebastian. She was impressed he had been carrying the dead weight of a sledgehammer. Her initial impression was confirmed—he did not fit the mold of a scientist. Shirtless, he revealed a set of abs that, beyond question, were not acquired by spending hours in the confines of a marine laboratory.

After ten minutes of brute force pounding, the boulder broke apart. Using his upper body strength, Sebastian lifted the heavy pieces out of the way and pushed the rest of the boulder into the mountain. A small rockslide revealed a large crevice that sloped at a steep angle into blackness. Sebastian jumped up with excitement, smiling at Maria, who ran over and anchored their ropes outside the crevice. After putting on a clean shirt from his pack, Sebastian joined Maria and they made their way down into the darkness.

Sebastian wasn't sure if he could hear the sound of rushing water over the howl of the wind, and he had no idea how deep they would have to descend to reach the stream. They alternated between sliding down on their butts and rappelling with their feet, and bumping into rocky edges. Sebastian began to notice ferns and fungus on the walls, a sure sign of moisture. The air was musky as well, with a hint of saltiness.

The crevice expanded from its initial size, and after about an hour, Sebastian's flashlight fell upon a small outcropping a few feet wide. They descended onto it for a brief rest, glancing down at the continued darkness past the outcropping. Deep in thought, Sebastian tried to understand the geology of the place. He moved his headlamp and flashlight around, soon finding a large cave-like opening a few feet away.

"I think we should go through that opening," he said, understanding that the success of their task was very much tied to their strict timetable, leaving no time for wrong decisions. They anchored themselves to the outcropping and unhooked from their ropes before inching over into the new opening.

The opening looked to be about four feet wide and three feet tall, forcing Sebastian and Maria to go through on their hands and knees. Sebastian felt moisture on his fingers, unsure if it was water or just sweat. Forging ahead, they came to large natural cenote, where they heard the unmistakable sound of rushing water.

The cenote was formed in the shape of a vertical cavern and was filled with turbulent water. Waves were crashing in and out, smashing into the walls, swirling in a vortex, then disappearing through an opening–only to reappear with the same violent intensity. "Okay," he said, "here's where I leave you and go alone."

Maria regarded the current. "Sebastian, you'll be tossed around like a rag doll. I think you shou–"

Not waiting for Maria to finish, Sebastian rappelled toward the water. Maria looked on, annoyed, as he continued to descend. He soon hung inches above the splashing water. He set his stopwatch and timed the flow. Twelve-second intervals.

Sebastian switched his flashlight and headlamp off. Hanging in total darkness, he saw a faint luminescence through the foaming waves, toward a far wall of the cavern. He waited for the torrent to rush out and dropped himself onto the cavern floor with a splash.

His legs and feet reacted by going numb in the freezing cold water. He focused on the far wall, but didn't see anything. Before he knew it, a wave lifted him off his feet and slammed him into the cavern wall, submerging him.

Underwater, the force of the current tossed him about. Out of the corner of his eye, he caught sight of that strange light again, but he still wasn't sure what he was seeing. The water spun him around and dragged him near the opening. He managed to cling to a wall, hanging on for dear life as the water rushed out. Able to breathe again, cold, his body in state of shock, he searched for the glimmering light. Like clockwork, the freezing water rushed in again. This time, Sebastian was ready. He took a deep breath and tightened his grip on the wall. Submerged, he saw them–small, luminescent snails, stuck against the far wall.

The raging water rushed out again and as before, the luminescence was gone. He stood there in the dark, chilled to the bone, his muscles tense. He waited for the turbulent water to return. Taking a deep breath, he used the force of the current to maneuver in front of the snails and peeled them off the wall. He was able to secure five snails and put them in a specimen bottle before the receding water spun him around and pulled him away. He scrambled and grabbed another wall and waited out the water. Once clear, he ran to the wall, where Maria had lowered another rope attached to a pulley she had set up. Sebastian grabbed the rope and wrapped it around his pulley, creating a loop.

He began hoisting himself up, climbing as fast as his exhausted body would allow, the cavern once again erupted with violence and the water missed him by inches. He turned back to glance again at the luminescent wall when something else in the water caught his eye. A beautiful light, something moving in the water, swimming free. Squinting, he tried to focus, but as soon as he saw it, it disappeared into the vortex rushing out.

"C'mon!" Maria shouted. "We're getting a flashflood in the crevice now!"

Sebastian pulled himself the last few yards to Maria, and they both crawled back to the outcropping.

"Whoa!" Sebastian exclaimed, looking up. The crevice had become a natural waterfall–rainwater cascaded down, making it almost impossible for them to climb out.

The noise of the waterfall was deafening. "We're going to have to improvise," Maria yelled. "It's going to take everything we've got to place new hooks as we climb out." Sebastian nodded.

Maria secured her first hook and ascended. While holding herself steady, she placed a second hook. They inched themselves up through the falling water.

After almost two hours, they pulled themselves out of the crevice and back onto the granite table. Drenched, and exhausted, they took a minute to rest as the rain continued to fall. They had the snails, but now it was a race against time to get back to the boat before it left without them.

During their rapid decent down the mountain, Sebastian

kept feeling the flask in his backpack, making sure it was still there. Once at the base, Maria reset her stopwatch. Attaching new hooks had added an hour to their adventure. "Ready?" she asked, somehow smiling, "We have two hours to get out of the jungle, instead of three."

Hands on his knees, Sebastian took a deep breath. He rose upright with a grin, and nodded. "Let's do this!"

They moved through the thickets in a jungle jog—a combination of jumps and short bursts of speed—balancing on fallen trees and ducking stray branches, all with as much energy as they could muster.

BACK ON THE boat, the captain realized it was forty minutes past the twelve hours he'd allotted them. What's more, the weather had taken a nasty turn—he'd been keeping a close eye on the steady rising waterline. Any longer and he risked drifting deeper into the jungle, only for the water to recede after the storm and leave him stranded. He fired up the engine and started to hoist the anchor, inching away from the bank.

SEBASTIAN AND MARIA broke out of the jungle, sprinting toward the boat as it pulled away. Maria reached it first with a hop, leap, and jump, followed close by Sebastian. They collapsed under the covered awning of the deck, exhausted, ignoring the captain's grunt on their return.

Breathing heavily, Sebastian removed his backpack and took out the flask. He peered into it and his snails were doing fine. Closing the flask his childhood neural condition flared up and rapid images started flashing in his mind. He started seeing pictures of glittering sand, ethereal humanoids wearing cloaks, and something that looked like a huge sparkling Russian Faberge egg.

CHAPTER FIVE
Defining Moment

SEBASTIAN AND MARIA were back outside the *Ultimo Rufugio* the next day. Sipping their beers, eyes on the ocean, they played out the adventure of the past twenty-four hours. Small bandages on Sebastian's fingers made souvenirs of the day. Maria, on the other hand, wearing a yellow sundress and her hair falling across her bare shoulders, appeared to be unscathed.

She broke the silence. "Sebastian, when you were pulling yourself up from the cavern, you stopped, as if you saw something."

Sebastian was surprised Maria had caught his momentary pause in the cavern.

"I think I saw a fish—the water was rough and it was hard to see. I may have been imagining things." He paused, debating if he should share the next bit of information. "I suffer from a condition called Pareidolia. In moments of severe physical or mental intensity, I get flashes of images that most often don't mean anything." His voice trailed off, unsure if he should continue.

Maria nodded. "Well, whatever the case, I hope your snails are the missing evolutionary link. How hard will it be for you to find that out?"

"The work isn't technically difficult, it's just time consuming and tedious," Sebastian replied. "It could take over three hundred attempts to isolate the DNA and confirm my findings."

The conversation drifted. Maria was going on an extended expedition that would take her all over the world–this was perhaps the last time Sebastian would see her in Panama. He wasn't sure why he felt sad that she was leaving. He lifted his beer.

"Well, here's to climbing mountains, crossing jungles, and finding new adventures. May our paths cross again."

Maria leaned forward and kissed him on the cheek. "Goodbye," she said with a smile.

Sebastian watched her head out of the restaurant through one of the open walls and down the path, toward a jet ski tied to the restaurant's pier. She stopped, placed her backpack on a nearby table, tucked her thumb underneath her spaghetti strap and removed her sundress, revealing a bronze bikini underneath. She tucked her dress into her bag and swung it onto her shoulders. Without glancing back, she shouted, "Sebastian, stop looking at me!" She hopped on the jet ski and took off. Sebastian smiled–he had indeed been staring.

He got up and paid the bartender for their lunch. A man with a paintbrush worked on the same large mural Sebastian had admired earlier. He had an assistant, a girl wearing a white painter's dungaree. She had paint on her clothes, her hands, and the side of her face. The painter stopped, picked up a rag and wiped the paint from her cheek. The girl turned around, as if she knew someone was staring. Catching Sebastian's eye, she smiled at him. He smiled back, making his way out of the restaurant.

As he was leaving, the two restaurant owners approached the painter about his mural. "Charles, this is incredible," one of them said. "You wouldn't believe how many customers have commented on your masterpiece. We wish you'd stay and paint one for our home, too. Please, please."

"You know I would love to," the painter responded. "But we're headed to New Zealand, where I've accepted a new commission." Resigned, the owners shook hands and went back to doting over their guests.

* * *

AT THE BOCAS del Toro Marine Research Center, Sebastian sat in front of his boss, Director Keira Morales. The conversation wasn't going well. Sebastian paused for the third time since their meeting started to let her finish texting. Dr. Morales was a thin, almost gaunt woman with dark, frizzy hair and piercing eyes that never sat still.

She listened to all the details of his adventure with seeming great difficulty, then pointed out that he might have found the well-known species *Hinea brasiliana*, which had already been studied by several institutions. In between texting and glancing at her computer screen, she went on to explain that Bocas del Toro didn't have the funding to research this any further.

"Hand these snails over to Doctor Cebrián Alveraz's group," she said without meeting his eyes. "They're already doing some research with luminescent marine life. I need you to support the group that's trying to figure out why Lake Erie has repeated occurrence of a foul-smelling algae bloom every summer."

Sebastian couldn't believe it. "Keira, are you kidding me? You want me to work on an algae bloom? Why did you even fund my expedition if you weren't going to give me the opportunity to prove my hypothesis?"

"I was sure you'd fail," she said. "I thought you'd come back empty-handed, which would have shut this whole affair down once and for all. We had already booked Maria for another expedition, and it was cancelled. And since we'd already spent the money..."

Her response was as frustrating as her personality. But Sebastian wasn't ready to give in.

"Okay," he said, "I'll meet with Doctor Alveraz and see where that conversation takes us. But how about this—what if I work nights on my project while doing the center's main research during the day?"

For the first time, Keira stopped shifting her eyes. They dropped to her table as she sighed. "Okay, fine," she conceded. "Whatever. Work on your pet project in the evenings only. No compromise on that." She turned back to her phone with deep interest. He had been dismissed.

* * *

SEBASTIAN MET DR. Cebrián Alveraz at his office the next day, and he found the doctor to be quite friendly. Cebrián was the senior scientist at the institute, and his lab boasted the institute's biggest research budget, with over twenty scientists on his team. He was credited with over a dozen major discoveries in marine biology, ecology, and oceanography. This also made Cebrián the center's main source of revenue.

Alveraz was fit and in his mid-fifties. He wore a trim goatee that accentuated his dark, golden-brown complexion and matched his light gray, wavy hair. He was authoritative, yet personable and wore a diver's watch on his right wrist and a blue activity tracker on his left. He had a charm about him that put Sebastian at ease.

He told Cebrián about his passion for discovering new species that would validate Step Evolution, and a quick summary of the adventure to acquire the snails.

"Sebastian," Cebrián said in sincere tone, "I love your story and want to help. Instead of giving my team the snails, use my lab in the evenings and find out if they are indeed the missing link," he said, to Sebastian's delight.

* * *

THE NEXT DAY, after working his full eight hours on the Lake Erie project, Sebastian grabbed the aquarium with his snails and headed to Cebrián's wing. As he got closer, the quality of furniture improved—even the paint on the walls was nicer.

Upon entering the main lab, he stopped in surprise. It was better equipped than any of the labs at Scripps. Each station had its own gear—everything from test tubes and beakers to microscopes and centrifuges. These were just the stations—on the other side of the lab there were incubators, aquariums, a NanoDrop 2000 spectrophotometer for measuring DNA concentration, and even a DNA sequencer. If his specimens were the big breakthrough he thought they were, this lab for sure had the equipment to confirm it.

Sebastian chose the workstation closest to the wall with all the major equipment, and placed the aquarium on the table next to it. He pulled his laptop out of his backpack and connected it. The network asked him to set up a new password. He thought for a second, then with a smile typed #LaraCroft.

He spent the next five hours developing the broad strokes of his research protocol, from identifying physical features to DNA sampling. His experiments were going to require long nights in the lab—he'd have to bring his sleeping bag from home.

At one in the morning, he shouldered his bag and left. On his way out, he noted that Cebrián's office light was on. He paused to peek in and saw Cebrián in his office, working.

Cebrián sensing a presence lifted his head. "Are you all settled in?" he asked. "Do you like the lab?" Sebastian gave him a thumbs-up. Alveraz paused, his expression turning thoughtful. "Sebastian, did you like your time at Scripps?"

Sebastian hesitated, surprised by the question. "It's a great place for marine research. Why do you ask?"

"Just curious," Cebrián replied, going back to the papers sprawled across his desk.

Sebastian stepped out of the research center into the warm night and crossed the parking lot toward his sole indulgence, a red Multistrada 1200S Ducati. He pushed down the black button to activate the dash and then pressed the red button all the way to start the bike. The roar of the engine was magnificent. As he made his way out of the center, he nudged the accelerator and felt the bike leap forward, the front wheel lifting off the ground.

While riding home, several thoughts drifted through his mind—Maria, the snails, Cebrián's lab—but one thought took control for the rest of his ride: What was it he had seen in the water, just as he escaped the cavern?

* * *

THE NEXT MORNING, Sebastian was back at the center at eight o'clock sharp. People rushed down the corridors, and a few groups in the main hall stood whispering.

He stopped to get coffee and found one of the scientists struggling with the coffee machine. "What's all the commotion about?" Sebastian asked, offering to help with the coffee machine.

"You haven't heard?" replied the bewildered scientist, stepping aside.

"Heard what?" Sebastian said.

"Doctor Cebrián Alveraz has accepted the position of director at the Scripps Oceanography Institute. He's leaving us."

So Cebrián's question from the night before wasn't so

innocuous! Sebastian thought. The scientist grabbed the half-filled, steaming coffee cup, not waiting for the pour to complete, and scurried away.

At around five o'clock, Sebastian picked up his backpack and was making his way to Cebrián's lab when he heard someone calling his name. He turned to find Cebrián, Keira, and a man wearing a bright, light-blue suit with large vertical stripes standing next to them. The man wouldn't have looked out of place in a mariachi band. He had a full mustache and wavy hair with lots of hair cream. Cebrián motioned for Sebastian to join them.

"I heard the good news," Sebastian said as he approached them. "I'm sure it's a wonderful opportunity for you."

Before Cebrián could say anything, Keira rolled her eyes, chiming in. "Wonderful news for Scripps, not for us. Anyway, I'm happy for you, Cebrián."

The doctor nodded, "Thank you Sebastian, yes. It is something I have been wanting to do for a long time."

"Hi, I'm Doctor Martinez Espino." The man with the mustache grinned. "I understand you're the scientist who went into the jungle to retrieve some snails. I hope they turn out to be valuable research. We have to be careful that we don't utilize our major resources on hunches."

"Hunches make us scientists," Cebrián countered with a straight face. "When we lose our sense of adventure and curiosity, we cease to be scientists."

Sebastian smiled. He was starting to like Cebrián. It was a shame he was leaving.

Keira explained to Martinez that she had given Sebastian permission to work on his quest in the evenings, as long as it didn't interfere with his day job. "Who knows," she said, shrugging her shoulder, "Sebastian's discovery may be the big break we need."

Eager to return to his research, Sebastian thanked them

and made his way to Cebrián's lab, where he began the long process of classifying his snails.

Sebastian's routine consisted of a full day's work on the Erie grant, followed by work on his snails starting at five o'clock, often until three a.m. There were times when he would sleep under the table for a few hours, head home to shower, then come back and start his day all over again.

This routine went on for several weeks, until one morning when a fellow scientist arrived earlier than usual. The lab was dark, except for a blinking computer screen, and switched on the lights. Sebastian, awakened by the light, glanced across at the blinking computer screen. The results of the last DNA sequence testing were in.

Groggy and stiff, Sebastian plopped down onto the workstation chair and tapped at the keyboard. The blinking stopped and an AGCT DNA model appeared on the screen. He stared at the model–this time something was different. He opened old pictures of DNA sequences of *Cerithideopsis Californica* and *Cerithideopsis Pliculosa* on a second monitor.

As he compared the models, he stood up, bringing his palms to his temples. He stood there staring at the monitors. He sat back down again, his sleepiness gone. Goosebumps prickled his arms. He called the other scientist over to see if he was correct in reading his results.

The scientist leaned closer to the monitor. "Is this the DNA sequence of your snails?" he asked, surprise in his voice. Sebastian nodded. "It appears that they're a genetic link to *Californica* and *Pliculosa*," he said carefully, after a few moments of comparison.

Everything that followed felt like slow motion for Sebastian. As word spread, scientists rushed in and out of the lab, congratulating Sebastian with vigorous handshakes, pats on the back, and typical South American-style full-body hugs.

* * *

KEIRA ROUNDED THE corner and saw Sebastian standing at the door of her office. "Yes, how can I help you?" She asked. "I have to get to a meeting in five minutes."

Sebastian said nothing, as he placed the printed results of his analysis on her desk. She scanned the printout with little interest. "What's this?" She jolted upright, gripping the report. "Does this mean what I think it does?" Sebastian smiled and nodded. "Oh, my God, this is huge!" she shrieked. Eyes wide, she picked up her phone and called Martinez, following with a flurry of texts to the center's Board members.

A short time later, Martinez was in the office too, waving the results in excitement. "Extraordinary!" he exclaimed. "We must celebrate. Keira, where are you hiding your good tequila?"

"Bottom shelf of the credenza," Keira replied, continuing to text.

Martinez poured three shot glasses and passed them around, shouting, "Cheers! Here's to solving the biggest mystery of evolution!"

* * *

THE NEXT TWO months passed in a whirlwind of writing, rewriting, and validating experiments. It didn't take Keira and Martinez long to approve and submit the paper detailing Sebastian's findings to the *Journal of Marine Biology and Oceanography*, and now all he had to do was wait. He took this time to recharge, riding his bike across the Panamanian countryside, climbing mountains, and staying with the locals in unknown villages. He heard their stories, and experienced their rituals and customs. All the while, he pondered what his next research topic would be.

Soon after he had returned home from his vacation, Sebastian received a cryptic email from the editor of the *Journal of Marine Biology and Oceanography*. He responded by setting up a time to call the editor.

"Hello, Doctor Miles," the editor said, sounding a bit

pensive. "Thank you for speaking with me. I have here...*impressive* submission from Bocas del Toro." He paused.

"Yes, I know, I made the submission. And please, call me Sebastian."

"Yes, yes, I spoke to Doctor Cebrián Alveraz at Scripps," the editor continued, distracted. "He too confirmed that you were the lead scientist on this incredible discovery." The editor went quiet, and after a few seconds, said, "Sebastian, that isn't what I have here in the official submission."

What the editor said next took the wind out of Sebastian. There were two names associated with the paper–Dr. Keira Morales and Dr. Martinez Espino. Sebastian wasn't mentioned in the submission anywhere. "I felt I should inform you, in case we need to make any corrections," the editor concluded.

"It must have been an oversight," Sebastian said, his mind racing. "I'll take care of it."

"I understand," the editor replied. "I'm prepared to hold off for twenty-four hours before the article goes to print. Since this is such a major discovery, it will be featured prominently on the front cover of the journal."

Bewildered, Sebastian hung up the phone. He headed for the research center, not caring where he parked his bike before heading straight to Keira's office. He found her at her desk, having a quiet conversation with Martinez.

"Keira," Sebastian said, stepping into the room without even a glance at Martinez.

"Hi, Sebastian," she said, more pleasant than usual. "How can I help you?"

Sebastian tried hard to keep a calm face. "There has been a misunderstanding," he said. "I just got off the phone with the editor of *Marine Biology and Oceanography*. He said he's going to publish my paper–however, my name isn't on it. Not even as a reference."

"Sebastian, there is no misunderstanding," Keira assured

him. "Please sit down and let me explain."

"No, thanks."

"Let me explain," Keira repeated, taking a sip of water. "Since Doctor Alveraz has left, we're under huge threat of losing the majority of the funding he was able to secure for his projects. Martinez is working with his donors, but they haven't confirmed one way or the other if they'll continue to fund them without Cebrián leading the research."

"So, what does that have to do with my paper?" Sebastian interjected.

For once, Keira wasn't texting—she was looking at him and not blinking. "We can't afford to lose that funding," she explained. "You're just a researcher. You don't have a brand. Martinez and I are senior scientists. We're known figures in the research world. That's why this discovery must be announced under our names—so donors notice us and what this center can do."

Sebastian couldn't believe what he was hearing. "Are you serious? This has been my goal for over five years, and now you want to take ownership of *my* discovery? You know what you're doing is wrong, and unethical, on so many levels, right?"

Keira's eyes grew large and piercing. "Sebastian, I didn't get here by playing nice. I do what I have to do to grow and maintain this research center. Martinez and I must own the credit for this discovery if we're going to fund our programs. Besides, when you accepted the commission, our contract stated that if we wish, we could assign credit of any and all discoveries to any of our senior scientists. As a visiting researcher, you knew that."

Sebastian glared at her. "Keira, this is no ordinary find of a new species, this is *the* species that proves Step Evolution. The fact that you guys aren't even mentioning me is pure theft. If this research was conducted under a senior scientist, I could maybe understand. But this was all my independent work, on my own time, against your judgment and support. You're hijacking my research."

"That is the whole point," Keira responded. "Sebastian. The fact no senior scientist even played a role indicates we all are sleeping at our jobs. It portrays a negative impression of the senior staff to the Board. And we can not have that."

"And listen," Martinez chimed in. "After all, it was in *my* lab that you worked to find this breakthrough. Cebrián had different rules when running his lab. This is now my lab, and whatever is discovered in my lab belongs to Keira and me."

"This is treachery and you know it." Sebastian snapped.

"We study evolution here," Martinez replied. "It's survival of the fittest."

Sebastian realized he was arguing with two people who had lost their moral compass. "I am going to put an end to your plan. I will contact the editor, submit the evidence, and shut your plan down. As he started to walk out, Martinez got up and put his hand on Sebastian's shoulder. "Sebastian, wait. Let's talk about this."

"Remove your hand," Sebastian growled, "or get ready to wear a cast." Martinez eyes grew large, and he recoiled.

Sebastian marched out, heading straight for Cebrián's lab to archive his electronic research materials and the results of his experiments. He emailed the .zip file to the editor and called him to explain what had happened.

"Sebastian, I've seen this more times than I'd like to count. It's a common occurrence in academia for senior researchers to take credit for work done by their junior teams. Even though there's clear evidence that you yourself made this breakthrough, the center does have the right to claim it as their discovery. I'm sorry, but you won't get credit for your research." His voice was heavy with sadness.

Sebastian sat at his workstation, numb. His snails glowed in the aquarium. A thought flashed through his mind to take them and release them into the wild, but he quashed it. Introducing them to a new habitat could play havoc with the ecosystem. After a few minutes, he picked up his things and rode out of the Bocas del Toro Marine Research Center for the last time.

* * *

SEBASTIAN'S ROUTINE FOR the next few weeks included long, seven-to-ten-mile runs in an effort to clear his mind. He also spent hours playing full-contact street soccer with the locals, each match, leaving him exhausted as he limped his way back to his apartment. Neither activity seemed to help him find the closure he was looking for.

One late afternoon, he was at home nursing a scotch and watching a documentary about pufferfish. The host, in his proper British accent, was whispering the narration, as if swimming among the creatures he didn't want to spook. *"This pufferfish is able to construct sand formations that look like underwater crop circles,"* the host said.

He heard the creak of the mail slot's metal flap on his front door as the courier delivered the day's mail. Sebastian jumped off the couch to pick it up. Every day since the incident at the lab, he had been awaiting and dreading the arrival of the *Journal of Marine Biology and Oceanography*. He had hoped the editor made an exception and gave him some credit. He saw the magazine nestled amongst the junk mail wrapped in a clear plastic bag. A picture of his snail was on the cover, accompanied by the headline MYSTERY OF EVOLUTION SOLVED. Underneath the headline, in bold black letters: BY DR. KEIRA MORALES AND DR. MARTINEZ ESPINO.

Sitting back down, he removed the magazine from the plastic and leafed through the article. As he had feared, there was no mention of Dr. Sebastian Miles.

As if on cue, his cell phone rang with a number he didn't recognize. Sebastian considered ignoring it, but it had a familiar area code—San Diego. After a few rings he picked up. "Hello?"

"Sebastian." It was a man's voice, deep and friendly. "This is Cebrián Alveraz."

It took Sebastian a moment to realize who it was. *Why is Cebrián calling me?* he wondered. *And how did he get my number?* "Hello, Doctor Alveraz. How can I help you?"

"I heard what happened at Bocas del Toro," Cebrián informed him. "I'm looking at the recent copy of the journal. Not a good situation." He paused. "But I haven't called you to discuss that. I have a proposition. Would you like to meet me at Scripps? I have a position that requires a daring researcher such as yourself."

Sebastian placed his drink on the side table and sat up. "Uh, thank you! Can you tell me what you're researching?"

"Let's just say it's a new evolutionary science I'm investigating," Cebrián said.

Sebastian waited to hear more. After an awkward silence, he realized Cebrián wasn't going to share anything further over the phone. At the same time, the doctor's offer helped him accept something he'd been struggling with for weeks—there was nothing more for him in Bocas del Toro.

"Okay, Doctor Alveraz, I'll meet you at Scripps," Sebastian said. With that, he signed up for an adventure that would shake the very foundation of what he believed to be true—and real.

CHAPTER SIX
The Blue Light

IT TOOK PHAM Kai all of his strength to get up and inspect the cabin—there was a big hole in the starboard wall, they had smashed his speedometer, and the housing of his compass was bent. He wasn't sure how they had missed the compass itself, because there was destruction everywhere. He started his motor, pulled the anchor up using his left hand, and made his way out of the reef.

His arms, shoulders, and legs ached. He had cuts and bruises over his entire body from the sharp edges of the reef, and most of all, his neck throbbed with pain. He moved his fingers over the holes left by the electric rod. They were the same marks he had seen on other fishermen in the village. He, too, was now branded. Using his left hand to steer the boat, he kept heading toward Vietnamese waters.

It was still pre-dawn when a soft blue light underneath his basket boat caught his eye. At first he thought the lantern was still on. Then he realized the brightness was different, almost luminescent, like a healing glow.

He stopped the engine and walked toward the round boat. As he got closer, he felt an odd feeling. A feeling that he was about to experience something powerful.

He lifted the bamboo boat and it wasn't a su vang fish–it was something else.

He had seen a glimpse of it in the water just before getting caught in the whirlpool. A spectacular specimen, unlike anything he had ever seen in all his years of fishing. A fish with a bluish-green, glowing nodule on top of its head that pulsed down to its dorsal fin. The fish was dead, but the nodule was still moving, as if it had a life of its own. He lifted the creature and took note of its eyes, gills, mouth and lateral fins. It was about a foot long, translucent and beautiful, a combination of yellow and pink. The nodule traveled in a unique, hypnotic pattern, a smooth, serene movement that was very addictive to watch. After staring at it for quite a while, he placed the fish in the cooler and filled it with seawater. He then placed all the remaining fish into the tin bucket and made his way home.

He dragged the basket boat onto the beach and stumbled into the house with the cooler and the tin bucket. Minh rushed to him, as she realized something horrible had happened–his shirt was gone, showing his bruised and battered body. He grimaced in pain, his entire body trembling.

Realizing that he was in no condition to talk, Minh prepared a poultice of powdered turmeric, salt, and ghee, cooking it on low heat over her small kerosene stove. She applied the warm yellow paste to Pham Kai's bruises with her fingers. He winced, yet soon found it soothing. After covering his bruises, she pulled a whitish piece of smooth crystal–*phitkari*, also known as potassium alum–from a rusty White Swan coffee tin. She submerged it in water and rubbed it over his cuts, focusing on the holes on his neck and right shoulder.

Between long pauses, Pham Kai narrated the entire ordeal to Minh. Her eyes widened with astonishment as she listened. When he was too exhausted to speak any longer, she took his hand and held it from shaking. "Pham Kai, please hear me, my dear man. No amount of treatment can ever cure me if I lose you. Please stop this folly. Let's get back to our regular life. We are not meant to be the type of people who take such risks." She embraced him. "Please, stop!"

Pham Kai stared at the cooler, and she followed his gaze to the bright light emanating from underneath its tilted lid. "What's in the cooler?" she asked. "Why is it glowing?"

"I'm not sure," he replied, sighing. "It's the most beautiful fish I've ever seen in my life. I think we need to take it to Haiphong and show it to the people at Tonkin Fisheries."

Minh walked over to the cooler and opened it. This was no su vang fish–it was something even more amazing.

"You're right, husband," Minh agreed. "You go ahead and sleep. I'll sell the rest of the catch in the market, and tomorrow, we'll head out to meet Hoang Binh."

Pham Kai slept for eighteen hours, waking up the next morning at six. Disoriented, he turned over to find Minh making breakfast. He glanced at the cooler and the entire nightmare came rushing back.

"How are you feeling?" Minh asked, happy to see the love of her life awake and in seemingly better condition than the day before.

"Much better," he answered.

"Good," she said. "Get up, wash up, and change. We have a long journey today."

Over the years, Pham Kai had made a friend named Hoang Binh, who on occasions visited their village to meet with the local fishermen. He worked for a large fishery and always shared stories of exotic fish found in Vietnamese waters. On his visits to the village, he had mentioned several times to Pham Kai to contact him if and when he caught an exotic fish, as he would try to fetch him a good price.

Minh had prepared half a dozen parathas–round flatbreads with layers like a croissant. She packed them along with cream mixed with sugar and pickled mango. Pham Kai had made this trip several times, and knew the course well. He steered their boat north, keeping the coastline on their left. By 7:30 in the morning, they were pointed toward Haiphong. Minh had helped Pham Kai clean the boat of all the debris and attach a cloth covering the gaping hole in the wall. She then took out a paratha, spread cream on it, rolled it up, and gave it to Pham Kai. He bit into it, realizing he hadn't eaten anything for well over a day. He handled the wheel with his left hand and ate his breakfast with his still-hurting right hand. She also handed him a bowl of hot, sweet chai. Pham Kai took another bite of the paratha and a sip of chai, the combination soothing his soul.

They reached the port of Haiphong by midday, bustling with container ships, large cranes, and thousands of boats. During the half-hour bus ride to Tonkin Fisheries, Pham Kai made sure to wear his lucky Tonkin Fisheries cap, which Hoang had given him several years ago.

Tonkin Fisheries was a large, white building fronted by huge main gates. Minh and Pham Kai got off the bus and made their way to the guardhouse. After they registered, the guard on duty called the reception desk to inform Hoang Binh that he had guests. His eyes lingered on Minh a fraction too long. He then got up and walked around the counter, asking Pham Kai to show him what was in the cooler.

Pham Kai didn't feel comfortable showing the fish to the guard. "This belongs to your boss, Hoang Binh," he said sternly, "and only he is allowed to look in this cooler."

Pham Kai's resistance surprised and insulted the guard. The guard moved toward them grimly, with the full intent of ripping the cooler from Pham Kai's grip.

Just then, the door opened and in walked Hoang. He quickly noticed the expressions on Pham Kai and Minh's faces. "What are you doing?" he shouted at the guard.

"I-I was just checking to see what was in the cooler," the

guard stammered.

"Pham Kai and Minh are my family," Hoang said. "Go back behind the counter or you won't work here again."

The guard scurried back to his station. Hoang bowed and walked the pair out of the guardhouse toward his building.

He took them to the company cafeteria, which had a full buffet with several hot dishes, salads, two types of rice, and a variety of desserts. The quantity and variety of food was something the couple had never seen before, and the aromas were mouthwatering. Hoang offered them lunch, but their humility prevented them from accepting, and they declined. They sat down and Hoang instead ordered them chai and biscuits.

Hoang watched with a smile as Minh dipped a biscuit in her tea, waiting for them to share the reason for their visit.

"Dear Hoang, we're very sorry to bother you at your work," Pham Kai said.

Hoang raised his hand, bringing it to his chest with a gentle bow. "The honor is mine, Pham Kai. Your visit is a delightful surprise. Tell me, how can I help you?"

"I think I may have caught a special fish," Pham Kai explained, pointing to the cooler he had set at his feet. "I've never seen anything like it, and we were wondering if it could be of some value to you."

Hoang nodded. "Yes, we're always interested in exotic fish caught in our waters. Take your time, finish your tea and biscuits, and then we'll check it out."

After they were done, Hoang took them to a freezing-cold room outfitted with long, stainless steel tables. He explained that this was their receiving area, where marine life was sorted into bins for processing. Pham Kai opened the cooler and placed the fish on the table. Hoang's eyes fixated on the glowing, bluish-green nodule—it was still moving, even though the fish was dead.

Pham Kai touched Hoang on the shoulder, waking him from his trance. "Both Minh and I have had the exact same experience," he said. "We can't stop staring at it, and we lose track of time. Do you think this is a new species?"

Hoang cleared his throat. "Yes, I think you may have caught something very special. I've never seen anything like this before either." He asked if he could show the fish to his team of experts to help determine its worth, it may fetch a premium price—he just wasn't sure how much. Minh and Pham Kai agreed.

The couple returned to the cafeteria, and for the next hour they watched people go in and out of the receiving area, all speaking in hushed tones. By three in the afternoon, Pham Kai and Minh needed to begin their journey back home. At this point, it would take them until midnight.

"I think you've done it, husband," Minh said with a smile. "You may have caught a valuable fish! Why else would they be taking so long?"

Hoang soon approached, pulling out a chair and sitting down. He smiled, choosing his words he spoke. "Pham Kai, we think you have caught a new species of fish." He paused. "Not just new to Vietnam, but perhaps to the world. There seems to be no reference or photographs of anything like your discovery anywhere. We think it should be presented to the Vietnam Maritime University for further analysis. We have a standing relationship with them. If we come across an unknown marine specimen, we sell it to them for a fixed price. With your permission, I'll process the paperwork and provide you with the money."

It wasn't what the two su vang fish would have fetched, but Vietnamese dongs worth eight hundred and sixty dollars was enough to get second and third opinions from private doctors. Pham Kai and Minh turned to each other and then nodded in agreement.

An hour later, they were headed back to their boat, the money tucked away in Pham Kai's inside kurta pocket. Pham Kai felt sad that even though they had some money now, it wasn't enough to get Minh her full treatment. Her option now was to wait and get the national health care, which would take months. Cancer needed to be treated now—even he knew that.

* * *

BACK AT TONKIN Fisheries, the experts examined Pham Kai's fish. They couldn't stop staring at the creature as they tried hard to identify and categorize it. Hoang pulled out his cell phone and called his friend Dr. Vu Ha.

Dr. Vu Ha was a pleasant-looking man with jet-black hair highlighted by a single streak of natural gray, as if someone had taken bleach and brushed it across his head. He had a round face that worked well with his diamond-shaped body. His beaming smile lit up the room, and he was well respected in academic research circles. Vu wasn't excited about the drive, as there was a lot of traffic, and he didn't expect the visit would lead to a new species. But he felt that the pictures and vague description Hoang had provided were enough to warrant an in-person inspection.

After the customary security registration and several handshakes and bows, he was escorted to the receiving area. There were a few fishery employees still gathered around, speaking in whispers. Hoang asked them to move aside.

Vu gasped as he approached the table. He ascertained that he was looking at a deep-sea prehistoric specimen. He grabbed the magnifying glass and moved closer to examine the nodule. It was a hexagonal cone structure with six surfaces, and each surface was a different radiant color. The color of each surface fluctuated between darker and lighter shades of the same palette. There were also these unique geometrical patterns like staircases indented into each surface. There was also an odd slit next to the dorsal fin, though he couldn't make out much of it.

The nodule revolved, pulsed and drifted across the body. *The fish is clearly dead, therefore how is it moving?* He thought. On closer inspection Vu realized that the nodule wasn't actually moving–it would appear and disappear between the head of the fish and the dorsal fin. Biological hexagonal structures were considered to be evolved mathematical wonders. This warranted further study, so he made arrangements for the immediate transfer of the specimen to his university.

Vu spent the next few days analyzing it with his researchers. They were having animated conversations, and Vu was enjoying the process. Just when they would find a feature of the fish upon which they could create a case for its morphology, another feature would refute it. Vu and his students couldn't stop thinking about it–it had taken over their lives.

During one such research session, the door of their lab swung open and the head of Vu's department, Dr. Cong Cuc, walked in. Everyone stopped talking. Cong ignored the students and ordered Vu to join him in his office.

The department head glowered behind his desk. He removed his glasses, licked them with his tongue, and began to wipe them with a cheap, blue printed handkerchief. "Vu, I've warned you several times not to get carried away with projects that waste my department's time and resources. What is all this talk about a fish?"

Vu shifted his weight. "Sir, I understand. But we've come across a unique specimen, and in my scientific opinion, it's going to be a great discovery in the marine field."

The department head gestured for Vu to stop talking. "Is this something that'll help reduce the hunger of our population? Will it help our fishermen catch more fish?"

Vu shuffled his feet again. He knew where the conversation was heading. He started to explain the specimen's importance and why it was necessary for them to continue their research.

"Stop delaying and answer my questions," Cong snapped.

Vu shifted his gaze toward the ceiling, taking a deep breath. "For now, the answer to both questions is, I don't know. It's too early to tell."

The department head furrowed his brow. "Vu, you know the mission of this university and our department. You know our strict policies against wasting government money. You and your team will see the inside of a jail cell if you don't stop working on this stupid fish. Dammit, you should have more sense." He turned his gaze to his computer monitor and gestured for Vu to go. Embarrassed, Vu bowed and left.

Frustrated and insulted, Vu went to his office and slammed the door. He dropped in his old office chair and stared at his computer screen. He couldn't understand how educated people like Cong could be so ignorant and arrogant. It always bothered him when Cong would refer to their department as *his* department.

However, though he had to follow orders, he needed to do something about this fish. An idea started to take hold–he could write a blog post describing the specimen. It was well within his rights as a researcher.

Perhaps marine biologists from a Western institute would read it and request to pick it up for further study. His post couldn't imply that he was reaching out to universities outside Vietnam, as that would be considered treason and theft of a national treasure. So he wrote the blog as an informational piece, stating only the facts.

As the days and weeks passed, not a single response or comment was made to the blog, adding to his disappointment. The creature was stored in the specimen refrigerator, and some days, he would take it out, stare at its still-glowing nodule, and return it with great care.

* * *

IT HAD BEEN several weeks since Pham Kai and Minh returned from their trip to Tonkin Fisheries. Pham Kai often wondered about the fish he had caught. What was it? Why was it so mesmerizing?

They began making daily bus trips to Qui Nhon city, spending their earnings meeting with specialists and getting chest X-rays, mammograms, bone scans, and MRIs. The results were always the same. Minh was suffering from an aggressive form of cancer.

The next few weeks were difficult. Minh felt betrayed by her body. They had never had children—maybe if she'd had children, maybe if she'd breastfed a child, maybe this cancer wouldn't have happened.

There were times during the day when, in private, she cried till her eyes went dry. She wasn't crying for herself—she cried for Pham Kai. What would he do when she was gone? They had been married for over thirty years. Their lives, routines, decisions, habits, even their styles of speech were so intertwined. They were one unit, one person. The thought of Pham Kai being alone, living his life without her, tore at her soul. She felt a deep sense of despair and guilt that somehow she had betrayed him.

Minh started to accompany Pham Kai on his fishing trips. She wanted to spend every waking hour with him while she waited for her turn at treatment, an agonizing ten months away.

Besides, she loved working alongside Pham Kai—he was her hero. She immersed herself in his routine of casting, hauling, sorting, and going to the market. She soon became too exhausted to think about her condition.

She also started making an old wives' tale recipe of tea. A concoction of a tablespoon of turmeric powder, a teaspoon of ghee, and two teaspoons of honey, all blended into heated coconut milk. She would sit on the edge of the boat and drink, watching Pham Kai gaze into the horizon for hours on end. One day, she asked him what was he looking for.

"A miracle," he whispered.

CHAPTER SEVEN
Paramarines

SEBASTIAN'S DUCATI MOTORCYCLE was made for distance. It took him through Costa Rica, Honduras, Guatemala, and Mexico before he crossed the border into Arizona, where he veered west toward San Diego. The further he got from Bocas del Toro, the better he felt. By the time he reached the Scripps Institution of Oceanography, he felt good. It was true what they said about long bike rides. The freedom on the road, the vastness of the Americas, even the bugs hitting his visor had a cathartic effect on him. The ride helped him leave the past behind him and focus on the future.

Sebastian cruised down to the Old Scripps Building, the very first marine research facility built on campus, and parked in the same spot he used for so many years. He walked the familiar, narrow corridors of Ritter Hall on his way to Cebrián's office. The smell brought memories of his time as a student at this prestigious research institution. An antique glass cupboard still held old artifacts of past scientists, including the famous dissecting microscope of Dr. Martin Johnson from 1936.

Entering a small vestibule at the end of the hall, Sebastian approached Cebrián's secretary, crouched in front of her computer screen with intense focus.

Hearing a shuffle in the doorway, she lifted her head to see a handsome man in a leather jacket holding a biker's helmet and smiling. "He's been expecting you. And wow, you're on time!" she said, motioning him toward an open office door.

Sebastian approached the office, noting how it reflected Cebrián's unique personality. The back wall was comprised of a large window overlooking the Pacific Ocean. In front of the window sat a sleek, modern desk with a bust of Einstein and a small statue of Gandhi holding his famous cane. To the right was a small round conference table with a whiteboard mounted on the wall, and to the left was a small cart with an espresso machine, and deep red Demitasse cups. On the walls he had pictures of Amelia Earhart, the Wright Brothers, a schematic of the starship Enterprise, and a copy of Alexander Graham Bell's patent.

Cebrián stood at the window with his back to the door, turning as he heard Sebastian come in. "You made it!" he exclaimed. "Good to see you again. Please, come sit."

He motioned Sebastian over to the conference table, where a towering stack of books on quantum physics were placed.

"How was your ride?" Cebrián inquired. "I'm sure it was an opportunity for you to think and reflect."

"It was great," Sebastian agreed. "It gave me much-needed time to recognize what's important for me going forward."

Cebrián's cell phone buzzed, and he ignored it. "Sebastian, I'm so happy you took my offer to come. Often, people who have experienced what you've gone through tend to lose their desire for research. I was hoping you wouldn't go down that path."

"I came close," Sebastian said, sighing.

"I know," Cebrián replied. "But you're here now." He picked up the books on the table. "You can see I'm doing some research of my own. I'm reading these because quantum physics is the closest field to a systematic and scientific study of the unknown. It's a subject where variability, chance, and random events are the norm." Sebastian leaned forward, listening.

"Quantum physicists," Cebrián continued, "have found subatomic particles that can be connected to each other when they are three thousand miles apart—meaning that when a quantum particle in San Diego turns clockwise on its axis, its partner particle in Philadelphia turns anticlockwise. Fascinating! Coffee?"

"Sure." Sebastian said.

Cebrián got up and walked to the espresso machine as Sebastian perused some of the books, confused but intrigued. Within a few minutes, the whole room smelled like a *finja* farm; the aroma was intoxicating. Cebrián went through the elaborate process of first grinding and then making fresh brewed espresso for the two of them.

He picked up the red Demitasse cups and placed one in front of Sebastian before continuing. "I'm building a team of scientists I call Paramarines. They'll be tasked with finding specimens that exhibit higher forms of evolutionary capabilities that tap into this quantum realm." Cebrián explained, pausing to take a sip. "These include intuition, telepathy, predicting future events, being at two places at the same time, and a number of other such unexplained phenomena. Scientists have known for a long time that certain animals have the ability to predict natural catastrophes before they strike. The tsunami in Southeast Asia that killed over three hundred thousand people didn't harm a single wild animal. Almost all of them took shelter on higher ground. And the animals that did die were the ones in captivity. There are dogs that lie next to terminal patients in a hospice facility twenty-four hours before they pass away. Pets have been known to get agitated when their owners have gotten into a car accident. We also know certain animals like dogs and cats start staring at an area of a room, where you and I don't see anything. They not only stare, but also show signs of distress, as if they see something. There are countless such recorded incidences."

Sebastian took a sip of coffee, considering. "So, your Paramarines will find specimens that exhibit measurable forms of such abilities?"

"That is our goal," Cebrián answered. "We've partnered with the world's leading computing and robotics university in Pittsburgh." And they've helped us develop a next-generation artificial intelligence supercomputer called Poseidon. We've populated it with over 1.2 million scientific research papers and given it access to over four billion real-time conversations related to events, meetings, seminars, and expeditions taking place across the globe. Any mention in a tweet, post, blog commentary, or picture related to a specimen that shows unexplained phenomenon, we capture it. We then use Poseidon to serve up the potential find for our Paramarines to investigate."

He stood up, setting his coffee on the table. "Sebastian, mankind is facing existential crises on a scale never seen before. We've polluted our oceans. Our food supplies are dwindling. We have rampant malnutrition and disease. Climate change is submerging coastal cities. We are experiencing greater forms of distrust, greed, corruption, violence, racism, and lack of tolerance than ever before. Humanity as we know it is falling apart. Something has to be done to solve these issues."

"And you think finding species that tap into the quantum realm would help us address these problems?" Sebastian asked, engrossed.

"Yes, the problems we're now dealing with need a new way of thinking to solve them. We as humans have to evolve to operate at a higher plane, like some of these species have evolved—that's why I see evolution as our solution. The best way to get there is to find such species and to learn to biomimic their capabilities."

"Doctor Alveraz, this is inspiring, I'll admit. But how do you propose a team of scientists even attempt to accomplish such a goal?"

"Please call me Cebrián and walk with me—I want to show you something," Cebrián said.

The duo made their way toward Vaughan Hall Building 8675. Inside, Cebrián led Sebastian into an elevator. Instead of pushing any buttons, he pulled a key from his coat pocket, inserted it into the panel, and twisted. He then pressed the floor buttons in a fast, code-based sequence. The elevator began to descend, as Sebastian's eyes grew wide. He'd been in this building countless times during his academic years, yet he'd never known there were more than three floors.

Several moments later, the doors opened onto a vast room the size of a large college lecture hall. What Sebastian saw shocked him—it was one of the most sophisticated command centers he had ever seen. The wall facing the elevator held five huge screens split into multiple panels, showing everything from maps and satellite images of water bodies and jungles to live feeds of major expeditions. A glass wall took up the entire right side of the room, and through it Sebastian could see a sophisticated marine biology lab complete with DNA sequencers, MRIs, portable X-ray machines, and mass spectrometers. The left side of the room held an open conference area with a large table. Situated throughout the space were several workstations with various transparent screens and tablets. Four individuals were spread throughout the space, two in the lab, another two at workstations. One in particular stood in front of his glass computer screen, opening files and zooming in and out of images with sweeping hand gestures.

"Welcome to the world's first Paramarine Operating Center, otherwise known as the POC," Cebrián said. He walked to the center of the room, turned his attention to the main screen and called out, "Poseidon."

The large wall-to-wall screens turned a deep blue, complete with colorful coral reefs and spectacular marine life. A pleasant, synthesized male voice emanated from the room's speakers. "How may I help you, Doctor Alveraz?"

"Anything new today that may be of interest to our Paramarines?" Cebrián asked.

"Certainly," Poseidon said. "I have been tracking Twitter feeds from a deep-sea research expedition off the coast of Baja, California. They have discovered a new bioluminescent specimen at a depth of four thousand feet. It appears to be a jellyfish that is being tested for cancer-fighting immunotherapies."

The Twitter feed in question showed up on a screen with its photo below it. Cebrián scanned the information as Sebastian stood, fascinated.

"Thank you, Poseidon," Cebrián said. Using the intercom, he requested that the four scientists working in the adjoining lab join him in the conference space.

The conference table was a large touch screen, and all the displays in the POC were duplicated on it. Cebrián touched a soft panel in one corner of the screen, and its surface assumed the appearance of a birch table with an aquamarine stripe running down the middle. A colorful coral fish would swim through the aquamarine strip from one end to the other. Sebastian took the aquamarine stripe to mean that Poseidon was present as well.

One by one, the scientists, or Paramarines, as Cebrián called them, entered and introduced themselves.

Shiloh was a marine biologist and mechanical engineer. He

was short and slim, with a warm complexion and shoulder-length black hair that he often tied back when working. His beaming, contagious personality emerged as he talked about his work on deep-sea submersibles, sensors, and aquatic technology.

Fabienne was another marine biologist with outstanding expertise in experimentation, research, and analytical deduction. Her fiery red hair was cut into a short bob with bangs, further adding to her natural intensity. She was outspoken and talked with her hands, was passionate about her work, and seemed to wear her emotions on her sleeve.

Of the other two scientists, Nidal was a geologist and Michelangelo was a data scientist. They struck Sebastian as idiosyncratic, but not in a bad way. He couldn't put his finger on it. They were twins, but not because they looked similar or were related–it was their mannerisms and how they spoke, as if they'd been working together for a long time and had picked up each other's expressions and non-verbal cues. Both were tall and appeared nimble, with a quiet and swift way of walking and moving. Nidal had dark hair that matched his dark-rimmed glasses and a serious face. Michelangelo had tousled blonde hair and a light scruff that gave him a soft, warm appearance.

Cebrián welcomed them all, introducing Sebastian as the researcher who had found the specimen that proved Step Evolution.

Fabienne's eyes widened. "Wait a minute. You're the one who found the snails? We've been wanting to meet you!"

Sebastian laughed. "Yes, but I just got lucky." He loved that his big discovery was referred to as "the snails."

Shiloh chimed in. "No such thing as luck. You rocked it, man!"

Like a big sister would, Fabienne rolled her eyes, and gave Sebastian a hint of the deep friendship the scientists had formed through their long hours working together.

"This place is impressive," Sebastian said, "When Doctor Alveraz invited me to Scripps to discuss an idea I couldn't have imagined in my wildest dreams what I'm seeing here today. Paramarines, artificial intelligence, and a command center with state-of-the-art equipment." He paused, turning his gaze to Cebrián. "Who's funding all this?"

Cebrián leaned back in his chair, folding his arms. "This has been in the works for quite some time. I submitted an ambitious proposal to our government explaining that nature has had over four billion years to evolve. There are species living in our world that have solutions to the global problems faced by mankind.

"If given the funding, I told them I would build a team of scientists whose mission would be to find such specimens and biomimic their natural capabilities, providing us with solutions far beyond anything we could imagine. After several years of discussion and debates, they agreed to fund my new initiative. This new research division has bipartisan approval, with a ten-year budget of three hundred million. This includes access to military transports, use of state-of-the-art government research facilities, and two of our very own Gulfstream G650ERs—private jets outfitted to transfer the POC and Poseidon anywhere in the world. We call them Panther One and Panther Two."

He paused, looking at Sebastian. "We're going to research the cutting edge of known science, and the key question is…" His voice lowered to a conspiratorial whisper as he subconsciously rotated the outer bezel of his watch. "Will you join us?"

"I'm not sure what to say," Sebastian admitted. "Your work here sounds exciting, but you're blurring the line between science and science fiction."

Cebrián laughed. "Good, we don't want anyone to take us serious. We're operating under the radar, until such time that we're ready to change the world. I think you're well suited to our task. You have a do-or-die, persistent attitude, you listen to your gut and apply scientific and logical deduction, and you're unafraid to search the farthest corners of the Earth to find your answers."

Sebastian nodded, looking down at the aquamarine wave on the table. Cebrián's words sounded sincere and compelling, and he wasn't kidding when he said he was working on a new evolutionary science. Sebastian folded his arms and rested his elbows on the table. Clasping his fingers, he spoke. "Searching for snails in the Panamanian jungle is not too far a cry from what I think you guys are doing here." He grinned.

Cebrián flashed his signature smile as the team began to walk over and shake hands with Sebastian. "I'll let you guys get to know each other. It's time for me to get back to my day job." He walked out of the conference area toward the elevator, giving Sebastian a pat on the back on his way out.

Sebastian spent most of the day getting to know the team. They all had similar stories: some had their PhD research topic stolen, others had lost their life's work to their senior team members. Cebrián had put the team together due to their common thread.

Shiloh walked Sebastian through the POC, explaining the various stations and their functions, the large hand-gesture navigation screen, and the power of Poseidon. Fabienne took him through the lab, highlighting new features of the equipment he may not have seen before. One was a hermetically sealed pod, complete with a bed, desk, and intercom. "What's that for?" Sebastian asked.

"It's a special portable chamber that seals off radiation, bacteria, and any unknown particles," Fabienne said. "We may have to use it if we come in contact with new specimens that may pose a danger. It can be taken apart and reassembled in minutes."

"Have we found any good specimen candidates for research?" Sebastian asked.

"Not yet," Fabienne replied. "But there are several potential leads. Well, now that we have an adventurer like you on our team, we may have better luck."

Sebastian shrugged. "We'll see." He got a feeling that Fabienne did everything by the book. She was detail-oriented, a true researcher. He could bank on her to ensure that all research protocols were followed. He thought they'd get along well.

Nidal and Michelangelo were walking Sebastian through their current work when the POC screens lit up and a submarine ping echoed.

"What happened?" Sebastian asked.

"Poseidon just got a hit," Fabienne responded.

"What does that mean?" Sebastian asked.

Before Shiloh or Fabienne could respond, Poseidon answered. "Doctor Miles," the robotic voice said, "I have found two data vectors that have cosine similarities, pointing to discrete events that may be connected."

Sebastian was taken aback upon hearing his name. He wasn't sure if he was supposed to respond.

Poseidon continued. "The first data vector is a blog post from a professor, Dr. Vu Ha of the Vietnam Maritime University, located in Haiphong City. It is about a local fisherman from the village of Nhon Ly who captured a fish around Paracel Islands that may be a new species. This fish has a unique glowing feature, a nodule that travels from its head to its dorsal fin. It seems to have a hypnotic effect on people. The blog did not go into too much detail, other than the fact that people would spend hours looking at it.

"The second data vector points to the Vietnamese fishermen from the same village. Some of them exhibit peculiar markings on their bodies that look like two puncture wounds. I found these images on local social media sites, with no commentary explaining them."

"Poseidon, please call me Sebastian," he said, trying to get comfortable with the idea of talking to a supercomputer. He turned to the team to see if they would be fine with him taking the lead. They all gestured for him to go ahead. "Poseidon, why do you think these two vectors are connected?"

"According to my correlation algorithm," Poseidon answered, "it appears that fishermen with these markings are those who most often search for unique species. However, I am unsure about causation."

"Okay, let's figure this out," Sebastian said. "Let's see if we can find the fisherman who caught this fish and determine if he has these puncture wounds. Poseidon, please show us the markings on the fishermen. Also, please bring up a map of the Paracel Islands, the South China Sea, the Gulf of Tonkin, and a satellite view of Nhon Ly village." In seconds, the images popped up. Sebastian was surprised how fast the data appeared. "Please transfer these images to the conference room," he requested.

The team made their way back to the conference table. Nidal stepped forward and pointed at a group of islands as he adjusted his glasses. "These are the Paracel Islands, not too far from Nhon Ly village. Geographically, this area is made up of large, rocky hills, deep caverns, and over a hundred coral reefs," he explained. "And this, nearby, is the area of the South China Sea where China is building a military base, which has lead the whole area into an intense territorial dispute with Vietnam. China is restricting all fishing by Vietnamese fishermen around these islands."

Michelangelo spoke, rolling up his sleeves. "Based on the information collected by tsunami sensors, there have been significant changes in water depth near one of the islands. The opening of a massive underwater cavern may be the cause."

Shiloh gestured across his section of the table to bring up pictures of Nhon Ly village—its streets, modest homes, and round, blue, basket-like fishermen's boats. With a flick of his hand, he started sending them to Sebastian. Images of the market and videos of fisherman pulling in their catches in big nylon nets floated around the table. Markings covered the fishermen's hands, necks, and faces, just as Poseidon had described.

"Take a look at this," Fabienne said, pulling one photo apart and shooting a copy to each person. "Notice the writing on his cap." It was a picture of a thin, wiry man with hardened lines of age and sea weather on his face. He was sitting on the beach with three other fishermen, an old boat in the background. He wore a green coat and gray track pants, with slippers on his feet. He was looking away from the camera, toward the sea. His eyes expressed his thoughts—he seemed lost in a dream. The words on his khaki baseball cap were hard to read, yet legible: TONKIN FISHERIES.

"Poseidon, I have a hunch," she said. "Can you locate where Doctor Vu's university purchases unique specimens?"

"Checking," Poseidon said. After a few seconds, it continued. "Tonkin Fisheries provides specimens to Doctor Vu Ha's university. The fishery is located near Haiphong City."

"Okay then, can we find the identity of this fisherman?" asked Sebastian.

"Sure," Michelangelo said. "We can cross-reference his face with the published database of registered fishermen in the village of Nhon Ly. The Vietnamese government requires all fishermen to be registered before they can get a fishing license." He started opening files and accessing information on the table in front of him. He had a name in a few minutes. "Pham Kai," he announced. "Registered fisherman. Fifty-three years of age. Inherited his boat from his father, who inherited it from *his* father. A generational fisherman."

Sebastian expanded Pham Kai's picture and found two markings on his neck. "Is there a way to find out if he's ever traveled to Tonkin Fisheries?"

"Let's see," Fabienne said. "Poseidon, analyze satellite images of this area, isolate Pham Kai's boat, and see if it's made the six-hour journey to Haiphong in recent months."

"How long will that take?" asked Sebastian.

"Approximately ten minutes," Poseidon answered. "I will have to analyze satellite images over the past year."

The team dispersed, checking phones and finishing a few tasks at their workstations while they waited. Sebastian took the time to explore one of the transparent gesture screens, familiarizing himself with the actions Shiloh had taught him.

Before he knew it, Poseidon's familiar nautical ping was heard. The Paramarines gathered at the center of the POC. "I have reviewed over hundred thousand images," it said. "Most of Pham Kai's navigation patterns have been in heavy fishing lanes. However, there are two departures from this norm. Around six months ago, he made several late-night or early-morning trips to the Paracel Islands, most of them near Bombay Reef. Later, he made a trip to Haiphong port. And importantly no other fisherman boat has made this trip."

"Fabienne," Sebastian said, "I think you're right. He appears to be our fisherman." He approached the man's image on one of the screens. "What have you found, Pham Kai?" he whispered. "And what are those marks on your neck?"

Sebastian turned away from Pham Kai's picture. His mind raced. "Shiloh, can we call Doctor Vu Ha?"

"Sure, what time is it in Vietnam?" Shiloh asked.

Someone shouted, "Eight o'clock a.m."

"On it," Shiloh said.

A few moments later, a man's voice came through the speakers. "Hello?"

Sebastian spoke up. "Doctor Vu Ha?"

A tentative "Yes?" came through the speakers.

"Doctor Vu Ha, this is Doctor Sebastian Miles from the Scripps Institute of Oceanography. We're calling about your blog post from several weeks ago referring to a new marine specimen. Are you still researching it?"

Vu paused, not believing that his blog post had worked. Controlling his excitement, he replied in his most professional voice, "We've stored the specimen for future research, for now. And please, call me Vu."

"Sure, please call me Sebastian," Sebastian responded. "Vu, you mention in your blog that the specimen has a hypnotic effect on people. What do you mean by that?"

"Sebastian, it's the most puzzling specimen I've seen in my academic life," Vu replied. "There's an unexplainable biological feature on it that defies any scientific explanation we can find. The fish is dead, but there's one part of it that appears to have a life of its own. It emanates some form of visible energy that moves from the head down to the dorsal fin. It's this movement that one can't stop staring at during examination. My students have often lost track of time while looking at it, and so have I. And there's a mysterious slit adjacent to its dorsal fin. We believe it's a new species—it certainly warrants further investigation."

"Okay, Vu." Sebastian said. "Would you be open to Scripps taking a look at it?"

Once again there was a brief silence. "That would be wonderful. My concern is that we don't have a reciprocal research agreement between our two institutions, and your request may be rejected," Vu replied.

Sebastian raised an eyebrow at the team, and they nodded their agreement.

Vu continued, "Send me an official request from your department, following the proper protocols, and I'll forward it to our department chair with my recommendation. Let's get the paperwork filed and we'll deal with the red tape if and when it shows up."

"Sounds good," Sebastian said. "Expect an email from us in the next thirty minutes. And Vu, thank you for working with us."

That afternoon, Cebrián joined the team in the POC. He walked over to the maps on the screen, looking at Haiphong. "Did you say this specimen is at the Vietnam Maritime University?" Cebrián asked.

"Yes, why?" Sebastian asked.

"I recommend you get ready," Cebrián replied.

"Get ready?" Sebastian repeated.

Cebrián folded his arms and turned toward them. "I don't think they will ship us the specimen. The Vietnamese government will bog down the process with red tape and bureaucracy. You'll have to go to Vietnam and try to convince them to give it to you. I'll call the state department and see if we can get your travel documents on the ground when you get there. It may be harder for them to refuse if you show up in person."

Shiloh fist pumped and yelled. "Hell, let's go to Vietnam and get this specimen!" The others agreed, though they seemed a bit unsure at the speed at which everything was happening.

They planned to meet at the private hangar housing Panther Two at six the next morning. Sebastian grabbed his helmet and backpack, and waved goodbye to the team. "See you bright and early."

He rode his bike out of the university, heading south for about half an hour. He turned into a secluded wooded area near Cabrillo National Park.

Over the years—as a teen, and later as a student working on his PhD—Sebastian had frequented this hidden spot many times. He took his bike right into the woods, parking it in a small clearing. He then made his way into the wooded area, but it wasn't a trail he walked along—it was a geological anomaly with twisted trees and odd shaped rocks, caused by an energy vortex in the area. After hiking through it for fifteen minutes, he came to a rock cliff surrounded by bristlecone pine trees.

These trees had been known to exist in California for over five thousand years. At the base of one in particular sat an opening covered by a large basalt rock shaped like a wheel-stone. He pushed it aside to reveal a natural manhole—a circular cave-like formation made of sandstone. He crawled military-style through it for a short while until it opened into a U-shaped cove surrounded by high cliffs, with a small tidal pond in the middle.

He couldn't remember how he'd found the place—since childhood, he had known it existed. His parents would joke with him, saying this was where they had found him, and indeed, his earliest memory of them was here. They said he was a gift given to them by the sea. They would tease him, saying he was a mermaid's child, hence his love for marine life and the ocean.

Making his way to the edge of the tidal pond, he sat down—the cove was how he had left it, pristine and undisturbed. He took off his shoes, folded his pant legs to clear the depth of the pond, and walked in. The instant his feet touched the water, he felt a combination of energy and relaxation, as if it had some element that rejuvenated every cell of his body. After wading for several minutes, he went back to the bank and sat until the sky grew dark. He thought about what had happened—meeting with Cebrián, the team of Paramarines, and the opportunity presented to him.

He got up. Before putting on his shoes, he walked back into the pond one more time. He leaned over and touched the luminescent plankton. Flashes of images flooded his vision. Since childhood, every time he touched the water with his hands, he would see these strange images. He used to chalk the experience up to his Pareidolia. He couldn't make out what the images were, but they would inspire and recharge him. Lost in thought, Sebastian made his way back to his bike and returned to Scripps.

THE NEXT MORNING, he stepped inside the Gulfstream G650ER, codenamed Panther Two, and was once again impressed with the technical resources available to the team. At the far end of the plane was a large screen with Poseidon's signature deep-blue water and coral reef. On one side were workstations, complete with portable incubators, aquariums, centrifuges, and a Nanodrop Spectrophotometer. The other side had comfortable, business-class-style. The plane was a mobile marine biology lab that could reach the remotest parts of the world.

The captain and copilot, both Texans with lilting drawls, came out of the cockpit to greet him. They shared the flight path to Haiphong, explaining that they would stop at Tokyo airport to refuel. "Folks," the captain said, "I recommend you get comfortable. It's gonna be a long flight. We just need a few last-minute clearances and we'll be on our way." He asked Sebastian to follow them into the cockpit.

The captain plopped down in his jump seat. "Doctor Alveraz shared all the details of your mission," he said with a grin. "I recommend we spend as little time as possible in Vietnam. Things in that part of the world can go real bad, real fast."

"I agree," said Sebastian. "Let's make it quick." He shook their hands and went back to join the rest of the team.

The plane took off, and after a few minutes, the vast Pacific Ocean appeared through his window. Sebastian gazed out as it stretched to the horizon. *How many unknown species are still hidden in the oceans?* he wondered.

Just then, his phone buzzed. He couldn't believe it, a text

from Maria: *Hey, heard what happened in Panama, not cool, hope you're on to a new adventure.*

The message brought a twinkle to his eyes. He started to respond, but it was hard to form the words. He had a lot to say, but he held back. He had just been thinking about Maria, wondering where she was.

He got some words out: *Where are you? You're not in a jungle or cave.*

Her response came back: *Yes, I just got done with my last expedition and now relaxing on the beach for some R&R.*

Sebastian replied, *Where?*

Somewhere you can't reach in a million years, she texted back, teasing.

Sebastian texted again: *Where?*

Guam, I was here for a blue hole expedition for the U.S. government, she answered.

Sebastian got up and walked over to the cockpit. "Captain, how hard would it be to land in Guam and refill there instead of Tokyo?"

"Hmm, we do have clearance to land at Andersen Air Force Base. Why?" the captain asked.

"We may have one more team member to pick up," Sebastian replied. "Can we do it?"

"Sure," the captain said. "We'll make the arrangements. Shouldn't be a problem. We'll land around eight a.m. local time."

Sebastian thanked the captain and texted Maria: *Get to Andersen Air Force Base at 8am and join me on my new adventure.*

Maria responded: *What??? What do you mean?? REALLY!!!*

Sebastian texted: *No joke, meet me and I'll bring you up to speed. I'll meet you at the main terminal. More instructions to follow.*

Sebastian realized he hadn't conferred with the team. Walking back he addressed them. "Guys, slight change in plans. We're going to land in Guam to pick up one more team member. She helped me with my last expedition climbing Cerro Tacarcuna," he explained.

Shiloh smiled. "I get it. We're picking up your old girl-friend."

Fabienne frowned at Shiloh, chiming in with a small hint of irritation. "Why do we need a mountain climber? Or for that matter, an expedition expert?"

"I have a feeling that getting the specimen from Vietnam will turn into an expedition. Plus, we'll need a person of her skill in the event we have to track and find its source. I believe our adventure is just beginning."

Fabienne pursed her lips before turning back to her laptop.

Sebastian walked over to the screen and requested Poseidon for any and all information on Vietnam Maritime University. Poseidon started displaying the main campus, the buildings, and layouts. Sebastian found the building that had the marine labs. It had a terracotta-tiled courtyard with a beautiful Bonsai plant in the middle. He rotated the picture—the front door of the building had a folding steel gate the kind that collapses and extends like an accordion with a standard padlock.

Fabienne walked over to him and glanced at the screen. "Preparing?" she quipped.

"Look at these pictures," he said. "Their graduation ceremony is a military parade. We're not headed to a private university. It's government-funded, with a focus on defense. I hope Vu succeeds in completing all the necessary paperwork for a smooth transfer."

"What happens if we're not allowed to bring back the specimen?" Fabienne inquired.

"Three days ago, I was riding my bike through the Arizona desert, bugs hitting my face," Sebastian said. "Today, I'm sitting in a near supersonic marine lab on its way to Vietnam, hoping to retrieve a brand-new species with unexplained biological features. I promise you, we are not coming back empty-handed. We'll come up with a fair solution that works for all parties." He paused. "Of course, if that doesn't happen, we'll just have to find Pham Kai and engage him to help us find another one."

Twelve hours later, as the plane made its final approach, Sebastian took in the beautiful beaches with turquoise water next to lush green topology. The island had a rocky structure, with elevations and sharp cliffs that ran right into the ocean. For a while, it appeared the plane was going to land on water, and then the runway came up.

"Welcome to Guam, folks," the captain announced. "We're stopping for ninety minutes to refuel, then we'll head out. You're more than welcome to go inside the base."

The plane came to a complete stop near the main building. Looking out the window, Sebastian spotted Maria standing in an army Jeep, wearing her signature hiking boots, shorts, and a white tank top with an open army fatigue shirt. A Ranger's cap sat on her head and she had sunglasses over her eyes, an army-style duffle bag over one shoulder. Sebastian opened the airplane door, and the hot, tropical air shocked him. Maria swung herself from the roll bar and landed on the tarmac, a big smile on her face, shaking her head in disbelief as they embraced.

She followed him back to the plane, where he introduced her to the team. As Sebastian brought her up to speed on the mission, Maria chewed on her bottom lip. She loved seeing Sebastian, but picking up a specimen from a university in Vietnam did not sound like an adventure. Shrugging her shoulders, she said. "I'm not sure you need me for this kind of mission."

"Well, hear me out," Sebastian replied. "We're all scientists going into hostile territory. I hope all goes well, but I'd feel more comfortable having you on our side. Plus, if the professor doesn't give us the specimen, we'll have to embark on an adventure to find another one."

Maria reflected at what Sebastian was saying. She gauged the expressions on the team, then her eyes lingered on Michelangelo and Nidal for a brief second before returning to Sebastian.

"Okay, but your reason for having me come along is weak," she agreed, smiling.

"That's what I thought, too," Fabienne blurted out.

* * *

VU FELT A sense of trepidation. Nothing ever went according to plan in Vietnam. But today, his wife had packed his favorite lunch—her famous Vietnamese barbecue, and that was great start to the day. He picked up the large black lunchbox from the dining table. It was quite elaborate, with a black canvas strap through the center and the words *MON BENTO* across it in white.

He made his way to the university, the whole time thinking about what could go wrong. He went straight to the lab, opened the specimen refrigerator and glanced at the polystyrene box that held the specimen. It was still intact—all looked good for the transfer. He then placed his lunch in the staff fridge next to it. But when he got to his office, a note from Cong lay on his desk, and Vu's heart sank.

As he walked into Cong's office, Vu saw a printed copy of his blog post and the paperwork Sebastian had sent him on the desk. The department head stared at him.

"When were you going to tell me, hmm?" Cong growled. "When were you going to tell me that you had gone behind my back?" Just as Vu was about to say something, the department head gestured for him to be silent. "Did I not order you to stop working on the fish?"

Vu's voice broke as he spoke. "Yes, you did, and I didn't work on it. I just blogged about it–"

Cong smacked his hand on his desk. Spittle flew from his mouth. "Shut up!" he shrieked. "I told you, stop thinking about that stupid fish, but instead you went ahead and wrote a blog about it!" He lifted the blog, crumpled it up, and threw it in Vu's face, causing him to flinch. "Do you understand the issue you've created for me? And now you have a bunch of Americans coming in from God-knows-where to pick it up. I'm amazed by your absolute stupidity! Did you think I'd give you permission to hand over the specimen because they sent me the paperwork? How stupid are you?" His bellowing voice carried out into the hallway. He pointed a finger at Vu. "You are going to tell those American bastards there is no fish. You've destroyed it."

Vu's eyes widened. "You want me to destroy it?"

"Yes, destroy it!" Cong shouted, beside himself with anger. "What, are you deaf as well as dumb now? We're not going to let Americans come into our university and take something that belongs to us! Do you understand? Now call them and tell them that the fish has been destroyed, on my orders. No need to come to Vietnam." He turned away from Vu in disgust and stared at his monitor.

Vu stood there for a moment. Never in his life had he been insulted this way. He wasn't sure why, but he bent down and picked up the crumpled printout of the blog post. Bowing, he walked out of the office with his fists clenched, shaking. Throwing the specimen in the incinerator was equivalent to burning down a library. He was being reprimanded for sharing knowledge with the world–sharing knowledge was his job.

He went back to the office, pulled out a folded paper from his pocket, and began dialing Sebastian's number.

* * *

POSEIDON BROUGHT UP Vu's picture. "Sebastian, Doctor Vu Ha is on the line."

Sebastian's phone was also linked to the communication system of the plane, and he put it on speaker. "Hi, Vu."

"Sebastian?" Vu asked.

"Yes, we can hear you," Sebastian responded.

"We have a problem," Vu said, his voice trembling. "Doctor Cong Cuc, my boss, won't give me permission to hand over the specimen. In fact, he has ordered me to incinerate it."

CHAPTER EIGHT
Kaleidoscope

"INCINERATE IT?" SEBASTIAN repeated, stunned.

Maria gestured for him to mute the call. Sebastian tapped his phone and nodded. "Ask him if there's any lab equipment they need," she said. "If we have it on the plane, maybe his boss would be open to a trade."

Sebastian tapped his screen again. "Vu, what if we offered you a trade? Is there any equipment Cong would be willing to accept?"

After a few moments, Vu spoke. "He's an illogical man. I'm not sure he'd be open to it. But there are a number of items we need for our lab. Our budget is so tight; we are always in need of equipment. What were you considering?"

"Fabienne? Shiloh?" Sebastian whispered.

Shiloh picked up a portable centrifuge. Fabienne grimaced and nodded. "Well," Sebastian said, "we have two portable centrifuge rotor packages on the plane. We can part with one."

"A centrifuge, you say?" Vu confirmed.

"That's right," Sebastian said.

"Cong is beyond upset," Vu pondered. "I'm fearful of even broaching the topic. But I think it's worth a try, let me talk to him."

* * *

VU SOMEHOW GATHERED the courage to go back to Cong's office.

"Now what?" Cong sneered. "Did you call the Americans?"

"Yes," Vu replied, shifting his weight, "and they've offered a portable centrifuge rotor package in exchange for the specimen."

"They're willing to give us a full-blown centrifuge complete with a rotor package?" The department head laughed out loud. "Fine! They're even bigger fools than you are. Tell them we accept their offer. Have them bring the equipment and you can hand over the fish. I'll call the appropriate government officials and tell them about the exchange. I want this chapter closed."

Vu couldn't believe the idea had worked. He hurried back to his office and sent a text to Sebastian. *We have a deal. Send me an official email and Cong will approve it. See you in a few hours.*

* * *

THE PILOT'S VOICE came through the speakers. "Folks, we're thirty minutes out. I reckon y'all better get ready for a quick touchdown and a rapid departure. The party that plans to go on this exciting excursion will be received by a U.S. State Department official, courtesy of Doctor Cebrián."

Landing in Haiphong was a beautiful experience—strings of green fields for miles, sloping mountains, rice paddies, and red-roofed buildings. The rice paddies ran right up to the tarmac. The airport had been built on swarm farmland.

The plane taxied to a stop near the terminal, a modest building. Sebastian and Maria stepped out of the plane, and like Guam, the hot, humid air greeted them. A sharply-dressed man wearing a dark gray suit greeted them next to a black Suburban with U.S. government diplomat plates. "Hi, my name's Zeke," he said. "I'm the assistant commerce attaché."

Sebastian placed the portable centrifuge inside the trunk, offered Maria the front seat, and climbed in the back.

Zeke drove to the guard post. He lowered all the windows so the guards could peer in, and he handed them a stack of paperwork while speaking fluent Vietnamese. The guards glanced at Sebastian. They lingered on Maria a few moments longer than necessary. She lowered her sunglasses and stared back at them, her expression all business.

The guards returned the paperwork and lifted the bar. Zeke drove out of the airport.

Soon, they were at the main gates of the Maritime University. It was eerie to see the actual building and the main monument with its big golden anchor and helm when Sebastian had been poring over pictures of them just a few hours earlier. Zeke parked, and as they made their way to the main building, two men slipped out of a nearby car and began following them.

Vu was already in the reception area, ready to receive them. Sebastian noted the streak of silver-gray that contrasted with the rest of his jet-black hair. Vu signed them in, and after getting them the appropriate badges, walked them over to his lab. Sebastian recognized and admired the bonsai tree in the center of the courtyard.

Maria stepped up and matched Sebastian's pace. "Don't look back," she whispered. "I think we're being followed by two plainclothes government officials." Sebastian kept walking, avoiding the urge to look.

They arrived at the lab, and Vu motioned Sebastian to place the centrifuge on the open countertop. He then proceeded to walk them toward the specimen refrigerator. Opening it he pulled out the polystyrene box that held the specimen and placed it on the table. "Here you go," he said, lifting the top cover. "I hope you're able to unravel its mystery."

Sebastian pulled a pair of lab gloves out of a plastic packet. The moment had arrived.

The glow of the fish lit up the ice that enveloped it in a soft, soothing luminescence. The instant Sebastian saw it, he knew they had made the right decision to come to Vietnam. He moved the ice around and lifted it out of the box. This was no ordinary fish—it was an amazing specimen. The fact that it was dead saddened him, but then he realized he'd seen it before—this was the fish he'd glimpsed in the *Cerro Tacarcuna* cavern, just before lifting himself clear of the rushing water.

Maria nudged Sebastian. The two men who'd been following them had entered the lab. He placed the fish back in the box and covered it with ice. Vu replaced the cover.

The two men spoke to Vu in strong, brisk tones. Vu bowed and asked Zeke to hand them their paperwork. One of them read through it while the other glanced at Sebastian, Maria, and the centrifuge. The one reviewing the paperwork spoke to Zeke in fluent English. "Did you complete this paperwork?"

Zeke nodded. "May I help you?" he asked.

"We need to call the Ministry of Commerce to make sure it's in order," the man replied. Dialing the phone, he fired off instructions to his partner in Vietnamese. The man walked over to the centrifuge and started fiddling with it.

"Sebastian, will you please go over and show the man that the equipment works?" Vu asked. "I fear he will damage it."

Sebastian made his way to the centrifuge and started explaining the unit to the official. Meanwhile, Vu opened the specimen fridge and began making space on a lower shelf, placing his polystyrene container inside. He then opened the staff fridge, pulled out his lunch box, and placed it next to the polystyrene container in the specimen fridge. Closing the door, he stood there watching the Vietnamese officers and then turned to Maria. "Maria, have you ever tried Vietnamese barbecue?" he asked. She shook her head, puzzled.

Ignoring her expression, Vu turned around, opened the specimen fridge, grabbed his lunchbox, and placed it on the table. "You know, my wife has a recipe that even the best restaurants in Vietnam can't duplicate. Guess where she got it from." Smiling, Maria shrugged. "She learned it from a famous street vendor in Haiphong," Vu confided. "The trick is to marinate the meat for forty-eight hours, then cook it over slow heat from actual coal."

The commotion in the lab grew louder, Sebastian showing the workings of the centrifuge, Vu explaining his wife's cooking. The officer on the phone snapped at everyone in Vietnamese, turning to Sebastian. "The Vietnamese government has denied your request to take the specimen. We thank you for your offer of the lab equipment. We ask that you please leave our country in the next two hours. We will return your equipment via the proper channels."

Zeke spoke up. "But our paperwork shows we have permission for this exchange."

The officer moved toward Zeke and unbuttoned his coat, exposing a Makarov semiautomatic pistol. "Like I said," he growled, "your guests must return to their plane. You can file a complaint through your consulate."

Sebastian spoke in a soft, authoritative voice. "Please keep the equipment. May I suggest we continue to work out a deal that your government would find acceptable?"

Vu interjected, his tone aggressive. "Thank you, Doctor Miles, but I believe the Socialist Republic of Vietnam has made its decision. It is in your best interest to return to your plane." He bowed to the officer, who was somewhat taken aback, though he appeared to welcome Vu's support.

"Okay," Zeke said. "We have our orders. Let's head back."

Vu bowed to the officer again. "Would it be acceptable if I were to offer a gift to this kind lady? They have come a long way, and the least I could do is give them my lunch."

The officer considered them both. "Fine, give it to her," he snapped. "We don't want them to feel that the Vietnamese are ill-mannered toward their guests."

Vu smiled and bowed again, handing the lunchbox to Maria. "Dear, please accept this food as a gift from my wife and myself. If you don't eat as soon as you board your plane, please do put it in the fridge." Maria accepted the gift, fumbling with it as she thanked him.

Vu led the group away, followed by the two menacing government officials. Watching them leave he returned to his lab, picked up the polystyrene container and dumped the contents in the incinerator.

Cong walked in as Vu was closing the incinerator door and switching it on. "Good, I'm glad you have destroyed that fish." Cong said. "Look something good came out of all of this. We ended up getting much needed equipment for your lab."

Unable to meet Cong's eyes, Vu nodded. Tears flowed down his cheeks as he stared at the incinerator.

AT THE STEPS of Panther Two, Sebastian and Maria thanked Zeke for his help and climbed aboard. Sebastian stopped by the cockpit. "Captain, please get us out of here, ASAP."

"We couldn't agree more," the captain responded. Within minutes, they were airborne.

Once the plane leveled off, Sebastian stood up, grinning. "Would you guys like to try some Vietnamese barbecue?" He brought the lunchbox to the main lab table.

"What's wrong with him?" Fabienne asked Maria.

"Not sure," Maria replied. "We couldn't get the fish, but the professor gave us his lunch."

"What do mean?" Shiloh asked. "We came all this way for a professor's lunch?"

Sebastian unclasped the strap of the lunchbox and lifted the lid. The smell of barbecue spread throughout the cabin, and the entire team gathered close. The first compartment opened into a sectional tray that contained a light green sauce and a red thick sauce. Shiloh dipped his finger in the green sauce and tasted it. "Oh man, coconut chutney with mint! I bet the red is a chili pepper super hot sauce."

Sebastian removed the first compartment, revealing a second larger tray containing small chunks of meat barbequed in an orange marinade. Shiloh lifted a piece and quickly put it in his mouth. "Wow this is really good," he said.

Fabienne yelled, "Will you stop touching the food."

Sebastian traced his fingers around the base of the second compartment and found a third compartment. He lifted the second compartment clear, and Fabienne gasped. Hidden in ice lay the prized specimen, its blue-green glow illuminating their surprised faces.

Fabienne moved in, grabbing a pair of gloves. "We need to be careful. We have to protect it from deteriorating." She lifted it from the bottom of the lunchbox and placed it on a backlit plate of opaque white glass. Switching the light on, she adjusted the magnifying glass on its metal arm and turned a control knob that lowered the temperature of the plate.

Sebastian was the first to peer through the magnifying glass. Like Vu, he too saw that the shifting nodule was a hexagonal structure, each side with a unique biological pattern. It glowed with the brilliance of its changing colors, quite similar to a kaleidoscope.

They all took turns at the magnifying glass while Shiloh uploaded pictures to Poseidon for analysis. Fabienne then carried it over to a temperature-controlled desktop incubator with glass windows. Placing the specimen inside, she set the temperature to four degrees centigrade. She also flipped a switch, turning the windows of the incubator opaque, protecting the fish from light.

Sebastian glanced at his watch: 8:00 a.m. in San Diego. He called Cebrián.

"Hello, Sebastian," Cebrián answered. "I hear you've had quite the adventure trying to get the specimen out of Vietnam. Zeke has apprised me of the details."

"Did he tell you we have the specimen?" Sebastian asked.

"No, he didn't!" Cebrián exclaimed. "How?"

"Some quick thinking by Doctor Vu Ha," Sebastian explained.

"Wow, that's wonderful! Have you guys taken a look at it?" Cebrián asked.

"Yes, and Cebrián—it's a miracle. I'm unaware of any marine life with such unique features." He shared their initial observations.

"Amazing," Cebrián breathed. "Okay, here's what I recommend. Instead of coming all the way back to San Diego, go ahead and land at Andersen Air Force Base in Guam. You'll have state-of-the-art equipment there, complete with a MALDI–ToF mass spectrometer and electron microscopes to peer into it at the atomic level. And you'll be closer to Vietnam, in case you need to find its source. I'll get you clearance."

CHAPTER NINE
Twenty-Two Minutes

SEBASTIAN WOKE UP to the thump of Panther Two's wheels touching down on the runway of Andersen Air Force Base. As the plane taxied, it took a sharp right turn toward a hangar. A field spread out in front of it, the tall grass waving in the wind.

The captain's voice came through the speakers. "We've been asked to pull into the hangar, where they've set up all the equipment for your work. We'll be able to connect Panther Two to the power and data grid, giving you access to the plane's equipment as well."

The sleek plane rolled to a stop on one side of the hangar and the team stepped out into the large climate-controlled building. "Sebastian," the captain whispered, "in the event of an emergency, text the code 113 to my number. I'll initiate a defensive protocol and ready the plane for immediate takeoff."

"Thank you, I appreciate it," Sebastian said, stepping off the plane. He thought the captain's words were strange, given they were on an American air force base.

A crisply-uniformed officer, holding her cap to her side, greeted the team. She explained that the middle of the hangar had been arranged with all kinds of lab equipment to aide their work. Sebastian recognized the ZEISS Gemini 500 electron microscope, capable of peaking at nano scales, as well as a MALDI-ToF mass spectrometer. In the middle of all the equipment were two fifty-inch screens mounted on movable stands, surrounded by counters, whiteboards, desks, lamps, magnifying glasses, a portable sink, and other essentials. Six foldaway spring beds with light army blankets sat against another wall.

"These are for your convenience, given that you may work at odd hours of the day," the officer stated. "It would've been difficult to secure you housing on such short notice, and having you stay off-base would have created all kinds of security issues. The chief brigadier general recommended we set you up here, though we were able to arrange a single hostel room for the two pilots."

Sebastian nodded. "Thank you. Any chance we can take showers and change?"

"Yes," she replied, "but the hangar doesn't have separate facilities. There's one set of shower stalls. The ladies will need to announce when they're taking a shower."

Fabienne spoke up. "Look, I don't care who sees me naked. I just need to take a shower and get into some fresh clothes."

Maria smiled–she was beginning to like Fabienne. "A woman after my own heart."

The officer broke a smile. "Understood," she said. "Once you've settled in, Brigadier General Pete Montgomery has invited you to join him for lunch. He's quite interested in hearing about your work. Also, here are your badges, which will allow you to access facilities on the base. Good luck with your research, and welcome to Andersen Air Force Base."

The lunch in the brigadier general's private dining room was excellent. The team had forgotten how good it felt to be on the ground, all cleaned up, with a good meal.

Their field of research fascinated the brigadier general. He was a massive man with a barrel chest and broad shoulders. He sported a beard and mane of wavy gray hair. Sebastian thought he looked like a unique combination of John Wayne and Arnold Schwarzenegger.

It was 1:00 p.m. and eighty-two degrees without a cloud in the sky when they finished lunch and left the brigadier general. As they reached the hangar, Sebastian waved at the guard standing outside. Three masons stood nearby, one of them cleaning the area with a broom while the other two mixed cement. Next to them were three large pallets of red bricks. It seemed they were in the process of building some sort of extension to the building.

The team got to work investigating the specimen. Before breaking for lunch, they had brought the incubator from the plane and plugged it in next to the rest of the equipment. Sebastian stood before the two mobile screens, a laptop positioned on the table in front of him. He clicked on a videoconference link.

Cebrián answered, appearing on the screen as his usual dapper self, wearing a navy blue sports coat with a white-collared shirt. "I can see you guys are all settled in after your meal with Pete," he said. "Good luck with your experiments!"

"Yes, we're eager to start." Sebastian said, and agreed to call Cebrián again as soon as they found something substantial.

Sebastian and Fabienne snapped on their surgical gloves and began to probe the fish. The nodule still glowed, appearing and disappearing along the length of the fish's body.

Gripping the laser scalpel, Fabienne made an incision and removed the nodule. She placed it in a Petri dish and poured saline over it. She peered at it through the magnifying glass with its built-in camera. "Wow, this is unreal," she whispered. "What are you?"

Sebastian flipped a switch on the magnification device,

and the nodule appeared on the main monitors. The team left their stations and gathered around the monitors, viewing it in detail for the first time. It was a biological wonder—a hexagonal, cone-like structure, each side with a unique biological geometric staircase pattern, almost like a symbol. And each side had a distinct color—greenish-blue, crimson or red, maroon, silver, rust, and pink.

"What do you think, guys?" Sebastian asked.

"It's unlike anything I've ever seen. Gotta be alien," Shiloh said. Fabienne shook her head at him. "No, I'm serious," he whispered.

"Let's run its cell structure through the electron microscope," Sebastian said. He took the laser scalpel from Fabienne and removed one cell layer from the greenish-blue side, placing it in the electron microscope chamber.

Fabienne returned the nodule and the fish to the incubator as the electron microscope's images came up on the big monitors. "I don't see a nucleus or mitochondria," she said. "And what are these small, round formations?"

"They're emitting the blue-green color," Sebastian said, squinting at the screens. He removed the greenish-blue cell layer from the electron microscope and placed it in the receiving chamber of the spectrometer. He then set the laser to a standard 266nm, to hit the sample for twenty-two minutes. The team stood in the center of the room, gazing at the monitors.

"This is it," Sebastian said. "Let's see what these formations are emitting."

He activated the laser and a loud click echoed in the hanger. The main monitor displayed an array of white dots. The receiving plate had registered the particles for a full minute. The click was heard again—the second firing sequence had occurred. More white dots appeared on the screen for the next minute. This repeated for twenty-two minutes, until thousands of particles had been collected on the receiving plate.

Fabienne studied the computer screen with excitement. "Okay, the particles have been collected, and the analysis is complete." She paused, confused. "They don't appear to be molecules of any known particle chemistry. They're like photons, but not photons. They don't have a magnetic field, and the identification column is blinking 'Unknown.' Not much to go on." She lifted her head and saw a strange, greenish-blue mist surrounding them—she couldn't see the walls of the hangar. Then the mist dissolved. Fabienne blinked, unsure whether her mind was playing tricks on her.

The second monitor lit Cebrián was calling. Sebastian answered the call, Cebrián's video appeared on both the monitors and he had changed into a new outfit. He now wore a gray blazer with a white pocket-handkerchief.

"So, how did it go?" Cebrián asked.

"We just started and—" Sebastian began, but Cebrián cut him off.

"What do mean, you just started?" Cebrián said with a frown.

"Well," Sebastian explained, "after we spoke, we removed the nodule from the fish. We just performed our first experiment using the MALDI. We collected some particles, but the data is inconclusive."

"It took you a day to remove the nodule and perform the first test?" Cebrián asked, leaning forward into the camera.

"What do you mean, a day?" Sebastian said. Now he was frowning.

"Sebastian, we spoke yesterday," Cebrián said with mild amusement.

"What are you talking about, Cebrián?" Sebastian replied. "We just spoke less than an hour ago."

"No, we spoke yesterday," Cebrián insisted. He pointed to

the Rolex on his wrist. "Twenty-two hours ago," he clarified. "Look at your phones."

The team checked their phones and wristwatches, and they confirmed that it had been about an hour since they had spoken to Cebrián.

"Cebrián, our watches and phones show that only an hour has passed since we last spoke," Sebastian said.

Cebrián motioned for Sebastian to wait and pressed a button on his table. After a brief pause, the brigadier general joined the call. "Hey, Pete, I just patched you into the team in the hangar. Can you solve a quick puzzle for us?" Cebrián asked.

"Shoot," said the brigadier general.

"When did Sebastian and the team have lunch with you?" Cebrián asked.

"What do you mean?" the brigadier general responded.

Sebastian, still confused, jumped in. "General, did we not just have lunch with you?"

The brigadier general squinted, as if he were checking to see if Sebastian was joking. "Sebastian, I had lunch with you and your team yesterday afternoon from 1200 to 1300 hours."

Sebastian turned to his team, as if both Cebrián and the general were pulling his leg. But his heart started racing. His team had gathered around him, their eyes fixed on the two monitors displaying Cebrián and Pete.

"Let me make sure I'm hearing you both," Sebastian said. He worked to keep his voice calm. "General, you're claiming that we had lunch with you *yesterday*?"

The general nodded. He was growing annoyed. "What's the matter, son? Yes, you had lunch with me yesterday. And now it's 1130 hours the following morning."

"Thank you, general," Sebastian said. He turned to Cebrián. "Let me call you back." He disconnected the call and sat down at the table and took a deep breath. "Does anyone want water?" he asked. No one answered. He walked over grabbed a couple water bottles from the kitchen fridge and sat back down. He drank half a bottle in one go. "Poseidon, what time is it?" he asked, clearing his throat.

"According to my system clock on the plane, it is three fifteen p.m." Poseidon's voice reverberated throughout the hangar. "However, when I sync my onboard server system clock with the Andersen Air Force Base system clock, the two do not match. The base's system clock is twenty-two hours ahead."

"How can that be?" Sebastian asked, not believing what he was hearing. "Do you think there's been a malfunction?"

"I have run diagnostics on my systems," Poseidon replied. "There is no malfunction. In the hangar, twenty-two minutes have passed. However, all the system clocks I am connected to throughout the world have advanced by twenty-two hours."

"Guys, what's happened?" Fabienne whispered.

"I'm sure there's a logical explanation for all of this," Sebastian assured her.

"What do you mean, a logical explanation?" Fabienne said. "You heard Cebrián, the general—Poseidon. All three can't be wrong. Something's happened."

"Let's get some fresh air and clear our heads," Sebastian suggested.

They all walked out and Sebastian noted that the sun was in a different position than when they'd walked into the hangar an hour ago. It should have been closer to setting, but in fact it looked like it hadn't yet reached high noon. The same security guard stood nearby.

Maria walked up to him. "Hi, how are you?"

The guard smiled. "All good, thank you, ma'am."

"Have you been on duty for the last few hours?" Maria asked. The team stood at a distance, trying to look casual as they strained to hear the conversation.

"Yes ma'am," he replied. "I got here at 0700. May I help you with something?"

"I do have a question," Maria said. "When did you last see us?"

The guard narrowed his eyes, trying to determine if it was trick question. "Ma'am, the last I saw you and the team was around 1300 hours yesterday, going inside the hangar."

Maria mustered a smile and thanked him, walking back to the team.

Sebastian noticed the three masons eyeing Maria and Fabienne. He approached them as the team looked on. By all appearances, he seemed to be having a normal conversation with them. The masons pointed toward a wall, and the magnitude of what had happened hit the whole group at once. The bricks they'd seen stacked high on pallets an hour earlier were gone, and in their place stood a fifteen-foot-long, shoulder-height wall.

Sebastian walked back to the group. "Let's play it cool. Did you notice the wall?" The team nodded, eyes wide.

"Things aren't making sense," Michelangelo said. "That wall couldn't have been built in an hour."

"The guard also said he saw us yesterday," Maria added.

The all stood there in shock, unsure of their reality. After a few awkward minutes looking around, they walked back in and returned to their stations, restarting their computers, phones, and lab machines. Poseidon and the Gulfstream computer had to be reset to the proper date and time. Maria sat down and swung her legs up onto the table, and Fabienne joined her. "Nothing tells me we've been awake for twenty-two hours," Fabienne said. "We're not tired or hungry. We're all operating normal. The guys don't even have stubble on their faces."

Sebastian was quiet, looking at the monitor with its array of white dots, when the most logical thought took control of his mind. "I think we may have just experienced a time-dilation event."

"Time dilation?" Shiloh repeated. He sat down next to Maria, running his hands through his hair. "I can't wrap my head around that. According to the laws of relativity, we have to be traveling at the speed of light to experience such a thing. Plus, the light from those frosted skylights in the ceiling didn't even change with the supposed sunset and sunrise."

"Shiloh, I think we were surrounded by blue mist the whole time. That must have obstructed our view," Fabienne said.

"What blue mist?" Shiloh asked.

"I'm sure I saw it," Fabienne insisted.

"I saw it too," Nidal chimed in.

Sebastian picked up a whiteboard marker, uncapped it, and then clicked it close. He did that a few times and then spoke. "Quoting Arthur Conan Doyle, 'If you eliminate the impossible, whatever remains, however improbable, must be the truth.' This whole experience is mind boggling, but let's run the experiment again to confirm our findings."

"I'm not sure we should do that," Fabienne warned. "We're dealing with some serious unknown forces here. Guys, the world outside jumped ahead by twenty-two hours while we experienced twenty-two minutes in the hangar."

Nidal stood up. "What if we run the experiment for one minute and see if time jumps by an hour outside?"

"Okay, let's try it," Sebastian said.

All this time Maria stood in silence, observing the team dynamic playing out. Sebastian, true to his nature, was pushing the team to take risks, and they were adapting to his way of thinking.

The team prepared the test again, this time with an added experiment. They set up two biological fungal reactions in separate Petri dishes. One was placed outside, where the time dilation wouldn't have any effect. The other was placed on

Fabienne's table.

The MALDI was set up to fire one-minute laser bursts. Poseidon synchronized the hangar server system clock with the base system clock.

Sebastian flipped the switch. They heard the click of the laser, and a new set of particles registered on the sensing plate. This time, the team took note of the opaque blue-green mist that surrounded them.

After a minute, the familiar click was heard again, and the next set of particles landed on the plate. "One minute has passed here," Shiloh marked.

"Poseidon, display the time of the base's system clock on the monitor," Sebastian said.

The team stood in silence as they all saw that one full hour had passed on the base's system clock.

Maria ran outside and came back with the Petri dish, handing it off to Fabienne. "This is scary, guys," Fabienne breathed, comparing it to the one on her desk. "The fungal reaction from outside has grown as if an hour has passed, and the one on my table shows a minute's worth of growth." She paused. "Do you know what this means?"

Shiloh interjected, "Somehow, this one side of the nodule is emitting particles that are having some kind of weird effect on our time in the hangar?"

Just then, Cebrián's name popped up on the monitor, and Sebastian answered the call. "So, how's it going?" Cebrián asked. "Were you able to solve how you lost track of time?"

"We have a theory," Sebastian offered. "I'm glad you're sitting down. We just ran the experiment again and confirmed our findings. Cebrián, as absurd as this may sound, we think we've experienced time dilation."

"Time dilation?" Cebrián repeated. He was reading something on the screen. "Poseidon is sending me the reports." He paused. "Wow, fascinating! How does it feel when you're experiencing time dilation?"

Fabienne spoke up. "Speaking for myself, I'm freaked out. It's like I'm living an episode of *The Twilight Zone*."

"I'm sure," Cebrián replied. "I can imagine how disturbing the feeling must be." He began scribbling in his diary. "How about this? Let's connect with the world's leading authority on particle physics, Giulia Valentina, and share our findings with her. I would love to get her perspective."

"Sure, we could use an external point of view," Sebastian said.

"Okay, let me see if I can get her this late in the evening," Cebrián said. He put them on hold.

Michelangelo jumped up from his chair and approached the screens. "Did he just say Giulia Valentina?"

"Yes," Shiloh said. "Why?"

"Well, she was on the team that discovered the Higgs Boson—the God particle. She's a legend in particle physics. This is so cool!"

Minutes later, a rather chic-looking lady with olive-toned skin appeared on the screen. She wore a teal silk nightgown. Her blonde hair was tucked into a layered bob. She was quite graceful, appearing closer to Cebrián's age, perhaps in her mid-fifties.

"Hi, Giulia," Cebrián greeted. "Sorry to call you so late."

"Not a problem, Cebrián," Giulia replied. "You know I'm always here for you."

The team raised their eyebrows. She appeared to be flirting with him. Perhaps they had some history. "But what is so urgent that you made me throw on my gown? You know I sleep in the nude. Couldn't it wait till tomorrow?"

Cebrián smiled. "You Italians are a passionate people, but I appreciate you putting something on before joining the videoconference. Meet my team, at present time located in Guam."

She adjusted her hair and made sure her gown was now covering her. "Hi, team. My apologies about the nude comment. I thought Cebrián was the only one on the call. My system doesn't always show every party, for some reason."

Cebrián continued, unfazed. "Giulia, you know about my work these days—"

"Yes," she interjected, "your name has come up. You're doing some science fiction stuff. And you know I'm a big fan of your work."

Cebrián ignored her comment. "I'm sending you the results of some preliminary experiments performed by my team."

Giulia read the report with a causal expression of intrigue. She squinted and pursed her lips. "Cebrián, what are you saying? This looks like time dilation."

Cebrián grinned. "That's why I called you so late."

"Okay, you have my attention," Giulia said.

Sebastian brought her up to speed on the specimen, the hexagonal nodule and their two experiments.

Giulia listened. "Incredible. This might mean the other sides of the nodule have time properties too. Some of us at CERN believe that gravity is a particle. We're searching for the elusive Graviton particle using the Hadron Collider. Maybe your team of—what did you say, Paramarines?—May have by accident discovered a time particle."

The team gazed at her, shocked, digesting the enormity of what she was suggesting. A time particle?

Giulia continued. "This is big! If you've found a time particle, this will change our understanding of time as we know it. No one has ever come across a find like this. I recommend we transfer the experiment to CERN and continue your research here."

"Thank you, Giulia," Cebrián said. "If what you're saying is true, then they must stay in Guam, away from the press and government influence. We have to proceed with extreme caution."

"Really, Cebrián?" Giulia said. "How do you propose keeping this quiet? This discovery—if it's indeed what I'm reading in these reports—will change the world from this time forward. No pun intended."

"Good point," Cebrián agreed. "I'll initiate the Honeycomb Protocol to safeguard our findings."

"Okay, if you invoke Honeycomb, then I agree," Giulia said. "Let the team stay in Guam and conduct their experiments. Just keep me in the loop." She smiled and blew Cebrián a kiss. "*Ciao*."

Cebrián disconnected the call with her and addressed the team. "So, how do you all wish to proceed?"

There was a moment of awkward silence. Sebastian turned to Maria, Michelangelo, and Nidal. "Do you guys think you can help develop a plan to find the source of the fish? Where did Pham Kai catch it? If he caught one, there must be more." The three of them exchanged glances and nodded their agreement.

He shifted his gaze to Fabienne. "Fabienne, would you help me develop the protocols to test the remaining sides of the nodule and find out what other time-related particles may be hiding there."

Fabienne nodded, a slight frown creasing her brow.

Lifting his head and speaking in the air he said, "Poseidon, I need you to figure out the parameters of the first particle. We need to determine and control the effects of the time dilation. Also, search for published quantum research that may shed some light on the type of particle we've discovered. I'd like you to develop the best scientific description of it.

"And Shiloh, I need your help designing a portable device using the 3-D printer that allows us to utilize the time control capability of the nodule."

"What do you mean?" Fabienne interjected. "You intend

to use these capabilities?"

"I don't know yet," Sebastian answered, "but it would be good to be able to generate these particles without bulky lab machines."

"Okay, you guys. We'll reconnect tomorrow," Cebrián said, signing off. The team saw Cebrián's lips curl into a hint of a smile. They knew what he was thinking–bringing Sebastian on board had been an excellent move.

The hangar was quiet except for the humming of laptops and the rush of air from the ducts. Maria was the first to break the silence. She shot a glance at Sebastian. "You know what works for me when I'm stressed? A good run! You guys wanna go for a run before we call it a day and catch up on some sleep?"

Nidal and Michelangelo declined, making up some story about having to stay back and process reams of data. Shiloh, Fabienne, and Sebastian welcomed the idea.

Four of them gathered outside. Maria was wearing a red tank top and loose fitting hip-length black running shorts. Her hair was tied in a high ponytail. Fabienne wore running tights and a worn-out, loosely fitted UC San Diego T-shirt. Shiloh and Sebastian were dressed in their workout clothes.

Maria recommended a five-mile run around the base and shared some basic rules. "We're going to avoid roads and run on paths. Let's try to stay in a two-by-two formation. And please don't put on headphones." There was an element of military precision to her instructions.

Fabienne and Shiloh surprised Sebastian. It turned out they were runners–they kept pace without a struggle. About thirty minutes in, they reached a coffee shop called Island Girl's Coffee 'n' Quenchers, a standalone structure with decorative bamboo siding in the middle of a strip mall parking lot, a drive-through on its side. It had a small table out front and big banners that read, COFFEE, SMOOTHIES, and

FRAPPES.

They all got drinks and sat outside, taking in the warm Guam breeze. Shiloh opened up the conversation. "So, what should we call this particle?" Fabienne frowned at him, thinking he'd lost it. Sebastian and Maria were intrigued.

Before anyone could answer, he continued sipping his drink. "I've been giving this some thought. Hear me out. We know it creates a time field that's slower than the time outside of it, which I'll call 'normal time,' for now. It's as if normal time sped away from us when we were in this field. I'd like to call these particles *Rahpido*. It's a made up word, but I like it."

"I like it too," Maria chimed in. "How do you pronounce it? Run it by me again. Sounds Spanish to me."

"Rah-PEE-doh," Shiloh enunciated. "And yes, it has Spanish roots," he added, smiling. "Imagine this. We're in a plane traveling from New York to L.A., and there are three classes—First Class, Economy and *Rahpido* class. It's a six-hour flight. Passengers settle in First and Economy, and start watching episodes of *Lost*. Some start working on their laptops.

"Passengers who paid extra to be in *Rahpido* class notice a device on the wall with a sign saying one hour equals six hours in normal time. When the plane takes off, this device emits *Rahpido* particles into their cabin and passengers are surrounded by this blue mist. Now, passengers in First class and Economy class sitting in normal time start watching episodes of *Lost* and experience the full six hours. They end up watching six episodes of *Lost*. The passengers in *Rahpido* class complete just one episode before landing in L.A. They paid extra to experience one hour of flight instead of the full six hours, even though it took them the full six hours to get to L.A."

"That's pretty good," Sebastian said.

Fabienne taking a sip of her drink saw an object hovering several hundred yards away. "What is that?" she said, pointing.

CHAPTER TEN
The Mist

MARIA DIDN'T EVEN turn her head. "It's a drone. It's been following us since we left the base. Courtesy of Cebrián and the brigadier general, I'm sure."

Fabienne's eyes widened. "Are we in some kind of danger?"

"No," Sebastian said, "but let's face it. It's like Shiloh explained. If this specimen is capable of creating time particles, then the implications to our world are nothing short of astronomical. Until we understand all the aspects of the nodule and how to control it, having added security isn't a bad thing."

They finished their drinks and headed back to the base. On reaching the hangar, there were two new guards stationed at the entrance. As they showed their badges, one of the guards informed them that a keypad security system had also been activated at the request of the brigadier general. He gave them the code and showed them the alert sequence in the event they needed to call for help. Word had spread that the team of scientists had discovered something big.

The hangar was quiet. Michelangelo and Nidal were fast

asleep. After they had all taken turns showering, they found a bottle of single malt whisky in one of the cupboards and spent a relaxing evening sharing their backgrounds and past lives.

Maria kept quiet and sidestepped the conversation. They all called it a night except Fabienne. She sat there on the kitchen table reading news on her phone. She was too anxious to sleep. She wanted to know what happened in the world during the twenty-two hours they had lost.

THE NEXT MORNING, spicy aromas of Spanish omelet, country-style potatoes, toast, croissants, and sweet maple syrup wafted throughout the hangar. Sebastian had awoken early and taken it upon himself to get groceries and cook up a storm for the team. It was the best way to wake up. He figured that the next few hours of work would lead to discoveries that would test their knowledge, perhaps pushing them further over the edge of human logic. It was important that they started the day off with a good breakfast.

One by one, the team walked up to the table where Sebastian had laid out the feast. The breakfast had the desired effect—it was helping them become a family. Maria and Fabienne were sharing a plate. Shiloh, true to his nature, was the most adventurous—he was pouring Finadene, a hot sauce from Guam, all over his helping of omelet. Michelangelo and Nidal had made their own omelet sandwiches with cheese. As they were clearing up, Poseidon's familiar ping sounded, and the coral screen appeared on one of the monitors.

"Yes, Poseidon?" Shiloh asked.

"I have an update on the research I conducted last night to determine the nature of these particles," Poseidon said. The team gathered around the monitors to hear the analysis. "I have reviewed well over two million scientific papers from different disciplines, from physics to quantum mechanics and almost all theoretical and physical sciences," Poseidon began.

"There is no mention—or even a hint—of the phenomenon we are experiencing. There is one area of science that is still unknown, and that is Dark Matter.

"As per known science, the majority of our universe is made up of dark matter. Scientists believe that it is comprised of particles that are at present unknown to us. We do know that dark matter has a massive effect on gravity, and as a consequence, on space and time. One can postulate that these particles emitted from the blue-green side of the nodule could be a type of dark matter particle."

"Poseidon, we have named these particles *Rahpido* particles," Shiloh said.

Sebastian added to Poseidon's research. "If these particles—sorry, I mean *Rahpido* particles—are indeed dark matter time particles, then it makes sense why particle physicists have never found them. In our call yesterday with Giulia, she mentioned that some scientists at CERN believe that gravity is also made up of particles. Why would time be any different?"

The team decided to perform limited experiments testing the *Rahpido* time particles for the next few hours. They discovered that by changing the wavelength and frequency of the laser that struck the film, they could control the range of the time field and the strength of the time dilation.

At 11:30 a.m., they once again synchronized all the system clocks. Sebastian clicked the conference icon on his laptop and connected to Cebrián.

Cebrián appeared, reading from a stack of papers. A rather large lapis lazuli ring adorned his right index finger. "Hello, team! You've been busy. Hmm, dark matter particles. Fascinating!" He put the papers down and regarded the team. "So, what is the plan?"

Fabienne gestured Sebastian to take the lead. Even though she was concerned about the effect time particles may have on the team, she had helped put together the protocol for their next sets of experiments. Cebrián gave them the go-ahead and disconnected the call.

The team took their positions. Michelangelo and Nidal returned to their respective computers, ready to compile and process the data the experiment would generate. Fabienne began the delicate process of removing a thin film of cells from the second side, the crimson side of the nodule. Shiloh was on the phone, searching the base for some crystals he would need to develop the portable laser device. Maria was also on the phone, asking for a gym mat to be set up in the hangar.

Fabienne placed the single-cell layer in the electron microscope chamber. She pressed a button, and the images of the cells came up on the two monitors. Similar to the greenish-blue side, the crimson side had the round, orange and red formations that burned with a crimson hue.

Sebastian placed the thin film in the MALDI chamber and set the laser to 266nm, as before.

"Okay, folks, this is our first experiment on the crimson side. What time is it?" Sebastian asked.

Nidal spoke up. "It's exactly 11:40 a.m."

Just then, there was a loud knock on the door, followed by the release of the locking mechanism. Several cadets marched in holding lunch boxes. The lead cadet approached Sebastian and clicked his heels in salute. "Sir, lunch has been sent with the compliments of the brigadier general."

"Oh, good!" Shiloh said. "Is it okay if we have lunch before we kick off the experiment?"

The cadet's eyes darted around their setup of monitors, computers, and lab equipment. Sebastian noticed that they lingered on the incubator. He was glad it was opaque, and that the specimen, for the moment, was hidden. He made a mental note to inform the guards not to let anyone enter when experiments were being performed.

"Let's break for lunch," Sebastian agreed. "Please express our sincere thanks to the brigadier general. The lunch boxes can go on the kitchen table."

The cadets set up the lunches and requested that the big hangar door be opened so they could install the gym mat Maria had requested. In about twenty minutes, as the team sat enjoying their lunch of assorted sandwiches, chips, and chocolate chip cookies, the cadets had set up the mat toward the center of the hangar. Between his bites, Sebastian kept looking at them—he wasn't very comfortable with them working in such close proximity to the equipment, let alone the specimen.

Once they were done, the lead cadet walked over to Sebastian and clicked his heels again. "Sir, we're done. Would you like us to clean up the kitchen?"

"No, thank you. We've got it," Sebastian said, smiling.

The lead cadet nodded and they all made their way out of the hangar, closing the main hangar doors behind them. Sebastian was relieved they had gone.

After clearing up the kitchen, the team returned to their stations. It was now 1:20 p.m., Thursday, May 6th. Sebastian set the laser to fire every minute for the next twenty-two minutes, similar to the first experiment, to keep all the variables exact. If this new particle was identical to *Rahpido*, then after twenty-two minutes, they would find the time outside of the hangar to be 11:20 a.m. on Friday, May 7th. Meaning the time would have once again jumped ahead by twenty-two hours.

Sebastian gave a thumbs-up and pressed the red button on the MALDI. The familiar click was heard and particles were registered. Two Poseidon server clocks were displayed on the monitors—one showing the server time on the plane and the other beaming in from the system clock on Andersen Air Force Base.

"Particles confirmed," Fabienne shouted. "Okay," she

continued, "the first minute has passed. Here we go again." She pointed toward the edge of the hangar. "Look!" A halo of red mist floated, fiery, luminescent and opaque. They couldn't see through it, yet it was brilliant and captivating. She then pointed to the clocks. "It appears our time is moving forward by one minute, and normal time outside the hangar isn't moving at all."

The experiment came to a close, and the red mist vanished. Eyes wide, the team passed glances back and forth as they pondered the effects of the new particle. They had experienced the full twenty-two minutes in the hangar, yet the world outside moved forward by only twenty-two seconds. The server clock in the hangar was showing 1:42 p.m. and the base server clock still showed 1:20 p.m.

"Guys, how come time didn't move outside?" Shiloh asked.

"Shiloh, time did indeed move outside—it just moved by twenty-two seconds," Poseidon answered.

"What do you mean? Did we just create time for ourselves?" Shiloh asked, his voice taking a higher pitch.

"I think that's exactly what happened," Nidal agreed, looking at his computer. "We could be inside this red mist for minutes, hours, even days doing our work, while outside, time would move at an alarming slow pace. This particle is the exact opposite of the first one."

"I think we need to run this experiment for a longer period of time to confirm," Sebastian said.

"Are you sure we should do that?" Fabienne asked.

Maria whispered to her, "We'll be fine. Relax, Fabienne."

Fabienne nodded, her eyes worried.

Sebastian called Cebrián, who listened to the results of the new experiment. "I thought the first particle, *Rahpido*, was game-changing," Cebrián said, "but this particle is even more amazing. A time particle that creates time in situations where we don't have any."

Sebastian nodded. "I'm recommending we push the envelope. I say we run the experiment for five hours. According to our calculations, we'd use five minutes of real time."

"I agree, if you're up to it," Cebrián responded.

"I believe we are," Sebastian said, looking at Fabienne.

"Okay, I'll let you guys make the call," Cebrián concluded.

The team gathered around the center table. "Boss," Shiloh said, "I recommend we start our experiment at 3:00 p.m. Guam time. We've come up with a busy schedule for the five hours. At Maria's request we're going to start off with a two-hour self-defense training session, something called Krav Maga. She feels that given the nature of our discovery, it'd be good to get the team familiar with some basic self-defense moves. After showering and changing, that should take us to 6:30 p.m. hangar time. We will discuss the time particles, and once time in the hangar reaches eight in the evening, the time outside the hangar should *only* be 3:05 p.m. We'll also have Fabienne's fungal experiment to validate that we in the hangar experienced the full five hours, whereas outside the hangar, time moved forward by only five minutes."

"Sounds good," Sebastian said. "Let's do this."

"**COMBAT NEVER HAPPENS** in perfect stances like you see in the movies," Maria began, not a hint of a smile on her face. "You don't just walk into a bar with your hands up in a boxing stance. In real life, combat happens when you least expect it—walking home, texting, talking to a friend in the safety of your own home. Krav Maga is an Israeli martial art focused on winning in real situations."

She stood at the center of the mat, looking straight at Sebastian, Fabienne, and Shiloh. "What I'm about to teach you could incapacitate someone, maybe even kill them." Sebastian was surprised that Michelangelo and Nidal had opted out of the training session.

"The main goal of the technique," Maria continued, "is to focus on finishing a fight as soon as it begins by attacking the most vulnerable parts of the body."

Shiloh and Fabienne once again surprised Sebastian. They seemed quite comfortable, performing the difficult, aggressive moves. At one point, Shiloh rushed toward Maria to see if she was able to employ her own training. She caught his approach out of the corner of her eye and drove her elbow into his solar plexus. Shiloh lost his balance, buckled with pain, and fell straight to the mat. She knelt next to him and placed her hand on his stomach, applying steady pressure instructed him to breathe. "Never expose your most vulnerable parts to your opponent," she instructed, leaving him to catch his breath.

Sebastian gave him a hand up, leaning close. "What were you thinking?" he whispered.

"Hey, she touched my stomach," Shiloh whispered, grinning. "It was worth it." Sebastian couldn't help but chuckle.

The team then had dinner, showered, and gathered around the conference table to discuss how the particles operated. It was clear they created some form of time field, evident with the red mist that surrounded them.

"Guys," Shiloh offered, "what about near-death experiences? When you're about to get into an accident, people say time slows down. What if that experience is due to this time particle hitting you?"

"Or the opposite, when you're having fun and then realize that three hours have passed," Maria added, "when you feel it should have only been like thirty minutes."

"Exactly," Shiloh agreed. "What if all our lives, we have been experiencing these time particles and never realized it?"

The team continued to share their collective experiences,

each one reflecting some strange effect on time. Before they knew it, Nidal yelled. "Team, it's now almost eight p.m. hangar time. Five hours have passed."

The team emerged from the hangar and walked out into the bright sunlight, squinting. They could see it was not even close to being 8.00 p.m. The sun was high in the sky. Shiloh spoke to the guard and verified that it was indeed just after three in the afternoon.

Fabienne picked up the Petri dish from its place outside the building and took it back inside, placing it next to the one on her table. The dish from inside showed fungal growth conducive to five hours. The blue color of the fungi had spread across the entire sample. The dish from outside had a small portion of the blue color, confirming only five minutes had passed.

The team gathered around the conference table, resetting their watches to the correct time. "We worked on the particle, had dinner, cleaned the dishes, got some serious ass-kicking combat training, and showered, all in five minutes of normal time!" Shiloh cried. "We created five hours for ourselves!" He let out a happy whoop, and it echoed up into the beams of the hangar. The team celebrated the experiment's success despite the worry of any unknown effects the time fields might be having on them.

"Shall we continue?" Sebastian asked.

They were tired, but also curious about the next side of the nodule. "Let's keep going," Michelangelo said. "It's only three p.m. We still have a lot of daylight left."

"Wait, what do we name this particle?" Shiloh asked.

Nidal spoke up. "How about *Lentio*?" he suggested. "No real meaning, except it lengthens our time to be able to do more stuff."

A smile spread across Shiloh's face. "*Lentio* it is!" he said.

This was too much for Fabienne, who had been fuming as

they talked. Raising her voice she said, "Guys, why don't you see the ramifications of this particle on our bodies? We all operate at a set circadian principle. There's a biological clock by which our body functions. It's precise and important for the normal functioning of our internal systems. Our heartbeat, our muscles, our senses, even our ability to think operates on an internal body clock. We just spent the last five hours working, eating, and training. Our bodies think it's nighttime, and in a few hours our pineal gland will start secreting melatonin, which will reduce our blood pressure and slow our systems down, preparing us for sleep. We are being too careless."

"I've been thinking about it too, Fabienne," Sebastian said. "I believe this specimen has evolved in a way that allows it to reset its circadian clock to be in sync with the time fields it creates. I'm sure that one of the sides of the nodules will have particles that align our circadian clocks."

"How can you be so sure?" Fabienne said.

"I don't know," Sebastian said in a calm voice. "Let's do the best we can to get through all of the nodule's sides. We have four left. Your anxiety is justified, but we can't afford to panic. We can't be afraid of what's going on here. If our circadian rhythms are off for a while, then we'll have to live with it."

Although the effects of the time particles disturbed Fabienne, the scientist in her was still curious to find what the other sides of the nodule did. "Fine," she said, pulling on a new pair of surgical gloves. She started to peel the single cell layer from the third side of the nodule, the maroon side.

They set up the MALDI to fire for twenty-two minutes. The hangar server and base server clocks were synchronized. Nidal and Michelangelo assumed their stations. Shiloh stared at the clock. Fabienne's hand rested on the red button, ready to press on Sebastian's signal.

Sebastian gave the thumbs-up. The laser clicked. They

were engulfed in a maroon mist and no time distortion or dilation had taken place.

No one in the hangar was prepared for what happened next.

* * *

BACK IN SAN Diego, Cebrián was in the midst of calling the Secretary of Defense, Richard "Dick" Richardson, to brief him on the latest findings from the Paramarines. He had a feeling they would need heavy security as research progressed. His call was brief and to the point, and the secretary listened. He knew of Cebrián's work—and knew that something extraordinary must have happened for Cebrián to call. The team had uncovered something big.

It took some time for the secretary to get his head around the time dilation phenomenon. "How is something like this even possible?" he asked. "If this discovery is what you're saying it is, we should move fast to bring it to the U.S. and have our military experts look at it."

Cebrián wasn't too fond of having to deal with the secretary, but he did have to brief him, since that was the structure the President had set up. Dick was a bit too nationalistic for his taste. Cebrián didn't trust him. Keeping the conversation polite, Cebrián said, "We're still investigating the phenomenon. And let's not forget the core agenda of my research—it's for the citizens of the world."

"Yes, of course," Dick agreed.

The call ended with the secretary agreeing that the team should remain situated at Andersen Air Force Base, with the security they needed. "Keep me updated on their experiments," he stipulated.

He then pressed a button on his intercom and asked his assistant to set up a time with the president. "Please tell him that his friend Doctor Alveraz has found something he needs to be briefed on." Dick could never understand why the president had such a soft spot for Cebrián.

He then pulled out his cell phone to make another call.

"Ready our team at Andersen Air Force Base. I might need them to extract a specimen there."

CHAPTER ELEVEN
Quantum Entanglement

"DO YOU GUYS feel something?" Shiloh asked.

"Like what?" Fabienne replied.

"I can't say for sure, it's like I feel a premonition of some sort," Shiloh responded.

The particles from the maroon side of the nodule had a powerful neurological effect on the entire team. Each of them had a strange psychic experience, a strong intuition regarding their most pressing need and current location. It was odd–to some it felt scary, and to others it appeared illogical. It was a bizarre conviction, a strong premonition to be at a certain place at a certain time. They weren't in a hypnotic state, gazing into the mist. For the next twenty-two minutes, they kept going about their work, but in the back of their minds, a spark of an idea formed, growing stronger. The premonitions were subtle, yet unyielding.

Maria had been thinking about finding an expert on the Paracel Islands and the underwater caverns of the region. She had been struggling to develop a strategy for Sebastian on how to get to the source of the specimen. Current maps, satellite pictures, and knowledge of the area weren't enough–she needed an expert. She felt a strong desire, almost to the point of certainty, that she needed to get to the Island Girl's Coffee 'n' Quenchers soon. There, she would run into this expert. Why she had this sense of clarity baffled her. She just somehow knew.

Shiloh had a similar conviction. He had been having difficulty getting in touch with the base's procurement head, who for the last day or so hadn't gotten him the crystals he needed for the portable laser device. He too felt a strong sense that if he went over to the mess hall—the Magellan Inn—in the near future, he would run into him having dinner. Why there, he didn't know—he'd never been to the place.

"What just happened?" Sebastian asked. "There was no time dilation or warping. Did you guys feel something odd?"

Maria walked over from her table. "I'm not sure how to describe it, but I believe that if I went to the coffee shop in the next two hours, I would end up meeting the expert I've been searching for. It's not just a random thought, rather an absolute feeling of surety. Don't ask me why I feel that way. I just know it to be true."

"Yeah, me too," Shiloh said. "I had this strong feeling to be at the Magellan Inn. I've never been there. Hell, I don't even know where it is. But I know without a shadow of doubt that if I go there, I'll run into the procurement officer who owes me my crystals." Shiloh's eyes ready to pop out of their sockets. "What's happening, are we all getting some kind of ESP?"

Fabienne spoke up. "I'm just glad we didn't experience any time dilation. But now we seem to have a dark matter particle that's connecting to the neurons firing in our brains, and the neurons firing in someone else's brain—which I think is even scarier. The first two particles were capable of creating linear, one-directional fast or slow time fields, whereas this time particle displays capabilities of quantum entanglement. The particle seems to connect the neurons in our brains that carry information of our most important goal with the neurons of people who may help us with it." She paused. "The scary thing is we all felt the representation of time and space for when and where that entanglement would occur." She stopped to think about what she just said. "In other words, our minds are telling us when and where to go to get what we need. Oh, my God, this is giving me goose bumps."

"Okay," Sebastian said, "let's test the theory. We'll go for a run in an hour and see if Maria's Paracel Island expert is at the coffee shop."

"I'll head out to the Magellan Inn and see if my premonition is correct," Shiloh offered. "He's been ignoring my requests. I tell you, if I end up meeting this guy, then this is some spooky weird stuff."

Sebastian turned to Michelangelo and Nidal. "What about you guys, what did you feel?"

Nidal glanced at Michelangelo, unsure if he should share his premonition. "I had a powerful thought to be here, close to the specimen tonight."

Sebastian nodded, feeling uncomfortable. "So did I."

Fabienne shook her head in disbelief. "Same here."

Shiloh's hair swung left to right as he shook his head vigorously in disbelief and made his way out of the hangar. He walked over to the Magellan Inn, a renovated facility capable of feeding 1,200 airmen at a time. It was about 5:00 p.m. and the place was filled with military personnel. Some were lined up at the counter picking out their meals, others were sitting at the tables, eating. There was a level of orderliness to the place, quite unlike a mess hall in a school or university. There was an air of respect, and when people spoke, they whispered. The only sound was the clinking of forks and knives on ceramic plates. The one very odd and out of place personal were several Dallas Cowboy cheerleaders in their NFL uniforms. They were moving from table to table taking selfies with the officers.

He chose a vantage point, darting his eyes around the tables to see if he could spot the head of procurement. He had seen the man's picture on the web and there was no sign of him. Just as he was about to leave, he spotted a man sitting by himself at the end of the hall. Shiloh, unsure of his actions, walked up to him, his heart racing. The man glanced up and immediately his facial expression changed. "Hi, you must be Shiloh?" he asked with a smile.

Shiloh flashed a smile. "Yes, I'm Shiloh. How did you know?"

The procurement officer didn't answer, instead asking him another question. "What brings you here?"

Shiloh wasn't at all prepared for the question and blurted out, "I was hoping to meet you here." The instant he spoke, he knew he'd made a mistake.

"Meet me here?" The officer said, surprised. "Did you call my office?"

"No, I just took a guess," Shiloh said, digging an even deeper hole for himself.

The officer chuckled and coughed. "It's just that I don't ever come to the Magellan Inn. Today the Dallas Cowboy cheerleaders are visiting and they are about to put up a show, so I decided to catch their act." He then sobered. "You know, I've been thinking about you. I have the crystals you ordered, they should be delivered tonight."

Shiloh nodded, still looking a bit dazed. He kept staring at the man.

The officer reached for something to say. "So, if my office didn't tip you, then tell me, how did you know I'd be here?"

Shiloh glanced about, uneasy. "Yeah, I took a shot in the dark. I thought since it was close to dinnertime, you might be here."

The officer looked like he wasn't buying Shiloh's explanation.

"Okay, thanks for getting me those crystals," Shiloh said, turning and walking away before the officer could ask any more questions. He was about to reach the door when a cheerleader jumped in front of him.

"Hi, you don't appear to be an officer, I love your hair." The cheerleader said flashing her signature smile.

Shiloh smiled back. "No, I am a visitor." He attempted to sidestep her.

"Stay, why are you going, we are just about to start our performance." She said moving her hands through her hair.

"Ordinarily I would have love to stay and watch. Today is not the day. Have a great performance." Shiloh said and then noticed that the procurement officer was now walking toward him too.

"I really have to go. Thank you." Shiloh said and hurried out of the hall.

"HOLY CRAP, YOU won't believe what just happened!" Shiloh shouted, bursting in to the hangar. "It worked, it really did! I met the procurement officer at the Inn. He never goes there, but today he'd made an exception for the cheerleaders. Look at my hands, they're shaking! How is this even possible?"

"Calm down, walk us through what happened," Sebastian said.

Shiloh explained in detail everything that had happened in the mess.

"Okay, why don't you relax and catch your breath," Sebastian advised. "We'll chat more in a bit."

Shiloh nodded—he knew what he needed to do to relax. He walked over to the kitchen and pulled a tub of chocolate ice cream from the freezer.

A LITTLE BEFORE 5:30 p.m., Maria, Fabienne, and Sebastian started their run to the coffee shop. Maria wore the same determined expression she had in Panama when she and Sebastian ran back from the mountain to catch the boat. Sebastian noticed that Maria was running faster than when they had jogged this route the last time. Her stride was effortless, her heels curling right up to her knees with every step in perfect running form. Her feet landed right under her body, her elbows were tucked in to reduce drag, and her head was straight, keeping her breathing uniform and consistent. Her eyes, however, kept darting around, checking their surroundings.

Fabienne, running along them noticed a unique wall art that she had missed during her first run. On the other side of the road ran a continuous half-wall that was painted with elaborate murals. Near the base, the art was of C130s, F16s and soldiers. The farther from base they got, the art began to reflect their surroundings—palm and coconut trees across from a park, then nuns, crosses, and churches when they passed a beautiful Mexican church. The art changed to represent the local population, in their native traditional clothes, and men fighting with wooden clubs and spears when they passed a building with a sign for Guam Social Heritage Center.

As they approached the Island Girl's Coffee 'n' Quenchers, Fabienne's eye caught a rare treat—an actual mural artist stood across from the coffee shop near a wall, holding a can of spray paint. He was working on a composition of coffee cups and coffee beans to represent the shop.

She headed toward an outdoor table and sat down, catching her breath, while Sebastian and Maria walked over to the window to grab their usual drinks. There were four people working inside the shop—the two owners, Franc and Sue, one staff member who stood at the counter, and another at the drive-through window. The woman at the window was new—she appeared to be a native of Guam, with strong Chamorro features of high cheekbones, almond shaped eyes and long straight black hair.

Franc came up to the window to greet them. The two owners had gotten to know Maria during her earlier visits to the shop when she was exploring the blue hole.

"Hi, Maria! How are you these days?" Franc asked.

"Great, thank you," Maria mumbled. Her eyes were fixated on the Chamorro woman. "Franc, who is she?"

Franc turned around to look, a bit surprised. "Why, that's Adora. She just joined us three days ago. Why, do you know her?"

"I was just curious. I hadn't seen her before," Maria said.

"Shall I introduce you?" Franc offered.

Maria smiled. "Let me catch my breath and drink some of this delicious tea first." She took her drink and walked back to the table with Sebastian.

They joined Fabienne and started scouting the coffee shop area. Other than the artist across the road, his spray cans making their familiar rattling noise as he shook them, there wasn't a soul in sight. A short time later, the rattling stopped and the artist began walking toward the shop.

The same Chamorro woman, Adora, came out and ran in his direction. She was an athletic girl, wearing the coffee shop's uniform of an orange tank top and a printed sarong. She embraced the artist, and it was more than a casual hug. They both walked back and sat at the table across from Sebastian and the others. She'd made coffee for him, which he sipped as they spoke in low, affectionate tones.

Fabienne observed the artist had heavy tattoos of strange animals all over his arms and legs. He wore a trucker's cap and had strong facial features not native to Guam, but more European. He had a square-cut jaw line with a heavy red beard and moustache, and he carried himself with an intellectual, rugged vibe.

Franc came out of the shop and walked over to the team,

sitting down on the other side of the table. "How are the drinks?" he asked.

"Good, thank you," Sebastian said. "I see you're getting your shop represented on the wall."

"Yes, I've been meaning to get that done," Franc said. "I was lucky to run into an artist. He turned around. "Hey, Adora and Charles, I'd like to introduce you to our friends." Adora looked over toward them, a bit surprised. She smiled as they got up and walked over. She and Charles sat on the bench next to Franc. Maria and Sebastian also noticed the large tattoos on Charles's hands. They were of roses with eyes, a spider web that had an odd insect, two eagle heads attached to one body, and a shape that looked like sails.

Sebastian started the conversation. "So, what brings you guys to Guam?"

Before Charles or Adora could speak, Franc got up. "Folks I will let you chat. Adora enjoy your break." He headed back into the shop.

Charles spoke up, his voice strong and understated with a slight cadence. "My wife Adora is from here, and we wanted to be close to her family. And since I love to paint, Guam seemed like a good place to find my favorite subjects." He paused and took a sip of his coffee, avoiding eye contact. Sebastian noted the uneasiness in Charles's mannerisms and his well-rehearsed, canned answer.

"Interesting," Sebastian continued. "And what are the subjects in Guam that you like to paint?"

Charles took another sip of coffee and glanced at Adora. Her eyes asked him not to say any more.

"It's a crazy hobby, and Adora wouldn't want me to go into it," he said, smiling at her.

"Well, we're scientists," Sebastian said. "Not much surprises us, so if you don't mind, please share."

Charles paused, almost sizing them up. "Okay, what the

hell. I'm a cryptozoologist."

"Cryptozoologist?" Maria asked, interested. "What do you mean?"

"It's a combination of zoology, geology, and folklore," Charles explained. "Cryptozoologists search for hidden animals, mysterious creatures upon which Hollywood has based a number of blockbuster movies. You may have heard of them as the Yeti, the Loch Ness Monster, Bigfoot, and the *Chupacabra*." Charles took a sip, blinking hard.

"So, you've come to Guam in search of these hidden animals?" Sebastian asked.

"Yes, and, no," Charles answered. "I'm not looking for the mythical animals from famous folklore. My research has been in a much different area. I've been searching for actual marine animals considered to be myths. For example, for the longest time, giant squid were considered to be a myth until one was filmed in 2004, and again in 2012 by a Japanese deep-sea research team.

"The blue hole in Guam is connected to the Paracel Islands via underwater caverns. In the world of cryptozoology, the Paracel Islands are a hotbed for hidden animals, and no one has explored them. And, they're now under the jurisdiction of the Chinese government."

Maria, Sebastian, and Fabienne shared a meaningful glance. "Fascinating," Sebastian said.

"According to myths and legends," Charles continued, "one such hidden animal has caused some of the world's most famous mysteries–the lost ships of the Bermuda Triangle. Even in today's age of technology, over a thousand experiences have been registered of captains stating that they lost track of time. Cryptozoologists believe these unexplained mysteries may be due to one or more hidden animals."

Adora stood up, adjusting her sarong. "It was a pleasure meeting you all. I have to get back to work." Sebastian stood up and shook her hand. Fabienne and Maria waved her goodbye. She gave Charles a kiss and walked back into the shop. His eyes followed her, full of affection.

"Charles," Sebastian said, "let me ask you this–you mentioned Paracel Islands. How familiar are you with them?"

Charles regarded them with surprise. "Well, in addition to being a cryptozoologist, I have completed my PhD in cartography at the University of Surrey. My dissertation was on the Paracel Islands." He said with a sheepish grin. "I guess you could say I'm quite familiar. I've studied blueprints and charts of the Paracel Islands dating back to 1747. I also met Adora at the University. She was doing her master's in ancient languages with a focus on hieroglyphs."

Sebastian asked for a moment. He took out his phone and pretended to take a picture of the mural, placing Charles's face within the frame. With a press of a button, he sent it to Poseidon. Within seconds, Poseidon ran a full background check against the FBI, NSA, Homeland Security, Interpol, and the national police databases of New Zealand, the U.S., and Australia. Poseidon sent a text message, *All clear.*

"Would you like to hear a fantastical story of coincidence?" Sebastian asked, putting his phone away.

Charles smiled and sat up. "Sure."

"We three are part of a special task force funded by the U.S. government. We're at present working out of Andersen Air Force Base, researching a deep-sea marine life that we believe originates near the Paracel Islands. In our initial experiments, it exhibited unique unexplained properties, or as some would call them, supernatural capabilities. I believe we may have found one of your hidden animals."

Charles's eyes grew larger by the second, shaking his head in disbelief. "Now I know how people feel when they hear my stories."

"Charles, we're dead serious," Sebastian said, trying to

calm Charles's nerves. He gestured toward Maria. "My colleague, Maria, has been looking for an expert on the Paracel Islands, and during one of our experiments with the marine life, she was exposed to certain particles emitted by it that gave her a strong premonition to be right here, at this precise time. And, strange things have been happening to us for the last twenty-four hours as we've continued to experiment on the specimen, and as outlandish as it appeared to us, we decided to test that premonition. So, here we are. And, lo and behold—here *you* are."

Charles's eyes grew even wider. "*El Sitio*," he blurted out.

"*El Sitio*?" Fabienne repeated.

"It means 'the place' in Spanish—being at the right place at the right time," Charles explained. "If what you're saying is true, then you guys may have found the hidden animal called *Isikhathi Isilwandle*, or translated from Zulu, 'The Time Animal.'"

He flipped over his left wrist and pointed to a tattoo. It was a clock with Roman numerals. The outer edge had waves representing sea or ocean, and the minute and hour hands were in the form of a fish. Maria and Fabienne leaned over for a closer look. It was beautiful.

"You see," Charles said, "there's old folklore among the Zulu tribe of Africa that says there's an animal residing in the deep caverns of the ocean. The Zulu god *Nkulunkulu* created this marine animal to control time. It's the one that has given grief to so many sea captains."

"Hmm, *Isikhathi Isilwandle*," Fabienne mused. "I like it, it's a great name."

"What other strange things have happened since you found this specimen?" Charles asked, leaning forward.

Fabienne turned to Sebastian, who nodded. Fabienne shared recent events about the specimen and its time nodule, including how the third particle had led them to meeting him here at the coffee shop.

"Cryptozoologists knew of *Isikhathi Isilwandle*, but we've never heard of these other details." He paused, then asked "How can I help?"

Maria spoke up. "As Sebastian mentioned, we believe this marine animal was found near the Paracel Islands. We need help navigating the islands to find its source."

"I can do that!" Charles said, unable to hide his excitement.

Sebastian recommended that he and Adora visit them at the base the following morning at nine o'clock.

Charles shook his head, almost interrupting Sebastian. "You expect me to wait until tomorrow morning to get a glimpse of something I have been searching all my professional life? Impossible. I can't wait that long. Please, I want to come along with you now, if you don't mind."

Sebastian checked his watch. It was almost 6:30. The sun was still high in the sky, but not as intense. "Give me two hours to get the proper clearance for you both. How about you come over around eight?"

Charles smiled. "Perfect. We'll be at the gates of the base at eight o'clock."

As they all got up to leave, Sebastian paused. "Hey, Charles, did you do the mural at a restaurant in Panama called *Ultimo Rufugio*?"

Charles's eyebrows shot up. "Yes, that's mine," he said, surprised that Sebastian recognized his work.

"Great work." Sebastian said. "I knew I'd seen you two before."

Charles nodded, sitting in a state of shock as the three marine biologists jogged into the distance.

He got up and walked over to the window. He asked Franc if Adora and he could leave for the night, they had an important meeting to attend. Adora looked over from her station and saw the expression on Charles's face. She had seen it before, something big had happened. Franc had no problem with Adora leaving early and would gladly close up for her. Adora wrapped up the order of the customer at the drive-through window, untied her sarong, neatly folded it, and placed it in a bin assigned for staff.

She waved at her colleagues, and quickly made her way to their car with Charles, who lowered the windows, reversed the car, and made his way out of the parking lot.

"What's going on Charles?" Adora asked.

"You will not believe what just happened." Charles said.

He then brought Adora up to speed in his meeting with Sebastian, Maria, and Fabienne. He shared with her that the people he met were actually marine biologists working at Andersen Air Force Base, and they may have found *Isikhathi Isilwandle*. The reason they had met with them was due to El Sitio, being at the right place at the right time caused by *Isikhathi Isilwandle*. Adora knew exactly what this meant.

She had supported Charles when he lost his job at the university, when he was repeatedly ridiculed by countless academics, through all the failed expeditions, the hours of waiting, searching, reading clues written on the side of Mayan statues, trekking through inhospitable terrain, getting innumerous bug bites, and carefully avoiding poisonous snakes. And most importantly, she had put her career on hold because she believed in him.

She had met him at the University of Surrey campus. He had a group of students around him, and he used a variety of chalk paint to draw animals on the sidewalk. These animals didn't look like any regular animal, his stories about them were fascinating. She had stood there watching him move and sway elegantly while drawing pictures and regaling the features of the animals. He had them fully engrossed, and that was where her love for him started. She wanted desperately to be a part of his life, and his passion. Now, after visiting three continents, draining their collective savings over the past many years, and working odd jobs, it appeared that Charles's wild ideas might finally be getting a break.

"Adora. Adora." She turned to Charles on hearing her name.

"Where were you?" Charles asked. "You were lost in some deep thought."

She found him so incredibly irresistible, and at the same time, vulnerable.

"Charles pullover there," she said pointing.

Charles was confused, but he noticed it was a parking lot of a building and the lot was empty. He chose a spot and brought the car to a complete stop. The office was closed.

Adora looked around and then opened her bun, her hair danced down her back and along her bare shoulders. She moved over to him, stared into his eyes, and began kissing him deeply. Charles was a bit surprised, but loved where this was going. They made passionate love in the parking lot of the Guam Social Heritage Center in the quiet, tropical evening. Their years of pent-up tension, frustration, and anxiety had finally been released.

Charles told her that Sebastian had seen his mural at Ultimo Rufugio. Pulling her tank top over her head and tying her hair back into a bun, she stopped. "That's where I think I saw Sebastian. I thought I'd seen him before," she said.

Charles was staring at her. "Okay, now stop staring at me. Let's get home, we have to change and get to the base tonight." She kissed him again on the lips. Charles was still a bit dazed, noting and loving the fact that Adora was such a flirt. If there was any delay, it was due to Adora's sudden and loving escapade. Adora to him was strong, sexy, and most of all, extremely intelligent. The fact that she was with him was easily the best thing that had ever happened to him. She was his true hidden animal.

BACK AT THE hangar, the click of the small door's electronic lock echoed into the rafters. Shiloh, Nidal and Michelangelo lifted their heads, expecting to see Sebastian and the team. Instead, two men walked in, and Shiloh's heart began to race.

CHAPTER TWELVE
Déjà Vu

"HELLO, SHILOH," THE procurement officer said. With him was the cadet who had delivered their mat. "I made it a point to deliver the crystals myself. I didn't have the necessary clearance, so I asked our lead cadet responsible for your security to accompany me. I hope you don't mind." The cadet once again appeared to be overly curious, looking at all the devices and honing on the opaque incubator.

Nidal and Michelangelo left their work and joined them.

"Thank you, you didn't have to make the trek. Couriers would have been fine." Shiloh opened the box, confirming it housed the crystals he needed.

"No problem at all, it was my pleasure," the officer said. Shiloh walked them to the door, thanking them again.

Moments later, Sebastian, Maria, and Fabienne busted in, sweaty and a bit out of breath from running hard. Maria and Fabienne headed straight to the showers, while Sebastian sat at the kitchen table and drank some water. He had Poseidon bring up pictures of Charles and Adora on one monitor, and their complete dossier on another. Shiloh, Nidal, and Michelangelo joined him.

"So, what happened?" Shiloh asked. "Did you guys find

the expert?"

Sebastian, between taking big gulps, spoke. "We did, and it is a fascinating story." He brought them up to speed.

"So, this validates our understanding of the third time particle," Shiloh said, listening to the details.

"Yes, that would be putting it mildly. Now I'm working on getting approval for them to visit us tonight," Sebastian said.

Maria and Fabienne emerged from the showers, and the team decided to make dinner. This time, Nidal and Michelangelo took the lead and began to prepare *spaghetti aglio e olio*. The aroma of fresh garlic being fried with dried red peppers filled the hangar and attracted everyone to the kitchen.

Fabienne decided to help by making a large salad. She opened the freezer, looking for green peas, and came across a full pomfret—a blunt-headed fish abundant in the Indian Ocean. It was packed in a service tray covered with plastic wrap. She stared at it for a moment. "Strange," she said to no one in particular. "We have one fish set to change the course of human history, and another all prepped for human consumption." She shook her head and closed the freezer, going back to her salad.

As they all sat down for the meal, Shiloh shared that he had gotten his crystals to make the portable device, and that the procurement officer and lead cadet had delivered them to him.

"What, they just barged in?" Sebastian asked. "We've got to develop a better protocol for people coming into the hangar."

They had just finished clearing up when Sebastian's phone buzzed. It was an automated text informing that Charles and Adora were being escorted to the hangar.

All eyes fell on them as they entered. Adora gave the impression of an Arabian princess with a swan like neck and straight back supporting her hip-length, bone-straight black hair. She wore denim shorts with a sleeveless red-checkered shirt, both ends of her shirt tied in a knot above her navel. Charles wore a black button-down shirt with the sleeves rolled up and black jeans. His strong hands and muscled forearms showed off his significant tattoos, and they were clear evidence that he had seen a lot of outdoor work. Both smiled, their eagerness visible in their eyes.

Sebastian and Maria shook hands and walked them toward the center of the hangar. Charles and Adora took in the jet parked to one side, and the series of scientific equipment arranged in a semicircle, forming a command center.

Shiloh glanced at the four of them walking over and could not help but observe the pairing. He stepped up to introduce himself. Adora automatically smiled at him, that elusive attraction Shiloh possessed instantly appealing to her. Maybe it was his innocent, boyish look, or his smiling eyes. She could not put a finger on exactly why but she felt a strong fascination for him nevertheless. Michelangelo and Nidal introduced themselves. Lastly, Fabienne wandered over and greeted them as well.

After the customary introductions, Fabienne led them to the incubator. "Are you ready?"

Charles nodded, not sure what he was about to see. Removing a pair of thin-framed glasses from his shirt pocket, he put them on and kneeled as close as he could to the glass. He also took out a soft leather-bound diary from his back pocket and a small pencil. "Ready," he whispered, taking in a deep breath. Adora leaned close beside him, her hand on his shoulder.

Fabienne flipped the switch and the glass cleared, displaying the hidden animal. "Oh, my God!" Charles gasped. He felt a sharp pain in his stomach, as if someone had punched him. The magnificent fish sat a mere twelve inches away from him, its hypnotic luminescent nodule in a Petri dish beside it.

He kept staring, unable to believe his eyes.

He lifted his hands and touched the glass. "Have you *any* idea what a significant find this is? What this means?" He began sketching making broad strokes in his diary.

Sebastian gestured everyone to gather at a table that faced the whiteboards, now covered with notes from the three particles already tested. He shared the details of their adventure, of finding the specimen, their trip to Vietnam, Dr. Vu Ha, and Pham Kai the fisherman, hinting at the possibility of finding the source of this hidden animal near the Paracel Islands.

Charles took copious notes as Sebastian spoke. "I still can't believe what I'm hearing. I do have a question," he said, holding his pencil in the air.

"Yes, go ahead," Sebastian, urged.

"When you *do* find the source of *Isikhathi Isilwandle*, what do you plan to do?" Charles asked.

"Protect it from poachers, safeguard its habitat, and learn to biomimic its capabilities," Sebastian replied. "This is why we all signed up for this job."

Charles closed his notebook satisfied with the answer and then asked a second question. "How secure are you guys here at the base? How many people know about this find?"

"Good question," Sebastian responded. "The brigadier general has increased security around the hangar, and a drone follows us around when we so much as go for a jog. Also, no one can enter this hangar without proper security clearance."

Charles nodded and did not push the question further.

Adora, taking advantage of the pause in the conversation, asked Fabienne, "You mentioned that the nodule has six sides, each with an indented mark, a sort of symbol. Can I see them?" Fabienne brought up the images on the two large monitors.

As Adora studied the images, her expression changed. "I

know these biological symbols!" She pulled out her phone and started searching it. "Yes, that's it," she said, handing her phone to Fabienne. "Can you display this picture on the monitors with the others?"

"Sure," Fabienne said. The picture was of an ancient Mayan stone tablet with rugged edges, about the size of a large book. There were dozens of small squares etched into it, and in each were two symbols.

Sebastian drew closer to the monitor. The symbols had faded over time and were hard to identify, but halfway through the tablet he recognized the biological symbol that appeared on the first side of the nodule. It was the side that emitted *Rahpido* particles, and next to it was a Mayan symbol of a man sleeping. "What does this mean?" Sebastian asked.

"I think this hidden animal may have been abundant in waters close to what we now know as Panama and South America," Adora explained. "We know the Mayans were a race of expert mathematicians and had a sophisticated understanding of astronomy and time. At several archeological sites, we've found elaborate tablets with symbols such as these etched in them. We never could understand what they meant, but now it's making sense. If the Mayans had somehow come in contact with *Isikhathi Isilwandle*, and if they had figured out how to mimic its abilities, it explains a lot about why the invading European armada had such a difficult time finding them. It also suggests some possible solutions to their many mysteries."

"Do you know what any of the Mayan symbols signify?" Sebastian asked.

She gazed at the monitor. "I do recognize them. They're varied representations of Mayan life and people. For example, the first side of the nodule that you tested and lost twenty-two hours in the real world, that accompanying symbol on the Mayan tablet signifies a human sleeping. I never could understand what this meant before today. But if that particle helps you pass time, maybe they somehow used it to hibernate during the winter months. They could have slept for eight hours and passed days or longer in real time."

"Wow, this is fascinating," said Shiloh.

"What about the second symbol?" Maria chimed in.

The second side of the nodule was accompanied by a Mayan symbol of a child and a man. Adora smiled. "Wow, this is unreal. For the longest time, archeologists have been fascinated by stories represented in hieroglyphs that during war times, Mayan baby boys were taken into a red mist, emerging as adult's only days later. Isn't that what happened to you guys? You spent five hours surrounded by red mist, and when you stepped out, only five minutes had passed in the real world. This is all making sense now."

"What about the third symbol–the time particle that gave us the premonition to meet you at the coffee shop?" Fabienne asked.

Adora stared at it. "Of course, the Mayan symbol connected to the third side of the nodule is of two men walking toward each other, one holding a bow and the other an arrow. Meaning they both have something of value to each other and meet at the right time."

"Adora, your analysis of the symbols on the first three sides is amazing," Sebastian said. "Can you decipher the three symbols on the remaining sides that we haven't tested?"

She nodded. The accompanying symbol of the fourth side of the nodule was of a Mayan king. It didn't make sense to her. She went back to her bag and consulted a notebook. "Oh, wow," she said reading her notes. "I don't believe this. There's an ancient myth about a king who never aged. He remained young for centuries. His people thought he was a god. It might mean that the particle emitted from the fourth side somehow stops our bodies from aging."

Fabienne gasped. And everyone sat thinking about the implications. Could the nodule really be affecting aging? She typed something into her computer. Scanning through an article, she started to read aloud. "'In 2007, three American scientists, Francrey Hall, Michael Rosbash, and Michael Young received the Nobel prize for their work on isolating the gene that regulates our body clock. They called it the 'Timeless' gene.' This time particle may somehow affect that gene.'"

Adora nodded and hiding the tremor of her hands she continued to leaf through her diary. "The fifth symbol is a set of twins, representing duality." She paused. "I'm not sure what a time particle has to do with duality."

Sebastian started pacing. "I think I may have a theory. What if the fifth particle allowed two people working on the same task to have the same thoughts at the same time? It's called the 'Twins Paradox,' because twins have been known to have the exact same thoughts at the same time."

"That could explain it," Adora agreed. She moved on to the sixth and last symbol. "If I'm reading this right, there are two Mayan symbols representing the sixth symbol, and they have been decoded as repetition and memory."

"What does that mean?" Fabienne asked.

Michelangelo spoke up. "This may be a stretch, but what if the time particle from the sixth side creates a time field that allows you to experience some kind of *déjà vu*? We all know *déjà vu* hasn't been explained by science, yet we've all experienced it at one time or another. What if this particle creates, for lack of a better term, a 'time memory,' or a 'time loop?'"

"What good would that do?" Shiloh asked.

"I think I may have a theory," Adora said, shifting through her notes.

"One unexplained area of Mayan culture that required years of practice was the Mesoamerican ball game. The objective of the game was to hit the ball with your right hip, right elbow or right knee and have it pass through a ring attached at the height of eight meters to win the game. It required perfect timing and body coordination, and archeologists had yet to explain how they had developed the incredible skill for playing it. I believe that this time particle may have helped the Mayans practice the game countless times, yet only remember practicing it once, thus reducing mental fatigue and frustration. Similar to a *déjà vu* experience."

"Fascinating," Maria said. "Becoming an expert in a skill without remembering all the failed attempts. Is that what you mean?"

"I think so." Adora answered.

Sebastian checked his watch. 9:00 p.m. He scanned the team. "I know it's late and we're all exhausted, but what do you say, guys? Shall we test out Adora's insights and see if the remaining three sides do what we think they'll do?"

He got unanimous agreement from the team.

Shiloh went back to his desk and retrieved a tablet in a blue casing. His eye twinkled at Sebastian. "Here you are, sir, all done. We're now mobile—we can create time particles without the big—and may I add, ugly—MALDI machine. All we do is insert the bio slide with the thin layer of biomaterial from any side of the nodule into this slot, set up the duration and intensity of the laser, and press the icon. This'll generate the exact time field with the strength and duration we need." Smiling, he handed the device to Sebastian.

Sebastian shook his head in disbelief. He took the tablet from Shiloh and laughed. The icon that activated the device was named "Time Warp." Grinning at the device, he said, "Great job, Shiloh!" He gave him a high five.

Adora and Charles stood aside, watching as the Paramarines sprang into action, setting up the experiments for the next three sides. Michelangelo reset and synchronized the system clocks between the servers, and Fabienne started developing the protocols for the experiments.

"Charles," Maria called, "We're working on a strategy to reach and explore Paracel Islands in particular Bombay Reef. Would you be able to look over the maps we have and help us out?"

"Sure, I'd love to," Charles said, joining her at her workstation. After poring through the materials for a few minutes, something caught his eye. "You see this dark area in the ocean," he pointed. "This shouldn't be there. This area is all shallow water, with reefs and littered with shipwrecks. This dark area indicates very deep water."

Sebastian, also peering at the screen, lifted his head. "Poseidon, would you please bring up satellite images of Bombay Reef from last year on monitor one, and more recent images on monitor two?"

The images appeared. The dark area hadn't been there a year ago. "What do you think this means?" Maria asked.

Nidal sat down on the center table with his feet propped on a chair, looking back and forth between the pictures. "Remember back at Scripps, Poseidon had pointed out a large shift in water levels registered by the tsunami sensors? What if this dark area is the reason for that anomaly?"

Charles, intrigued by Nidal's thought process raised his hand and said, "Good point! Sebastian, do you mind if I ask a few questions of Poseidon?"

"Sure, go ahead," Sebastian replied.

Charles glanced around and then said, "Poseidon?"

"Yes, Doctor Charles Shine, may I help you?" Poseidon responded.

Charles cleared his throat. "Do you have access to GOES-Sixteen?"

"I do," Poseidon confirmed. "Please allow thirty seconds for me to establish a live link to Geostationary Operational

Environmental Satellite-Sixteen." Precisely thirty seconds later, Poseidon came back. "I have now established a direct link to the satellite."

"Amazing," Charles whispered. "Could you access their onboard storage and bathymetry pictures of the ocean around the Paracel Islands?"

"Yes," Poseidon replied, "please give me a few moments."

Charles explained to the team, "As part of my PhD, I studied the process of mapping the ocean floor. The National Oceanic and Administrative Agency, or NOAA, owns one of the most state-of-the-art satellites for mapping ocean floors using bathymetry. When a satellite orbits and takes hundreds or even thousands of bathymetry readings using gravitational algorithms, a supercomputer like Poseidon can create an accurate picture of the ocean floor of an exact location."

Poseidon returned. "I have the bathymetry maps of the area." A colorful topographic map of the ocean bed appeared on a monitor. The team could see a yellow and green landmass, and a red geological hole with a swirling pattern.

"Poseidon, please overlay the bathymetry picture onto the satellite picture," Charles requested. As Poseidon adjusted the frames, the dark area on the photograph aligned with the red hole.

"I think we may have just found your source. This is a deep underwater cavern," Charles said.

"What are these swirling patterns in the middle?" Maria asked.

Nidal explained, "I'm not certain, but I believe the swirls indicate massive movements of sand."

Fabienne announced that the experiment protocols were complete, and they were ready to test sides four, five, and six of the nodule. Sebastian motioned Adora and Charles to follow him to the kitchen table.

"Guys, I want to warn you that testing the three remaining

sides is going to get hairy. The first three have destroyed our scientific understanding of time. We're dealing with forces of nature that we don't comprehend. If you remain with us during the experiments, we may all experience serious psychological trauma. Nothing prepares you for the shock you feel when twenty-two hours of your life are gone. Fabienne was so disturbed that she spent several hours catching up on world news."

"Sebastian," Charles spoke lowering his voice, "all my life I have dreamt of this day, and for the last few years I've dragged the love of my life through the most dangerous and inhospitable terrain on earth searching for hidden animals and aquatic life. We're not going anywhere. Right, Adora?"

Adora flipped her hair away from her face with her hand and nodded.

"That's great to hear. We would benefit from your collective expertise. Let's get to it." Sebastian said.

FABIENNE'S SCREAM ECHOED through the hangar as she backed away from the microscope and placed both hands on her cheeks. "Oh, my God, what have we found? Is this our Ponce de Leon moment? This time particle will change our current understanding of longevity and how we practice medicine," she said, almost yelling. They had just tested the time particles emitted from the fourth side, and Adora's explanation of the King who didn't age now made sense.

These time particles created a luminescent silver mist that not only stopped the biological clock of the fungi cells, it *reset* them to behave as if they were in the early stages of formation. Certain biological cells coming in contact with these time particles wouldn't age, and could possibly even repair any damage they had suffered.

Charles chimed in, "I told you guys *Isikhathi Isilwandle* is one powerful hidden animal."

Given what the team had just experienced with the fourth time particle, the fifth time particle didn't faze them too much. It confirmed that when two or more people working on a task were exposed to it, they have the same thoughts at the exact same time, making the accomplishment of their task faster and more seamless. They tested the particle by choosing two team members, Adora and Nidal, who had never worked in the past as a team. The task should have taken them two hours to complete, but being in perfect sync with each other, they were able to complete it in forty-five minutes.

"How did it feel Nidal, when you and Adora were exposed to the time particle?" Sebastian asked.

"Smooth. It wasn't as if we could read each other's mind. It was more like we both knew what the other had to do at the precise time, and passed control to each other at the exact time," Nidal explained.

This led the team to the final experiment. The symbol on the sixth side of the nodule was connected to the Mayan symbols of repetition and memory. The team had hypothesized that this time particle created some sort of *déjà vu* experience.

The team devised a narrow, complex laser maze on the exercise mat using laser pointers and mirrors. It was designed as a kind of obstacle course, requiring the participant to traverse it by contorting their body in precise movements—bending, twisting, and shifting their weight as they went. It was thought that if a time loop was created by the sixth particle, it would allow the participant to repeat the exercise again and again until they mastered the maze, yet only remember doing it once.

The team didn't know how it would affect a person's psyche. Whoever participated in this experiment would have to have nerves of steel.

Maria volunteered. The sixth time particle created a pink mist, and unlike the others, the team could see through it. They watched her stand at the start of the mat and begin her first attempt through the maze. After a few moves, she tripped a laser for the first time. A beep sounded throughout the hangar, and she reached into her pocket to click a counter Fabienne had given her. Then the unthinkable happened. Maria stopped moving, and a second Maria appeared at the start of the maze and began to move through it again. Every time she tripped a laser, a new frozen image of her remained, and a new Maria began the course all over again.

The team stood around the mat, staring at the physical miracle unfolding in front of them. They were witnessing Maria in each moment of time like an animated flip-book. Almost an hour later, she completed the course and Shiloh shut off the time field. The many frozen images of Maria vanished, and she approached the team with a smile. "You're staring at me as if you've seen a ghost," Maria said. "What happened?"

"You tell us," Shiloh replied.

"Well, I completed it in my first try," Maria answered.

"Not really," Fabienne said. "Look at the counter in your pocket."

Maria took out the counter and her eyes grew wide. "What? This can't be right. I didn't attempt the maze thirty times."

"Yes you did, Maria," Fabienne answered. "It appears this time particle somehow helped your conscious mind forget your actions so you didn't feel bored or fatigued while repeating them. Yet it allowed your subconscious mind to remember your actions."

"This time particle will be the hardest of all to understand," Sebastian said.

Maria, still not believing what happened, made a beeline for the kitchen. "I need a stiff drink."

Charles followed her and sat across the table while she nursed her drink. He showed her his notebook, where he had sketched many images of Maria in different positions navigating the maze.

"Charles, my body feels like it's gone through a two-hour workout, yet I'm sure I completed the maze in the first try," Maria said, taking a sip.

Charles didn't respond.

She continued, "I've been involved with some daring and dangerous expeditions, but none of them come close to what we're experiencing here."

Realizing the need to lighten the mood, Sebastian tossed the whiteboard marker to Shiloh. "How about it, man? Names for the fourth, fifth, and sixth time particles?"

Shiloh, still reeling from the shock of the last few hours, moved robotically to the board. He uncapped the marker and started writing, becoming more like his old self the more he spoke.

"We've completed testing of all six sides of the nodule. The first particle somehow affected our time in such a way that we experienced a couple of minutes when hours had passed in the real world. We called this particle *Rahpido.*" Shiloh wrote the name. "Great particle to use when one needs to pass large amounts of time without feeling or experiencing it.

"The second time particle affected our time in the other direction. We called this particle *Lentio.* We can see humanity using this particle when doing mundane tasks, such as working out, doing laundry, studying for an exam, or napping. This particle creates time when we don't have any. I can see myself using it to take hour-long naps and only losing five minutes." Everyone laughed.

As Sebastian had hoped, Shiloh's laid-back summary of the findings had a positive effect on the team's mood. They congregated around the center table, listening, clapping their hands and celebrating the power of the time particles they had discovered.

these two particles weren't powerful enough," ed, "then we were introduced to the third particle, e Charles' use of the term *El Sitio*. When we first experienced *El Sitio's* effects, we all had individual premonitions to be at a certain place at a given time. And that is how we met Charles and Adora, and how I met that ugly procurement officer." Again, everyone laughed.

"As for the powerful fourth time particle, well, this one somehow connects with our cell physiology, removing age and damage. By now, you may have caught the pattern in my naming convention. I put a suffix of *–io* after each word to make it sound Italian or Spanish. It's been scientifically proven that names sound cooler in these languages."

The team chuckled as Fabienne spoke up. "How about *Fisio*, since it affects the physiology of our cells?"

At first, Shiloh was surprised that Fabienne had joined in the fun of naming the particles. He then scratched an imaginary beard, adopting the air of a wise professor. "Yes, that will do, perhaps. What do you think, team?" Everyone voiced their agreement, offering scattered applause.

"Excellent!" Shiloh exclaimed. "From here on out, the fourth time particle shall be called *Fisio*!" He continued with the next particle. "This one causes two or more people in the time field to experience incredible coordination of thought." Adora unsure raised half of her hand. "Yes, Adora?"

"When Nidal and I were in the experiment together, it was almost as if were a single mind," Adora shared. "It felt as if we were connected through some divine force. How about we call it *Divinio*?"

"*Divinio*," Shiloh repeated. "I love it!" he shouted, adding the name to the board as the team laughed and applauded. "Okay, now for the last particle. We all saw Maria navigate the maze many times, yet she felt as if she had done it once."

"I'd like to name this particle, if I may," Maria announced.

"Sure, please go ahead." Shiloh said.

"I'm in love with the poetry of Rumi, a thirteenth-century Persian Sufi poet. He touches upon the phenomenon of time, and that too, *déjà vu*. So, I suggest we call the sixth time particle *Rumio*, in honor of the great Rumi."

"*Rumio* it is!" Shiloh exclaimed, writing it on the board with a flourish. Throwing his arms wide, he presented the names like the great P.T. Barnum, his voice booming throughout the hangar. "There you have it, folks! The six! Particles! Of Time!" The team burst out laughing, climbing to their feet with cheers and applause as Shiloh bowed. As an afterthought, Shiloh commented, "I'm sure once the scientific community gets hold of our research, they'll try to give the particles names like *beon*, *meon*, *ceon*, etc. But for the Paramarines, they will always be *Rahpido*, *Lentio*, *El Sitio*, *Fisio*, *Divinio* and *Rumio*." He put the cap back on and placed the marker atop the table.

The team gathered around the kitchen to celebrate, pouring drinks and toasting each other. Minutes later, they were interrupted by Poseidon's nautical ping. His voice flooded the speakers. "Team, we may have a dangerous situation developing."

"What is it?" Sebastian inquired, making a beeline to the monitors.

"I have hacked into the CCTV security feed. Switching to infrared, I have identified armed personnel in camouflage gear, hidden in the tall grass surrounding the hangar," Poseidon replied. "They appear to be readying an attack formation."

Sebastian sprang into action. "Charles, Shiloh, Maria—get the incubator onto the plane. Shiloh, secure the time warp device. Fabienne, secure all hard copy evidence of our research. Nidal and Michelangelo, wipe the drives and erase the whiteboards. Poseidon, kill the lights on my mark."

He texted *113* to the number provided by the pilot and

Panther Two's internal lights turned on, the door opened, and the stairs extended. At the same time, he got a call from Cebrián.

"Sebastian, Poseidon has made me aware of the situation. I've contacted the brigadier general–he's sending his elite security detail to the hangar. It'll take them ten minutes to get to you."

"Okay, we'll reconnect once we're in the air," Sebastian responded, hanging up.

"I thought we came here to experiment in complete safety. Go figure," Shiloh said to no one in particular.

"Why are we having to run from our own military base?" Fabienne shouted.

"Good question, Fabienne," Sebastian answered, helping with the evidence. "Let's first secure our work and ourselves. Then, we'll get to bottom of all this."

Sebastian told everyone to board the plane and seal the door. He and Maria were going to stay outside and try to talk to their aggressors, stalling for time. He did a final check of the hangar door, making sure it was locked, then joined Maria at the conference table. Michelangelo and Nidal took up seats next to them. "I guess you guys didn't hear me," he said. "You need to get inside the plane."

"We heard you," Michelangelo replied, "but we would prefer to stay with you." Sebastian scrutinized them before letting it go.

They sat tense around the table, waiting. They could hear some commotion outside the guards were doing their job. There was some intense arguing, but no bullets were flying. Yet.

A muffled bang was heard, blowing the door lock apart. Sebastian stood as six armed men in masks came through the smoke. Four of them took up offensive positions, and two walked up to the table. They removed their masks, revealing the procurement officer and lead cadet.

"We're not here to hurt you," the officer said. "All we need is the specimen."

"Are you under orders from the brigadier general?" Sebastian demanded.

The procurement officer replied, "We're under orders from the highest office of our government. The sooner you hand it over, the faster we'll be out of your hair." By now, the rest of his men had joined them at the table.

"What's with all the theatrics?" Sebastian pressed. "Why not just use the code to open the door?"

One of the men announced in a clipped tone, "Sir, we have a few minutes before the elite guard arrives." The officer nodded and approached Sebastian even closer. He was at least three or four inches too short to meet Sebastian eye-to-eye. He threw his chest out. "Where's the specimen?"

Sebastian breathed an internal sigh of relief as he glimpsed the pilots crouching at the blown door. He glared at the officer. "I'll give you thirty seconds to leave this hangar. Otherwise, I promise you that the next time you wake up, it'll be in a hospital bed."

Surprised by the steely eyes of the scientist, the officer glanced at his team and coughed.

Realizing this was his opportunity, Sebastian shouted, "Poseidon–lights!" and the hangar went dark.

CHAPTER THIRTEEN
The Escape

THE PILOTS SCANNED the scene. The two hangar guards were on the floor with hands and feet secured, their heads covered with burlap sacks. Six men were gathered, pointing their guns at Sebastian and three other Paramarines. Peering in, they saw that all the plane's systems had been activated—they'd be able to fire up the engines and punch the plane through the hangar. All they needed to do was get aboard, but the plane's steps were retracted and the door was sealed.

The captain typed a different code into his phone, activating the silent release of a hidden pneumatic bay door near the rear wheels of the plane. He heard Sebastian shout and the hangar went dark, triggering the emergency lights to kick on with an eerie illumination. Now was their chance.

Moments before the hangar went dark, Nidal and Michelangelo had assessed their attackers. First, the safeties were off on all their firearms—these men were not messing around. Second, they were not part of a trained force such as the Navy SEALs or Green Berets. One key giveaway was their positioning. Instead of taking self-protective flanking positions, they were all gathered around their two leaders—the procurement officer and the lead cadet. Third, their stances were all over the place—some had a casual hand on their weapons, while others showed no trigger discipline whatsoever.

Before their assailants' eyes could adjust to the sudden darkness, Maria capitalized on their advantage, leaping onto the table. Pivoting on her left hand, she tucked her left knee in and stretched her right leg out and brought her hiking boot across the jaw of the lead cadet, the impact throwing him onto Fabienne's workstation. Using her momentum, she leapt from the table and landed on her feet, standing over the motionless figure.

Sebastian moved with equal speed. He slammed his elbow into the chin of the procurement officer, whipping the man's head back. Using his palm, Sebastian struck the dazed man in the mouth, knocking him to the ground.

The biggest surprise to those watching from the plane came from their two unassuming colleagues, Nidal and Michelangelo. They both moved with professional precision, a cut above Sebastian and even Maria. Their coordinated hand-to-hand combat took out two of the armed men closest to them, taking their sidearms and neutralizing the last two men with clean shots to their knees. The team on the plane jumped as the hangar thundered with gunshots.

"Poseidon—lights," Sebastian ordered. The hangar lit up again. Maria and Sebastian stood over the still forms of their adversaries. Nidal and Michelangelo were in similar positions, scanning the environment for movement.

The main hangar door began to crank open like a garage door, and a few men from the elite guard rushed through the blown opening. Guns raised, they spread throughout the hangar, shouting, "Clear, clear!" Michelangelo and Nidal placed their guns on the table and raised their hands, assuring the guards that they weren't a threat.

The head of the elite guard, a major by rank, came through

the main door and approached Sebastian. "We were ordered to scramble in response to an imminent attack, sir. Are you folks okay?"

"We're fine," Sebastian replied, "but who are these guys?"

"Unsure, sir," the major responded. He called Brigadier General Pete Montgomery to report. "We're at the hangar, sir. There was indeed an attack. Six hostiles have already been neutralized. Orders?"

"Neutralized? How?" Pete asked.

"Unsure, sir," the major replied, glancing at the Paramarines.

"Let me talk to Sebastian," Pete barked. The major handed the phone over.

"Sebastian," Pete said, "I'm getting all kinds of mixed orders and reports—I'm not sure who authorized this attack on you. I'm receiving orders to retrieve the specimen and all related research data and deliver it to the Pentagon. There was a transport plane ready to take these men and your specimen to Washington D.C."

Sebastian wasn't shocked to hear Pete's rundown. The decision had been made at the highest levels to take control of their research. What Pete told him next, however, did surprise him. "Sebastian, I don't understand the politics of it all, but you do what you need to do to protect the specimen. Understood?"

"Loud and clear, general," Sebastian responded. "Thank you."

"Good," Pete said. "Now, hand me back to the major."

In the meantime, paramedics had arrived at the scene, and all six injured men, accompanied by military police, were carted off on stretchers. As the ambulances pulled away, the noise of their sirens was eclipsed by the sudden ignition of jet engines. The tables, equipment, even the floor of the hangar started vibrating. The major turned to see that Sebastian now stood alone—the rest of his team had disappeared, they had boarded the Gulfstream. The major shouted over the noise, "Brigadier General Montgomery is arriving! I recommend you wait for him! He wants to conduct a full investigation!"

Sebastian acted as if the engines were drowning out the major's voice. He pointed to the airport terminal, shouting, "We need to move out of here! Tell Pete we'll meet him in the terminal!"

The major looked confused, but ordered his guards to move out of the way. Sebastian gave him a nod and boarded the plane, retracting the steps behind him. Once inside, he yelled to the pilots, "Get us out of here!" The plane leaped forward.

The pilots radioed the tower, requesting emergency clearance. Oblivious to what had happened, the tower had no reason not to allow it.

The major watched as the plane headed straight to the main runway. Realizing what was happening, he jumped into his jeep and barked at the cadet to drive. The cadet gunned the accelerator and they sped off in an attempt to intercept the jet before it could take off. The major then pulled out his cell phone and punched a code that connected him to the tower. "Abort that Gulfstream's takeoff!" he shouted.

"Sir, that plane has clearance from Brigadier General Montgomery himself," the air traffic controller responded.

The major cursed under his breath. "I'm Major Jo Jackson, head of base security, and I'm giving you a direct order. Stop that plane!"

The control tower came through the pilots' headsets. "Panther Two, abort takeoff. You do not have clearance for takeoff. I repeat, abort takeoff."

The pilots ignored the warnings and the vehicle with pulsating emergency lights heading straight down the runway toward them.

"Initiate short takeoff protocol," the captain instructed the copilot, ignoring the tower's order. He then got on the cabin intercom. "Folks, I recommend you buckle up real fast. Takeoff is gonna be a bit aggressive."

The captain rammed the throttle forward, awakening the roar of the jet's Rolls Royce engines. True to its name, Panther Two raced down the runway in the direction of the speeding jeep.

The major realized the plane was still attempting to take off, but he felt confident they could still force it to abort. He ordered the cadet to speed up. The cadet holding the steering hard floored the accelerator. The major knew he was reducing the length of runway available to the plane. He also knew that most private jets needed five thousand feet for takeoff.

The Panther Two captain watched his ground speed, flaps at twenty degrees. He needed to reach 108 knots in three thousand feet.

The major, standing on the seat of the jeep, noted the distance markers on the side of the runway with growing apprehension. They had already shortened the runway by half. He was sure the plane would abort takeoff. It'd be impossible to get the lift they needed.

The scream of the jet engines was deafening. The wind tunnel created by their air intake was so intense that it pulled the jeep closer to them. Watching his panels and ground speed, the captain grabbed the control stick and pulled it, lifting the nose of the plane.

Major Jackson couldn't believe what he was seeing–the plane was attempting takeoff in less than three thousand feet.

Out of sheer fear and self-preservation, the cadet slammed on the breaks, bringing the jeep to a screeching halt. The Gulfstream took off only three hundred feet from it, clipping the windshield with its landing gear. The turbulence was so powerful that it knocked the major over onto the back seat.

Dazed and dismayed, he lay on his back as the blinking red lights of the plane faded into the distance.

The Paramarines were rattled by the G-forces of the takeoff, their hearts pumping with adrenaline, strapped in and still clutching their seats. The jet leveled off, and they all started clapping and cheering. The captain and co-pilot had pulled off an amazing takeoff maneuver.

Sebastian turned around to see both Adora and Charles seated with the rest of the team, their hands clasped on the table exposing white knuckles, expressions of slight concern on their faces. When Sebastian had pointed out that things were going to get weird in the hangar, they had never imagined it would include escaping a group of armed men.

"Sorry, Adora and Charles!" Sebastian exclaimed. "We had to make some quick decisions. As soon as we get to a safe location, I'll make arrangements for you to get back home, complete with proper travel documents. I know this isn't what you signed up for."

Charles shook his head. "Sebastian, please, we want to be part of the team. Adora and I wouldn't miss this once-in-a-lifetime opportunity of finding the source of the specimen."

Sebastian thanked them both for continuing to pursue the adventure, then walked up to the cockpit. "Thank you," he said to the captain and copilot. "Is our transponder on?"

"No, I turned it off," the captain replied, smiling. "We don't want to be tracked right now."

"Great, thank you," Sebastian said, going back to the team. "Is everyone okay?"

Maria nodded, shifting her gaze to Michelangelo and Nidal. They nodded as well.

"So, you guys are Navy SEALs or Green Berets?" Sebastian asked.

Both Fabienne, who appeared most shook up by all that had happened, and Shiloh, who for once appeared serious, leaned forward to hear the answer.

"Yeah," Shiloh chimed in. "What were those moves? You disarmed and destroyed four men in less than five seconds. And Maria! Wow, that roundhouse kick was insane. And boss, what you did to the procurement officer was unreal–he went down like a rock."

"Michelangelo and I were Navy SEALs," Nidal said. "It was a difficult part of our lives that we don't share."

Sebastian didn't want to dwell too much on it either. "Well, all of that isn't important now. I'm grateful you were there."

Just then, the monitor in the back of plane lit up and Cebrián's face blinked onto the screen, catching everyone's attention. He skipped his customary greetings. "Is everyone okay?" They all nodded, staring back at him. "I've been in contact with the Pentagon, the secretary of defense, and even the president," Cebrián continued. "We're trying to find out who ordered the attack. There are several conflicting reports, but whoever it is, they're running a dangerous secretive group. They're loyal to a fault to their leader, and here's what's most interesting and disconcerting–they aren't breaking any laws by attacking you. They're protected under the new regulations of Homeland Security. Their use of force was meant to intimidate you so you would hand over the specimen without any resistance. However, they didn't expect such opposition from a group of civilian scientists."

"Hey, we protected what rightfully belongs to all mankind," Sebastian said.

"Hmm . . ." Cebrián lifted a paper. "A broken jaw, broken nose, broken cheekbones, dislocated kneecap, and two flesh wounds from gun shots." He placed the paper back on the table. It was hard to tell, but it appeared one corner of his mouth broke into a hint of a smirk. "Okay, what are your plans now?"

"Charles has identified a geological anomaly near Bombay Reef," Sebastian replied. "We believe that's the source of the specimen."

Cebrián regarded the pair. "Hello, Doctor Charles Shine and Adora Celestine. I've learned about you two from Poseidon's reports. Thank you for the support you've given us in these last few hours." Unsure how to respond, they nodded and turned their gaze to Sebastian.

Shiloh spoke up. "Cebrián, if we're being hunted by a secret government force, wouldn't they be tracking this call?"

Cebrián nodded. "Good question, Shiloh. I've activated block chain security protocols. All communications, interactions, Poseidon's analyses, and the team's findings over the last few days have been broken into small bits, encrypted, and distributed across global servers, making it impossible for anyone to retrieve any valuable information.

"Furthermore, your cell phones have been electronically burned, so they're as good as paperweights. And Panther Two is coated with a special carbon nanotube-infused paint that once the captain changes the angle of the flaps, you become invisible to radar. I'm working on finding out who's putting you in danger, trying to sabotage our work. Now get some rest. Good luck!"

The captain's voice came over the speakers, asking Sebastian to join them in the cockpit. "Sebastian, we're on a flight path heading west from Guam, with no real destination programmed. You got somewhere in mind for us?"

"We're planning our next steps," Sebastian answered. "All we know at the moment is that we have to go to Vietnam first—the village of Nhon Ly."

"That'll work, though I'm sure they don't have an airport," the captain said.

"I'll ask Poseidon to find us an airstrip in the area," Sebastian replied. "Ideally an obscure one."

Sebastian left the cockpit as Maria walked over to him. He wasn't sure if it was the altitude or the time particles or the combat and subsequent escape, but he grabbed her by the waist, gazed into her eyes, and kissed her on the lips.

Maria wrapped her arms around his neck, reflecting on just how much it had taken for him to show his fondness for her.

* * *

BACK IN NHON Ly, Pham Kai sat up straight on the old wooden bench in his yard, looking out to sea, hoping and wondering. In some essential way, he felt broken by the fact that his wife was dying—at worst, her prognosis was six months, and at best, two to three years—yet he still had a quiet dignity and grace about him. Minh gingerly lowered herself next to him, holding out a cup of turmeric tea. They sat together, gazing at the water. Minh had no words left to console her husband.

They had just finished dinner, and the evening dusk lit up the sky with shades of orange, yellow, and pink before darkness fell. Pham Kai was contemplating the sea and sky when he noticed a slight movement to his left. Down the pebble path, he saw two well-dressed men walking in their direction. Squinting his eyes in the falling twilight, he realized one of them was his dear friend Hoang Binh.

Delighted to greet Hoang and meet his new friend, whom Hoang introduced as Dr. Vu Ha, Pham Kai invited them in. Minh insisted they have plate of her rice and spicy fish curry. They all sat on the jute mat. Huang's friend loved the meal, and he seemed to relish the simplicity of Pham Kai and Minh's life and their strong representation of old cultural habits and famous Vietnamese hospitality.

After polishing off their plates with much praise and thanks, Hoang addressed the reason for their visit. Darkness had fallen, and Pham Kai lit a couple oil lanterns. With the rhythmic shushing of the waves and the dim flickering light, Hoang dropped his voice to low tones. Pham Kai and Minh sat riveted, listening to him.

"Immediately after you left Tonkin Fisheries, I called my friend Vu and told him about the fish you had brought in. Vu also thought there was something special about it. But before he could do a full examination of it at his university, an American team arrived and negotiated to take it." Hoang smiled at Pham Kai. "Vu hasn't been able to get the fish out of his mind. He has taken a four-month leave from his university, and using his own savings, he wishes to engage you for an expedition to find it one more time. He'll pay you two months full earnings, plus expenses."

Minh felt herself overcome with anxiety as the conversation progressed. The last time her husband had gone on such a mission, he had come back injured and incoherent. The chances of being caught a second time by the Chinese Navy were unacceptable.

Vu surprised by the uneasy expressions on their faces, asked what was bothering them.

Pham Kai shared with Vu and Hoang some of the ordeal leading to his capture, torture, and eventual escape. He then pulled aside his collar and showed them the two burn puncture marks on his neck and right shoulder. Vu found the marks very disturbing, and Hoang was moved by the fact that neither of them had shared any of this during their visit to him at the fishery.

"I'm a professor and a researcher," Vu explained, "and I have in my possession special documents from the Chinese embassy that, if required, will give us safe passage. I'm also willing to increase the compensation to make it worth your risk. The specimen you found is the most unique I've seen in my entire career."

Pham Kai requested that he and Minh step out to discuss

it. Both their guests nodded and bowed.

Minh stood unwavering that Pham Kai refuse to take any more risk in order to pay for her treatment. Pham Kai, for his part, insisted that if he didn't make every effort to find a way to get her treatment, he would regret it for the rest of his life. After hearing Pham Kai's emotional plea, Minh agreed that if Vu offered the means to cover her treatment for six months, granting her the best possible chance for longer-term survival, which would be enough to take such a big risk. Perhaps Vu's special government papers from the Chinese embassy could provide some protection.

Vu placed his right hand on his heart after hearing about Minh's condition. He agreed to finance Minh's treatment, and as a final condition, Minh insisted that she accompany them on the mission–she didn't want her husband going alone. Vu bowed, though he did point out that she should consider starting her treatment, rather than delaying it. Minh smiled, silent and defiant.

With the agreement now made, Pham Kai glanced around the room and found a scrap of paper. Using a broken pencil, he started writing. Hoang peeking over his shoulder saw it was a supply list. He laughed, telling Pham Kai to dictate the list and he would put it in his phone. With a gentle shake of his head, Pham Kai explained that by writing the items down, he wouldn't forget any of them. He assured them that as soon as they had secured the items, they would set sail.

Looking at the list, Hoang and Vu noted typical items like fishing nets, weights, motor oil, fuel, and food rations. Collectively, they determined that the safest way to proceed would be at night, meaning during the day they would need to be well within Vietnamese waters. This would reduce their chances of being caught by Chinese patrol boats.

Vu agreed with the plan. They shook hands, bowed, and made their way outside. Hoang walked Vu back to his hotel, where he bid him goodbye and good luck.

It was a restless night for Vu—the excitement of searching for the specimen kept him awake. Not wanting to linger in bed too long, he got up at six the next morning and decided to go down and book a TATA Super Ace Mini truck—a vehicle designed to navigate the small streets and gullies of Vietnam's villages.

The mini-truck driver and Dr. Vu Ha pulled up to Pham Kai's house that evening. Vu had all the supplies Pham Kai had requested, as well as some additional items, including a flare gun, a spear gun, oxygen tanks, scuba gear, a fish tank, laminated nautical maps, a sleeping bag, and rubber boots. Pham Kai smiled at the laminated nautical maps, which would be useless. Only the maps drawn by his grandfather and father would do.

Vu once again urged Minh to stay back and start her treatment. She brought both of her palms together forming the gesture of Namaste, refusing—she wouldn't let her husband go alone.

It took them several trips on the basket boat to load all the supplies onto Pham Kai's fishing vessel. Vu noted some serious damage in the cabin—he surmised that it was caused by the Chinese patrol boat incident, and asking them would reintroduce their fears of the risks involved.

Pham Kai checked one last time with Vu. "Shall we head out?" Vu nodded, stepped out of the cabin, and strolled toward the stern of the boat. There was a small wooden bench and table, anchored to the deck with screws—a great place to spread out the maps, chart their course, and strategize about how to find the fish.

Even in her frail condition, Minh pulled in the anchor. She had already stacked all their supplies against the front wall of the cabin. She had also strung up three hammocks. She wasn't going to let her health slow her down.

A loud shot broke the quietness, followed by a sputtering of engine, and diesel smoke poured from the exhaust pipes. In the pitch darkness of the night, they made their way out to open sea.

* * *

DICK FUMED AS he listened to the report from his team leader. Major Francrey Williams was trying hard to calm him down. He and Major Williams had spoken just days ago about the situation, and Major Williams had been overconfident.

Today, that confidence was still present, which only served to further exasperate Dick. Taking the fish and research data was supposed to be a simple, discreet extraction, not a complete and utter failure. Cebrián's team of scientists hadn't just neutralized his men, they'd dropped them like rag dolls.

"What do you mean, you can't track their plane?" Dick shouted into his cell phone. "With the surveillance satellites we have at our disposal? Are you saying they disappeared after taking off from Andersen Air Force Base?"

"Yes, sir," Major Williams responded. "They're not showing up on any radar. It appears their jet has stealth capability. We're not getting any transponder pings, no cell communications, and no Internet server traffic."

"Major Williams," Dick said, "your team's incompetence is astonishing. They only brought unwanted attention by storming the hangar." His voice trailed off, but he caught himself and launched in again, stronger than ever. "I need you to fix this, Major. Find that plane. They have to land and refuel at some point. I need you to invoke Goliath–we have to track, intercept, and retrieve that specimen. As of now, this is your *only* job. Don't fail me, understand?"

Major Williams hurried through the corridors of the Pentagon to a special command center. He scanned his ID badge and punched in his code, stepping inside a room bustling with activity. Several duty officers were monitoring live missions in Syria, Iraq, Afghanistan, and Somalia. He walked over to the officer in charge and ordered him to initiate the Goliath Protocol. The officer pulled together a team of four experts trained to find covert operations.

Activating a network of surveillance, GPS, and multiband image processing satellites, the Goliath Protocol also authorized tapping into the NSA's visual and voice monitoring servers. This allowed them to track cell phone conversations, live camera feeds from all over the world, and deep web traffic in real time. If a way to find Sebastian and the team existed, then Goliath was it.

* * *

AFTER SPEAKING WITH the team, Cebrián made his way to the NOC using the same route he had taken with Sebastian–past Ritter Hall, into Vaughan Hall, then deep underground via elevator. The command center stood empty and still, its five huge screens showing maps of various locations. "Poseidon, please invoke the Honeycomb Protocol," Cebrián ordered. "Include all research on the specimen."

Cebrián had set up Honeycomb for just such a day. Unbeknownst to the politicians who had approved the funding of his research, he had recruited thirteen of the best scientists from top university research labs, private enterprises, and even secret government research. They were aware of Cebrián's research, and they knew that the day his team found something important enough, they would come under immediate threat from governments all over the world—those looking to militarize it, monetize it, or both, depriving humanity of any benefits the research uncovered. These thirteen scientists didn't subscribe to the concept of imaginary borders that divided countries–they were loyal to science and its ability to uplift humanity.

The first scientist to respond to the Honeycomb call was Hamza Hamad from Pakistan, a genius in applied mathematics, astrophysics, and a savant at communicating with machines. Sitting in his living room, he could remotely hack into and take over any machine in the world that had a control panel.

The second scientist to sign in was from Israel, Talia Goldman, a brilliant quantum physicist, futurist, and another celebrity hacker.

As each scientist responded, their images appeared on the oversized screens in the NOC. Hamza started tossing his hair with his hands when he saw that Talia had logged in. The third scientist was from the UK, then India, Japan, Germany, France, Italy, Spain, Algiers, Iran, Switzerland, and Russia.

Hamza was the first to speak, reading his screen. "Cebrián, what are you saying in this report? I don't believe it, this is amazing!"

The Honeycomb team scanned through the documents as Cebrián took control of the conversation. "The reason I asked Poseidon to initiate Honeycomb is that members of our hive need immediate protection. As you can see, we've found a marine specimen that has evolved to use time as a defense and survival mechanism." Spellbound, the team didn't utter a syllable as Cebrián continued. "When we got the specimen, it was already dead. We don't know for certain if there are more in the South China Sea. Its presence and capabilities have leaked within the U.S. government. Around 2300 hours Guam time, a covert team attacked the Paramarines. We don't yet know who they are, but we can no longer trust the United States.

"On my orders, the Paramarines have gone stealth. They're making their way to the possible source of the new species. If they find it, they'll work toward securing it from poachers."

Some of the experts held their heads in their hands, shocked at the enormity of what they were reading. Some even got up and started pacing their labs and offices. Without exception, they all understood the astounding significance of the discovery.

Kabir, the scientist from India, spoke up. "Reading this report mandates that if such a discovery is to be applied, we'll need to create a multinational and multi-disciplinary council of officials to develop and manage our first World Temporal Organization, one that sets the rules of application for these time particles."

The scientists continued to share their collective astonishment. One scientist, however, had remained quiet all the while, and that was Omar Tabreze from Iran, a brilliant geneticist. "Cebrián, what if your team doesn't find the source? What if it's the only surviving specimen due to its miraculous capabilities? Does it even have the evolutionary need to reproduce?"

Having expected the question, Cebrián offered, "I then hope we might find some living stem cells in the specimen, and I would ask you to develop a cloning capability for the nodule. I don't think farming this specimen is an option." Omar nodded, and moved his hand to touch his forehead—an Eastern gesture of deep respect.

"Okay, Cebrián," the Russian scientist said in a gruff voice. "What do you need us to do?"

Cebrián laid out the plan. "Ordinarily, I'd be using my own resources. But given the attempted infiltration by the U.S., we have to employ a covert approach. I want the geneticists to start developing a plan to clone the nodule. The quantum biologists, please formulate some hypotheses concerning the time particles—for lack of better understanding, we're calling them dark matter particles. I need our geoscientists to figure out how to find the specimen. I also want the anthropologists, cognitive psychologists, and neuropsychologists to determine the effects of these particles, from individual to societal levels.

"Finally, Hamza and Talia, I need two things from you.

First, find and access any available autonomous, remotely controlled vehicles that our Paramarines may use in the field. Second, find out as much as you can about this secret U.S. government faction that's after our specimen."

Talia texted Hamza on the chat screen that she would take care of getting into the Pentagon, and he should work on finding the transport. Hamza responded via chat, *Cool.*

"Oh, I almost forgot," Cebrián said. "Kabir, you're right. We need you and Omar to start developing the framework for the World Temporal Organization."

Hamza, whose fast strokes of keyboard could be heard by all, spoke up. "Cebrián, I've found a Skjold-class boat, a small, stealth-shielded catamaran warship operated by the Royal Norwegian Navy, anchored at the port of Haiphong." Tapping away, he continued, "The boat's crew are on a week-long shore leave. There isn't a single person on board, and according to the logs, they won't be returning for another five days."

Cebrián, hearing Hamza, picked up his phone and started searching for a phone number. Alfred Burland III, the Fleet Admiral of the Royal Norwegian Navy, was an old friend of his. "Great, Hamza. I'll speak to my friend in the Royal Norwegian Navy and take care of approvals and authorizations."

Poseidon spoke up. "I have found an airstrip close to Nhon Ly village. It belongs to a closed Nike factory. There are no workers managing the facility, except for a security guard."

Hamza piped up enthusiastically, "Oh, hi, Poseidon! Good to hear your voice! If our team is landing near Nhon Ly, I can navigate the boat there."

"Good to hear your voice too, Doctor Hamad," Poseidon replied. "And yes, positioning the boat as close as possible to Nhon Ly would be ideal."

"Thank you, Poseidon," Cebrián said. "I'll ask Zeke to meet the team at the Nike factory." He then addressed the assembled scientists. "Friends, thank you for responding so readily to Honeycomb. What we're about to do to secure the specimen and get our team home safe will no doubt be in violation of several laws, both national and international. My sincerest thanks to each of you for your support. Good luck, and be safe."

Just then, Talia spoke up. "Wait guys, someone in the Pentagon has invoked the Goliath Protocol."

"Well then," Cebrián said, with beaming determination, "it looks like it's going to be Goliath versus Honeycomb."

CHAPTER FOURTEEN
Return to Bombay Reef

VU SAT ON the old trunk in the cabin while Pham Kai steered the boat toward the north side of Bombay reef. It was 1:30 a.m., and they had just arrived in the area. There were no signs of the Chinese patrol boat. Pham Kai had beads of sweat on his forehead–due to the heat, and due to the memory of what had happened to him the last time he was in this area. He reduced the speed of the boat as he found the channel his grandfather had mentioned in his notes–the same channel he'd taken deep into the reef before transitioning to the basket boat and getting caught in the whirlpool.

Minh came inside the cabin where the two men were standing. "Is this where you found that fish?" she asked. Pham Kai nodded. She stood next to him and whispered, "Pham Kai, something is wrong with this place. There's mist everywhere."

Pham Kai didn't have an answer for her–he too had felt this way during his fishing trips to the area. However, he'd always been more worried about being caught by the patrol boats.

Vu watched as Pham Kai managed the fishing net. After untangling it, he folded it over his left shoulder. Standing on the starboard side of the boat, he swung it over the water. It was hard to see much in the lantern light, as Pham Kai insisted they not use the spotlights. Vu had already explained to them that since he was paying for the trip, he didn't need them to store the catch in the hull—he was looking for that one specific fish. This was hard for Pham Kai and Minh to accept. Releasing them back into the sea was so contradictory to their way of life. However, since Vu was paying for everything, including Minh's medical treatment, they didn't argue. Pham Kai did make one request, however—if he happened to catch a su vang, he could keep it to sell. Vu agreed.

They cast the nets for three hours from both sides of the boat, each time emptying their catch into the large tin tub filled with seawater. Pham Kai and Minh would then stand aside and watch as Vu brought the lantern close for inspection. Each time, he would shake his head. He'd hand the lantern to Pham Kai, so he could check for su vang fish, then both men would lift the tub and empty it into the sea, feeling the bite of disappointment a little more each time. This went on more than a dozen times in the course of a few hours. By 4:30 a.m. they were exhausted.

Frustrated, Vu sat at the table facing the dark outline of the reef. Pham Kai joined him, and Minh made them some chai. Vu, in between taking careful sips of the hot tea, kept glancing at Pham Kai, who sat on the floor with Minh. Their faces lit up with the soft light of the lantern. They both looked tired, but not broken. They kept whispering to each other—something he had noticed several times during the trip. Minh would whisper her thoughts to Pham Kai. Vu found it quite endearing.

"What are you two whispering?" Vu asked. Pham Kai shook his head. Minh then whispered again, and Pham Kai shook his head again. Vu pressed on. "Obviously, she's saying something important to you. What is it?"

"She is reminding me to share with you the details of the

night I caught the fish," Pham Kai said.

"Go ahead then, tell me." Vu said.

Pham Kai explained to Vu what had happened that night—how he had rowed his basket boat deep into the most treacherous part of the reef and gotten caught in the dangerous whirlpool. He then described how he had escaped, complete with his boat and net. That was how he had caught the fish Vu was so interested in.

Vu's eyes grew large—that was an important piece of information Pham Kai hadn't shared in the past. Being a marine biologist, he knew that if a whirlpool had formed in this area of the reef, then a deep underwater cavern must exist to cause it. This meant the specimen may have come from the cavern itself—a cavern that may have yet to be explored by humans, which would explain why the specimen had gone undiscovered.

Vu asked if Pham Kai knew where the whirlpool formed. This was why Pham Kai hadn't volunteered the information—he knew the instant Vu heard about the whirlpool, he would want to fish as close to it as possible.

Pham Kai explained the incredible danger of attempting to reach that location. But he agreed to try to get the boat as close as possible the next night.

Pham Kai started pulling up the anchor when Vu requested that they try one last time for the fish before leaving. Pham Kai looked around—it was still pitch dark, now around 5:00 a.m. Dawn would start to break in an hour. Pham Kai shook his head no and kept pulling up the anchor.

"Pham Kai please, you don't understand, it's very important that we make this catch," Vu pleaded.

Pham Kai paused, sensing Vu's deep commitment—a familiar feeling to him. Against his better judgment, he agreed to keep going. Letting go of the anchor, he picked up the net and cast one more time. He swung the net out and let it sink a bit longer than usual before pulling it in. Vu helped him haul it, and they sorted through the catch. Once again, disappointment set in for both of them. They emptied the tin tub into the sea as Minh hoisted the anchor.

Pham Kai started the engine and made their way out of the channel. Vu went back and sat on the bench at the table, looking back at Bombay Reef, like a child walking away from a playground.

Pham Kai felt they had delayed a bit too long getting out of the channel. He still needed to head closer to Vietnam for a good two hours before he would feel safe. He had been maintaining a steady speed of thirty-five knots when he saw a small light about two miles ahead. The sun was starting to rise, and he could make out the horizon line, which was at about three miles—so this had to be a boat speeding in their direction. He didn't like the intensity of the light or its movement. It behaved like a spotlight. As he tried to figure out his next move, Minh walked into the cabin and pointed to the starboard side. There, at approximately the same distance, was another light coming closer. Pham Kai looked to the port side, thinking he could move in that direction, but a third boat with the same kind of light-headed coming closer. His heart skipped a beat. This was the situation he had wanted to avoid. The three boats were surrounding them. He slowed down, starting a full turn back toward the channel. He figured if there was any chance of escape, he needed to go deeper into the channel to the lagoon and hope the patrol boats wouldn't follow him.

Realizing the sudden change in speed and direction Vu asked Pham Kai what had happened. Pham Kai pointed to his right. Vu turned and saw the approaching light. "Relax, Pham Kai, I have proper papers," he said, tapping his pocket.

* * *

***YOULING CHUAN*, THE** Phantom Boat—this had

become the call sign of the Chinese patrol boat that had allowed Pham Kai to escape. When Wang Li had gone back with a broken nose and stories of how an old, feeble Vietnamese fisherman had gotten the best of him, his commanding officer had given him this call sign to punish him. There was no tolerance for such failure in the Chinese Navy.

The fact that he hadn't sunk the fisherman's boat, instead escaping the area to avoid being stranded by the changing currents of the reef, was further insulting to his superiors. His officer had told him that he should be glad he wasn't stripped of his titles and dishonorably discharged. Other patrol boat captains had informed the commanding officer there wasn't any sign of the fisherman or his boat—so they had to conclude he had survived. Even worse for Wang Li, the two su vang fish he had confiscated hadn't brought him any recognition—they'd become property of the People's Republic of China.

From that day, Wang Li had become obsessed with one and only one mission—finding the fisherman who had taken his dignity. He couldn't care less if it sparked an international incident between China and Vietnam. He'd punish him with such cruelty that the fisherman will become an example of Chinese wrath.

Today's patrol was no different than any other—they would get to the south side of Bombay Reef, head out five miles into the open sea, and then turn around and approach the reef from the north side. The navy had added two more boats that would patrol from the east and west. They knew that the news of two su vang fish being caught at Bombay Reef would cause an influx of Vietnamese fishermen willing to tempt fate. The addition of the two patrol boats to the area further angered Wang Li.

They had been patrolling the area for several weeks, confused that not a single fisherman had been seen. In fact, no activity of any kind had occurred. The three patrol boats would get to Bombay Reef at 5:00 a.m. and disperse to their assigned routes. They all hated the reef—it was a dismal island, always misty and mysterious.

Dawn started to break up the pitch darkness of the sea. As Wang Li settled in his captain's chair for their routine patrol, the boat's VHF radio crackled. It was one of the other captains—they'd spotted a vessel. He peered through his binoculars, searching for confirmation. He ordered the commander to speed up and head for the reef.

Through his binoculars, he recognized the shape and size of the boat with the orange and yellow accent stripes running along its length. He couldn't believe his luck—it could be the fisherman! His heart started to race, but he didn't want to get too excited. Then the fishing boat made a move that reminded Wang Li of how Pham Kai had tried to escape the last time.

The three patrol boats converged at the mouth of the channel simultaneously, only to see Pham Kai navigate deeper despite the crashing waves and ever-present mist. The captains of the other boats weren't at all familiar with the channel—they knew they had to have precise nautical maps to navigate it. They kept their engines idle, waiting for orders.

Wang Li commanded them to follow him in, flanking in a tight V formation. The channel turned and twisted as the waves churned, and there were rocky protrusions everywhere. After an hour of careful navigation, they closed within a half-mile of Pham Kai's boat, deep within the channel.

* * *

PHAM KAI KNEW he only had a few minutes before the three boats came bearing down on them. He ordered Minh to retrieve his grandfather's notes from the trunk. She removed the rubber band, unwrapped the plastic, and started laying out the old, tattered papers on the boat's helm. Vu watched, amazed that Pham Kai's family had kept such valuable information to themselves.

While navigating with one hand, Pham Kai started flipping through the papers. He was looking for one that had a small drawing and a brief note on another opening in the channel. The channel was part of an ancient caldera forming a large letter *C*. In theory, one could enter the reef from the north side, navigate to the center, and then continue on and come out almost a mile south through the southern opening. His grandfather had written in big letters never to take the southern opening, as it was narrow with sharp rock walls. Pham Kai had always known about it, but given the warnings by his grandfather, he'd never attempted to navigate through it.

Vu, baffled by Pham Kai's desire to avoid the patrol boats, glanced at the notes. "Are you planning to navigate south?" he asked. Pham Kai nodded. "Pham Kai, I must insist on a safer course of action," Vu said, pulling the folded papers from his breast pocket. "This expedition is approved by the Chinese government. There's no need for us to avoid the Chinese, we have every right to be here. Stop the boat, and I'll talk to the captains. I promise you, we'll be fine."

One hand still on the boat's wheel, Pham Kai scanned the waters of the southern opening. His eyes darted to the warnings scribbled in his grandfather's handwriting, then over to Minh. He searched Minh's worried eyes a final time, and then idled the boat's engine.

Vu thanked him and stepped to the stern, waiting for the boats to catch up. Soon, full daylight was upon them, and Pham Kai could make out the southern opening about a hundred yards away. He could see why his grandfather had written such explicit warnings. Unlike the northern opening, with choppy waters, and shifting currents, the southern opening was calm. He had to step out of the cabin and walk to the bow to see any signs of danger—a series of jagged rock tips made a long, narrow corridor just beneath the waves. Since the current was so calm, there was no splashing of water on rocks to indicate they were even there. The rock walls of the corridor were twelve feet apart, even narrower in some places—far too close to gauge from the position of the helm. He began to feel that stopping had been the right decision, whatever the consequences.

Wang Li understood why they had stopped. According to his computerized nautical maps, the fishing boat couldn't go any farther. The channel stopped here—there was shallow reef in front, and the only way to get out was to turn around and head back the way they had come. There was a man standing on the stern of the fishing boat, waving at them. He saw two other people in the cabin, but he still wasn't sure if it was the same fishing boat. Whatever the case, the waving of this portly, well-dressed man confused and irritated him.

As his boat made the final approach, Wang Li came out of the cabin and stood on the bow, resting a hand on his gun. He ordered the engines cut and let the momentum take them closer. He shouted in Chinese, "You're trespassing in the sovereign waters of the People's Republic of China! Step aside and prepare to be boarded!"

To Wang Li's surprise, the stupid Vietnamese man continued to smile with a sense of surety as he bowed and stepped to the side. Wang Li and his two lieutenants jumped onto the boat. The man continued bowing, his head down in respect, both hands extended in front of him holding official-looking papers. Wang Li walked up, and still speaking in Chinese, asked him who he was and what this was all about.

Even more surprising, the man replied in fluent English. "I'm professor Doctor Vu Ha of the Vietnam Maritime University, with full permission to be here to conduct my research."

Wang Li took the paperwork and scanned it. To his surprise it was legitimate—it had a seal from the Chinese embassy in Vietnam, giving permission for research. Wang Li read the paperwork as the other patrol boats maneuvered to either side, hemming the boat in from the port, starboard, and stern.

While Wang Li read the documents, one of the lieutenants walked up to the cabin and saw Pham Kai and Minh sitting on an old trunk with their heads down. He called out to Wang Li as he brought them out onto the deck, kneeling them down with their hands on the backs of their necks.

Still reading the paperwork, Wang Li glanced up. There, to his immense joy, was Pham Kai.

He immediately drew his gun and pointed it at Vu. "You've recruited a criminal who was caught fishing these waters without permission! He is wanted by the Chinese government, and since you're working with him, you too are a criminal." He put the gun to Vu's head, grabbed his collar, and dragged him to Pham Kai and Minh. He pushed Vu down, forcing him into the same position.

Shocked, the professor began to protest, but one of the lieutenants slapped him with such force that his head whipped to the side. Vu's eyes watered.

Wang Li then stood in front of Pham Kai, staring at him for a while. This was the man who had brought him so much pain—and now, here he was again, kneeling. Fate had given him another chance, to make an example of this defiant Vietnamese fisherman. He was going to do everything to him he had planned and more. And then he glanced at Minh—something about her disturbed him. It was as if she were unafraid to die. For that matter, Pham Kai held the same expression. Neither of them appeared defiant—it was more of a sad expression, with eyes staring straight into the sea, as if they had accepted death. "Who is this woman?" he asked Pham Kai.

"She is my wife," Pham Kai replied.

"Why have you given up on life?" Wang Li asked him.

"You knew that coming back here would mean imminent capture, torture, and death. Yet you came back anyway, and you even brought your wife. Why?"

Pham Kai, looking straight into the sea with tears rolling down his cheeks, said, "We have only a few months left together. She has a disease that will soon take her life."

"So, you came here to die. Why did you bring this idiot professor along?" Wang Li asked.

"He has promised us enough money to get my wife her treatment, if we helped him with his research," Pham Kai replied.

Wang Li's stared at Pham Kai and Minh's defeated form for a long minute. His superstitious nature began to get the best of him. Taking an involuntary step back, he said, "No wonder my luck has gone bad since I met you. You have the shadow of death and ill fortune, and you've transferred it onto me." He wiped his hands on his shirt, as if to cleanse himself of it.

Vu expressed his apologies, reiterating that they had permission to be here.

"You know," Wang Li sneered, "these documents you so proudly carry are no better than the toilet paper on my boat." He unbuckled his belt and stuffed them down the back of his pants, then crammed them into Vu's breast pocket. "There, your paperwork has been processed." The gathered sailors laughed.

"But I have official permission from your government to be here." Vu insisted.

"Shut up!" Wang Li yelled. "Take him to the boat. I'll have our authorities deal with him." Focusing back on Pham Kai, he lowered his voice into a snarl and said. "I was going to inflict so much pain on you that you would have begged me to kill you. However, since fate doesn't have mercy on you, I'm not going to jinx my life any further with your filthy luck." He now stood several feet from their huddled forms, unwilling to be near them. "Instead, I think we should all watch you steer your boat straight into the reef, sinking it with you two aboard. I'll give you this gift–you'll both die together."

The lieutenants grabbed Vu and started forcing him toward their boat. Vu knew that getting arrested by the Chinese government would mean torture, imprisonment, and many years of bureaucratic court battles. He started pushing the lieutenants away, resisting their orders. Wang Li ordered them to hold him down in a kneeling position. Scared out of his mind, Vu started begging for forgiveness.

"Calm down, professor," Pham Kai whispered in between all the shouting. "You're making things worse."

But Vu went into full-blown panic mode. He thrashed his feet and hands, screaming at the top of his lungs. "But I have papers! I have papers!"

The two lieutenants were having a difficult time getting him to kneel. Vu's wails and pleas carried over the entire reef. The crews of the two other boats stood on deck, watching the situation unfold.

Wang Li shouted at his lieutenants to hold him down, as he pulled a set of brass knuckles from his pocket. Slipping them over the fingers of his right hand, he stood behind Vu, who continued to thrash and scream for forgiveness. Pham Kai and Minh watched in horror as the decent man who had come to their home, full of life and excitement, descended into animalistic terror.

Wang Li clenched his fist several times, testing the brass knuckles. He grabbed Vu by the hair, aligning the back of the man's head with his fist. He wound his arm back and smashed his fist into the base of the professor's skull and upper back. Vu yelped, and his eyes stopped moving, his mouth opened and his tongue jut out. The lieutenants released his arms, and Vu slumped to the ground like a sack of potatoes.

Pham Kai and Minh could see that his eyes were open, but they lacked any indication of awareness. They could hear him breathe, as if he were trying hard to say something, but only soft grunts came out. Worst of all was the sudden silence. Had the great mind been lost?

Wang Li called out to Pham Kai. "Look over here, this was supposed to be you." He nudged the limp doctor with his boot and ordered his lieutenants back to their boat. He too jumped aboard, turning to Pham Kai. "And now, it's your turn to die. Navigate straight into the reef and sink your boat."

CHAPTER FIFTEEN
Sixteen-Century Figurehead

PANTHER TWO LANDED at the Nike factory as Zeke waited, ready to greet the Paramarines. On entering the plane, he was amazed at the sophistication of the equipment. It was a flying science lab. The team was listening to a voice coming out of the speaker system—Poseidon was explaining Goliath, and the Skjold warship. Then it added, "Sebastian, based on today's satellite images of the Paracel Islands, Pham Kai's schooner is near Bombay Reef. The Chinese Navy have increased their patrols of the area, so his odds of capture have gone up."

"Poseidon, please connect me to Doctor Hamad," Sebastian said. Noticing Zeke, he stood up and shook hands, gesturing for him to take a seat with them at the main table.

Hamza's voice came through the speakers. "Sebastian, good to speak with you and the team."

"Thank you, Hamza, for arranging the boat," Sebastian responded. "Tell me, how far is it from us?"

"It'll reach a cove five miles north of Eo Gio beach in about thirty minutes," Hamza answered.

Zeke nodded, he knew the location. The Paramarines piled into his Suburban, loading it with their bags, scuba gear, the specimen slides and Shiloh's time warp device.

Sebastian was the last one to join them—he was still speaking with the pilots. They informed him that they would head to Singapore. They'd remain within a two-hour radius, waiting for instructions from Cebrián or Sebastian. Sebastian agreed with their plan. The team had also decided that the specimen and glowing nodule should remain on the plane, where there was power to keep the incubator charged. Before stepping out of the plane, Sebastian gave a last look to the incubator. It was opaque—on and operational.

Before he hopped in the Suburban, he went to the back to take a final look at their gear, noticing Vu's Monbento lunchbox tucked away on the side. He found it funny—this was where it had all begun, with the professor's Vietnamese barbeque. He shut the back hatch and hopped into the Suburban.

Zeke pulled out of the Nike factory—the guard still hadn't returned. Zeke had given him money to go and have a beer while the plane landed. He made sure to get out and close the gates so as not to attract any suspicion. They were a mile from the factory when they heard the roar of Panther Two's engines at low altitude.

Zeke asked Sebastian to open the glove compartment and pull out a bag. "I was asked to pick up phones for you. These are untraceable satellite phones. Cebrián wanted to make sure he and Poseidon were able to connect with you in the South China Sea. As you know, your current phones have been deactivated for security reasons." Sebastian passed the new phones to the team.

Adora was sitting in the back and pulled her cell phone from the sleeve of her bag. She decided to test if it was deactivated. The phone turned on, and she was even able to connect to a cell tower. Maybe Zeke meant only Sebastian and his team's phones had been deactivated.

She received a message in English and Vietnamese

regarding roaming charges. After accepting, she typed out a text message to her mother in Guam and one to Franc at the coffee shop: *Charles and I have the opportunity to join an expedition. We're in Vietnam for the next couple of days and will be back soon. Cell coverage will be spotty, so please don't expect updates. I'll ping you whenever I can. All good! Love you guys.*

She waited for the icon that indicated the texts were sent and placed it back in her bag.

The drive to the cove was dark and quiet. The team was thinking about the enormity of the task that lay in front of them. Dawn started to break as Zeke slowed his Suburban and turned down a winding dirt road. Gradually, the terrain changed from low-lying farms to rugged coastal cliffs. They heard the low rumble of the waves far below them, and Zeke came to a stop near a natural canal formed by seawater rushing inland during high tide. "We're here. We'll have to carry our gear on foot."

The team picked up their bags and scuba equipment, climbed down to the edge of the canal and walked in single file. Zeke handed out a couple flashlights, and after about fifteen minutes of walking in the pre-dawn gloom, the canal opened up into a cavern with high, rocky ceilings. There was a stale, rotting smell. Sebastian pointed his flashlight up and found the source. A colony of demon bats swarmed the cavern roof. The team entered, and continued along a rocky ledge, finding that the water in the canal got deeper the farther in they went. It was a natural tunnel that opened into a semicircular cove—the perfect spot to anchor a boat. Sebastian stood on the ledge and could see the open sea ahead of him.

"Good morning!" Hamza's voice echoed through the cove.

Flashlights swung around to the voice, and the team discovered the marvel hiding close to them. Several yards down the canal, the towering bulk of the Norwegian attack patrol boat floated in the water.

"Please stand where you are," Hamza's booming voice requested from the ship's loudspeakers. "I'm moving closer so you can climb aboard."

He fired the lateral navigation jets, and they could hear bubbles surfacing as the boat glided closer. Sebastian jumped on the deck first and opened the main door, climbing a set of stairs to the bridge, where six chairs occupied the ship's various control stations.

After the team had loaded their gear onto the ship, some of them made their way to the bridge, where Sebastian and Zeke stood admiring the sophistication of the vessel. Nidal and Michelangelo identified the weapons stations and started to acquaint themselves with the controls. Shiloh took over navigation, and Charles and Maria took over the mapping station. Fabienne and Adora were still going through the rest of the boat—there were sleeping cabins, showers, a galley, a mess area, laundry, and a medical bay. The boat was also stocked with rations, which included several bars of Toblerone chocolate, a favorite of Fabienne's. They estimated the boat could sustain a three-month open-ocean mission for their small team of six.

Zeke shook Sebastian's hand and wished them luck before making his way back to his SUV to call Cebrián with an update.

Hamza helped Shiloh figure out all the navigational controls, and then handed him full control of the boat with a couple of taps on his keyboard. Three thousand miles away from where he started, his time as a pirate had come to an end.

Poseidon's familiar voice came through speakers on the bridge. It had already downloaded the last known coordinates of Pham Kai's boat onto the mapping station, along with all of Maria's and Charles's research and bathymetry maps of the Paracel Islands.

Sebastian stood on the bridge, admiring the smooth ride

of the ship—an air-cushioned catamaran hull capable of high-speed rapid maneuverability and a water jet propulsion system. It was the perfect vessel for their mission, with a shallow draught of about a meter that gave them the ability to navigate the rocky reefs of the Parcel Islands. He walked over to Nidal and Michelangelo at the controls of the weapons station. It was a modern two-touch screen interface. The first screen was dedicated to weapons selection. The second was for targeting and guidance systems. The two soldier scientists briefed him on the ship's arsenal.

Maria and Charles were immersed in deep discussion at the mapping station, which was a flat touch screen table. There were icons on the side that allowed them to pull up maps, satellite images, and bathymetry layouts of the seabed. The whole table was a working screen. Charles brought up satellite images and superimposed them on the bathymetry layouts downloaded off the GOES-16. They were trying to get within a one-mile radius of the deep-water cavern.

After several minutes, Maria said to Shiloh, "I think we've got it. I'm transferring the coordinates to your station." With a touch of a few icons on the screen, Shiloh's navigation station received a popup indicating new coordinates. He confirmed, and they were locked in.

"Okay," Maria continued, "now I'm sending you the last known coordinates of Pham Kai's boat. Looks like it isn't too far from the first set of coordinates."

They all knew the plan. First, they were going to try to find Pham Kai, and then they'd head to the general location of the deep-water cavern. Shiloh informed them that their ETA was approximately two hours.

Sebastian left the bridge, curious to see the rest of the ship, and soon ran into Adora and Fabienne in the medical bay. They were amazed at how well equipped it was, capable of handling two patients at any given time.

Sebastian then made his way to the cabins, avoiding the captain's quarters. He found a small cabin at the stern of the ship and sat at the small desk attached to the wall. He pulled out his phone and made a call. There was a pause, followed by a series of tones, as if it were going through an intense network of satellites and servers.

"Hi, Sebastian," Cebrián answered.

"Hey, Cebrián," Sebastian replied. "I figured we'd catch up. We're on our way to the possible source of the specimen, but first we're going to try to find a friend who we think may come under threat from the Chinese Navy."

"Ah, yes," Cebrián said. "Pham Kai."

Sebastian paused for a moment, then asked a question that had been on his mind all day. "Cebrián, what's your plan to deal with the secret faction in the U.S. government that's trying to take our work?"

"Sebastian, I've initiated several countermeasures to neutralize the impending threats," Cebrián assured him. "I can't get into details, but you're already aware of the Honeycomb. We're also meeting in Sweden with their navy to develop a strategy that gets you guys safely out of the South China Sea. I'm working on a multi-national plan involving several government leaders. Above all, our goal is to find, protect, and preserve the sanctity of the specimen."

"Sounds good," Sebastian said, relieved. "I'll keep you posted as we make our way to the source."

* * *

ON PHAM KAI'S boat, still on her knees, Minh crawled over to Vu. He was listless, but alive. His eyes were fixated, staring at something in the distance. She whispered his name, but he didn't respond, not even a blink. It was as if he wasn't there anymore. It was a painful thing to watch—he made grunting noises, like his body was trying hard to breathe. He still lay flat on his back, his hands and feet spread out, his neck turned on its side. Some of his shirt buttons around his belly had popped open. She felt sad for him–just hours ago, he had been a man of dignity and presence. She squeezed his hand while whispering his name, hoping to get some sort of response. The documents he was so proud of stuck out tauntingly from his shirt pocket. Tears flowed down her face.

The captains of the patrol boats were on the radio, arguing about why Wang Li didn't sink Pham Kai's boat with machine gun fire. "Why all the drama of the fisherman ramming his boat into the reef, and then sinking it?" one of them shouted.

"Shut up! I have my reasons," Wang Li snapped back. "I want to see him take their lives through his own actions." The other captains fell silent. They knew they were dealing with an illogical, deranged sadist, but they were also certain it was his superstitious nature that drove his decision.

Pham Kai stepped out of the cabin and walked over to the stern, bypassing the spread-eagle form of Dr. Vu, his head resting in Minh's lap. He called out to Wang Li, shouting that in order to sink his boat, he would need to gain speed. He asked if they would all move back three-quarters of a mile. He would then speed up to ten knots, steer through the channel to this same spot, and ram his boat into the reef–that would guarantee the damage needed to sink the boat. Wang Li ordered the boats to pull back. It took them almost half an hour to navigate back near the center of the channel. The three boats regrouped in a V formation and the crews came out on deck. They had folding chairs and binoculars set up, as if they were going to watch a live entertainment show.

Having reversed his own boat closer to the center of the channel, Pham Kai pointed it toward the reef. He took in his surroundings, noticing it had turned into a beautiful day–the sun was out, and the mist had lifted too. Wang Li shouted out to get going. "We don't have all day to watch you die!" he yelled through a bullhorn. The crew was excited to witness a real live suicide.

Pham Kai walked back into the cabin and Minh followed. He increased his speed to ten knots—a dangerously fast speed for the channel. The patrol boat captains and crews watched his boat grow smaller. Commenting on his steering skills—it had taken them a long time to catch up to him, and now they noticed he was zigzagging through the channel at much higher speeds. His boat would crash into the reef any moment now. They all smiled, waiting for the spectacular end.

Pham Kai had been planning their escape since the moment they boarded. He hoped the captains were unaware of the southern opening to the channel. But if he slowed the boat down, the captains would know something was amiss and fire their machine guns. He needed to keep his speed at ten knots with no signs of slowing.

He shared his plan with Minh. She offered to stand at the bow and guide him, helping him avoid the rock walls on either side. He nodded.

Minh went to the bow and leaned over the edge, her hand on her forehead to shield her eyes, looking ahead for the beginning of the treacherous rock walls. To Pham Kai, her graceful form became a sixteenth-century ship's figurehead that had come alive to guide and protect her vessel.

With the rhythmic rocking of the boat and the seawater splashing in her face, it was hard to make out where they were. She wiped water from her eyes, knowing that one wrong direction from her would mean a fatal crash. Pham Kai shouted through the front cabin slats, asking if she could see the rocks yet. She shouted back, "No!"

Pham Kai was about to slow the boat down and risk raising suspicion when he saw Minh gesturing with her left arm—he heard her calling out to steer to port. A wave of nervous relief came over him. He was so glad she had insisted on coming with him. He turned the boat to port. Minh then pointed with her right arm, shouting, "Starboard! Starboard!" Pham Kai responded, turning the wheel to the right.

A creaky scraping sound erupted from the starboard side of the boat as it ground into the rock wall, just as Minh gestured again to the port side, calling for him to adjust course. The noise stopped as the boat escaped the starboard wall.

Almost halfway through the southern opening, a mere three feet on either side, they careened through the rocky corridor at ten knots. Minh began gesturing and shouting, "Port! Port! Starboard! Port!" Pham Kai followed her instructions blindly, doing his best to keep up.

The patrol boat captains watched with eager anticipation, as Pham Kai's boat headed nearer the reef. One captain spoke up. "Why hasn't he hit the reef yet? He's right on top of it!"

"Wait, it's about to happen," Wang Li replied. Another minute passed and still no explosion. He then got up from his chair, his eyes fixated on the boat. Even with binoculars, they couldn't see the rapid left and right movements from Minh's instructions–the boat just appeared to be heading away from them at a strong, steady speed.

He looked to the other captains for their opinion. They too stood up, peering through their binoculars. They exchanged looks with each other. Could it be? Had this pathetic Vietnamese fisherman found a second opening out of the channel? If so, how was he navigating it at such speed? That was impossible.

Just then, the two lower captains started laughing. Pham Kai's boat appeared to gain more speed, having crossed the reef boundary into open sea. "It appears your Vietnamese fisherman has made a fool of you again."

Rage overtook Wang Li. He unstrapped his sidearm, and screaming at the top of his lungs, started shooting the metal cabin door of his own boat. The bullets did little harm to the tempered metal, but the crew dove for cover to avoid ricochets.

On the open sea, Minh came into the cabin, her face, hair, and clothes soaking wet. Pham Kai grabbed a towel and started helping her wipe off the water. They both started laughing and crying—they had pulled off a miracle.

Still, the chase was on. It took the three patrol boats over an hour to navigate through the channel and reach open sea. They knew that even though Pham Kai's boat was old, he would have covered over ten miles in that time. This was now a matter of great pride for all three captains.

Minh went back to check on Vu. He was still limp and lifeless. Pham Kai asked how he was doing. She shook her head. He then asked her to see if the patrol boats were visible—if they were, then they had crossed the horizon line and were within five nautical miles.

The three captains pushed the very limits of their engines, pursuing the fishing boat at full speed—fifty knots to Pham Kai's 25-30. Given enough time, they would catch him. They also spread out a mile from each other laterally. This would help ensure they caught him if he tried anything tricky.

Almost two hours later, the far-right patrol boat spotted Pham Kai's schooner about five miles away, forty-five degrees east of its location—deep within Vietnamese waters. The captain radioed the other boats, and they all adjusted course. Minh ran back in to inform Pham Kai that patrol boats were now visible. He wasn't surprised, but all he needed to do was get close to an international tanker, and that should deter them. They'd think twice before firing on him if he were in the shadows of commercial traffic. The problem was there wasn't any such traffic. All he could do was keep gunning toward Vietnam.

It took the patrol boats another forty-five minutes to get within firing range, but precision was impossible. They had to barrage him with rounds. The firing cadets for each boat sat behind their respective controls, using visual cues and radar measurements to align their shots.

Pham Kai's heart skipped when he heard the crack of the machine guns, and several huge holes ripped through the patched-up starboard wall of his cabin. He and Minh dove to the floorboards, narrowly surviving the first volley. Pham Kai used one hand from his position on the floor to yank the wheel port and starboard, creating a rapid zigzag motion. They heard the distinct whine of rounds flying overhead and pattering into the water all around them.

The second volley, however, ripped through the stern of the boat, creating a gaping hole in the transom. The satisfied captains ordered the cadets to fire along the pitch, hoping to cut the boat in half vertically.

The couple covered their heads as the roof of the boat was torn to splinters. Grabbing each other's hand, they jumped behind the trunk in the back of the cabin. The rounds tore into the engine room, killing the boat's momentum. Dead in the water, Pham Kai knew that the next volley would be their end.

CHAPTER SIXTEEN
Fire

SEBASTIAN AND THE team were racing to the last known coordinates of Pham Kai, when the Skjold's proximity system Senit 2000 sounded an alarm. "There's a small vessel on the starboard horizon, heading our way," Nidal called out. "And three more vessels behind it in a flanking formation, following at high speed."

Sebastian shot up from his chair—the entire team heard a repetitive cracking sound in the distance.

"What was that?" Fabienne asked, joining them on the bridge.

"Machine gun fire," Maria replied.

"Shiloh, slow down," Sebastian ordered. Shiloh tapped his navigation screen, and the ship slowed to a crawl.

"Nidal, does the Senit have telescopic camera capability?" Maria asked.

Nidal's fingers flew over the icons on his screen and the team saw an old, deep-blue fishing schooner bobbing in the waves with black smoke coming out of an old pipe on top of its cabin. Nidal changed the focus of the cameras past it, to the three patrol boats with their Chinese flags snapping in the wind.

Converging on the small vessel, the patrol boats were formidable in comparison. The team saw fiery sparks spewing from their machine guns, followed by the sound of a second volley. The tiny boat was struck several times, sending splinters of wood and metal flying everywhere. The black smoke sputtering out of the exhaust pipe stopped. The boat bobbed in the water.

Poseidon's voice came through the speakers, "Sebastian, image recognition confirms that is indeed Pham Kai's boat."

Sebastian's decision was swift and clear. "Can we neutralize those machine guns?" He asked, turning to Nidal and Michelangelo.

Their fingers danced across the icons of their screens, as the laser-guided grenade launchers were brought online. At approximately two miles, the weapons system was made for just such a situation.

Nidal locked the laser guidance system to each of the three boats' machine guns—no matter their movements on the choppy seas, the system would ensure the grenades flew straight to their targets, successfully delivering their payloads.

"Yes we have a lock on them." Nidal answered.

"Open all weapon bays," Sebastian ordered. "I want those patrol boats to see what they're up against."

"Got it," Nidal replied, fingers tapping. "Ready to fire."

Sebastian stared at the monitors. "Fire!"

CHAPTER SEVENTEEN
The Rescue

BASIL BELEN WAS a wiry man with a nervous tic—his jaw twitched to the right at the same time his left shoulder jerked upward. The tic, like the stutter that accompanied it, was most prominent when he shared important news. He flew through the corridors of the Pentagon and took an elevator down, his foot tapping between floors. He reached the unassuming office with no nameplate, just a number painted on the door.

Basil was the Goliath Protocol project lead, a civilian analyst responsible for finding and tracking Sebastian and his Paramarines. He had a small team of three specialists, and they had been working on the project for over twenty-four hours straight without so much as a break. Major Williams had instructed Basil to inform him immediately if they had the slightest hint as to the Paramarines' whereabouts. A hacker by trade, Basil was amazed at the sophistication by which Sebastian and his team were eluding him. It was like they'd disappeared from existence after taking off from Andersen Air Force Base.

After exhausting every technical approach, Basil had instructed his team to go old school—look at manual systems that didn't require connected computers. Maybe a physical log, notes, shopping lists, receipts, anything that could show the team's habits. They called the base and had a team of cadets comb through the entire hangar for every single scrap of paper, including the garbage. After a few hours of study, they were still empty-handed. The only habit they found of any interest was the team's frequent visits to Island Girl's Coffee 'n' Quenchers.

"They might have had civilian visitors from off-base we could look at," said one of the team members.

"H-h-how will that help us?" Basil asked.

"We could investigate their backgrounds, maybe they'd be able to provide some clues," he explained.

Basil nodded and gave the go ahead to contact the base visitor center.

Within minutes, they were entering civilian names from the logs into Goliath, bringing up photo IDs and social media footprints, looking for any connections to the information found in the hangar. Before long, the hunch paid off.

Two civilians had visited the hangar around 8:00 p.m. on the night the team escaped. Adora Celestine and Dr. Charles Shine. And, there were no exit time stamps in the logs—their visitor badges hadn't been returned. That implied they could still be with the Paramarines.

Goliath went to work, finding every detail on the two civilians—social security numbers, bank accounts, cell phone numbers, email addresses, passport details, fingerprints, job histories, citizenships and physical addresses. Their entire lives were accessed.

Basil's team then used firmware to ping their cell phones. As expected, the phones were shut off, so they installed a program that would track the phones anywhere that had cell phone coverage the moment they were turned on.

As luck would have it, Goliath soon brought up a red-box

alert–Adora had turned her phone on. Basil and his team scrambled, their fingers tapping their keyboards in a flurry. One set up the tracking protocol, another isolated and triangulated cell towers to get the phone's precise location, and another placed a software code on her phone that would give them control over it, even if she turned it off.

Moments later, an outgoing text message appeared on their screens: *Charles and I have the opportunity to join an expedition. We're in Vietnam for the next couple of days and will be back soon. Cell coverage will be spotty, so please don't expect updates. I'll ping you whenever I can. All good! Love you guys.*

Basil immediately had one of his analysts bring up all satellite images from the last four hours in a ten-mile radius of the cell phone signal. The team must have landed somewhere–there had to be an airstrip close by.

It didn't take them long to isolate an old airstrip at an abandoned Nike factory. Standard images didn't show anything of interest. However, infrared images taken approximately two hours ago told a different story–the heat signature of a private jet appeared in the middle of the runway. They could only make out its engines, as the body of the aircraft appeared faint, probably due to stealth mode.

Basil smiled. He knew what needed to be done. Tapping his fingers on the table, he said, "Increase the resolution of the engine, isolate the exhaust, and run a spectrograph analysis. That'll give us the precise chemical composition of the exhaust. Instruct the satellite to send us real-time video of the airstrip with the spectrographic analysis superimposed."

The satellite video started to come through with a multiband color stream showing the jet's exhaust in a line stretching the length of the runway. This technique hadn't been possible at Andersen Air Force Base–too much air traffic. But here, they had the chemical signature of the plane's exhaust, giving Goliath something to track.

They knew the team was in Vietnam, near Nhon Ly, and Goliath's tracking of the Gulfstream told them it was headed to Singapore. Basil grabbed his cell phone and dashed out of the command center.

Major Francrey Williams didn't offer Basil a chair. "I hope you have something positive to share," he said, giving Basil a piercing look.

Basil nodded in acknowledgement. Without getting into the details, he informed the major of their success.

"Where's the plane headed?" the major demanded.

Basil's jaw and shoulder twitched as he spoke. "Si-Si-Singapore, w-w-we think."

"Is the team still at the same coordinates?" the major asked.

"No," Basil said. "Th-they're on the move. We've placed tracking code on one of their phones, which also allows us t-t-to listen in on their conversations when the phone is nearby. They're near the beaches of a small village called N-N-Nhon Ly."

"Okay," the major said, "keep tracking both the plane and the team until further notice, and send me live updates of the coordinates." He motioned with his hand, indicating that the meeting had ended. Not sure why, Basil almost bowed before turning to leave.

He shook his head as he made his way back, upset with himself. All his life, people like the major had been rude and dismissive to him. He couldn't understand why—was it his physique, his tics, or just the fact that he accepted such behavior from people? Back at the command center, he told his team they did a great job and were free to go home. He picked up his messenger bag, took out two rubber bands, and secured each pant leg to his ankle. Grabbing his cycling helmet, he left the facility, irritated.

Major picked up his cell phone and made a call. He

activated his team in Singapore, ordering them to board the plane as soon as it landed and extract the specimen. He then called Secretary of Defense Richard Richardson to share the good news.

"Good," the secretary said. "Secure the specimen, but leave the team to me, I'll handle them. That specimen must still be on the plane. They wouldn't risk exposing it to the Vietnam heat. And Major–get it right this time."

The secretary hung up the phone and called Captain Francis Drake of the *USS Bainbridge*, a destroyer currently deployed testing a new weapon. Captain Drake, as his name suggested, came from a long line of famous navy men.

"Captain Drake," Dick said, "I need you to find a vessel in the South China Sea and seize all scientific materials on board. It's manned by a group of American scientists, and their work is a matter of national security. I need you to confiscate their laptops and any other equipment in their possession, and if they resist, place them under arrest."

Drake paused. "Where in the South China Sea? And did you say scientists?"

"Yes, scientists," Dick confirmed. "My team will be sending coordinates as soon as they become available. Just start sailing toward Vietnam."

Drake knew better than to ask for details. "Understood. I'll wait for further instructions."

On hanging up with Captain Drake, secretary asked his assistant to call his general counsel. He wanted to ensure that he had full authority to move forward under the Homeland Security Act. Secretary took a moment to think about what this discovery would mean. *Cebrián needed to understand the national security threat his specimen imposed. It could give America an unprecedented advantage over its enemies. The nation that gained mastery over time would become the next superpower. Under no circumstances should Cebrián be allowed to share it with the world.*

This was bigger than splitting the atom.

* * *

NIDAL TAPPED THE blinking red icon on his screen, and three small rocket grenades fired, the thunderous sound startling some of the team members. Sebastian stepped out on the deck and watched them hiss nearer the patrol boats. Moments later, he saw three small puffs, followed by three muffled booms.

The patrol boat captains also heard the explosions, and the subsequent silence of their guns. They shot glares at the firing cadets, who kept pulling their triggers, baffled expressions on their faces.

Wang Li ordered all boats to a full stop, and the officers and the crew all stepped on the deck, staring in shock at their machine guns. A six-inch hole had been bored through each of them—something had pierced the inch-thick, solid steal exteriors and exploded inside them, causing complete destruction of the firing mechanisms.

One of the lieutenants yelled and pointed to the open sea. Wang Li shouted for his binoculars. As the lieutenant brought them out, he snatched them, swearing under his breath. He brought the binoculars to his eyes, and what he saw almost made him take a step back. Two miles away, a formidable black catamaran warship floated with its weapon bays open, ready to engage. On the deck stood a man who seemed to be staring back at them, his hands on his hips.

Wang Li was flabbergasted—why would an unmarked catamaran warship come out of nowhere to help this low-life fisherman? He stood there in silence, studying the ship's arsenal. He knew he was beaten. Any further provocation would result in a battle that he couldn't win. Frustrated and angry, he ordered his boats to retreat.

Pham Kai and Minh, holding onto their old trunk for dear

life, couldn't understand what had happened. The machine guns had stopped firing after the three mysterious explosions. They stayed huddled in their destroyed cabin for what felt like a lifetime. Eventually, they stood up, peeking through the gaping holes in the cabin wall. At the starboard side, they saw the three patrol boats racing back for the Paracel Islands. Trembling, they turned port side and realized what had caused the Chinese to run. A Westerner stood on the deck of an amazing warship floating near them, grinning as if he knew them.

Sebastian released a folding ramp and guided it gently onto Pham Kai's boat. Climbing down the plank he stretched his hand out, helping the frightened couple aboard the Skjold. Pham Kai pointed at a figure of a man lying motionless on the deck.

Maria and Fabienne joined Sebastian. Maria gave Minh a bottle of water and draped a blanket over her shivering form while Sebastian and Fabienne headed toward the back of Pham Kai's tattered boat. Sebastian was shocked to see it was Dr. Vu Ha. His mouth was open, tongue was hanging out. His eyes were open but unseeing. Using a stretcher, they transported him to the Skjold's medical bay.

There, Fabienne and Sebastian went into triage mode. They stabilized Vu's breathing with oxygen and started a saline drip. They also found morphine and gave him a small dose to ease his pain.

Sebastian stepped out of the medical bay and walked over to the mess area, where Pham Kai and Minh sat, close together, drinking tea. "Poseidon, I need you to translate English to Vietnamese and back so we can talk with our guests."

He sat down at the table and for the first time got a good look at the man whose discovery would change the world. They exchanged a meaningful glance, a feeling of deep respect coming over them both.

"Greetings," Sebastian said. "My name is Sebastian. You're both safe with us." Poseidon's voice came through the speakers in Vietnamese. Pham Kai and Minh looked up with surprise at hearing their language. Pham Kai introduced himself and Minh. He thanked them for saving their lives.

Sebastian went on to explain that they were a group of researchers, and Pham Kai's discovery of the fish had led them here in search of its source.

The couple listened, nodding. Pham Kai explained that this was why they were there, too. Dr. Vu Ha had wanted to catch another specimen. The main reason they were risking their lives to help him was to get enough money for Minh's treatment.

Pham Kai went on to describe the whole ordeal with the patrol boats and their risky escape through the southern opening of the channel—including how the Chinese captain had boarded his boat, and ignoring Vu's paperwork, inflicted the injury to Vu's upper back with a metal device he wore on his hand.

Charles joined them, and Sebastian requested that he and Maria ask for details about how Pham Kai had caught the specimen. He went back to the medical bay, sharing the details of Vu's injury with Fabienne.

Her eyes widened with shock. "Who in this day and age uses brass knuckles? It's more a weapon for street thugs, not a captain in the navy."

They set up the portable X-ray machine and took a series of images. The damage was clear, and quite serious—the 3C, 4C, and 5C vertebrae were fractured. They stood outside the medical bay, discussing the team's options. They couldn't continue the mission with the professor in this condition. Even with a neck brace to stabilize him, any sudden movements—even the rhythmic rocking of the ship—could cause a catastrophic worsening of his condition, up to and including death. They had to stay put until a medical team could reach them and airlift Vu to a hospital in Qui Nhon.

"We can't stay here, we can't move on, and we can't come out of stealth mode," Sebastian whispered. Fabienne nodded, deep in thought. He pressed a nearby intercom, asking Shiloh to join them. The trio found a small meeting room and sat around the metal conference table.

Their best idea involved contacting Zeke to see if he could arrange for a medical chopper. Fabienne's eyes sparkled. She shot up and started pacing the small room. "Remember what happened to the fungi cells that were exposed to *Fisio* time particles?"

"Yeah," Sebastian said, "they stopped aging."

"No," Fabienne shook her head. "They didn't just stop aging. They acted like stem cells—they were becoming younger. What if this time particle could activate the stem cells in Vu's spinal column? They would start to repair his cranial nerves and rebuild his fractured vertebrae."

Sebastian got up and started pacing too. "Do you think that could work? How long would Vu need to be exposed before his condition improved?"

Fabienne eye darted around, unsure. "Hours? Days? I don't know. I recommend we run the experiment for two hours, then stop and examine him. If we see any improvement, we can run it again for another two hours. This way, we'll be checking on his progress at timed intervals."

"Let's give it a shot," Sebastian said.

Shiloh retrieved the time warp device from his cabin. Fabienne made sure Vu's vitals were strong, and gave Shiloh a thumbs-up. He placed his device on the table next to the wall, already loaded with the slide containing a single-cell layer of the *Fisio* side of the nodule. He then walked out of the medical bay with Fabienne and closed the door. Sebastian watched him, noticing that he hadn't activated the device.

Shiloh had made another modification—Bluetooth compatibility, allowing him to operate the device with his phone from a distance, so as not to be affected by its time field. He pulled out his cell phone and opened the time warp app. They soon saw Vu surrounded by the silver mist created by the *Fisio* time particles. With the time field set for two hours, all they could do was wait.

The trio was still standing in the corridor when Sebastian's phone buzzed.

"Now what?" Sebastian muttered.

It was a text from the captain of Panther Two. Reading the text, his heart sank. *Armed men have boarded the plane, and they're taking the incubator. They claim to be with our government. They also tried to access the server data and our logs, but Poseidon had already erased everything, so they didn't get any information. Unfortunately they have possession of the incubator.*

"Dammit!" Sebastian cursed, shaking his head.

"What happened?" Shiloh asked.

"The specimen has been taken by armed men," Sebastian answered, more than frustrated with the turn of events.

Fabienne shook her head and whispered, "Not really, follow me."

She took them to her cabin. Her bags and equipment sat on the bed, and a small fridge occupied a corner. She opened it and pulled out Vu's lunch box.

She placed it on the table and opened it. In the top compartment, Sebastian saw two small, powerful batteries attached to wires that led down into the second compartment. Removing the top portion, she exposed two small nitrogen cylinders with rudimentary circuitry. It appeared they were wired to fire a burst of nitrogen at set intervals to cool the lunch box. Fabienne then removed the second compartment, and there rested the *Isikhathi Isilwandle*, its nodule glowing magnificently.

Sebastian couldn't believe what he was seeing. The prized specimen was right there with them—it was never left on the plane. "How?" he asked.

"Just before the attack in the hangar," Fabienne said, "I asked Shiloh for a favor. I needed him to create a portable device that could store the specimen inconspicuously. Vu's lunch box fit the bill."

"So, what's in the incubator?" Sebastian asked.

Fabienne laughed. "There was a pomfret fish in the kitchen's freezer. I replaced the specimen with that."

"A pomfret," Sebastian repeated in a hushed voice. "So, they've boarded the plane and walked away with a pomfret." He wrapped Fabienne in a hug as the three of them burst into laughter.

Sebastian headed back to his cabin and texted the captain: *Not to worry. Take off as soon as you can. I'll send you new coordinates. Be sure to maintain stealth mode.*

The captain replied: *Yes, sir. They're not interested in detaining us – they have what they came for. We've refueled and all systems are go.*

Sebastian's phone buzzed again—this time it was a call, and a smooth voice with a unique accent he couldn't quite place greeted him. "Hi, Sebastian, this is Talia Goldman. I'm one of the Honeycomb scientists."

"Hi, Talia, thank you, we appreciate all the support," Sebastian replied.

"Don't mention it," Talia said. "I'm calling to inform you that I've tracked a hacked phone belonging to one of your team members."

"Really?" Sebastian exclaimed.

"I'm not sure whose phone it is," Talia continued, "but it sent a text to a cell tower in Guam. I can't access the content of the text, but it's a Guam number."

"Thank you, Talia. I think I know who it may be,"

Sebastian said.

"Sebastian, you need to destroy that phone," Talia warned.

Sebastian hung up and hurried to the mess area, where Maria and Charles still sat with Pham Kai and Minh. "Charles," Sebastian said, "where's your cell phone?"

"I don't have it with me. I left it in Guam, in our apartment." Charles replied.

Sebastian nodded and took the flight of steps to the bridge. Adora sat on a chair, looking out at sea.

"Hey, Adora," Sebastian said, "did you send a text to someone in Guam recently?"

Adora turned to him, a bit startled by his voice. "Yes, why?" Then, as if knowing she had messed up, continued to explain herself. "I was concerned that my family would start searching for us, since we'd just got up and left."

Sebastian motioned for her not to speak. He grabbed a paper and pen from one of the stations and began writing. *Where is your phone now?*

She fiddled with a bag next to her chair, pulling the phone out and handing it to him. He took the phone from her and wrote on the paper: *Sorry, Adora. When you texted your family, the group hunting us hacked your phone. They're listening in and tracking us. I have to destroy it.*

The warm, wet heat of Vietnam hit him as he stepped out on deck. Taking a couple strides and reaching the edge of the boat, he cocked his arm and threw the phone into the sea. The phone hit the surface of the water, skipped, and sank.

He stepped back onto the bridge and hugged an embarrassed Adora. "Relax. We rushed out of the hangar in a hurry. I understand you had to inform your family."

She nodded and looked like she felt a little better as they joined Charles and Maria in the mess. Pham Kai and Minh had been given a cabin and had gone off to rest.

"How'd it go with Pham Kai and Minh?"

"Good, we have what we need," Maria replied. "Pham Kai insisted he could fix his engine and they could make their way back to their village. I requested that they relax, and that we'd drop them off. His boat is done, anyway. It'll sink in a day or so. How's Vu?"

"I'll gather the team and update everyone." Sebastian pressed the intercom button and invited the team to the mess area.

"So, folks," he began, "here's the situation. Doctor Vu Ha has some fractured vertebra. Any sudden movements could be fatal. This means we can't continue on to Bombay Reef or head back to Nhon Ly village. And Panther Two was boarded by a group of armed men who've taken possession of the incubator."

"What? They have the specimen?" Nidal asked, alarmed.

"Actually, no," Sebastian smiled. "Thanks to Fabienne and Shiloh, we have the specimen here, stored safely onboard."

A cheer went up from the team, for Fabienne.

"Stop it, guys. It was nothing," she said.

"We can't move Vu, we can't head to the reef–is our mission over?" Michelangelo asked.

"Not yet," Sebastian responded. "We're trying something new. Fabienne had another breakthrough idea–use the *Fisio* time particle to stabilize Vu's condition to the point that we can continue on."

"So," Nidal said, "when will we know if we can start moving again?"

Just as Sebastian was about to respond, the intercom crackled, followed by a hiss of static. A weak, barely audible voice came through. "H-Hello?" They glanced at each other in confusion, not sure what they were hearing.

Fabienne was the first to realize what was happening. She ran out of the mess, down the corridor, and yanked open the medical bay door. There on the edge of the bed sat Vu, his quivering finger trying to hold the intercom button.

Sebastian came running behind her, and they both stood frozen at the door. Shiloh's time warp device had stopped firing. All the mist was gone, and it appeared that Vu had regained the use of his limbs. His face was almost back to normal as well.

They approached, still unsure of what total effect the *Fisio* time particle had on him. They'd hypothesized that the particles would support the body's normal repair functions by activating the stem cells near his neck, but it was all conjuncture. They never in a million years expected this–and with such speed.

They couldn't localize the *Fisio* time particles to his neck area specifically, so his whole body had been exposed to them–which could mean that the stem cells in the other parts of his body had also been activated, repairing any and all ailments at once.

That was when they both realized why he appeared so different–the thick wave of gray hair on his head was gone, replaced by its original jet-black. His hair follicles had begun producing melanin again.

He was alert, but incoherent. His hands moved like he was intoxicated. He gave Sebastian a puzzled look, as if trying to recognize him. He stretched his hands to Sebastian's face, and something wonderful happened–he gave a faint smile. It wasn't his usual beaming smile, but it was a huge improvement over his initial condition.

They took a second round of X-rays as the team gathered at the bay door, looking on with wonder. The images came up on the monitor, and what they saw shocked them–his fractured vertebrae were repaired. Sebastian and Fabienne whispered back and forth in amazement, not wanting to alarm the professor–it would take years to understand the science behind this. Each time particle was proving to be a miracle unto itself. Given Dr. Vu Ha's remarkable recovery, Fabienne recommended no further exposure to the *Fisio* time particles. They still weren't sure as to the long-term effects. Sebastian agreed and they left him to rest.

With Vu resting again, the team moved all the gear and personal items off Pham Kai's boat, including his old trunk and brought it onboard. They placed Vu's gear in a cabin, setting it up for him to use once he was ready to move out of the medical bay. They then sat around the mess table, discussing their plans to head straight to Bombay Reef in search of *Isikhathi Isilwandle*.

* * *

AS THEY SAT discussing their plans, Sebastian's phone buzzed once more. "Hey, Cebrián," he answered, heading to his cabin.

"Sebastian, I've learned who ordered the attack at the hangar," Cebrián informed him. "Talia was able to hack into Goliath and get me the facts."

"Who was it?" Sebastian asked.

"The secretary of defense," Cebrián said matter-of-factly.

"The secretary of defense?" Sebastian repeated, bewildered. "I thought he supported our research."

"He did, until we found the specimen. He wants to militarize it," Cebrián said, and then he shared that armed men had boarded Panther Two in Singapore and taken the incubator.

"Yeah, I know, but we have the specimen and the nodule," Sebastian said.

"What? How? That is great!" Cebrián said, shocked.

Sebastian filled him in on everything, adding that they were now back on track, headed to Bombay Reef.

"This is excellent news. Okay, you investigate Bombay Reef, and I'll continue to work on my plan to convince the Swedish Navy to help us out. Be safe," Cebrián said, hanging up.

Sebastian, standing on the bridge next to Charles, was looking at the approaching island of Bombay Reef on the monitors when he caught a movement from the corner of his eye. He turned around and saw Pham Kai standing outside the door of the bridge, peeking. Sebastian walked up and stretched out his hand, and welcomed him onto the bridge.

Pham Kai entered the bridge, looking at the stations, when the image on the monitor caught his attention. He spoke in Vietnamese, pointing to the monitor. Sebastian asked Poseidon to translate.

"Pham Kai is saying he knows this area well and is here to help you," Poseidon responded.

Sebastian smiled, appreciative of the Pham Kai's support. He turned to Charles. "How far are we from the cavern?"

After doing some quick calculations, Charles answered, "About half a mile northeast of our current location."

"Let's make two teams," Sebastian said. "One to check out the lagoon, the other to perform an investigative dive of the area near the underwater cavern. Our scuba gear will only allow us to get to ninety-five feet. The seabed is less than thirty feet, so we can explore the cavern up to sixty feet deep. Hopefully, we'll find something interesting that may shed some light on our specimen." He looked to Charles. "I forgot to ask, how deep could you dive?"

Charles nodded. "I'm fully certified up to one hundred feet."

"Great." Sebastian said, relieved. "Okay, Shiloh, get us close to the reef. Nidal, Michelangelo, Fabienne, you guys check out the lagoon. Maria, Charles, and I will search for the cavern. Adora, may I request you stay on the bridge to support Shiloh, and also check on Vu and our guests?" Adora nodded.

Everyone met up on the main deck. "Shiloh," Sebastian said, with a hint of humor, "you have the bridge."

Shiloh smiled back at the Star Trek reference. "Aye, captain."

The cavern team jumped off the diving deck while Nidal, Michelangelo, and Fabienne left for the lagoon in a rigid inflatable boat (RIB). They had to be careful navigating the reef and of the changes in current. When they reached the beach, the first thing they realized was this was no tropical beach paradise with pristine white sand. It was rocky, with a thick carpet of sharp stones.

Bombay Reef was shaped like a bean, and the lagoon conformed to its odd shape. Thanks to their scuba boots, the walk was uneventful as they made their way through the vegetation, which was comprised of patches of short bamboos, occasional orchids, and an abundance of rubber plants.

They soon noticed a distinct lack of any birdlife. It didn't make any sense—they heard insects everywhere, and they'd seen a multitude of snails on the beach, both of which made up the main food supply for many birds.

"I think I have a theory," Nidal said. "Birds, out of the entire animal kingdom, are most sophisticated in their use of their biological clock. Time plays a pivotal part in their lives, from hatching eggs, to pushing their babies out of the nest, to migrating. I believe birds know there's something wrong with time here, and their genetic memory avoids this reef." Both Fabienne and Michelangelo paused, strained to hear any birds and then nodded in tacit agreement.

After about an hour of trekking, they came across a geological anomaly. The vegetation gave way to an open area with a large sand dune made of soft white silica sand. They started climbing it, unsure how and why it was there. Upon reaching the top, what they saw took their breath away. Fabienne almost fell, holding onto Nidal to stabilize herself.

Looking down at the lagoon, plants, fish, leaves, and other bits of natural debris, were all hovering in mid air. Schools of fish glided along without any water. It was a symphony of colorful marine life miraculously suspended in air. The three of them stood there in silence, hypnotized.

"Oh, my God, what is all this?" Fabienne whispered. Nidal and Michelangelo didn't answer. They kept staring at the gleaming beauty of the illogical moment.

They skidded down thc dune closer to the suspended marine life, and then realized what they were experiencing–the water was so incredibly clear, they couldn't even see it. With no ripples or waves, it was impossible to see where the edge of the water started. The three of them stepped forward and squatted on the edge of the dune, stretching their hands until they touched the water. Fabienne cupped her right hand and lifted it, seeing the water as it trickled through her fingers.

"What do you think causes the water to be so clear?" Michelangelo asked.

"Several factors," Fabienne replied. "Lack of wind, no waves, no tides, and light bouncing off the silica in the sand dune, creating a perfect mirror. I've seen a similar effect on the beaches of Cala Macarelleta in Spain."

Michelangelo didn't buy it. "I have a different theory. I think it's a remnant of the time particles."

"How do you figure?" Nidal asked.

Michelangelo sat down on the dune. "Look at the suspended bubbles–they appear to be still. We still don't know how these time particles work. I think the water here is under a much slower time field. That's why everything so vivid."

Fabienne did not give a counter argument. She was unconvinced, and there wasn't enough data to form any hypothesis.

After several minutes admiring, they climbed back to the top of the sand dune and started walking the length of the lagoon. They soon saw a set of unique geological formations in the water. Large obsidian boulders were spread throughout the lagoon, seemingly at random. There was another interesting feature, a botanical formation. A coconut tree had sprouted on the dune and grown at an angle over the years. Its trunk now hung over the water, crossing four or five feet over it—they couldn't tell where the tree's branches ended and where the water began.

Fabienne climbed over the tree, and straddling the trunk, slowly moved over to the part that hung over the water. She then flipped over, dangling with her head down, arms stretched out and her crisscrossed legs holding onto the tree, her face and arms submerged in the water. It was the best representation of the optical illusion. The schools of fish and plants all appeared to be suspended in the air, level with Fabienne's eyes.

Nidal pulled his phone out and took pictures, as he had been doing all along their walk.

After a thorough exploration, they decided to head back to the boat. Other than the spectacular appearance of suspended marine life, they didn't find any evidence of *Isikhathi Isilwandle.*

* * *

SEBASTIAN, MARIA, AND Charles descended to the sandy seabed. Brightly colored fish swam around them, darting through and around the reef. They saw a massive coral field, which appeared untouched by humans. There were over two thousand species of coral in the world, and many of them were present here. Sebastian recognized *Acropora*, *Panova*, *Montipora*, and *Porites*, among many others. In between the corals were strategically placed oysters the size of their hands, filtering the water to ingest planktons.

They swam on top of the reef, searching for the cavern, when they came across another spectacular sight—a set of unique sand structures, like underwater crop circles. Six to seven feet in diameter, with two concentric rings, they were true works of art–amazing geometrical representations of the Fibonacci sequence.

As they swam over the structures, they found the little pufferfish responsible, busily carving a new masterpiece in the sand with its fins. Sebastian, found the moment to be uncanny, he had been watching a documentary of this exact species when he'd gotten the call from Cebrián.

The divers were careful not to create turbulence that would disturb the intricate patterns. Several minutes later, they neared the coordinates of the cavern.

Charles, oblivious to all the beauty around them, constantly checked the ADCP he had found on the Skjold. An Acoustic Doppler Current Profiler worked on the principles of Doppler, emitting a "ping" at a constant frequency. The sound waves hit suspended particles in the water and returned to the device, allowing it to measure the speed of the current. If there was a whirlpool in the area, the ADCP would track it.

Reading the device, he pushed on his fins hard and swam in front of Maria and Sebastian. Stopping their forward movement he pointed at the device. According to the reading there was an incredibly strong tidal movement few hundred yards away, comprising up to three hundred million cubic yards of water. Such a volume was capable of creating a giant whirlpool over forty feet wide and fifty feet deep.

Sebastian shook his head at Charles in disbelief–nothing indicated that such an intense event was happening. A whirlpool this massive should be felt well over three miles away, possibly more. It should be pulling plants, fish, and all kinds of material toward it. Charles inspected the device, looking for any sign of malfunction.

Sebastian pulled out an underwater marker from his pocket and lifted a flap on his sleeve, revealing a white plastic surface. He wrote on it like a whiteboard: *Keep going. Readings not making sense. Yes?*

Charles took the pen and wrote: *Dangerous? Can't risk it.*

Sebastian then pointed at the small plant next to him that had long, wiry leaves—it was flowing normally, not being pulled in any direction. Charles knew what Sebastian was saying. He nodded, not fully convinced, and reluctantly gave the "Okay" sign.

They continued to swim for several more minutes, realizing there was nothing in front of them but clear, blue, open sea—there was no marine life anywhere ahead. The ADCP was indicating a difference of speed in the water particles right in front of them, yet they could not feel or see any evidence of it.

As they were considering their next move, the same pufferfish joined them, appearing to debate whether or not to cross the invisible threshold. Proving itself the more daring of the group, it propelled itself forward and vanished right before their eyes. It was gone.

Sebastian swam to where the pufferfish vanished and stuck his hand out in a piercing motion. Just like the fish, his hand disappeared. He pulled his hand back, wiggling his fingers, checking for damage—it was fine. He gestured for them to wait, and before Maria could stop him, he too vanished. Maria gestured to Charles that they should follow.

On crossing the threshold, Sebastian didn't feel anything resembling the force registered on Charles's device. In fact, he was surprised to find that this area was the same as the one he had left—vibrant and full of marine life. But for some reason, it was all invisible from the other side, except for the open blue sea.

He turned to Charles and Maria, and what he saw shocked him. They were still, picture-perfect, not moving at all. The bubbles created by their regulators hung around them, like hundreds of sparkling jewels. He could see every fish, plant, and coral for miles, just like looking into a massive fish tank, except everything was still.

He understood what was happening. Time was moving faster in this area.

It wasn't long before Maria and Charles joined him, equally shocked by what they saw. They stayed in the area for fifteen minutes, according to their watches, searching but finding nothing. Sebastian made the diver's sign for "boat" and they headed back.

Back on the Skjold, Adora and Shiloh were going through the galley, trying to figure out what to make for dinner. With all the action and stress, they realized the team had not had a full meal for over fifteen hours. While going through the freezer, Adora turned and saw Minh standing at the galley entrance, watching them shyly. She gestured for her to join them. Adora had the kitchen freezer open. It had large rations of beef, chicken, shrimp, and fish. Minh gestured to Adora, seeming to ask if it was okay if she took over. Adora nodded.

Minh took out two bags of chicken and two bags of beef. She placed them on the stainless steel counter and started opening various cabinets. She found soy sauce, brown sugar, ginger paste, hot chili-garlic paste, and lime and lemon juice concentrate. In the spice cabinet, she found the usual salt, pepper, ground and crushed red chilies, and peppercorn. She also found a large bag of rice, cans of condensed milk, cream cheese, and unbelievably, coconut milk–a staple ingredient in Vietnamese cooking.

Adora and Shiloh were fascinated by her speed–Minh was in her element. She soon had the chicken cut into pieces, which she placed into a thick mixture of soy sauce, brown sugar, ginger paste, red chili paste, and lemon juice. While the chicken marinated, she used gestures to ask Adora and Shiloh, who were busy making a salad, how the stove and oven worked. She'd probably never seen one so sophisticated.

Minh arranged all the pieces of chicken she'd prepared on

a baking sheet. Adora then placed the tray in the oven and set the temperature to three hundred degrees and the timer to forty minutes.

Minh then found celery, broccoli, peas, potatoes, and carrots, and started to stir-fry them in oil and soy sauce. She added a tablespoon of brown sugar and chili paste, and some red crushed peppers. She also did something very odd—she found a peanut butter jar in the pantry, opened it, and smelled it. Unfamiliar with it, she could tell it was some kind of peanut paste. She took two tablespoons and added it to the mix. The incredible aroma of the stir-fry flooded the galley.

Shiloh and Adora both clapped. They knew this was going to be an amazing meal. Minh took the two large slabs of beef and sliced them into long, thin strands. She then placed the beef into a separate pan and fried it with some red pepper. Once the color of the beef turned brown, she added it to the stir-fry pot, turning up the heat, making a high-pitched sizzling sound.

Pham Kai, hearing the commotion–or smelling the wonderful aromas–joined them too. On seeing Pham Kai, Minh lit up. She said something in Vietnamese, and Pham Kai picked up the bag of rice and took out six cups. He first washed it, which they guessed was a Vietnamese thing, then placed it in the boiling water. He was making sticky rice, Pham Kai style, he added a little bit of milk, a teaspoon of condensed milk, and a quarter cup of coconut milk.

The cavern team was back first, followed by the lagoon team, both heading straight to the showers. Adora and Shiloh surmised that neither of them had been successful in finding the specimen. However, they didn't look disappointed–they had found something. They set the table, placing the dishes that Minh had prepared.

About half an hour later, they gathered around the table. The sight of the freshly prepared food made them smile with anticipation. Just when they were about to start eating, Sebastian noticed that Pham Kai and Minh weren't there. He knew Vu was still resting–perhaps they were checking on him. He got up and searched the galley on his way to the medical bay and stopped. What he saw was achingly beautiful and humbling.

Minh and Pham Kai were sitting on the floor of the galley–they had laid out a hand towel, with pots and a pan from the stove on it. Minh sat at one end, and Pham Kai sat at the other. They had made their own small dining area, and Sebastian knew why. In the Indian subcontinent and Southeast Asia, there was a common practice that people didn't eat with other people if they felt they weren't of the same financial and cultural status.

He sat down next to them, gesturing for them to please join the rest of the team in the mess hall. Surprised, Pham Kai bowed, and shook his head, declining the offer. Sebastian insisted that they both join them, or he would bring the entire team into the kitchen. He didn't know how much of his rapid gesturing was understood, but it did the trick. Pham Kai picked up his plate and said something in Vietnamese to Minh, who picked up her plate.

They followed Sebastian into the mess hall. As soon as the team saw Minh and Pham Kai walking in with Sebastian, Shiloh started clapping and cheering. The rest of the team joined in, applauding loudly. Both Pham Kai and Minh were beaming, unable to bow enough to share their happiness. They all sat at the table as equals.

The dinner was a blessing. It fired them up–their sinuses were running, and some of them even had sweat beads on their foreheads, yet they couldn't stop eating. The combinations of flavors Minh had created were out of this world.

After the team cleared the table, Nidal transferred his pictures from the lagoon to his computer, displaying them on the monitor at the far end of the mess area. He then brought up the picture of Fabienne dangling off the coconut tree. It was a spectacularly colorful picture, wonderfully clear, in perfect focus, and it didn't make a lick of logical sense. It was evident that Fabienne was dangling off the tree in midair—but why were schools of fish, and sea plants suspended in the air around her?

Fascinated, the whole team walked up to the monitor as Nidal cycled through photos. Picture after picture was shockingly beautiful. Even Pham Kai came closer, looking at them intently.

"What do you think is causing such unbelievably clear water?" Shiloh whispered.

"I think it's the time particles," Michelangelo said.

Fabienne rolled her eyes. "We don't know that."

"We do," Charles said.

Everyone tore their gaze away from the screen and focused on him.

"I think when time is slower in water, the effect is the opposite of the mist we're used to seeing with time particles in air." Charles said, putting his pencil and notebook down. "But one thing is for sure—we now have clear evidence that *Isikhathi Isilwandle* is in the area!"

They all decided to call it a night. Fabienne went to the medical bay to check on Vu, who was fast asleep. He was much better, breathing steadily, with color back in his face. Adora and Charles found their cabin, happy to crash for the night. Nidal and Michelangelo went back onto the bridge to confirm that all systems were operational, and to make sure the proximity warning system was functioning in case the Chinese Navy made a move.

Sebastian, Maria, and Shiloh, instead of going to their cabins, stepped out onto the deck. It was a typical Vietnamese night—hot and humid and pitch dark. The stars were out, and they could see the Milky Way with incredible clarity. Sebastian sat down, and Maria and Shiloh joined him.

Sebastian peered up at the stars and just when he was about to say something.

Shiloh bolted upright. "Look!" he yelled, pointing.

CHAPTER EIGHTEEN
The Two-Headed Monster Awakens

CAPTAIN FRANCIS DRAKE stood inside the combat ready room of *USS Bainbridge*, a formidable Arleigh-Burke class guided-missile destroyer with a full complement of missiles, torpedoes, and a battle-hardened 270-man crew.

Bainbridge's deployment meant two things—the mission was of the utmost importance to national security, and the need for enemy pacification was paramount. The crew knew they were on a seek-and-retrieve mission—they were going deep into enemy territory to extract their asset. Drake knew that being activated by the secretary of defense meant the situation was serious, and carrying out his orders was his only priority.

But it was the nature of his orders that confused Drake. Ordinarily, he would be engaging terrorists on hostile ships representing governments that were sworn enemies of the United States. However, this time he was ordered to apprehend a team of scientists and their research. Most confusing, that research involved a fish. All this might and power for a small team of scientists and a fish? These orders certainly didn't fit the profile of previous operations.

Drake was leaning over the navigation station, reviewing

the course set by his new executive officer. His previous XO was removed due to disciplinary issues. The new XO, John Paul Jones, had a stellar record, but was a bit nervous explaining his strategy to Captain Drake.

John believed avoiding commercial traffic wasn't a good idea. He had a list of container ships en route to Vietnam, and had identified two that belonged to companies based out of the UK. He'd already contacted them, and they had agreed to have the *USS Bainbridge* come in between them. Chinese radar would register the *Bainbridge* and not react, being that they would be in internationally recognized shipping lanes. This would allow them to enter deep into the South China Sea before changing course to find their target.

Drake approved the strategy, and the course was locked into the navigational computer. They were still two full days from reaching the general area of the last ping from Adora's phone.

He then ordered an immediate meeting of his senior staff.

"Officers, our testing of 'Trident' will have to wait. I've been on two calls with a very irate Secretary of Defense. We're headed into South China Sea. Our mission is to apprehend a team of scientists and all the research they have in their possession, including a specific type of marine life that's of the utmost importance to national security. Two attempts have been made to retrieve it, both of which failed–one in Guam, where the researchers neutralized six armed men assigned by the secretary of defense, and the other in Singapore, where the scientists switched the marine life with a worthless specimen which was flown all the way back to D.C. As I said, the secretary is beyond upset. He has now appointed us to carry out the mission."

"Sir, are we hearing you right?' asked one of the senior officers. "We're going into hostile territory to apprehend a team of scientists and bring back a fish?"

"Why are the scientists and this fish so important?" John asked.

"I won't go into details," Drake said. "Suffice to say it's an important fish, and its retrieval is priority number one." He paused, eyeing each of his senior staff in turn. "All we know from the secretary is that it's aboard a small vessel near Bombay Reef. These scientists have commandeered the vessel in an effort to find the specimen's source, and they plan to share their findings with the world. We need to stop them at all costs. If required, we've been authorized to apply lethal force. Keep in mind this is a dangerous mission, deep in Chinese waters. Most importantly, we can't under any circumstance let the Chinese take control of the research or the specimen—even if it means sparking an international incident. Do I make myself clear?"

The staff voiced their affirmation in unison, even those who found the mission to be absurd.

* * *

WANG LI, THE infamous captain of the *Youling Chuan*, and the two other captains of the Chinese patrol boats raced toward mainland China. They were less concerned about their fate—which could include a court martial, and dishonorable discharge—and more concerned with the unidentified, armed warship that had initiated hostile action. It represented a direct attack against China itself. They had already radioed the incident to their naval headquarters, describing the black warship in detail. The Chinese Navy had deployed their version of the AEWAC—an Airborne Early Warning and Control drone—over the Paracel Islands. They had also started using satellite surveillance of the area, so far with negative results.

It took the patrol boats over four hours to get to their base. On arriving, they were received by military police that took the captains and crews to the barracks for questioning.

The forensics team collected the residue from inside the machine guns to run a series of tests. This would help them identify the make and model of the ship involved. Based on the description from the crew and captains, they were sure it was a Norwegian Skjold-class attack ship—China had recently placed a large order with Norway for the very same ships to replace their current patrol boats.

According to the captains, the ship that attacked them didn't have a flag—it didn't belong to any country. It was as if they were dealing with a private group that came in to save the Vietnamese fisherman. One theory they had was the Vietnamese government had hired mercenaries to protect their fishermen from harassment and potential attacks from the Chinese.

The grilling of Wang Li wasn't half as bad as he'd expected. The captains were reprimanded, but the interrogation went no further. The report from the forensics team had been shared with their superiors, and there was clear evidence that the patrol boats had indeed been attacked by a Skjold-class attack ship. The three boats would have had no chance of surviving, had they confronted the aggressor. Retreat had been the best course of action. They had, nevertheless, brought shame to the People's Republic of China.

The supervisor of the investigative team read the report aloud, almost shouting the last sentence. "Your actions, though correct, have brought shame to our nation!" He removed his reading glasses and conferred with his colleagues. The rest of the investigative team had somber expressions on their faces. "You two," he said, pointing at the subordinate captains, "You will perform menial work on your boats for the next thirty days."

Then he turned to Wang Li. "You are a whole different story. You deserve severe punishment for not sinking the fisherman's boat. However, I want you to report to Captain

Zheng He of the Luyang-I and provide him with support in locating this mysterious ship."

Wang Li couldn't believe his superstitious nature had paid off. By not attracting any more bad luck from Pham Kai and his wife, he wasn't being dishonorably discharged—at least, not yet. Without making eye contact with the other two captains, he saluted and walked out.

The Luyang-I class destroyer was a multipurpose attack ship with approximately similar armament to the *Bainbridge*. Commissioned in 2004, it was the workhorse of the Chinese Navy. Designed for deep-water missions, the ship was equipped for heavy battle. It was undergoing routine maintenance of its engines, weapons, and electronics when Captain Zheng received the message regarding Wang Li and the mission from naval GHQ. Just then, an intercom announcement came through that a patrol boat captain was requesting permission to come aboard. He took a deep breath and pressed the intercom, telling his purser to hold the captain on deck.

Upon seeing Zheng, Wang Li saluted him. Zheng responded half-heartedly, surprised to see how much starch the man had applied to his uniform. "I'm not sure why GHQ has assigned you to my ship," Zheng said, a hint of disdain in his voice. "I have all the information needed for the mission. We don't need you."

Wang Li wasn't sure how to respond. He kept quiet and stared straight ahead, not making any eye contact.

"Well, you're here now," Zheng continued. "The purser will escort you to your cabin, and you will remain there until I ask for you." Zheng started to walk away.

"Yes, sir. When do we plan to cast off?" Wang Li asked, still staring straight ahead.

Zheng turned, annoyed at Wang Li's direct question. "Get comfortable," he replied. "We're not going anywhere for at least forty-eight hours. We're overhauling several major systems."

"Yes, sir," Wang Li said with a salute. Zheng again responded half-heartedly.

Wang Li sat in his cabin. Zheng's sophistication, education, and class annoyed him—most high-ranking officers were part of the privileged class, and being the captain of a destroyer was a far cry from being the captain of a patrol boat.

It had been four hours since Wang Li was shown to his cabin, and he seethed with anger. There was obviously more to the black ship than just saving the Vietnamese fisherman. No one comes into Vietnamese waters with that kind of firepower to save a fisherman. But he was glad the destroyer would blow it out of the water. *That is, if these lazy idiots decide not to take their sweet time cleaning their ship or whatever the hell they're doing*, he thought.

There was a knock on his cabin door, and a voice announcing his name came through. It was the ship's petty officer third class. The junior-most officer had been sent to retrieve him! If he were anyone else, they would have sent a senior officer. Wang Li had a pretty clear indication of how he was regarded on this ship.

He almost saluted the petty officer before realizing that he outranked him. Wang Li waited for him to salute, but to his surprise, the petty officer instructed him to follow. They went through several floors of the ship, turning and twisting, avoiding people in the corridors. He felt a new level of energy in the crew. Maybe he imagined it, but something had changed. They reached a secure door where the petty officer entered a code and gestured for Wang Li to enter. He'd never seen a room like it. The premier war room had large monitors on the walls, a big conference table in the middle, and several tactical stations were manned by crew wearing headsets. A large radar screen displayed with several live satellite feeds of the Paracel

Islands. A larger-than-life portrait of Mao Zedong hung on one wall, and the whole room had a plush carpet that changed shades from deep red to light red depending on where you stood in the room.

Zheng sat at the head of the conference table, and he gestured for Wang Li to approach. Wang Li came up to the right side of him and waited for an invitation to be seated. To his annoyance, Zheng didn't offer any such privilege.

"We've been informed that the ship that attacked you may have gone stealth. This raises our suspicions as to who they are. We've tried everything at our disposal, but we're unable to track them. We can't find them anywhere near the Paracel Islands. We need you to provide a guess as to where you think they would be." Zheng didn't so much as complete his sentence.

Wang Li blurted, "If they're in the area of the Paracel Islands, my bet is they're going to be near Bombay Reef."

"Why Bombay Reef?" Zheng pushed back. "There's nothing there. Even birds don't visit that island."

"That's where I've run into the Vietnamese fisherman. Twice," Wang Li answered.

"Why do you think the fisherman goes there?" Zheng inquired, sipping a cup of green tea.

"I think he's searching for su vang fish," Wang Li offered.

"Su vang fish?" Zheng repeated with surprise. "How do you know that?"

Wang Li hesitated. "I confiscated two from him the first time I encountered him, and like any good officer, I submitted them to the service of the People's Republic of China."

Zheng chuckled at Wang Li's attempt to ingratiate himself. "Why did the fisherman return? Did you not teach him a lesson the first time?"

Wang Li defended himself, sharing the details of his encounters with Pham Kai, including injuring the professor.

He explained that the main reason why the fisherman had defied his orders not to return was because he was trying to save his wife. Apparently, she suffered from a disease that would take her life, and su vangs were his way to earn money for treatment.

"So, you took the only hope he had of saving his wife," Zheng almost shouted at Wang Li. "What kind of a man are you? You know we aren't at war with Vietnam–they're our allies. Why did you take the su vang he caught?"

Before Wang Li could respond, Zheng got up and walked to the screen, stroking his chin as he muttered, "Why did you come back, fisherman? And why did the stealth ship save you?"

Zheng turned around and ordered his senior officers to the conference table. Zheng debated for a moment, and then gestured to Wang Li to take a seat. He asked his team for their ideas about the stealth ship, and they started coming up with reasons for its strange location, all related to the mineral resources found near the Paracel Islands.

Zheng cut them off. "You're missing a big clue. It's hidden right in front of you–the professor. According to the report, there was a third person on the boat." He turned to Wang Li. "Do you remember his name?"

Wang Li paused. "Vu Ha," Wang Li said, almost spitting on the officer next to him. "Doctor Vu Ha."

"Bring up his information," Zheng ordered an officer. Within seconds, Dr. Vu Ha's full profile was displayed on a screen. The officer brought up his research and blog entries–the last of which, from almost six months ago, was about a local fisherman who had caught a fish that may be a new species. As they read the entry, it highlighted that the marine life had special properties.

"You idiot," Zheng said, disgusted with Wang Li. "The fisherman wasn't there to find su vang. He was helping this poor doctor catch this new species. And I'd bet my career this stealth boat has come here to find the same marine life. That's why they took the risk of engaging our patrol boats, scaring them away like rats." He turned to his officers. "Complete all maintenance in the next six hours and prepare to cast off. We need to find this stealth boat, confiscate their research, and if they've found this new species, claim it for the betterment of the People's Republic of China." He directed Wang Li's gaze to a monitor on the far wall. "Is that the ship that attacked you?"

An image of the Skjold warship appeared on the screen. Wang Li nodded, feeling embarrassed.

"Good," Zheng said. "We've ordered several of these ships from the Norwegians. Now we'll have one more to add to our fleet." He turned to his team. "Gentlemen, do not take this mission lightly. This is a dangerous stealth ship capable of high-speed attack. It won't register on any of our electronic surveillance–we'll need visual confirmation of its presence. We're dealing with a sophisticated group that's working in secret on behalf of a hostile government. Anyone care to guess what government that would be?"

"Meiguo!" one of the officers shouted, loosely translated as "the United States of America."

Zheng nodded, wrapping up the meeting with orders to plot a course for Bombay Reef. He then said something that shocked Wang Li. Speaking to his weapons officer, he said, "I need this to be a precise surgical strike. We can't damage that boat–if it's indeed the Skjold as we believe it to be." Zheng turned to his commander of Special Forces. "We won't be dealing with prisoners or the drama of negotiating their release with other governments. This group of arrogant mercenaries has attacked our sovereign nation, and we're well within our rights to terminate them. We need to send a message to whichever government supports them that China is not like other countries, where they can inflict aggression without consequence. And if we do find them near the Paracel Islands, their presence will be considered espionage, which is punishable by death. There will be no prisoners, do you understand?"

The commander nodded. "Aye, aye, sir!"

CHAPTER NINETEEN
Event Time

"LOOK!" SHILOH YELLED again, running to the side of the Skjold. "What is that? They look like northern lights, but they're underwater."

Sebastian and Maria joined him. The water all around them had become bright maroon, glowing with a unique luminescence. It was still, and they could see every living sea creature, plant, shell, and coral underwater. It was similar to the photos of the lagoon, except more dramatic and otherworldly against the backdrop of a night sky and bright stars.

Shiloh ran in and alerted everyone to join them on the deck. Within seconds, the whole team was outside looking at the glowing, transparent water. In all his years of fishing, Pham Kai had never witnessed such a spectacle, and neither his father nor grandfather had ever mentioned seeing such a sight. Adora and Charles were the first to remove their clothes and jump in the water. Their hands and feet swayed back and forth, surrounded by radiant, maroon light. It appeared they were suspended in space turning and somersaulting like aerial acrobats. The entire team removed their clothes and jumped in. Even Pham Kai and Minh joined in, except they wore their regular clothes–they were much too modest to undress in front of strangers.

Maria swam up to Sebastian. She wrapped her legs around his waist from behind and climbed onto his back, enjoying the moment without having to do any work.

"That's not fair," Shiloh shouted, his head bobbing up and down as he splashed in the water. He was wasting way too much energy treading. He swam up to Sebastian and grabbed hold of his shoulder. Sebastian smiled at Shiloh's unabashed nature.

Adora and Charles's joined them. "Good idea," Adora said, noticing what Maria had done. She got on Charles' back and wrapped her legs around his waist. Fabienne swam close to Adora, who held her hand out. Now Charles was treading for three. Pham Kai said something to Minh in Vietnamese, and she climbed on his back too. They formed a large circle, with three men treading and the rest holding on. Nidal and Michelangelo had swum away, snorkeling in the clear maroon water.

The team's swim gave them an entirely new perspective, showing them the true beauty of Bombay Reef. They could see how dangerous it could be for inexperienced sailors. The underwater terrain had no uniformity to it—random small hills of corals, sharp rocks, and mounds of shells and stones made for treacherous sailing. Large, jagged slabs of igneous rocks were also scattered throughout the ocean floor, formed by constant eruptions of lava. Another interesting geological phenomenon caught their interest—at almost five feet tall and three inches wide, vertical pole-like structures, sharply pointed at the end, jutted out of the seabed—obsidian glass spikes. They appeared to be spread all over, but their layout seemed to have some kind of geometrical pattern to them.

There was something beautiful about the seabed—as if every rock, pebble, stone, and coral had been placed in perfect harmony.

The team also realized that the marine life in these maroon transparent waters were behaving oddly, displaying a special ritual. Schools of mandarin and angelfish with green, blue, and orange hues were swimming around and through the gaps between the Paramarines—they weren't trying to avoid them, showing no signs of fear at all. Even aggressive species like stingrays and barracuda accepted the team as their own, as if they were here by invitation.

A family of manta rays started touching them with their large wings, and minutes later a group of endangered hawksbill sea turtles joined them. They swam in between them, some even exposing their underbellies, the most vulnerable part of their bodies.

Charles was the first to address the miraculous development. "Guys, I'm sure we're in the presence of the *Isikhathi Isilwandle.* Look at how the marine life is acting—I know it, we're witnessing a miracle."

Sebastian chimed in. "I think, given the maroon, luminescent water and the fact that it's so still, it appears we're experiencing the time particle *El Sitio.*"

Nidal and Michelangelo swam up to the group, removing their masks. "We've been scouting the area," Nidal said, "and the marine life is displaying really odd behavior. They're swimming toward us, almost trying to touch us."

"Yes," Sebastian said, "we experienced that too. How far did you guys check out the reef?"

"We swam about a hundred yards in all directions," Nidal replied, "and except for the beautiful display of marine life, we couldn't find any evidence of our specimen or the cavern." He treaded water easily, continuing, "There are some unique geological structures. Long, obsidian spikes. They must have been here for tens of thousands of years. It takes millennia for these types of crystals to grow just a few inches. These are almost five feet tall. Amazing!"

"Let's head back to the ship, and form two dive teams to investigate all this," Sebastian said. "The first team can be Michelangelo, Charles, and me. The second team can be Maria, Fabienne and Nidal. We'll alternate with an hour's surface interval each between dives. If we're here by invitation, let's meet our host."

The two teams dove for two hours, with no luck finding the elusive *Isikhathi Isilwandle*. In that time, they had explored most of the luminescent area. Tired, they gathered in the mess room. Shiloh had patched in the camera feed from the bridge, and they could see the maroon ocean still lit up with all the marine life lazily swimming about.

"What do you think is happening? What are we doing wrong?" Sebastian asked while taking a sip of hot coffee. "The species is here somewhere. Why can't we find it?"

Shiloh was snacking on Freia biscuits. Maria had made a plate of leftovers from their dinner of sticky rice and baked chicken. All the diving had made her hungry again.

"That's a good idea," Fabienne said, seeing Maria's plate. She ran into the galley and made one for herself.

The team sat, thinking, eating, sipping, wondering what their next move should be, when Sebastian had an idea. "I think it's time to have some of our big guns brainstorm with us. I know we're missing something here."

He punched a button on his phone, and through the speaker, the same new tones were heard, indicating a secure connection was being established.

"Hello, Sebastian." Hearing Cebrián's voice silenced the room. The team leaned close as Sebastian shared the details of their earlier investigation of the lagoon and the whirlpool, followed by the current phenomenon of the brightly lit maroon ocean. He concluded with the outcome of the four dives, yielding zero results.

Cebrián listened, then recommended that the team upload

all the underwater pictures to Poseidon. Within minutes, he had two of the Honeycomb scientists on a conference bridge—the geoscientist and the Russian seismologist. Hamza and Talia also joined the call.

"Congratulations, Paramarines!" the Russian said. "My name is Dmitri Fedorov, and on behalf of all of us, excellent job."

"Thank you, Dmitri," Sebastian said, "but we have to find the specimen first."

"I know, I know," Dmitri said. He continued in his gruff, deep voice. "We've been working behind the scenes to help you figure out how, and these pictures of the underwater terrain and lagoon are very helpful. These jagged, igneous rocks on the seabed are a very rare seismic phenomenon. In the notes we have from Poseidon, there's mention of a large cavern near you. Were you able to investigate it?"

"Not yet," Sebastian answered. "We haven't been able to find it."

"Fascinating!" Dmitri bellowed.

"Hi, this is Josephine Tharp. Tell me about these vertical obsidian spikes I see in the pictures." A soft new voice came out of the phone speaker.

"Josephine Tharp?" Nidal said with a hint of surprise. "Are you in any way connected to Marie Tharp?"

"Yes, she was my aunt," Josephine responded, her shyness evident.

"Marie Tharp?" Shiloh whispered, looking at Nidal with a confused expression.

"Yeah, Marie Tharp!" Nidal confirmed with fan-like exuberance. "Only the most famous geologist in history. She mapped the ocean floors—the bathymetry analysis we used to find the location of the cavern. She invented the science for it."

"Yes, she was an amazing person," Josephine responded warmly. "Now, what can you tell me about the obsidian crystals?"

Nidal took the lead. "Sure, these are vertical spikes, almost pole-like in shape, five to six feet tall, three to four inches wide. They appear to be growing out of the seabed. The soil around their base is soft, undisturbed, and smooth. They're crystalline in form, black, and shiny. We couldn't determine if they were growing randomly or in a geometrical formation—but they appear to be equidistant from each other. If I wasn't a geologist, I would've thought they were man-made and placed there intentionally."

"Are they all obsidian?" Josephine asked. "Or have you found other spikes made of other natural material?"

"The ones we've found are all obsidian," Nidal replied, wondering where she was going with her line of questioning.

There was a moment of silence before she continued. "Can you estimate how many there are?"

"We've counted over a dozen," Nidal responded. "My guess, given the size of the luminescent area, there should be about two dozen such spikes. And one more thing—I saw obsidian boulders in the lagoon. They weren't spikes like these, but they were definitely obsidian."

"Cebrián," Josephine said, "can we get a live satellite picture of the area? Since the ocean is crystal clear and lit up, we may be able to see how these obsidian poles are placed."

"Sure," Cebrián said. "Poseidon, did you hear that?"

"I am on it," Poseidon responded.

Accessing the satellites on top of their location, Poseidon produced the live images. It was a sight to be seen—a round area approximately a quarter mile in circumference appeared on the monitors, lit up brightly in a maroon hue. The Skjold was near one side of the large circle.

"There's no sign of the cavern, and look at the obsidian crystals—they appear to be in a hexagonal arrangement," Sebastian said.

"Such hexagonal obsidian formations have been found in different oceans and seas, even in the Baltic Sea," Josephine said. "The most recent were found in Sydney Harbor. I'm intrigued to see them here too, where the specimen may be found." She paused, hesitant. "Wait a minute. Obsidian crystals are known to have a time frequency at which they vibrate. They all resonate together."

There was a moment of silence—everyone could feel that they were close to figuring out the puzzle. "Paramarines," Cebrián said, "Based on Josephine's point, I would venture a guess. You're searching for the specimen in the right area, but not at the right *Event Time*. I think your Event Time is off."

"Event Time?" Shiloh repeated.

"Hmm, good point, Cebrián!" Dmitri bellowed. "Event Time is the precise moment an event occurs. It could be a second or even a microsecond. If you miss the Event Time, you miss witnessing the event. How many times have you stood with others looking at the night sky, when your friend sees a shooting star and you're left saying, 'Where, where?' This is because you either blinked or looked away and missed the precise Event Time. This is how the species has remained undiscovered. Observing it has been an infinitesimally small probability."

Sebastian got up from the table and walked over to the monitors. "Obsidian crystal poles surrounding this area are forming a time lattice. And if we're able to tap into the frequency of it, our specimen may appear." He turned around and faced the team. "Shiloh, do you think we could use your portable time warp device underwater to emit *El Sitio* particles while we swim close to the obsidian poles?"

"I don't see why not," Shiloh said, getting up from his seat. "I can put it in a waterproof container."

"Great, let's do this." Sebastian walked up to the table, addressing the Honeycomb team. "Thank you, this was the breakthrough we needed. Shiloh's going to prepare the portable device, and we'll dive in thirty minutes. This time, we'll match the Event Time of the specimen and hopefully spot it. I'll call you again to share the results."

"Sounds good, we will reconnect after your dive," Cebrián said, disconnecting the call with the Paramarines.

Cebrián thanked Dmitri and Josephine before hanging up with them too. Hamza and Talia remained on his monitor. "Okay, what's the update?" he asked.

"We have two major problems," Talia said. "I've been tracking Goliath and everything else that's in play trying to find our team. I've also been tracking Chinese naval movement." She paused. "Cebrián, the situation doesn't look good. According to Goliath's logs, the *USS Bainbridge* has reclassified their mission. Use of lethal force has been authorized."

Talia continued. "There has also been Chinese naval movement. A Luyang-I class destroyer made an unscheduled departure from the Chinese naval port of Shantou, and it appears it's set a course for the Paracel Islands. That's a lot of firepower for such a small area. I'm sure this is in response to our team neutralizing the three patrol boats."

"Okay," Cebrián mused. "We have the *Bainbridge* approaching from the west, and a Luyang-I destroyer approaching from the east. What are the ETAs for each?"

"Approximately twenty-four hours for the *Bainbridge*, they have been heading toward our team's coordinates for over a day," Talia replied. "And about six hours for the Luyang."

"Hamza, what can we do to slow them down?" Cebrián asked.

"It's going to take some doing," Hamza responded, "but I should be able to access some of the systems on the *Bainbridge*, mostly noncritical—their weapons and propulsion systems are independent, not connected to a network I can hack. As for the Chinese ship, I'll have to see what I can do. Talia, can you give me a hand with this?" Talia nodded. "Okay, Cebrián, give us a few hours."

"Thank you," Cebrián said. "Keep me informed."

* * *

BASIL BELEN WAS intrigued by the anomaly in Goliath's logs. Still upset by his interactions with Major Williams, he was back in his control room at the Pentagon, performing routine maintenance on Goliath's system backup files and control codes. Apparently, the office of the secretary of defense had accessed the log file that contained the mission status for the *USS Bainbridge* twice in one day. He didn't think much of it, continuing to look through other system files, but his compulsive nature made him go back. The second code that accessed the log files appeared to look like the code from the office of the secretary of defense, but it was a hack.

Basil twitched, impressed that a hacker had been able to break through all the seven security layers. In his opinion, there were two people in the world who could accomplish such a feat. One he knew well, even fancied—an Israeli quantum physicist and gifted hacker named Talia Goldman. The other, a friend of Basil's, was an applied mathematics and astrophysics savant named Hamza Hamad, from Pakistan. He respected both of them.

Being a hacker himself in his previous life, Basil knew there were certain protocols, one of which dictated that he not report them to the Pentagon. Besides, they weren't doing anything specifically harmful.

Hamza and Talia were coding ferociously, using Goliath as their main entry point into the *Bainbridge*'s systems. They needed to see if Goliath had other information on the *Bainbridge*, as well as anything on the Luyang-I destroyer. As they worked, a message popped up on each of their screens: *Hamza, Talia, what are you doing hacking into Goliath?*

"It's Basil Belen," Hamza said, still on video chat with Talia. "He's found us."

"Yeah," Talia replied, "I got the message too. He's using a secure three-way text line."

Hi, Basil, she typed. *How did you know it was us?*

On receiving the message, Basil put his coffee down and typed. *I know your work, Talia. I took a guess that Hamza had a role in this as well.* He paused for an answer, but his excitement got the better of him. *So, what are you doing poking around useless log files of a random mission in the South China Sea? What's the story here?*

Talia chuckled at Basil's response, glad he was following the hacker's code of ethics. Before shutting them down, he wanted to know why they were hacking his system. *We're trying to save our team of scientists from imminent attacks by the U.S. and China*, Talia typed.

I know, Basil messaged. *We were the ones who found them. Why is the secretary of defense up in arms about your scientists?*

Talia and Hamza decided to be straight with Basil. They explained what the scientists had found.

Unbelievable, Basil responded. *You're not pulling my leg? Time particles?*

Yes, Talia messaged. *Time particles. And believe me, neither Hamza nor I would be hacking into your system if this wasn't a world-altering situation.*

Okay, what do you need? Basil asked.

Talia and Hamza sat up. They knew Basil was a hacker, but they didn't know he'd be willing to commit treason to help them.

We need to access the systems on the Bainbridge and any information you have on the Luyang-I destroyer, Talia responded. *We need to slow them down so our team can do their job and get out of there in safely.*

There was a pause before Basil responded: *You know I can't share technical information on either the Bainbridge or the Luyang-I.*

I'll send you what I have that is classified as level one, basic information. There's no need to keep hacking Goliath. I'm going to delete the code you've written and scrub any trace of your presence. I'll also be changing Goliath's security protocols. Please don't try hacking it again. Next time, I won't be so friendly.

Thanks, Talia typed: *We hear you.*

Basil downloaded all the nonessential information he had on the two vessels and sent it to them in a secure packet.

On reviewing the files, Hamza and Talia realized how little they had to work with. Most systems on the *Bainbridge* were standalone—they could only be accessed by physically plugging into them. And as for the Luyang-I, they had even less.

"What do you think?" Hamza asked.

Talia continued going through the documents. "Not sure. I don't see what we can do. This information on the *Bainbridge* isn't very helpful. Let's go through it line by line. Maybe we're missing something."

After a few minutes, Hamza whistled. "Look at this. There's a number on the bottom of page seven. It looks like a handwritten cell phone number."

Hamza started hacking into the registry database of cell numbers and discovered the number belonged to the current XO of *Bainbridge.*

"Wow, do you think Basil put it there for us to find?" Talia said, smiling.

"Not sure," Hamza replied. "I do find the coincidence a bit too convenient. This is all we needed from him. We'll be able hack the phone and use it to piggyback onto their maintenance servers. Let's look at the information on the Luyang-I."

After poring over the documents on the Chinese destroyer, they realized Basil had given them another break—the email address of the captain.

"Do you see it?" Talia asked.

"Yes," Hamza answered. "It'll do nicely. I can use it to get into the captain's laptop and then gain access to the ship's Wi-Fi network and systems."

"What do you have in mind?" Talia asked.

"I might be able to create chaos on the *Bainbridge* by randomly shutting down their nonessential systems. I have to figure out a way to make them realize they've been hacked, causing them to slow down to repair. According to military news website RealClearDefense, there is a theory that Russians have hacked into U.S. warships causing them to crash into commercial traffic. If I can somehow create an illusion that Russians have hacked into *Bainbridge*, that would do the trick. As for the Luyang-I, I'll access the CPU boards on their engines and use machine code to make one propeller run two RPMs faster than the other. In theory, they should lose their ability to steer the ship straight."

"Wow, brilliant." Talia said, flashing a thumb's up gesture.

They both worked in silence, racing to slow down the two warships.

CHAPTER TWENTY

Miracle of Isikhathi Isilwandle

THE TEAM WORKED in silence, getting ready for a monumental dive. It was as if nature itself had come to a standstill to pay tribute to the big event.

Charles, standing next to Sebastian, whispered, "Thank you."

"Let's hope our theory is right," Sebastian said, looking down at his mask. While adjusting it, he thought about what Charles had been through for most of his professional life, searching for hidden animals—all the criticism and ridicule he'd faced from colleagues, family, and the vast majority of the academic world. To them, he had been a wasted mind, a lost soul who had given up a promising career in academia to chase myths. Sebastian looked up at Charles, and even though it was dark, the luminescent maroon waters of the reef were bright enough to show that those years of failure had taken their toll. His face had lines of sadness and stress beneath the childlike innocence and enthusiasm.

Charles wanted to say so much more, but his emotions got the best of him. He cleared his throat and walked over to Maria and Fabienne to help them inspect their scuba gear.

Nidal sat on one of the diver's benches, checking his

diver's camera attached to his helmet and going over notes on the white plastic surface of his sleeve. If he felt any excitement, Sebastian couldn't tell.

Sebastian sat down on the edge of the boat on the diver's platform, fins touching the water. Like the others, he knew in his heart that this dive would be special—they would come face-to-face with the specimen.

Maria, Fabienne, and Charles came over and sat down next to Sebastian and Nidal. They were ready.

"Remember, everyone," Sebastian said, "the specimen is most likely ancient—it's had eons to develop its abilities. Once we align ourselves with the frequency of the obsidian crystals, we may be able to see it. We may find some unnatural formations, or face some sort of defense mechanism that we've never seen before. Let's swim in pairs—Fabienne, you're in the lead with Nidal. Maria, you're with Charles. I'll control the time warp device and swim between the four of you. We'll swim in formation, with pairs breaking off when something needs investigating. And Charles, please double check you have your Doppler device."

Charles gave his underwater backpack a pat, indicating he was ready. Looking out toward the dark outline of Bombay Reef one final time, Sebastian took a deep breath and said his favorite sentence: "Okay, let's do this."

Maria already had her mask on and moved into position. Sebastian rinsed his in seawater to keep it from fogging. One by one, without making a splash, they slid into the water.

It was still an incredible experience—they could see every detail in the clear, luminescent water, rich with marine life. The coral under the maroon light reflected all the colors of the rainbow, the sand on the seafloor was a carpet of glitter, and everything around them glowed.

They swam to one of the obsidian crystal spikes and floated around it.

Sebastian pointed at the time warp device, now in its waterproof casing, and gave a watch-and-look signal, indicating that he was going to activate it. The others gave him the "Okay," signal in return. He activated it with a special switch and it started emitting *El Sitio* particles.

The team waited, casting about for any change in their environment, focusing on the approximate center of the hexagon formed by the crystal spikes.

Sebastian brought the device close to his mask to make sure it was working properly. As he did so, the glittering sand of the seabed started to move—it was falling down. The movement could best be described as how sand falls in an hourglass. The falling sand made a series of mathematically precise swirls. The swirls converged at the center in a logarithmic spiral, similar to an ammonite shell.

The team watched in awe as the phenomenon unfolded. The swirls kept forming and the sand kept falling, giving way to a gigantic swirling funnel going deep into the earth.

Sebastian noted the similarity to the famous staircase in the *Sargrada Familia* church in Barcelona. This funnel, however, was a thousand feet in circumference. Its glistening walls formed six sides, just like the time nodule. Each side was luminescent, with the same colors and symbols—and the maroon wall representing *El Sitio* particles was pulsating.

From each luminescent side, a long tube protruded to the center into a large red oval that sparkled with crystals. The crystals appeared to be connected to each other in a hexagonal pattern via glittering, gold-laced tubes. The structure resembled a massive, beautiful Faberge egg. Sebastian realized that his Pareidolia condition had sparked this image in his mind.

The tubes that extended from the walls were translucent, and inside them were pulsating spheres that traveled toward the egg.

Fabienne held Sebastian's shoulder, trying hard not to

panic. It was so much to take in.

Sebastian then gestured to investigate the amazing structure. They swam cautiously, deeper into the opening of the funnel.

Charles tapped Sebastian on the shoulder, showing him the message he'd written on his sleeve. *The Isikhathi Isilwandle?*

Sebastian nodded. He was forming his own thesis. The cavern and swirls they saw in the satellite pictures were actually this structure—there never was a cavern.

Sebastian also realized that the structure was too large to be carbon-based. The precision of each spiral, the tubes, and the pulsation were mathematical in nature. In his opinion, this was the first ever sighting of a non-carbon-based, multi-cellular life form. The enormity of the moment dawned on him—this was a new evolutionary branch unknown to mankind.

Having reached the red oval structure, they were now several feet below the seabed, taking in its immense size, almost as big as a single-story building. They soon realized the glittering crystals weren't crystals—they were clusters of time nodules, similar to the one on the fish. Hundreds of thousands of them crowded the surface of the red oval mass.

It took them some time to realize another miracle—fish just like the one on the boat swam all around the oval mass. The team gestured wildly to each other, ecstatic that they had found more like their specimen. Seemingly at random, the fish would align the slit near their dorsal fin next to the nodules, and the mass would pulsate, transferring a single nodule into the waiting fish's body. Having received their precious cargo, the fish would then swim deeper into the swirling funnel and disappear.

Sebastian motioned that he would swim closer to the oval mass and see if he could remove one of the time nodules. The team gave him an "Okay" sign.

As he got close to the oval, something strange happened.

He felt a strong sense of familiarity, almost a kinship with the life form, as if they had always known each other. He felt a burst of energy flow through his body, just like when he walked through the pond at his secret retreat. Images started to flash in his mind.

Maria swam up to him and touched his shoulder. On feeling Maria's touch, he came out of his trance and indicated with a gesture that all was good. Stretching out his hand, he touched a single time nodule. The large oval mass pulsated, and the nodule floated into his hand. It was an exact replica of the one they had. He touched another nodule, and as before, the oval mass pulsated and the nodule floated into his hand. He held them out to Fabienne, who had already pulled out an underwater bag.

Maria followed suit and touched one of the nodules, but nothing happened. Surprised, she turned to Sebastian. He touched the exact same one, and again, the mass pulsated and the nodule floated into his hand. It appeared the life form was only reacting to Sebastian's touch. One by one, each team member touched a nodule, and in each case, nothing happened. The one person who could collect them was Sebastian.

Charles swam up and held out his arm. *Collect 300 nodules*? Sebastian nodded. He knew why Charles had picked that quantity. There were 195 countries and almost 92 stateless nations—each would get one for their own research.

It took him about twenty minutes to gather all the nodules. Fabienne's special underwater bag was full and glowing brightly. Nidal, Maria, and Charles collected cell samples from the walls, the tubes, and the red mass using special duct tape. The team started heading to the obsidian crystals that marked the boundary to the life form.

Maria looked back, shocked to see that Sebastian hadn't joined them—he was swimming rapidly toward the swirling staircase, going deeper into the funnel. She alerted the team—they couldn't stay down much longer. They treaded for a few seconds, trying to comprehend what Sebastian was doing. He had now broken protocol. And it didn't appear he had any mind to turn back.

Maria signaled to follow him down, and they all nodded. He appeared to have a clear purpose—maybe he knew something they didn't.

The team caught up with Sebastian, and Maria grabbed his shoulder. He turned and gestured for them to go back. Maria shook her head vehemently. Sebastian turned away, aligning himself with the twisting wall that showed *Rahpido* symbols. The team continued to follow him. Maria detected that the shade of maroon light all around them was changing—the opening of the creature was starting to close, and they were nearly a hundred feet deep. She also noticed that the marine life was maintaining underwater pressure conducive to human survival. This meant they would not have to worry about any pains caused by decompression sickness.

Maria pointed at the opening, then toward her dive computer. Sebastian nodded and gave her the signal to continue on. She ordinarily appreciated Sebastian's confidence, but he was seriously jeopardizing the safety of his team and himself.

The team kept following him, and although it appeared they were swimming deeper into the creature, their depth gauges didn't indicate any change. Maria realized they had also lost their spatial orientation. Her dive computer was not making any sense—she didn't know if they were swimming down, up, or laterally.

Then the entire *Rahpido* wall started pulsating, and the area around them turned greenish-blue. The wall converged around them, forming a tunnel, and soon they were no longer swimming—they glided along the walls of this newly formed

Rahpido tunnel, propelled either by current or some mechanism of the life form. Maria checked her watch, marking one minute since she'd last grabbed Sebastian by the shoulder.

* * *

BACK ON THE boat, Shiloh paced around the bridge. Through the monitors they had witnessed clouds of glittering sands being expelled. The swirls, the walls, and the abyss had faded and the cavern was closed. The water had become dark again—the maroon luminescence had disappeared. He had switched on the underwater lights, and they couldn't see beyond twenty feet.

Shiloh and Michelangelo stepped out on the deck. It had been ninety minutes since they had last seen the team disappear into the swirling funnel. "I'm getting really worried they don't have enough oxygen to be underwater for so long," Shiloh said, checking the surrounding water.

"Remember, they may have experienced some form of time dilation while coming in contact with that thing. For us it has been ninety minutes. For them it may have been just a few minutes," Michelangelo said and then changed the topic. "How far did you say we are from the lagoon?"

Shiloh squinted trying to focus through the darkness. "Almost the same as before, about a mile, give or take. Why?"

"Are you game for a boat ride? We have to get to the lagoon," Michelangelo said.

"Why?" Shiloh asked.

"I think it's the *El Sitio* particles we were exposed to in the maroon sea. I have that same premonitory feeling we experienced back at the hangar," Michelangelo explained.

"Okay, what is it?" Shiloh asked anxiously.

"I think, I have a role to play," Michelangelo hypothesized. "Remember how the particle works—maybe someone on the dive team is thinking the same thing I am, and we've connected. I am not sure. I have a strong feeling we need to get to the lagoon."

"Okay, let's go," Shiloh said.

Michelangelo confirmed the Skjold's stealth mode and requested that Adora and Pham Kai keep an eye on the monitors. In short order using their RIB, Shiloh and Michelangelo reached the lagoon.

Michelangelo moved rapidly through the vegetation, stopping to let Shiloh catch up. He also carried the last pair of oxygen tanks—something told him he would need them. After about an hour, they stepped into the clearing where they had a clear view of the dune.

It was now almost three hours since the team had gone missing. Shiloh followed Michelangelo up the sand dune, hoping in his heart that the team would be sitting safely on the other side. The last twenty feet, they ran to the top, out of breath and searching wildly.

The lagoon was dark, the water still. They couldn't see anything. Michelangelo was half expecting to see the same phenomenon he had seen during the day, with the transparent water. It would have made it much easier to find the team. He pointed his flashlight at the lagoon, switching it on and off several times—a signaling technique. Shiloh applied the less sophisticated method, yelling their names.

Michelangelo's hand shot up to his pocket. His satellite phone was buzzing.

* * *

INSIDE THE LIFE form, Sebastian and the team were still gliding through the *Rahpido* tunnel. Maria was tracking their time carefully, mindful of how long they could stay down. It had now been eight minutes. The *Rahpido* tunnel was at least fifteen feet across, and it was lit by a pulsating blue luminescence. Maria saw that they were in some kind of self-contained ecosystem, almost like a pod compatible with carbon-based life forms. And it wasn't they who were gliding through the tunnel—this newly formed pod was doing the traveling, with all of them inside it. It was biological in nature, with transparent walls, almost like glass. They were still underwater, but the pod itself was part of the *Rahpido* tunnel. It was quite like the pulsating spheres they saw in the tubes connected to the red oval mass.

She tapped Charles on the shoulder and pointed to his bag, making a gesture with her hand. He realized she wanted him to use the Doppler device to gauge how fast they were traveling, so he took it out and pointed it toward the tunnel wall. What he saw made no sense. He flicked the on/off switch and pointed it again for a second reading. Shocked, he handed it to Maria.

They were traveling at a blinding 760 miles per hour. The pod was keeping them safe from G-forces, acting like an inertia damper to keep them from being bounced around. Coupled with the effects of the *Rahpido* particles—allowing them to experience minutes compared to hours in the outside world.

They kept twisting and turning for another five minutes in their relative time. Maria saw she was getting low on air, when pod stopped moving and the wall opened up onto a shallow seabed. The pod they were in dissipated and they were soon floating in normal seawater, the opening they had just emerged from a few yards below them.

This opening wasn't the same as the one they had found at Bombay Reef—it was a blue-green luminescent circle, lighting up the ocean around them, with obsidian crystal spikes in a hexagonal formation around it.

Dazed, the team swam to the surface and removed their masks. Fabienne, still holding her bag of time nodules, was trying to get her bearings, splashing around wildly. "Oh, my God, what just happened?" The team had fallen quiet. She faced Charles, Maria, and Nidal, who appeared to be in shock.

Fabienne turned around, following their gaze and let out a scream.

A few hundred yards away sat the unmistakable outline of the Sydney Opera House. They had just traveled from Bombay Reef to Sydney Harbor in a relative time of thirteen minutes.

Sebastian swam over to Fabienne and put his arms around her. "It's okay, we're fine." He then turned to others. "You guys okay?"

Charles was still staring at the Opera House, barely able to nod.

Maria asked the most obvious question. "What's wrong with you? You broke away from the group!"

"I know, and I'm very sorry," Sebastian said, embarrassed. "I couldn't risk losing the opportunity."

"How did you know this was going to happen?" Nidal asked.

"I'm not sure," Sebastian said. "It's hard to explain. When I touched the giant red mass, I felt something, as if the life form had somehow communicated. It wasn't telepathy–it was more like a transfer of information. I think it lives deep beneath the surface of the Earth, and these tubular tunnels are connected to the obsidian crystal formations."

"So, how did we get to Sydney?" Nidal asked.

"I'm not sure about that either," Sebastian admitted. "I saw flashes of images. Most of them didn't make any sense. I did however recognize locations. And one of them was Sydney Harbor. I knew if I thought about the location and went down the Rahpido wall, I'd somehow end up reaching it. I know it doesn't make any logical sense."

"Couldn't you think of a place closer to Bombay Reef?" Nidal asked. "And wait a minute, we all touched the red mass, none of us felt anything. Why is it you're the one with this information? And what was that we traveled in? According to Charles's device, we were traveling over seven hundred miles an hour."

"Nidal," Sebastian replied, "I really don't have answers for you. Once we get back, we'll figure out the science behind it all."

"So, how do we get back, Peter Pan?" Maria demanded, still upset with his risky move.

"I guess I'll think of the obsidian crystals near our boat and then touch the walls," Sebastian replied. "In theory, that would take us back."

Maria shook her head in disbelief, turning toward the others. "Check your oxygen. What's your meter reading?"

"1200 PSIs," Nidal said.

"800 PSIs," Charles said next.

"500," Fabienne blurted out.

"1000," Sebastian replied.

"1000 PSIs," Maria finished. "If we go back the way we came, we'll need a minimum of thirteen minutes."

"Not if we exit in the lagoon at Bombay Reef instead of the cavern, those Obsidian boulders are actually another opening." Sebastian said. "It'll shave three to four minutes off the return journey."

The team exchanged an uneasy stare. This whole connection between Sebastian and the life form was getting weird.

Ignoring what she was thinking, Maria said, "Well, we still need oxygen for Fabienne, who's at 500 PSIs, and Charles, who has 800. That is, if everything goes perfectly according to plan."

"I'll share my tank with Fabienne when she runs out," Sebastian suggested.

"And I'll share my tank with Charles," Nidal offered.

"It's incredibly risky," Maria said. "I guess we'll have to make it work."

"Nidal," Sebastian said, "see if your satphone is still working and call Michelangelo. Tell him to meet us at the lagoon."

Nidal unzipped a waterproof bag and pulled out his phone. He found several missed calls from Michelangelo and Shiloh. "Guys," he said while dialing Michelangelo, "I think the other team has been trying to get ahold of us. If it's been less than thirty minutes since we first started the dive, it's been over three hours in real time."

"Sydney?" Michelangelo's voice came through the speakerphone. "Sydney, Australia? What the hell are you guys doing in Sydney, Australia? That's three thousand miles from here. How did you even get there in three hours? And what about your oxygen?"

"We'll explain everything when we get back," Nidal answered.

Maria asked for the phone. "Michelangelo, I'm not sure how this will play out, but we should be resurfacing in the lagoon about three hours from now, about seven or eight in the morning, your time. Be ready with oxygen tanks."

"We're already at the lagoon, and we have the oxygen tanks," Michelangelo replied, still in disbelief. "We figured you guys might show up here."

"Thanks, good thinking," Maria said, handing the phone back to Nidal.

"Okay, let's head back," Sebastian said, then pulled his mask back on and adjusted his regulator.

They swam down to the opening of the life form. This time, Sebastian was with Fabienne, and Nidal was with Charles. Maria swam in between the four of them.

As soon as they entered, Sebastian floated close to the wall and touched it with both hands. The wall pulsated. They started to swim deeper, and the same behavior repeated itself. They started to shoot through the tunnel, turning and twisting in a self-contained marine pod.

Sebastian kept an eye on Fabienne and her oxygen

monitor, and Nidal did the same with Charles. Five minutes into their journey, Sebastian took a slow breath and handed his regulator to Fabienne, who took hers out and grabbed his.

Maria checked her pressure meter. Once again, it wasn't registering any changes. Even if they were going deep inside the earth to come out the other side, the life form was maintaining an ecosystem conducive to their survival.

Nine minutes in, the tunnel opened up into the seabed of the lagoon. The team had approximately a minute till they ran out of oxygen in their collective tanks. They swam out of the opening, and realized they could not reach the surface.

Nidal recognized what had happened. Given that the obsidian spikes and boulders were ancient, a geological dome covered the natural floor of the lagoon. The team was stuck between the lagoon seabed and the dome and they had all taken their last deep breath.

CHAPTER TWENTY-ONE
Trouble Onboard

CAPTAIN DRAKE UNDERSTOOD the significance of his mission, but he was still having difficulty moving against a group of American scientists. His XO was off duty, and he wanted to have an off-the-record conversation regarding their mission.

John Paul Jones, the XO of *Bainbridge*, was in the gym, working out on an elliptical machine, a TV remote in his hand. Every time he switched the channel to ESPN, it would automatically jump to a channel playing *Judge Judy*.

He preferred to distract his mind while he worked out, and watching sports did that for him. After about forty-five minutes, he got off the elliptical, frustrated. He made his way to the mess hall to refill his water bottle with juice and to see what was on the menu.

The mess hall wasn't too busy. Most of the tables were empty, and he realized he'd already missed the main dinner rush. The tables were covered with blue plastic tablecloths with the words, READY TO ROLL printed on them in red. There was a rather large bulletin board with *a Sailor of Distinction* sign on it. Several pictures of distinguished sailors were tacked on it. Next to it was a flat-screen TV with cables dangling from it, similar to the one in the gym. To his surprise, *Judge Judy* was on it as well. *What's with this show?* he wondered, filling his water bottle.

To the side of the fountain lay the standard dinner buffet with several meat dishes like pork chops, beef tenderloin, and barbecue chicken, paired with several vegetable dishes and rice. The chef had also added cheeseburgers, fries, and a platter of small pizzas. That was a change–John was expecting macaroni and cheese. He loved a plate of macaroni and cheese after a good workout. He peered through the window to the galley and called out to the chef, who snapped a salute. "Sir, yes sir."

"At ease," John responded. "Why don't we have macaroni and cheese today?"

The chef, looking a bit flustered, blurted out, "Sir, the boiler stopped working for some reason. I'm having the electrician look at it. I had to even microwave the rice. Sir, we have a different menu for the officer's mess. Don't you want to eat there?"

John knew it was a polite hint for him to leave, but he liked the menu in the main mess hall. He made his way to his cabin, noticing a group of sailors running down a corridor. He stopped, wondering where they were heading. Another sailor ran past him. "Sailor, what's the rush?" he almost snapped.

"Oh, sorry, sir," the sailor said, coming to a halt with a salute. "The game is about to start, and we're headed to the break room."

"Okay, no need to run," John replied. The last thing he wanted to deal with was an unnecessary injury during a live mission.

Just as he turned to go, he heard voices yelling from the break room. "What the fuck is wrong with this thing? Why does it keep switching to *Judge Judy*?"

John smiled, making his way back to his cabin. He no sooner stepped in than his intercom buzzed. Captain Drake's voice came through. "XO, please join me in my office."

He pressed the intercom button. "Aye, sir. I'll meet you in zero ten minutes." He showered and changed into his navy-appointed cargo pants and blue T-shirt with the U.S. Navy seal printed on the chest. He was off duty, and he knew Drake wouldn't want to see him in uniform.

Ten minutes later, he knocked on the door of the captain's office. "Come in," Captain Drake's muffled voice came through the door.

Captain Drake was a man of taste. He had three leather sofas placed in a U-shaped pattern on a large, handmade Turkish rug. He had framed historic documents on one wall, with a large scale model of the *USS Bainbridge* mounted in the middle of them. On the side sat a credenza with bottles of whisky and gin, along with a martini shaker and glassware placed on a tray. He also had a small kitchen on the side with a large dining table that also worked as a conference table for meetings. On the other side of the room was a rather large mahogany desk with a glass top. It appeared to be an antique, featuring beautifully carved wood with inlay patterns in a lighter stain.

Captain Drake sat on the single sofa with a drink in his hand–whisky with two ice cubes. He gestured for John to take a seat. He lifted his glass questioningly. John, who had yet to eat dinner, declined.

"XO, what do you think of the mission we're on?" Drake asked, getting right to the point.

"What do you mean, sir?" John responded with a hint of hesitation.

"I mean," Drake said, "we're going into hostile waters to apprehend a group of American scientists to retrieve a specimen they've discovered. It seems wrong." He paused, shaking his head and taking a sip of whisky. "I respect the secretary of defense, but such aggression toward our own civilians isn't sitting too well with me. Additionally, I've been reading the research documents the secretary sent over. This group works for Doctor Cebrián Alveraz, a highly respected and influential academic and researcher, and a favorite of not only the current president, but past presidents as well." He took another sip from his glass. "Did you know he spearheaded the creation and passage of a bipartisan, $300 million budget proposal for his research? I'm not sure what's happening here, but I think we're involved in some kind of political drama."

John was surprised by Captain Drake's candid commentary. "Sir, you've given us specific orders to use force to neutralize the team, if necessary," he reminded him.

"I know," Drake whispered. "And I fully intend to see our orders carried out." He paused again, seeming to come to a decision. "XO, this specimen can control time."

John had always kept a tight rein on his emotions, but his eyes grew large. He stared at Drake as if he were joking. "What do you mean, sir, 'control time?'"

"I mean exactly what I said," Drake responded. "They found a fish that has the ability to speed up and slow down time."

"How is that even possible?" John asked, incredulous. "Control time? I'm sorry, sir, but are you being serious?"

"I'm completely serious," Drake answered, looking worried. "Why do you think we're having this conversation? I think what Doctor Cebrián and his team want to do is share this discovery with the world, and our secretary of defense doesn't want that to happen. We're walking into a political, social, and ethical minefield."

They both sat in silence. Drake kept nursing his drink, gazing at the model of the *Bainbridge.*

"Sir, how do you wish to proceed?" John asked.

"Keep on course," Drake said. "We have our orders, even

if we don't fully agree with them. As much as I hate this situation, we have a job to do." He got up, indicating the meeting was over.

"Sir, permission to speak freely," John requested and then hesitated. Drake nodded, gesturing to him to speak.

"Sir, I don't fully understand the motive of our defense secretary," John explained, "but I do believe this isn't what you and I swore to defend as officers. We should be providing the scientists with protection and safe passage instead of apprehending them and taking over their research."

"This is why I wanted to hear your thoughts. Duly noted," Drake said, stretching his hand out.

John stood up, shook hands, and saluted before making his way to the door.

"XO," Drake stopped him, "I keep getting *Judge Judy* on TV. Have someone take a look at it." He pointed a remote at the TV on the wall, trying different stations.

"Aye, sir," John said. "I'll have media look into it. Thank you, sir."

* * *

JOHN JUMPED OUT of his bunk and checked his cell phone. It was 0430. The screen appeared to be locked, annoyed he shut the phone off and switched it on again. His phone had been giving trouble over the last twenty-four hours. It all started when he had gotten a message to update his phone and since then it had been acting up. He made a mental note to have his IT folks look at it.

This was going to be a big day. They were less than eleven hours from reaching the Paracel Islands. He turned on his shower to find that the cold water wasn't working. He waited for a few moments—he couldn't take a shower in scalding hot water. After what seemed like an eternity, he shut the shower down and walked back to his room, entering the code for engineering in his intercom. A hurried voice responded.

"What's happening to our cold water, sailor? I need to take a shower," John demanded.

"Sorry, sir," the duty engineer responded. "It's been one helluva night. We're not sure what we're dealing with. We've had fire sprinklers going off, electrical systems shutting down, water being routed to places where we've shut the valves off. I'm speaking with facilities management, but they're not sure either. It appears the maintenance server is acting up."

"Well, get it fixed," John ordered. "We're on a mission, sailor, and we need to be one hundred percent ready."

"Aye, sir," the engineer replied. "I'm manually rerouting cold water to your quarters and the captain's quarters. Please give it a minute and you should be good to go."

"Fine," John replied, letting go of the intercom button.

As promised, cold water started running again. John showered, changed, and headed straight to the officer's mess. The instant he entered the room, he knew something was wrong. For one, instead of Fox News, CNN or ESPN, *Judge Judy* was still on, and the buffet trays—which ordinarily would have scrambled eggs, hash browns, and pancakes—were all empty. There was a side table with crackers and cheese, bread, peanut butter, jelly, and small bowls of oatmeal. On a smaller table, there were three jugs of juice, and jugs of regular and chocolate milk.

He poked his head into the galley and found the captain's personal chef, Mess Specialist 3rd class, holding his forehead, looking at the microwave.

"What happened here?" John asked.

The chef turned and fired a salute. "Sir, we've had nothing but problems since 0300. All the equipment is acting up. It works for a few seconds and shuts off randomly. None of the stoves, microwaves, or ovens are working. I haven't been able to make breakfast. The cooks in the main dining hall are having the same problem. You can imagine how upset the sailors are, especially because there's no coffee." He started to fiddle with the microwave, as if it would magically start working.

"I see," John replied. "I'll look into it. Not having coffee isn't an option."

"Thank you, sir," said the chef with a sigh. "Engineering has been working on it, too."

John grabbed two slices of untoasted bread and spread peanut butter on them. He ate his sandwich with a cold glass of chocolate milk while watching a woman sue her boyfriend for leaving his dirty socks lying around the house on *Judge Judy*.

Drake was already on the bridge, looking out at sea. They were still cruising between the two commercial ships. Drake acknowledged him and John saluted. "At ease," Drake said. "Have you heard of all the problems we've been having?"

"Yes, sir," John replied, frustrated. "I've been made aware of them, including one I experienced personally while trying to take a shower."

Drake grunted in response, and they proceeded to the Combat Information Center. The plan was all systems go. The *Bainbridge* was at optimal combat readiness, and they were making good progress toward Bombay Reef. The CIC team also informed them that according to the latest satellite surveillance reports, a Luyang-I class destroyer had left the Chinese naval port of Shantou, and it appeared to be headed to Bombay Reef.

"Dammit," Drake cursed. "XO, meet me in the war room at 0900 hours, as planned," he ordered, exiting.

"Aye, sir," John said. He stayed behind, catching up on the latest reports. Before he knew it, it was 0845. He made his way to the war room.

Captain Drake and his team of senior officers were already seated when John joined them. They had pictures, schematics, and crew manifests of the Luyang-I destroyer on the main screen.

"So," Drake said, "we have a potentially messy situation on our hands. The Chinese have dispatched a destroyer to Bombay Reef, and it can't be a coincidence. Either they know about our mission or our scientists have done something to piss them off. Per our calculations, they should've reached the Paracel Islands several hours ago, but for some reason, they've slowed down considerably. We're not sure why. We need a plan that'll get us to our scientists first."

"Are there any theories as to why they've slowed down?" one of the officers asked.

"They're exhibiting weird navigational patterns, as if they've lost steering control," another officer replied.

"We can push our engines to full capacity," the chief engineer offered, "and switch on our auxiliary engines. That should give us an extra ten knots."

"Good," Drake said. "Let's get to work. Dismissed."

The officers dispersed, except for John. He wanted to address the ship's recent nonessential systems issues. Although mostly irritants, they were becoming serious. "Captain, about the series of bizarre events concerning nonessential systems—"

"XO," Drake said wearily, "not having cold water, working ovens, or ESPN hardly constitutes an emergency. As long as we've got propulsion, weapons, and we remain combat-ready, we'll be fine."

"I understand captain," John persisted, "but this is different. I think there's a pattern developing."

As if on cue, the General Quarters alarm sounded and an automated announcement started blaring. "All personnel report to the deck. This is not a drill. All personnel report to the deck. This is not a drill."

"What the hell is happening? Who authorized General Quarters?" Drake shouted as they ran to the bridge.

The officer of the deck (OOD) was frantically flipping switches at his station, trying to turn it off. "No one, sir!" he shouted, wide-eyed. "It just came on! We're trying to shut it down."

"XO, get on the goddamn intercom and order the chief engineer to override the alarm," Drake shouted, furious.

John was already on with the engineer when the alarm stopped. A soft rhythmic chorus of men and women singing replaced it.

The words were unrecognizable. "*Rossiya svyashchennaya nasha derzhava, Rossiya-lyubimaya nasha…*"

After a few moments, Drake directed the officer to break formation and stop the ship.

"XO, we're listening to the fucking Russian national anthem." Drake said.

CHAPTER TWENTY-TWO
The Powerful Spleen

HUE, THE NAVIGATOR of the Luyang-I, clicked off the notification that the ship was drifting to port by a tenth of a degree. Nothing out of the ordinary—this kind of deviation happened all the time due to changes in sea current. He approached the pitch darkness of the front windows to look at the stars, eventually returning to his post. His monitors showed that all was normal—speed, revolutions, fuel, engine temperature, and pressure. The ship was purring.

The directional monitor then showed a deviation of a fifth of a degree. Once again, not worth adjusting. It was interesting, however, that the deviation was all on one side. The current must be coming from starboard.

He walked over to a nearby station, poured some tea, and grabbed a cookie. A pontificator by nature, he stood there thinking about how the whole world only knew one type of Chinese cookie—the fortune cookie. He shook his head and returned to his station. The directional monitor showed a deviation of three-tenths of a degree. Using the helm, he adjusted course to starboard, but the port deviation increased to two-fifths of a degree. He compensated further, only to find it climb to half a degree again.

He asked his second officer to call engineering to see if

they were experiencing anything unusual. The answer came back negative. His second officer handed him the phone. "So, what's the big deal?" an engineer barked over the engine noise. "Adjust course."

"The more I adjust, the more it deviates," Hue explained, raising his voice. "It appears there's something wrong with either the helm, or the directional computer."

"There's nothing wrong with the any of the systems," the engineer declared, taken aback.

Captain Zheng was finishing his dinner when his intercom buzzed. "Yes, what is it?"

"Captain, would you mind coming to the bridge?" Hue asked hesitantly. "We may have a technical issue."

"Have you asked engineering to look into it?" Zheng asked.

"Sir, the chief engineer is standing next to me."

Zheng entered the bridge and the crew saluted him, standing aside as he made his way to the two men next to the navigational computer. "So, what's the problem?" he barked.

"Sir, we're unable to steer the ship properly," Hue replied.

"Explain," Zheng ordered.

"Sir, the ship is drifting to one side," Hue continued. "Every time we course-correct, it drifts even more. We're going in a large circle."

"How is that possible?" Zheng asked. "The ship can't deviate a full degree without our explicit instruction."

"That's what I said," the chief engineer added.

"Have you run diagnostics?" Zheng asked.

"Yes, sir," the engineer continued. "And all systems are working fine. The rudder angle indicator, helm control, gyro compass, and rate-of-turn indicator are all fully operational.

"Clearly not!" Zheng shouted. "We're going in a fucking circle!" He pushed the men aside. "Let me see what's happening."

Holding the joystick, Zheng started to adjust for the drift, but every adjustment created an even bigger problem.

"It's as if the ship has a mind of its own," Zheng said, frustrated. "I hate these updates and overhauls. Something always breaks down. I'm sure something corrupted our systems while we were docked." Letting go of the joystick, he asked. "What are our options?"

"We have to shut down all systems," the chief engineer said "Upload my last backup, and restart all systems one by one."

"That's not an option!" Zheng shouted. "That would take twenty-four hours. The Skjold may be gone by then." He paused, rubbing his chin. "Maybe it isn't a steering problem." He pressed the intercom and ordered his senior officers to the war room, then ordered a full stop. He didn't want to burn any more fuel.

Wang Li heard the drowning of the ship's engines. He opened the door of his cabin and peeked into the bulkhead, finding nothing unusual.

He hesitated for a moment and stepped out. With strong, confident strides, he made his way to the bridge. He was about to turn onto the bulkhead when he heard Zheng shouting and sounds of steps around the corner. He stood still and waited for the voice to subside and then peeked. Zheng and his senior officers were all heading for the war room, and in their hurry the last officer hadn't fully shut the door.

"Why the hell is my ship going in circles?" Zheng demanded of his officers. "Every diagnostic test has come back negative." They stared straight ahead, unable to provide any answers.

Just then the war room door swung open.

Zheng too turned around to see who it was, but no one walked in. "Who the hell is it?" he barked. "Either come in or shut the door."

Hesitantly, Wang Li entered and saluted.

Zheng's face broke into a disgusted expression. "What the hell are you doing here?"

"I-I-I h-heard our engines had stopped and wanted to offer help," Wang Li stammered.

Zheng was too angry to deal with him, returning instead to his officers. "I need an answer, now. Why are we going in a circle?"

The engineer started narrating all the diagnostics he had run and their results.

"Speed differential," Wang Li muttered, looking at his shoes.

Zheng heard Wang Li over the loud voice of the engineer. He lifted his hand to silence the engineer. Turning to Wang Li, he said, "What did you say?"

"Speed differential," Wang Li repeated. "Navigating the reefs requires high-speed turns, and our rudders don't turn us fast enough. We increase the speed of one propeller and reduce the speed of the other, causing the boat to turn at sharper angles."

Zheng looked at his chief engineer, who nodded in agreement. "Of course, but I've already checked our propeller speeds, and they're identical to each other." Mid sentence, he went quiet and started to type on his laptop. "Unless…"

"Unless, what?' Zheng asked. "Spit it out."

"Unless in the last update, the control chip code got corrupted," the chief engineer said, reviewing the machine code of the control chips of the engines. "We're not dealing with corrupted code. We've been hacked. Whoever's done this is highly skilled. The code is extremely sophisticated. It's made one propeller run faster than the other."

"Hacked?" Zheng said. "How?"

"Not sure, sir," the chief engineer said. "But we can fix it without rebooting every system. I'll upload my backup onto the control computer and reboot this system. It'll take three or four hours at most."

"Do it," Zheng said. He called over an officer from a nearby monitoring station. "Shut down internet access and begin a ship-wide scrub of all computer systems, all the way down to crew laptops, even mine. We'll use secure protocols to communicate with headquarters for the remainder of the mission." He then addressed Wang Li. "If I see you in this room uninvited again, I'll throw you in the brig. Now, return to your quarters."

Wang Li saluted and left the war room, unsure why the captain despised him so much.

* * *

SITTING ON TOP of the dune, Michelangelo and Shiloh waited patiently as daylight broke across the horizon. "I'm going to get into the water with the oxygen tanks," Michelangelo said. "The others should be surfacing any time now." He strapped the tanks to his back and waded into the lagoon, swimming into the center and keeping watch for any sign of the team.

As the water started turning bluish-green and transparent, Michelangelo also saw the big issue–the domed floor would keep the team from surfacing. He started swimming from one end of the lagoon to the other, looking for a weak area where he could punch a hole. After a good deal of searching, he found a four-inch gap about ten feet down, where the blue-green light was brightest. Using the base of an oxygen tank, he started to bang at the hole with all his strength.

His timing couldn't have been better. The dive team had just emerged from the opening, the last of their oxygen depleted. Nidal gauged the varying levels of panic setting in on the team's faces as they struggled to hold their last breaths. He gave his regulator to Charles, relying on his Navy SEAL training to remain calm. A rhythmic banging sound vibrated through the water from above, and he saw debris floating down. Following the debris, he swam up and found a small crack in the bedrock and someone bringing the base of an oxygen tank down. Using his fingers he began to pry at the crack.

Maria realizing the seriousness of their situation took charge of the team. She knew that even though they were seasoned divers they could only last two to three minutes without oxygen. Making hand gestures she communicated to follow her movements.

Bending her legs back, she placed her hands behind on her heels. This move arched her back naturally lifting her hips up and stretching her neck back. In yoga it is called the Camel pose, a backbend that creates space around your sternum, elongating the spleen. The reason she had the team do this pose was to activate the spleen to excrete highly oxygenated red blood cells into the bloodstream. This allowed them to hold their breath longer giving them much needed additional minutes.

While the team looked like convex floating life forms, both Michelangelo and Nidal were able to break the bedrock. The oxygen cylinder came through, and Nidal rushed it back to the team. Fabienne was the first to inhale a deep breath, followed by Charles, Maria, Sebastian, and then himself. After taking a few breaths, Nidal went back to the opening and took the second tank through the same hole.

For now, they had survived, but they were still trapped underneath the bedrock dome. Michelangelo surfaced and swam to Shiloh, who stood on shore anxiously.

"I need a heavy rock, quickly!" Michelangelo yelled. Shiloh shot up one side of the dune and down the other, running toward the rocky terrain of the reef. He found a rock that probably weighed over forty pounds and carried it over the dune, almost tumbling down the other side. Michelangelo lifted the rock with one arm and swam back down to the bedrock. Nidal was still at work, his hands expanding the edges of the crack.

Michelangelo brought the rock down with all his strength, but water resistance wasn't letting him get the leverage he needed. He wedged the rock into the opening and kicked it through the crack, creating a hole big enough for the team to pass through.

Fabienne was the first to go through. Michelangelo helped her to the surface as the rest of the dive team followed. They were soon sprawled on the sand dune, catching their breaths in the morning sun. Shiloh handed his water canteen to Maria, who gave him a big hug before taking several large gulps.

Michelangelo stood nearby, giving them time to recover. "So, what did you get me from Sydney?" he asked.

Everyone laughed, exhausted but happy to be alive. "Nothing from Sydney," Fabienne said, "but we did get you time nodules. Three hundred of them." She lifted the glowing bag.

They gathered their things and made the short trip to the anchored Skjold, glad the excitement was over and nobody had gotten hurt. The dive team disappeared into their cabins to shower and change. Fabienne used the galley freezer to secure the time nodules, also transferring the cell samples of the walls and red oval mass they had taken.

Upon hearing the good news, Minh and Adora started preparing breakfast. The team gathered around the mess table after their showers, exhausted, starving, yet incredibly excited about everything they had seen and discovered. For the moment, however, they were immensely grateful to Minh and Adora for preparing the food.

Sebastian took a bite from an impromptu omelet and spicy potato sandwich he'd made, asking Poseidon to connect them to Cebrián. It was time to share the good news.

One by one, Cebrián connected the entire Honeycomb team to the call and shared video clips from Nidal's diver camera. Everyone stared in silence, absorbing the first ever footage of an entirely new life form.

Sebastian kicked things off. "We've collected three hundred time nodules to be equally distributed around the world. We've also collected samples of the walls and the big red structure to conduct DNA analysis. We think this may be the first living example of a non-carbon based life form. As you all know, Felisa Wolfe-Simon of NASA was the first to suggest the existence of arsenic-based microorganisms in California's Mono Lake. But leading scientists refuted her research, and I think they were too quick to judge her."

He paused to see if there were any questions before continuing. "As you can see, the cavern we were searching for all this time was this life form. It appears to be a complex structure of networked circular Fibonacci staircase formations that either lives in the deep caverns of the world, or perhaps even forms them itself. It has evolved to coexist with carbon-based life forms. The slit we see in the original fish is the means by which the time nodules become a part of them."

Dmitry spoke up. "Sebastian, I'm confused. Is this footage of the Sydney Opera House?"

Sebastian smiled awkwardly. "We haven't had the opportunity to discuss internally how that event occurred, but, yes—that's the Sydney Opera House. We traveled about three thousand miles and back. The *Rahpido* wall of the life form created a tunnel that operated like a high-speed Hyperloop."

"How is that even possible?" Dmitri's voice boomed through the speakers. "If that's true, you must have been going close to Mach speeds. The G-forces should have killed you."

"It appears the life form creates a biological pod that envelopes and protects the traveler," Sebastian explained.

"I don't understand it. You had no oxygen for three hours?" Dmitri questioned.

"Well, you're surrounded by *Rahpido* particles, so you're experiencing minutes while hours pass outside," Sebastian replied.

"Okay, one last question," Dmitri said. "How did you know to go to Sydney and back to the lagoon?"

Sebastian shifted in his chair and then lowering his voice he revealed, "When I touched the red oval mass, I experienced snapshots of information. For instance, I now know that the life form consists of a series of tubular tunnels spread across the Earth, from the U.S. to China, from Paris to Panama, and these structures are constantly changing, evolving, and forming new caverns throughout the Earth's crust and mantle.

"These *Rahpido* tunnels open up wherever the obsidian crystal formations are. I remembered Josephine mentioning that a new set of them were recently discovered in Sydney harbor. So when I touched the *Rahpido* tunnel wall and thought of that particular location, somehow that information was transferred to the creature, and it took us there."

His explanation was met with silence as everyone grasped the enormity of it all.

"Fascinating," Omar Tabreze broke the silence. "I'm glad you were able to pick up DNA samples. They'll help us truly understand this creature."

"I hate to break up the party, Sebastian," Cebrián said, "but in a few hours, a Chinese destroyer and the *USS Bainbridge* will be closing in on your location. They both have hostile intentions to board and take control of your research. I need you to get out of Bombay Reef. I'm working on a plan to get you guys home safely. I'm sending you new coordinates."

"Wait, I have one last question," Kabir interjected. "Why did the life form choose to communicate solely with Sebastian?"

"Great question," Cebrián said. "It's something I was wondering too. Unfortunately, we don't have time to unravel that mystery. It'll have to wait until the team is safe. Okay, signing off." Cebrián disconnected the call.

Sebastian felt the stare of the team. He could see that they, too, wanted an explanation. "Guys, this whole mission has been nothing but a series of improvisations. We had to smuggle the specimen out of Vietnam, then fight our way out of Guam, almost kidnap Charles and Adora, borrow a Skjold warship, take on Chinese patrol boats, and now this dive to find the life form.

"What I'm trying to say is we've had to make some pretty major decisions on the spur of the moment. And when interacting with the creature, I had a choice to either return to the ship and hope to find it again, or take advantage of what I thought I understood. I chose wrong. I put the team in great danger in order to understand the power of this species."

Nidal spoke up. "We all know what we signed up for. We knew there would be risks. And improvisation is part of that risk. No matter how much we plan, we're still building the plane as we fly it." He looked around at the team and back at Sebastian. "We're Paramarines."

The team dispersed to make preparations to cast off, but Maria tugged at Sebastian's shirt, asking him to stay behind. When the others had left, she stared at him critically. "Sebastian, you know something that you're not telling us."

Sebastian's ocean-blue eyes had that mysterious look again. "Maria, I'm still trying to figure out what happened to me."

Fabienne checked in on Vu, who was now fully coherent. She took him to his room and settled him in, then went to the galley and brought him some leftovers. "Please eat something and gain your strength."

"Thank you," he said, lips quivering.

"We have a lot to update you on regarding the specimen," Fabienne continued. "Join us after you've eaten and cleaned up." She gave him a reassuring smile and headed back to the bridge.

Vu scanned the small, clean cabin, complete with an attached bath. He was happy to see his things were there as well. He was still wearing his torn, bloodied shirt and the gruesome memories rushed back in, making him tremble. He distracted himself with the food, surprised at his appetite. After finishing his meal, he decided to take a shower and change into a new white shirt and khaki trousers. He stood in the bathroom, staring at his reflection in the mirror. Something was different about his appearance–he looked younger.

He picked up his tray and stepped out of the cabin, unsure where to go. He started down the corridor and stopped at the galley, noticing a familiar face.

On seeing Vu, Minh almost screamed with joy. She couldn't believe he was standing in front of her. She ran up to him to greet him and gave a bow, both of them started tearing up.

Minh spoke rapidly in Vietnamese. She took him to the mess area and had him sit in a chair at the main table. She ran up to the bridge and brought back Pham Kai, who was equally glad to see him up and about.

They sat next to the professor and gave him all the details of the last day-and-a-half, including their bold escape from the patrol boats and miraculous rescue by the Paramarines.

It was an information overload, especially coming from two Vietnamese who at best were guessing at a lot of what was going on. Vu couldn't understand much–their stories sounded more like fairy tales. From the luminescent maroon waters to the life form that went inside the earth for miles, much of it must have been supposition.

The three of them didn't notice Sebastian approach. He'd

never heard Minh speak much, and it appeared she was doing most of the talking. It was as if three friends had met after a long time apart. He realized that for Pham Kai and Minh, being around them had been a foreign experience—reuniting with Vu gave them some much needed social interaction and camaraderie. After a few minutes, he knocked on the door and entered. "Hello, Doctor Vu Ha. It's good to see you awake and feeling better."

"S-Sebastian," Vu stammered.

"Yes, how are you feeling?" Sebastian asked. "

"Thank you, I'm feeling much better," the professor replied. "I know you have hundreds of questions, Vu, and I promise we'll answer all of them," Sebastian said. "But for now, I need Pham Kai on the bridge to help us get out of our current position."

"Pham Kai on the bridge of this ship?" Vu asked, eyes wide.

"Yes, he's the most qualified to navigate these waters," Sebastian said.

Pham Kai had a fair understanding of what was being said, even though Poseidon wasn't translating. He gave Vu a nod and walked back to the bridge with Sebastian.

"Do you know where the bridge is?" Vu asked Minh.

She nodded, and he followed her through the ship. He marveled at the five large stations of the bridge, with buttons and touch screens, each manned by one of the Paramarines. In the middle were two large monitors, one displaying the scene outside of the ship, and the other a topology map of the area. He recognized Bombay Reef.

Sebastian stood next to Shiloh, noticing Vu and Minh peeking in. He invited them in, pointing to seats next to Adora and Fabienne. He introduced his team. "Vu, that's Nidal, Michelangelo, this is Shiloh next to me, over there is Maria and Charles, and his wife Adora sitting next to Fabienne, whom you already know."

Maria turned around when she heard her name. "Vu, we loved your Vietnamese barbecue," she said, flashing her signature smile.

The team laughed as they greeted Vu, welcoming him to the bridge.

"Okay, folks," Sebastian said, "we have less than two hours to get out of the area and as close as possible to Cebrián's coordinates. Pham Kai, help us get out of here."

* * *

ONCE AGAIN FULLY operational, the two warships raced to intercept the Skjold–the *Bainbridge* from the west and the Luyang-I from the east.

Captain Francis Drake sat in his war room, giving final instructions to his Navy SEALs. "Your mission is a go. Your RIBs will reach the Skjold faster than us. Take control of the boat, subdue to the scientists and navigate the boat toward our ship. Godspeed."

Their plan was simple–upon spotting the vessel, the Navy SEALs would surround the vessel as quickly as possible. They would then pacify any crew they encountered, employing stealth for as long as possible. They had pictures of the scientists, and would use extreme caution when apprehending them–especially the two retired Navy SEALs and the leader of the team, Sebastian Miles.

"Aye, aye, sir," Captain Rudy Shepard acknowledged, ordering his men to move out. The RIBs headed out in a parallel formation, creating discrete Kelvin wake lines, a beautiful site in the deep blue waters of South China Sea.

CHAPTER TWENTY-THREE
The Attack

IT TOOK THE team longer than expected to navigate out of the treacherous channel and head out to open sea. They had just begun to make good progress when the Senit 2000 sounded an alarm. The system had identified two warships in close proximity, as well as small inflatable boats heading rapidly toward them.

Michelangelo recognized them as Navy SEAL RIBs. "Folks, we have company. Those RIBs are in attack formation. I believe they're Navy SEALs."

"How long before we get to the coordinates?" Sebastian asked.

"Two hours. Not enough time. We're going as fast as we can," Shiloh said.

"The two warships are an hour away," Michelangelo informed the team, "and the Navy SEALs should reach us in about fifteen minutes."

"Shiloh, slow down and bring us around. Michelangelo, open all weapon bays." Sebastian said.

"What? Slow down?" Shiloh asked, alarmed by the orders.

"Yes," Sebastian confirmed. "Running away from them won't work."

"What do you have in mind?" Nidal asked. "I don't recommend hostile action against our SEALs."

Sebastian nodded. "We need to slow them down."

"How? Are you thinking of a standoff?" Maria asked, looking at the monitors.

"Something like that," Sebastian replied. "Except we'll add the element of shock and awe."

"What do you mean?" Nidal asked. "How?"

"I have a wild idea," Sebastian explained. "Remember when Maria was solving the laser maze challenge, and we ended up seeing multiple images of her in different positions?"

"Keep going," Shiloh said, slowing the ship and turning it around.

"What if we generated a *Rumio* time field and moved our boat laterally several times?" Sebastian said.

Shiloh shot up from his chair. "I think I know where you're going with this. *Rumio* particles create a temporal loop, where we repeat our actions, but don't remember repeating them. Viewers outside the temporal field would see multiple images of us."

"We'd create multiple boats ready to engage. We may confuse them enough that they may call off their attack," Sebastian said.

"It would buy us some time," Michelangelo chimed in. "But how will we track how many times we repeat our movements?"

"Easy, we'll give control to Poseidon via Bluetooth," Shiloh answered. "Poseidon will shut down the time warp device after we repeat our actions ten times. The mental effects of the particles only work on biological entities. No offense, Poseidon."

"None taken," Poseidon answered.

* * *

CAPTAIN DRAKE, THE XO, and the senior officers were gathered in the war room when Rudy's voice came over the speakers. "Captain Drake, sir, did you not say there was just one Skjold to board?"

"Affirmative," Drake responded, frowning. "The operation involves the boarding of a single vessel."

"Sir," Rudy said, "we're facing a fleet of ten fully-armed Skjold warships. They have weapons bays open and stand ready to engage. There's also a kind of pink mist all around them."

"Ten ships?" Drake yelled. He turned to his radar technician. "What is he talking about?"

The officer typed away on his keyboard, bringing up a live satellite image of the area. "Sir, I'm not sure how this happened, but he's right. There appears to be ten vessels."

"Where did they come from?" Drake shouted. "For the last forty-eight hours, we've been chasing down a single Skjold. How is this possible?"

"Sir, shall we continue our approach and attempt to board one of them?" Rudy asked.

"How would you know which one to board? No, abort the mission and return to the *Bainbridge*," Drake ordered. "We'll need to figure this out before attempting anything else." He turned to his senior staff. "I need answers. What in the name of God is happening?"

"Sir, if I may?" The XO requested.

"Go ahead," Drake replied.

"I think they may be using the very technology we've been sent to retrieve against us," the XO explained.

"Open a channel with them," Drake ordered.

Moments later, Skjold's bridge speaker crackled, and an authoritative voice came through. "This is Captain Drake of the *USS Bainbridge*. We're ordering you to close your weapon bays and prepare to be boarded. Any resistance to my orders will be met with lethal force."

Sebastian walked over to the communications station and pressed a button. "Captain, we're private researchers on a sovereign Norwegian vessel. With respect, you have no jurisdiction to board us."

"This must be Doctor Sebastian Miles," Captain Drake replied. "I've been reading reports about you and your team. For the national security of the United States of America, we can't allow you to continue. Close your weapon bays and stand down."

"Captain," Sebastian said, "since you know so much about me, you must also know that my team and I are not ones to give up. We'll not close our weapon bays, and we'll do everything humanly possible to defend our research and our lives."

"Sebastian," Nidal said, "what are you doing? We can't take on a destroyer, not to mention the Chinese. It's game over. We've come as far as we can."

Sebastian regarded the team one by one as he spoke. "We *cannot* surrender the research. All the good this nodule can do for the world will suffocate in the hands of a few powerful nations. And if the true potential of this nodule dies, the next stage of mankind's evolution dies with it."

The bridge fell silent as the team took in Sebastian's words. Moments later, Maria came to his side. "He's right. We can't surrender. We have to stand and protect our discovery."

Captain Drake's voice came through. "Doctor Miles, I know you want what's best, but I have my orders. If you refuse to stand down, I'm afraid I won't be able to vouch for your safety."

Sebastian realized Captain Drake didn't want things to get ugly. "We understand your position, Captain. But we cannot in good faith let you take our research. Do what you have to do."

Captain Drake was hoping it wouldn't come to this. "What

are our options?" He asked, turning to his XO. "I didn't expect this level of resistance from a bunch of scientists."

The communication's officer spoke up. "Sir, the Chinese captain of Luyang-I wishes to speak with you."

"Dammit! Put him on the speakers," Drake responded.

"This is Captain Zheng He of the Luyang-I. This is the sovereign territory of the People's Republic of China. We strongly advise you to leave immediately to avoid any misunderstanding."

Captain Drake rolled his eyes. "This is Captain Francis Drake of the *USS Bainbridge*. We're a sovereign United States naval vessel on a military mission, conducting lawful activities beyond any UN-recognized coastal waters of any state. We're operating with due regard to international law governing these waters. We're here to bring a group of American scientists into our protection, at which point we'll exit the South China Sea," Drake responded.

"That boat and its people have attacked three of our patrol boats, recognized as an act of war against China. They must stand trial in our courts for their crimes," Zheng stated, maintaining the same civil tone.

Drake continued. "We cannot allow you to capture and detain American citizens. The United States government will investigate your accusations and determine the right course of action."

There was a moment of silence and the crackle of the microphone, followed by the Chinese captain's voice. "We'll allow your citizens to be taken into your custody, provided their vessel and all materials on the vessel are taken into ours, remaining the sole property of the People's Republic of China." Zheng then terminated the call.

At that very moment the radar officer of the *Bainbridge* called out, "Captain Drake, our sensors show that the Luyang-I has launched RIBs. They're speeding toward the Skjold."

"Son of a bitch, he was stalling us. Get Zheng back!" Drake shouted.

"Sir, they're not responding," the communications officer said.

The weapons officer shouted, "Sir, the Luyang-I has gone into full combat alert."

"XO, apprise the secretary of defense," Drake ordered, "and request permission to engage." He turned to his tactical action officer (TAO). "Issue general quarters, and fire a warning shot across the bow of the Luyang."

"Aye, Captain." The TAO activated the targeting system, locked a spot three hundred feet from the Luyang's bow, and fired a projectile explosive that sent a geyser of water high into the air.

"Sir, the Americans have just fired a warning shot!" the Chinese XO yelled.

Zheng had the schematics of the *Bainbridge* displayed on the monitors. He had early on made the decision that he wasn't going to let the Skjold and all its research leave the area, especially after seeing its logic-defying capability.

"I want a measured response, something that will send them a message. Target their auxiliary machine room. I believe they have weapons batteries there. That will neutralize them with little casualty. Do we have a lock?"

"Aye, sir," Zheng's tactical officer replied. "We have a stealth ship-to-ship low impact air missile locked," an officer replied.

"Okay, let's give this arrogant American a taste of Chinese weaponry. Fire!" Zheng ordered. Zheng didn't know that, due to the earlier hack, the engineers of the *Bainbridge* had rerouted power. Weapons were no longer connected to batteries in the auxiliary room.

An explosion rocked the *Bainbridge*. Catching the edge of a workstation, Drake looked to the monitors displaying ship functions. Red and yellow alarm signals popped up everywhere, indicating damaged or nonfunctioning systems.

"Why didn't our sensors alert us sooner to the incoming missile?" he shouted at his weapons officer.

"Sir, the Chinese have used a new weapon. I'm reconfiguring the system to detect it," the weapons officer answered, typing on his keyboard.

The XO ran to the phone that connected to the engine room. "Status!" he shouted.

"It's bad, sir!" the chief engineer yelled. "The auxiliary machine room's been hit. It's taking on water. The doors have sealed and we have sailors trapped inside. The bulkhead leading to the room was also taking on water, so we closed it, too. They knew exactly where to hit us."

The XO repeated everything to the war room. "Casualties?" he demanded.

"Unsure, sir," the chief engineer reported. "We're rigging a makeshift pump to remove the water. We're working as fast as we can. I have to go, sir!"

"Copy that," the XO said, hanging up the receiver.

Captain Drake stood in the middle of the war room, looking at schematics of the Luyang-I displayed on the top two monitors. He knew where their engine room was and the batteries essential to operate their weapons.

"Do we have weapons control?" Drake shouted.

"Aye, sir!" the TAO responded.

"I want a spread of three guided missiles targeting their two weapon batteries and their main engine room. Cut their fucking feet out from under them."

"Aye, sir!" the TAO shouted. "We have a lock!"

"Fire!" Drake yelled.

The *Bainbridge*, alarms blaring and smoke pouring from its hull, fired three guided ship-to-ship missiles at the Luyang-I. Drake and the officers watched the monitors as the three missiles made contact with their targets. The Chinese evasive counter missile measures were no match for them.

"Captain," the TAO said, "direct hits have been confirmed. They're not going anywhere, and their weapon batteries are down. All three impacts are above the waterline. They're neutralized, but aren't in danger of sinking."

"Very good," Drake responded. "Get Zheng back on the line. We're just getting started."

"Captain Drake," Zheng's voice came over the war room speakers, alarms and commotion loud in the background, "you have committed an act of war against the People's Republic of China. We'll respond with nothing less than our full might."

"You're in no condition to make threats, Captain," Drake replied. "Call your boarding party back or prepare to be sunk."

Zheng slammed the receiver back in its cradle. None of their weapons systems were operational. The *Bainbridge* had neutralized them in a single retaliatory strike.

"Contact GHQ and tell them to dispatch the two Luyang-III destroyers to support us. And tell the boarding party to stand down and return to the ship." Looking at his XO, he asked, "Casualties?"

"Several wounded, so far," Zheng's XO answered. "No casualties, all are accounted for."

"Good," He breathed a sigh of relief. "Focus on the batteries. Our weapons need to be operational ASAP."

Wang Li was rapidly approaching the Skjold in an inflatable speedboat. He'd been asked by Zheng to join the Chinese boarding party, as he was most familiar with the capabilities of the Skjold.

His excitement was interrupted when his boarding party heard explosions behind them. They turned around to see smoke billowing from both the *Bainbridge* and the Luyang-I. Wang Li realized that their boat had slowed down. The team lead was getting new orders. To his extreme disappointment, they started heading back to the Luyang-I.

"Why are we returning?" Wang Li yelled at the team leader. "We're so close! Come on, finish the operation!"

The leader stared at him as if he were an exasperating child. Wang Li shot up from his seated position and opened his mouth to argue further, a crazed look in his eyes. Without hesitation, the team leader smacked the butt of his rifle into Li's forehead.

Wang Li sat down hard, rubbing his head. He *couldn't* go back, he had come too close. His enemy was right there. The inflatable hadn't gained full speed. Wang Li made a snap decision and rolled over the side, hitting the water with a splash.

Hearing the splash, the leader's surprise turned to disgust. "Leave him!" he yelled to the helmsman.

Back on the Skjold, the Paramarines watched the ongoing saga as dusk settled over the sea. Nidal shot up from his chair. "I don't believe this. The Chinese fired on the *Bainbridge*. And the *Bainbridge* has retaliated."

"Oh my God, have we started a war?" Fabienne shouted.

"According to my limited knowledge of these ships," Michelangelo said, "the Chinese have hit the auxiliary room of the *Bainbridge*, and the *Bainbridge* has taken out the Luyang's weapons batteries and engine room. Should we make a run for it and try to reach Cebrián's coordinates?"

Sebastian clasped his hands behind his head, thinking for a second. "No, we're not running from this. Bainbridge appears to be seriously damaged. Shiloh can connect us to Captain Drake?"

Captain Drake was rapidly barking orders. The XO had informed him that a team of engineers were working on reaching the trapped sailors. They would need two hours to pump the water out from the bulkhead and adjoining rooms and cut a hole through the wall to reach them.

"What are you saying, XO?" Drake asked.

"Sir, our men will suffocate. They're running out of oxygen," the XO hurriedly reported. "The rescue has to happen underwater. All the adjoining rooms are flooded."

"You mean to say they're good as dead?" Drake asked.

Just then, Sebastian's voice came over the speakers. "Captain Drake, this is Sebastian Miles, we can see your ship has been damaged. Is there anything we can do to help? Have you suffered any casualties?" Sebastian asked.

Drake reared back, surprised at the call. "Sebastian, we're dealing with a serious situation. I need to go."

"Sir, please wait. That's why I'm calling. Maybe we can help," Sebastian insisted.

Drake shook his head. "How? We have maybe a dozen sailors stuck in the auxiliary machine room with fifteen minutes of oxygen remaining. It'll take my men two hours to get to them. If you had listened to us, we wouldn't be in this situation."

"Captain Drake, I know this will be hard for you to understand, but we can save your men."

"What? How?" Drake asked, looking at his XO to make sure he'd heard Sebastian correctly.

"Captain," Sebastian said, "this is why you've been ordered to take control of our research. We have a scientific breakthrough that would come in real handy right about now. We'll use it to save your men. How close can you get me to them?"

The XO jumped in. "If you're willing to swim, the ducts can get you close."

"Okay," Sebastian said. "We can rendezvous with you in just a few minutes. Allow us to board, and we'll save your men."

Drake glanced at his XO, who consented by shrugging his shoulders.

"Fine, come on over," Drake said. "But what makes you so sure we won't arrest you?"

"We'll deal with that when the time comes," Sebastian replied. "For now, let's focus on the rescue." Sebastian ended the call and turned to Shiloh. "Get the time warp device ready with the *Rahpido* slide. Michelangelo, take the helm and get us to the *Bainbridge*."

Treading in the water, Wang Li could see the Skjold a few dozen meters away. It was now fully dark, and then two large spotlights switched on, right at the waterline, and the engines started making an intense, high-pressure noise. As he treaded, unsure what was happening, the ship took off in the direction of the *Bainbridge* with incredible speed. Li couldn't believe his rotten luck. He started smashing the water with his fists. With no other option, he started swimming toward the *Bainbridge*.

Sebastian, Shiloh, and Nidal boarded the *Bainbridge*, and to their surprise, Drake and his XO were there to receive them. Nidal saluted them.

"At ease, soldier," Captain Drake said, after returning the salute.

"How close can you get us to the men?" Sebastian asked, not wasting any time.

The XO took the lead. "The bulkheads and the adjoining rooms are all flooded. If you swim through the ductwork, you can get on top of the auxiliary machine room. They only have about five minutes of oxygen left."

"How long is it going to take your men to break through and get to them?" Sebastian asked while following the XO through the ship.

"My men have been cutting through the walls. We've gotten a break—we think we can get through to them in sixty minutes or less," the XO answered, almost running.

"Get me an oxygen tank," Sebastian said. "You'll have the full sixty minutes to get to them."

"In sixty minutes, they'll be dead, remember they only have minutes of oxygen left," the XO reminded him, radioing ahead for the tank.

"Just trust me, and keep cutting until you reach them," Sebastian said.

They reached a boiler room with an opening in the floor and water bubbling up through it. There was an oxygen tank on the side, complete with scuba gear.

Sebastian didn't need the full gear, just the mask, the regulator, and the tank. The XO gave him directions to get to the opposite side of the auxiliary machine room. "Go fifteen feet right and then ten feet left. You'll come to a submerged vent in the auxiliary room. My men are on the other side, which hasn't completely submerged yet."

Sebastian nodded and jumped into the opening. It was just large enough for one person. He switched on his flashlight and swam to the vent. He set the time warp device for a 1:20 *Rahpido*/real time ratio and activated it. Three minutes of *Rahpido* relative time would give the engineers a full hour to cut through the walls.

Shiloh had configured the time warp device in such a way that it only covered Sebastian and the men in the room, who noticed that the water and remaining air space above their heads had become a radiant blue-green.

Outside the room, the engineers worked frantically. As they continued to cut through the steel walls, they knew it was already too late. It was now a retrieval operation, not a rescue operation. The thought sickened them, but they didn't slow their pace.

Cutting through the last wall they waded through the water and came into a radiant blue-green air pocket holding the sailors, still alive and looking shocked. One by one, the divers helped them swim out of the room to safety.

The XO, Shiloh, and Nidal had been standing next to the

opening for an hour. It was awkward—they didn't know much about what Sebastian was doing. They just stood there in silence, waiting.

The wall speaker hissed on and the chief engineer's excited voice came through. "Attention, all hands. The rescue operation is a success. All sailors by some miracle are alive and well. They're reporting to sick bay."

Pandemonium broke out across the entire ship as cheers, clapping, and whistling echoed through every corridor.

"How—how did you guys do this?" the XO asked Shiloh and Nidal. Sebastian's head popped out of the opening, and they helped pull him out. He stripped off the mask and regulator as Shiloh and Nidal clapped him on the back and congratulated him.

XO glanced at Sebastian's pressure gauge, shocked that the psi meter hadn't moved at all.

Drake walked in and stuck his hand out to Sebastian. "I don't know how you did it—okay, maybe I've read a few reports and know how you may have done it—but I want to say thank you."

Sebastian nodded and shook his hand. They were escorted back on deck and stood next to the brow that would take them to the Skjold. The group fell quiet as Sebastian asked Captain Drake, "Permission to disembark, captain?"

"Sebastian," Drake said, "Thank you, once again. Would you and your team do us the honor of dining with us? Our boat is under repairs, and even though we're on high alert, the Luyang isn't a threat. I promise this isn't a trick to arrest you or take over your research. I owe you this."

Sebastian turned to Nidal and Shiloh seeking their thoughts, he paused. "Let me go back and speak with the team. The last few days have been anything but normal. I'm sure we'd all like a break."

"Sounds great, take your time. Radio us when you're

ready," Captain Drake replied earnestly.

They all shook hands and the Paramarines walked down to the Skjold. Drake and the XO could hear the excited celebration coming from the Skjold as the rest of the team heard the news of the successful rescue. Drake turned to the XO and smiled wryly. "Well, I imagine the secretary of defense has a court-martial waiting for me."

It took the team an hour to clean up and prepare for their evening. The Paramarines made their way to the *Bainbridge*, where they were met with a salute from the XO and all of the senior officers. They were then escorted to the captain's dining room.

"Captain Drake," Sebastian said, "please allow me to introduce Charles, Adora, Maria, Michelangelo, Nidal, Shiloh, and Fabienne."

Drake met them with a big smile, welcoming them aboard the *Bainbridge*.

The conversation, to no one's surprise, focused on the nodule and the time particles. Drake and the senior officers listened raptly as the team described them, the subterranean life form, how they had discovered it using the time warp device, and how they had traveled to Sydney in a matter of minutes. Sebastian didn't feel there was any need to hide the facts any longer. Drake had read the reports from the secretary—he already knew the broad strokes of their research.

"How are you going to 'manage' the secretary of defense?" Sebastian asked Drake in a hushed voice.

Drake lifted his glass of water and took a sip. "I've known Dick for a long time. His heart is in the right place, but I think he's gone way overboard." He chuckled. "No pun intended."

"His heart may be in the right place, but he's created a lot of problems for us," Sebastian said, sharing the attack in the hangar and how they had escaped. "And now, sending a warship to the South China Sea to take control of our research," he continued. "Had it not been for your civility, Captain Drake, we would most certainly not be having this conversation, or this gracious meal."

"Well, I'm glad how things have turned out, honestly," Drake admitted. "I've had trouble with this mission from the start. I couldn't in good conscience attack my own countrymen. Whatever the politics of the situation, it just felt wrong."

The team rolled with laughter as the XO described the fallout from being hacked, including the cold sandwiches and scalding showers, and how he was now a reluctant fan of Judge Judy.

The idea of having dinner was excellent, they were all able to enjoy a little R&R and forget about the weight of the world for a while. Minh, Pham Kai, and Vu had requested to stay back for a quiet meal of their own.

Tucked away in a dark corner of the Skjold deck sat a shadowy form dripping salt water and sweat, involuntarily shaking from excessive adrenalin. Brass knuckles glinted in spite of the darkness.

CHAPTER TWENTY-FOUR
Heroes Rise Up

PHAM KAI, MINH, and Vu were enjoying their meal in the mess area, happy for the peace and quiet. Vu was still recovering from all that had happened since he woke up. Sebastian had given him all the notes documenting their experiments in Guam, and he had seen the video of the life form that created the nodules.

He read Sebastian's notes while taking a spoonful of the sour soup Minh had made. She was able to prepare a simple meal called Canh Chua, based on tamarind-flavored broth with pieces of pineapple, chopped tomatoes, bean sprout, scallions, and garlic. She had added hot sauce liberally on top. She also added noodles and pieces of chicken to give it more weight. It was beyond scrumptious.

Vu felt beads of sweat appear on top of his head as he took continuous bites. Minh and Pham Kai were happy to see him eating. He was starting to look good, but they were surprised that his hair had lost its distinguished gray wave. How he was able to recover from that injury was beyond their ability to understand–they knew it must have had something to do with the special fish Pham Kai had caught.

"What are you reading, if you don't mind?" Pham Kai asked. "Is it about the fish I caught?"

Vu was startled to hear Pham Kai's voice, even though they were all sitting together. He was so engrossed in reading and enjoying the soup that he had forgotten. "Yes, Pham Kai. You have caught the biggest discovery in the history of mankind."

"What is it?" Pham Kai asked. "Why was the sea maroon and glowing at night, and what was that big thing we saw on the TV? I've never seen a creature like that in my life."

Pham Kai and Minh listened to Vu's explanation with extreme interest, taking in everything from the six time particles to the large, subterranean, arsenic-based creature.

"So, one of these time particles healed you from your injury?" Pham Kai said.

"Yes," Vu confirmed. "It appears one of the time particles they call *Fisio* has the ability to help the body regenerate its cells. It seems like a miracle."

"In our culture, we believe the sea has all the medicine needed by mankind," Pham Kai said then turning to Minh meaningfully.

"Stop, I don't want you to ask…" Minh said.

Pham Kai looked at her in bewilderment. "Minh, this is the miracle we've been searching for all these months," he whispered.

"I know, but what if it doesn't work for me?" she said.

Vu brought both his hands together, palms facing each other—a gesture of forgiveness and respect. "I don't know if this will work for your condition, but I'll ask the team and see if we can test these particles on you."

Minh nodded and smiled, but her heart was heavy with sadness. Pham Kai stared down at his bowl of soup. In all that had happened, Minh had forgotten about her condition—but her loving husband was still searching for a miracle.

Vu continued to share more details of the nodule and the subterranean creature as he read the reports.

"What do you mean, this fish can slow down time?" Pham Kai asked.

Vu explained while reading aloud about the *Rahpido* time particle.

"Vu, I remember there are stories—and it also happened to me, when fishing near the Paracel Islands—of people losing track of time," Pham Kai said.

Vu nodded, smiling. "Like I said, you have discovered something great. What would you like to name it?"

"Name it?" Pham Kai smiled humbly, shaking his head.

"Yes, you discovered it, and I'll make sure the world knows it. So, what would you like to call your fish?" Vu asked again.

"I don't know, Vu. I don't think I would like that," Pham Kai said, feeling awkward.

For a moment, Minh thought she saw a shadow from the corner of her eye. She turned to look at the door, thinking someone from the team had returned from dinner. Her scream startled Vu and Pham Kai. They followed her gaze behind them, unable to believe who stood in the doorway.

Wang Li, dressed all in black, water dripping from his frame, regarded them with a menacing expression. Instant panic struck them, though Vu took a few extra seconds to recognize him.

Pham Kai whispered under his breath, "Poseidon, help!" He knew Poseidon was in charge of the ship and would somehow alert Sebastian and the team.

"What was that, you stupid fisherman?" Wang Li taunted. "A prayer for your friends to return, perhaps? I watched them leave. No one can save you now."

He then focused on Vu, and his expression turned pale, as

if he'd seen a ghost. "How is this possible? I broke your neck. How is it you're standing here? And why do you look different, almost younger? What's going on?"

Just then, Pham Kai's demeanor changed. He stood up.

Wang Li's eyes whipped around, making sure they were alone. He appeared nervous, confused. For the first time in their presence, he felt vulnerable.

Pham Kai stared straight into Wang Li's eyes. "You can't kill us or hurt us. It's not meant to be. You've lost against us twice–you will continue to lose if you keep going. Your hatred toward me is costing you everything you love and respect."

Minh and Vu stared at Pham Kai, shocked by this formerly quiet man.

Wang Li was also taken aback by Pham Kai's words. "Tell me what magic is taking place on this ship!" he demanded. "I have to take control of it and hand it over to the captain of the Luyang."

"Listen to me," Pham Kai said. "This ship is operated by a computer, and we don't control it. You'll never be able to take control of it–none of the systems will start. I know this because I've been studying how it operates for the past two days."

Wang Li knew one thing about Pham Kai–he was a masterful seamen. Only a brilliant sailor could perform the stunt he'd pulled off while escaping. If Pham Kai was saying a computer controlled this ship, then it must be true.

"Pham Kai is right, Wang Li," Poseidon's voice came through the speakers.

Wang Li jumped, wild-eyed, trying to look everywhere at once. "Who said that? How do you know my name?"

"I am Poseidon, the computer controlling this ship. And yes, you heard Pham Kai say my name when he first saw you. I not only know your name, Wang Li, but I know your rank, your reporting officers, your address, the names of your family members, and everything contained in your official record. Pham Kai was also correct about something else—I will not give you control of this ship."

A mix of fear and anger contorted Wang Li's face. "Well, if you don't give me control of the ship, I'll kill these three, right here and now."

"I cannot agree," Poseidon said. "I have already informed the *USS Bainbridge* of this hostage situation. Several American Navy SEALs presently have their sniper rifles trained on you."

Wang Li tucked his chin, and saw that Poseidon was right. Three red dots danced across his shirt. But he couldn't accept defeat. He couldn't let Pham Kai win again. "You broke the law," he growled at Pham Kai through gritted teeth. "You were fishing in the Paracel Islands, a sovereign territory of the People's Republic of China. You were not allowed to be there. I told you—"

"You forget, captain," Pham Kai interrupted, "that those islands are not China's territory. You attacked me. You tortured me. You tried to cripple a man who had paperwork in accordance with the laws you pretend to care so much about. You tried to force me to commit suicide with my wife. And when that didn't work, you chased us all down and destroyed my boat. But know this, captain." He paused, searching Wang Li's eyes. "My will to save my wife is stronger than your will to destroy us. It's stronger than the entire Chinese Navy. And far bigger forces are at work here than just you and I. Perhaps our destinies are tied—perhaps we both have bigger roles to play, bigger than we can see or understand. Whatever the case, I'm done running from you."

"Bah!" Wang Li spat. "What destinies? All I know is, ever since I met you, my life has been nothing but hell! I've lost my commission, and I'm the laughingstock of the navy. I have to fix this!" His eyes were desperate, almost pleading with Pham Kai. "I need my life back."

"And I want my wife to have a full life," Pham Kai replied seriously.

Wang Li stared at the floor. Pham Kai's new demeanor and his words were starting to break him down.

Sebastian and the team were right in the middle of their dessert when they got a message from Poseidon that a hostage situation had occurred on the Skjold.

Captain Drake activated his SEAL team to neutralize the threat. They had the Chinese captain in their sights, through two five-inch windows on the Skjold. Wang Li was standing straight in their line of sight.

"Sebastian, who is this joker?" Drake asked.

"I think he's the Chinese patrol boat captain," Sebastian said, holding his cell phone to his ear with Poseidon on the line. "He has a grudge against Pham Kai. He's working alone."

WANG LI WAS exhausted, more so than he'd ever felt in his life. He just wanted to lie down and go to sleep. "You don't understand," he said weakly. "I'm a loyal soldier, following orders. All I want is respect and recognition."

"And you think respect and recognition comes from hurting people who are weaker than you?" Pham Kai asked softly. He stepped between Wang Li and the snipers, placing a hand on the man's shoulder. "I will not let them shoot you. You've lost your way. Your ego and pride have gotten the best of you. It's time for you to rise up and become a man who defends the weak."

As the red dots disappeared from his chest, Wang Li truly saw Pham Kai for the first time. The man he loathed and wanted to destroy was reaching his tormented soul. "Who are you?" Wang Li asked.

"I'm just a fisherman trying to save the love of his life," Pham Kai answered.

For the first time in years, Wang Li felt something he had

never experienced—his soul felt at peace. He removed the brass knuckles from his hand and placed them in his pocket, lifting his hands into the air.

Navy SEALs boarded the Skjold and escorted Wang Li onto the *Bainbridge*. Minh was visibly shaking, looking weak and frail. Pham Kai hugged her tightly and spoke in her ear. "It's over, we're fine. Relax, all is well." She hugged him back, sobbing.

Vu bowed, offering deep respect for how Pham Kai had diffused the situation. Pham Kai bowed his head in return, still holding Minh close.

After Wang Li had been escorted off the Skjold, the team came over from the *Bainbridge* to check on them. On seeing the team, the three broke into a collective embrace. After all the hugs, Shiloh walked in holding a bowl of soup Minh had made.

"What? Stress makes me hungry," he said, feeling their judgment. "And wow, this is heaven." Mumbling with his mouthful.

They all broke out laughing as he devoured his second meal of the evening.

* * *

WHAT DO YOU mean, you didn't arrest the scientists and confiscate their research?" the secretary of defense shouted over the *Bainbridge* war room speakers. "Drake, you had direct orders! This is insubordination, Grounds for court-martial! You're throwing away your career on a bunch of idiots who don't know what's good for their country. I expected more from you. You're the fucking captain of one of the most powerful destroyers in the U.S. Navy. Act like one!"

"Dick!" Drake yelled, trying to get the secretary's attention. "These scientists saved my men, they know what's good for our country. I'm taking them to a secure location to give them an opportunity to explain their position to you."

"Drake, you have lost your mind!" the secretary continued. "These scientists are sharing their discovery with the entire world, which is a huge threat to the national security of our country! I'm ordering you to arrest them!"

"Dick, I don't have time for your political games," Drake replied.

"Drake, I'm releasing you of your command," the secretary ordered. "XO, you are now in command of the *Bainbridge*."

The XO responded without a pause. "Sir, on behalf of myself and the entire crew, Captain Drake is our chief and we'll continue to support him."

"You're a bunch of idiots!" the secretary somehow shouted even louder. "I don't understand what those stupid scientists have done to you, that you're willing to face a court-martial. That's where you're all headed!"

"Dick, you do what you need to do," Drake said, "but just to be clear, I'll protect these folks with everything at my disposal. These are American citizens, and they mean no harm to the United States of America or any of our allies. They're not our enemy. I recommend you stand down." He pressed the button, ending the call.

The war room was quiet, but only for a moment. Applause broke out from the senior staff. "No need for that," Drake said, holding a hand up for silence. He turned to the communications officer. "Patch my office into all active duty captains. I need to bring them up to speed and make sure they understand what's at stake here." He headed from the war room, gesturing for the XO to join him.

* * *

AFTER EIGHT HOURS of repair, *Bainbridge* was ready for travel. The goal was to escort the Skjold to a friendly port safe from any threats. They were barely underway when the

TAO announced urgently, "Sir, two Luyang-III class warships are approaching, one from starboard and the other from port. The three ships have us surrounded."

At the same time, the communication officer announced, "Sir, the Luyang-I captain wants to talk to you."

"Put him on the speakers," Drake ordered.

"Captain, the Peoples Republic of China orders your unconditional surrender," Zheng's voice echoed through the war room.

"Captain, if you think we'll surrender without a fight, you don't know me or any American warship captain," Drake fired back.

"Captain, you're surrounded and outgunned," Zheng argued. "The best course of action is to surrender unconditionally. We'll resolve our differences through diplomatic channels."

"Captain, all three Chinese warships have crossed the five-mile mark," the XO informed him.

"Fire warning shots at all three of them," Drake ordered.

The weapons officer fired three projectiles programmed to detonate two hundred feet in front of the approaching ships.

"This is a warning to you," Drake spoke into the speakerphone on his conference table. "If you don't cease your forward progress, we will engage you."

"Captain Drake, all three warships have locked missiles on you," Zheng replied. "We haven't fired because we want to end this amicably. In our last altercation, no one was killed. Let's not allow this to become deadly. After all, our nations are not at war."

"Well, if you don't want this to get deadly, stop your forward progress," Drake said. "If you cross the three-mile mark, we will fire upon you."

"Sir, six warning projectiles have been fired from the Chinese warships," the *Bainbridge*'s TAO announced.

A series of explosions thundered one hundred feet from the *Bainbridge*—two on the starboard side, two off the bow, and two off the port side.

Zheng raised his voice. "You are hereby ordered to surrender in the name of the People's Republic of China! You are not to move from your current location, or we'll fire."

"Captain Drake, I repeat, we have six missiles locked on you, and we will fire. You must stand down," Zheng ordered again.

"Captain Zheng, we're not surrendering, nor are we handing you the Skjold or the scientists. Do what you have to do. We're ready to engage," Drake said, hanging up.

Zheng conferred with the other captains. They agreed that they couldn't let the Skjold leave the area.

"Sir, the Chinese have fired low-impact laser-guided stealth missiles. Impact in three minutes," the TAO shouted.

Drake turned to his TAO. "Activate Trident."

"Aye, Captain," he confirmed, punching a code into the keyboard.

The top six monitors displayed a grid pattern representing the *Bainbridge* and the three Chinese warships. The prototype XN-1 Laser Weapon System, code-named "Trident," had been under testing prior to their current mission. Drake was ready to see it in action.

Trident immediately identified the missiles, converging on them to create the shortest vector. A silent, invisible laser was fired from the deck of the *Bainbridge*, and each of the projectiles disappeared from their monitors, destroyed in midair.

"What happened?" Zheng shouted. "Where did our missiles go?"

"Not sure, sir. They appear to have been destroyed," the Chinese TAO responded.

"How?" Zheng demanded.

"Sir, I don't know," the officer replied, his voice quavering.

Zheng got on the phone to the other captains, and they were equally perplexed. The Chinese warships soon launched a second volley.

"Sir, we have additional incoming bogeys," *Bainbridge*'s TAO reported. "Time to impact, three minutes."

Once again, Trident locked its laser and fired its lethal beam, neutralizing them in midair.

The three Chinese captains conferred over radio, wondering what new technology *Bainbridge* had deployed.

Drake pressed a button on the speakerphone that connected him to the bridge of the Luyang-I. "Captain, you can see that your weapons are powerless. We can neutralize anything you throw at us. Disengage and let us go our separate ways." He waited, but static answered.

"Captain, they've fired another volley of missiles," the TAO reported. "Time to impact, three minutes." A blinking red light appeared on his screen.

But the XN-1 grids weren't adapting to the incoming missiles. "What's the problem?" Drake asked.

"Sir, I'm running diagnostics. It appears Trident needs to cool down."

"Cool down? What the hell!" Drake shouted. The bridge waited in silence.

"Two minutes to impact, captain," another officer shouted.

"We need it operational immediately!" Drake ordered.

"I'm trying, sir!" the TAO acknowledged, typing hard on his keyboard.

"Sir, direct hits are imminent!" the XO shouted.

"Sir, Trident is offline," the TAO confirmed.

The war room became silent as they all watched the monitors highlighting the missiles headed their way.

Just when the impact was imminent eight independent projectiles breached the water far off the *Bainbridge*'s bow. Going at near supersonic speed, they reached the missiles in seconds, destroying them.

"What was that?" Drake shouted.

"I don't know, sir! The Chinese missiles have been destroyed by a defensive counter attack," the TAO replied.

"How, who fired?" Drake yelled.

The speakers of the war room crackled, and a strong voice came over. "Luyang warships, the Gotland-class attack stealth submarine of the Swedish Royal Navy orders you to stand down. You are firing upon our ally, the United Stated of America. The slightest additional provocation will result in the firing of torpedoes that are locked onto all three of your positions."

Several hundred yards off the bow of the *Bainbridge*, the black submarine breached the surface of the water.

"Sir, the Chinese ships have come to a full stop," the TAO reported.

The speakers crackled again, and the same voice came on. "Captain Drake, this is Cebrián Alveraz, pleased to meet you."

"Cebrián, your timing is impeccable," Drake replied. "Pleased to meet you too."

"Captain, shall we head out before the Chinese fleet sends more ships?" Cebrián offered.

"Gladly," Drake agreed. "May I recommend we proceed to Okinawa Naval Base? It's a short trip, and it'll deter the Chinese from attempting anything stupid."

There was a brief silence. "That's a splendid idea, captain," Cebrián replied. "We're plotting the course now."

Captain Drake reconnected with the Luyang-I captain, who was none too happy with the outcome. "Captain Zheng, we're heading out immediately. Before we go, I'm sending over your patrol boat captain. He tried to hijack the Skjold. My

Navy SEALs will drop him off shortly."

"Understood," Zheng replied, fuming. He knew he was beaten, between the new secret weapon on *Bainbridge* and with the arrival of Swedish submarine the odds of winning had dramatically gone down.

* * *

A CHINESE COMMANDO team on the deck of the Luyang-I stood ready to receive Wang Li. Their guns were drawn, and they ordered him to get on his knees and clasp his hands behind his neck—just like he had ordered Pham Kai, Minh, and Vu a few days prior. He heard the RIB pull away, making its way back to the *Bainbridge*.

They escorted him through several bulkheads and a series of stairs, deeper into the bowels of the ship. They walked through another set of locked doors to an area containing five cells. The commandos kept walking, opening another door to reveal a room with several bunk beds, lockers, and a bathroom.

"Wait here," one of the commandos barked. "The captain will meet with you shortly."

They left the room, shutting the door behind them, a series of locks clicking into place. He sat on one of the bunk beds and waited. He knew they were going to process him and hand him over to the authorities once they got to the port of Shantou. His career, his dreams, his life, and his identity were gone. The government would make an example of him, showing everyone how not to act as an officer in the Chinese Navy.

Minutes later, Zheng walked in, the door locking behind him. Wang Li stood and saluted.

"Sit down!" Zheng ordered. Wang Li obeyed, staring straight ahead.

"Wang Li, you're the dumbest sailor I've ever met," Zheng said, disgusted. "Why the hell did you jump off the inflatable boat? Why did you swim toward the Americans? Don't you have any common sense?"

Wang Li didn't say anything—he had been reprimanded by senior officers enough to know to never respond. Zheng waited, expecting him to defend himself. "You are one lucky son of a bitch. I wanted to see you court-martialed, but the head of Naval Intelligence wants to meet with you—you're one of the few sailors who've ever been inside the *Bainbridge*. He thinks you might also know something about their new defensive weapons."

Wang Li couldn't believe what he was hearing. He kept looking straight ahead, still unsure if he was in trouble, or if he was going to be rewarded for his actions.

"I'm going to have you detained here until we arrive at Shantou," Zheng said, walking toward the door. "They may think you're some kind of espionage superstar, but I certainly don't. As I've already made clear to you, I don't believe you're worthy of your uniform."

"How d-dare you say that." Wang Li responded. Zheng stopped in his tracks and turned around as Wang Li stood. "I *am* worthy of my uniform. The Chinese Navy is my life."

"Sit down!" Zheng barked, approaching him swiftly. "Who gave you permission to stand?"

Zheng caught the briefest glimpse of a fist, brass glinting in the light.

Wang Li struck the captain squarely on the mouth, breaking his front teeth and splitting his lips. Zheng's head jerked back violently, blood and saliva spraying upward as he fell to the floor. He lay there in shock, sprawled out. Instinctively, he raised his hands, shouting for the guard, who unlocked the door and stepped in.

"Arrest this bastard and throw him in a cell!" Zheng shouted. The guard drew his sidearm and cocked the trigger. "You idiot!" Zheng screamed at Wang Li, holding his bleeding mouth. "You're finished! You're a dead man!"

Wang Li smiled, raising his hands and following the guard. "Just be glad I didn't kill you," he told Zheng. "Nobody tells me I'm not worthy of my uniform."

Wang Li didn't know it at the time, but his career was truly starting to take off.

* * *

THE PARAMARINES TRANSFERRED over to the Gotland. Both ships were now headed to Okinawa Naval Base. Hamza had taken control of the Skjold and was returning it to its original location. The team made sure the boat was cleaned up and in good condition.

The team went down the narrow opening into the submarine. Even though it was formidable, it still felt cramped. Fabienne held the box that had all the nodules and slides—she didn't want anyone else to carry them.

The officer who greeted them took them through several different levels to reach a conference room where Cebrián was waiting. "Welcome, Paramarines!" he exclaimed with a broad smile.

Fabienne and Maria hugged him, and everyone else shook hands. Cebrián was delighted to see them.

"Hello, Charles," Cebrián said, shaking Charles' hand.

"Doctor Alveraz, good to meet you," Charles responded.

He greeted Vu, Pham Kai, and Minh with a bow. "Vu, would you please share with our honored guests that you have informed us of Minh's medical situation, and we would like our ship's doctor to take a closer look at her?" he requested.

Vu nodded and whispered the news. Pham Kai bowed with gratitude. Cebrián requested the officer standing outside the conference room escort Pham Kai and Minh to the medical bay.

"Fabienne, I understand you're holding the prized nodules," Cebrián said. "Let's move them to a secure location. I've arranged for a special cold storage facility on the ship that we'll house them in. But let me have a look first!" She handed him one, and he studied it closely. "What wondrous miracles of evolution."

"Nidal," Cebrián continued, "please connect your diver's camera to the monitor. I'd like to see the video again of your adventure with the subterranean specimen. Start it from the time you saw the maroon sea and found the obsidian crystals, and play it until the point you guys return from Sydney."

For the next hour or so, they were all transfixed by the monitor. They could barely believe what they'd experienced.

The video wrapped up and Cebrián addressed the team. "So, Paramarines, how are you feeling about all that has happened?"

"Where do we start?" Fabienne said. "In the last few weeks, we've completely changed our understanding of time and space—more accurately, we understand them less than we did previously."

Cebrián nodded in agreement.

"Shiloh, tell me about the portable time warp device you've built. That's quite an ingenious machine."

Shiloh shook his head, running his fingers through his hair. "It's nothing big, it's based on the principles of MALDI-ToF operations. All I did was miniaturize it and add a software application that helps us create and manage the time fields."

"Excellent job," Cebrián said. "Okay now, let me bring you guys up to speed. While you all were locating the source of the specimen, the Honeycomb team has been busy working out the manifesto for the proper use and application of the time nodules. We were also debating where we should have their research center. We've decided that we aren't going to harvest them from the subterranean species. We'll work on cloning them instead."

"Where is this cloning research going to be conducted?" Fabienne asked.

"I knew you'd be the first person to ask that question," Cebrián smiled. "There's a small fishing village one hour north of Boston called Gloucester. I'm helping the town develop a new Marine Genomics Research Institute. We'll house our research there."

He turned back to Shiloh. "Shiloh, you'll oversee the development of a robotics facility in Lawrenceville, near Pittsburgh. There's a large blue building on Hatfield Street that's fast becoming the hub for all robotics research in the country because of its close proximity to Carnegie Mellon. All major corporations are moving into that location to develop their robotics. The goal of this research lab is to create robotic machines that will use the time nodule to create time fields for major tasks like removing plastics from our oceans within months instead of decades." Shiloh stretched his hand out and gave Cebrián a high five.

Cebrián then looked to Sebastian and said, "Our third research facility will be the home of the World Temporal Organization. At this facility, we'll conduct additional research on the time particles—what they do, how they work, and their various applications. We'll also research the subterranean travel you experienced, which I call 'Dune Travel.'" He pondered for a moment and then continued. "This facility will be responsible for developing the rules and laws of temporal applications."

"Where will it be located?" Sebastian asked.

"That's still up in the air," Cebrián replied. "Dmitry is requesting we set up operations in Russia. I'm leaning toward a politically neutral place whose government lacks an agenda. Placing this facility in the U.S., Russia, China, the UK, France, or any other such country creates that risk. I believe the World Temporal Organization should be remote as well. I've been in touch with the head of India's scientific research, and he has recommended that their Bharati facility in Antarctica may be a good option. It's remote, we can equip it with all the latest scientific gear, and freely perform experiments without causing any major social repercussions."

"Doctor Cebrián, could you please report to sick bay?" The submarine captain's voice came through the speaker.

CHAPTER TWENTY-FIVE

Minh

FABIENNE, SEBASTIAN, AND Cebrián rushed to the infirmary. "What happened?" Cebrián asked.

"I'm not sure," the doctor replied. "She was fine when I started my examination. Per the information I've received from you, she is indeed suffering from some form of breast cancer. We were performing a routine checkup when her blood pressure fell and her pulse slowed. I think she was running on pure willpower and adrenalin. She collapsed while I was performing my examination. I have her on oxygen, but looking at her eyes, we believe she's fallen into a coma."

"A coma?" Sebastian asked.

"Yes, I've seen this several times," the doctor explained. "It appears that late-stage cancer patients often run on adrenalin, and when they relax and calm down, it is then that their bodies give up."

"But she's been fine thus far," Sebastian said, realizing the big burden both Pham Kai and Minh had been carrying all this time.

Pham Kai was seated next to Minh, holding her hand. They all hugged and reassured him, telling him that all would be fine.

On Sebastian's request, Minh was transferred into the hermetically sealed pod Cebrián had brought from Scripps. She looked frail, but peaceful. Pham Kai sat outside the pod, looking in through the glass window. Sebastian sat with him for hours. It was going to take them another twelve hours to get to Okinawa Naval Base, where modern Western medicine could be applied. According to the Gotland doctor, it was likely already too late. He didn't have the ability to perform a CT scan or an MRI, but based on his professional experience and looking at her vitals and responses, it was now a matter of days.

Fabienne walked in to check on Minh. She placed her hand on Pham Kai's shoulder and stood next to him. She opened the pod door and walked inside, taking Minh's vitals and noting them on the clipboard next to her bed. She stepped out and shut the door, looking at Sebastian. "I know what you're going to ask."

"So, what do you think?" Sebastian asked turning to her.

She shook her head, searching for the right words. "Look, it's a long shot. We have no idea what the *Fisio* time particles would do to Minh. They may make the cancer cells stronger, we really don't know."

"Fabienne, Minh has already gone into a coma. We're biologists—we know that once that happens, the end is close. I've spoken to Pham Kai, and he agrees. Even if there's close to zero probability that Minh's condition improves, we have to try it."

"Sebastian, it may hasten her demise," Fabienne insisted. "Please explain to Pham Kai that this isn't a tested medical practice. Once we activate the *Fisio* time particle field, we won't know how she'll react. He may lose her."

"Yes..." Pham Kai said, understanding. He couldn't speak

English, but he had picked up a few words. Pleading he repeated. "Yes."

Fabienne hugged him and nodded.

Pham Kai had a permanent set of worry lines across his forehead, which had become further pronounced in the last few hours. Sebastian had already explained the risk, and he was willing to take it.

Seeing the gaunt face of his wife through the window was tearing at Pham Kai's heart. His partner, who had lived her life courageously, who had stood by him all these years, who had given him the strength to live the daily grind with dignity, was now lying in a plastic bubble. He had to try.

Fabienne wiped her own tears. "Okay, let's do it. I'll work with Shiloh and set it up."

* * *

HOURS LATER, MARIA joined them. "How's she doing?" she whispered.

"She's been under the *Fisio* time field for some time," Sebastian explained, hands clasped behind his head. "Since cancer spreads when a chromosome signals the cells to multiply, we're hoping the *Fisio* particle shuts it down so the cells don't receive the signal."

Maria noticed Sebastian's worry. Through all the impossible situations they'd been through, nothing had fazed him. But this was different—she knew he felt helpless. She hugged him, knowing there wasn't much she could say.

Fabienne, Shiloh, and Sebastian kept quiet during the ride to the hospital. They had reached Naha military port, and per Cebrián's instructions, a medical team and chopper were already waiting. Minh and Pham Kai were on the chopper, headed to the hospital.

The SUV pulled in front of a modern-looking building, and they registered as guests with the receptionist, who gave them directions to head up to the third floor, turn right, and follow the blue line on the floor. They sat in a small florescent-lit waiting room for forty-five minutes.

Just when Sebastian was about to check with the nursing station, a doctor approached them, reaching out her hand. "Hi, I'm Doctor Matsumoto. You must be Sebastian."

Sebastian shook her hand and responded, "Hello, Doctor Matsumoto."

"I have some conflicting news," she continued. "Minh is currently stable, but her MRI indicates a rather large nodule in her cerebral cortex and another in her left breast. I have a team of doctors looking over her reports, lab results, and MRIs. We're unable to make any sense of it based on the size of the nodule in her brain and the fact that her cancer has metastasized to such a large scale." She paused. "I'm not sure how to say this, but she shouldn't be alive."

Sebastian nodded. "I understand, doctor. We've performed an experimental treatment to help stabilize her. You're seeing the results of our work."

"What kind of work is this?" the doctor asked. "Her cells are behaving as if they were reversing the effects of the cancer."

Ignoring the comment, Sebastian asked, "What are our options, doctor? How can we cure her?"

Fabienne and Shiloh came over to hear what was going on. Dr. Matsumoto asked them to join her in the examining room where a monitor displayed Minh's brain. "You see, this dark spot on the cerebral cortex, we need to remove it. Two surgeons perform this type of surgery—one exposes the area, and the other removes one cell layer of the tumor at a time. Both surgeons have to work in perfect synchronization. This type of surgery takes many years of practice, with twenty years of experience required between the two surgeons before they can do the procedure. Over the years, they form an unspoken language—one practically knows what the other is thinking."

"I'm still not seeing the problem," Sebastian said.

"My partner, who performs this surgery with me, has gone on a hiking trip in the mountains of Nepal. There's no cell coverage there. I can't reach him, and he won't be checking in for another two weeks. I have another surgeon, but she's new—performing the surgery with her would require a precise modeling of the tumor, cell-layer by cell-layer, and that would take weeks of lab work. We have a few hours, or maybe a day at best, before we lose her. I'm sorry. I really don't know what else to do." Dr. Matsumoto took a step back from the monitor.

Fabienne glanced at Sebastian. He nodded. "Doctor Matsumoto, what if we told you that we can help?" Fabienne said.

Matsumoto raised an eyebrow at her.

Fabienne continued. "You and your new surgeon would be in perfect synchronization. You'll operate as a single mind."

"How would that be possible?" the doctor asked. "I've performed this kind of surgery with the new surgeon once, and it was nearly impossible. You don't fully understand the complexity. We use the Da Vinci robot. She manages the two left arms, and I manage the two right arms. Both surgeons have their precise 3-D model, and we follow it. To further complicate matters, we also have to have another surgeon removing the breast cancer, so there will be three surgeons operating at the same time. It just can't be done! Finally, she has fallen into a coma. It's simply too late."

"Doctor Matsumoto, the same technology that stabilized Minh can be used to help you perform the surgery," Fabienne explained.

Dr. Matsumoto paused. She kept looking at the floor, thinking. "I'm not sure how all this will work out, but I feel I must listen to you. Let's meet in the conference room, and you can share how your technology may help." Dr. Matsumoto pulled out her phone and walked away, giving instructions to her team.

Fabienne turned to Shiloh. "Let's get the time warp device ready. Do we have the *Divinio* slide?"

"Yes, I packed all the slides in case we needed them and the device is all charged and ready to go," Shiloh said.

The three of them sat down with Pham Kai, and using a hospital-provided interpreter, they explained what was happening. Given the location of the tumor, Minh could have serious disabilities if something went wrong. He listened to them, giving a nod for them to proceed.

The conference room was fitted with monitors, and they could see Minh's MRIs of her brain and torso. Three doctors sat reading reports, and four nurses were seated in the rest of the chairs. Dr. Matsumoto was seated at the head of the table. "So, tell us about this new technology of yours."

"Doctor Matsumoto, without going into the details of our research," Fabienne said, "we'll share the facts with you. We have here a device." She gestured at Shiloh, who pulled out the time warp device and placed it on the table.

They all stood up to look at it. "What is it?" Dr. Matsumoto asked.

"It's a portable Matrix-Assisted Laser Desorption/ Ionization device," Shiloh answered.

"What does it do?" one of the doctors asked.

"It's a device that emits time particles," Fabienne said.

Pin-drop silence filled the room. "I'm not sure I comprehend what you're saying." Dr. Matsumoto said folding her arms across her chest.

"Doctor Matsumoto," Fabienne explained, "for the last three weeks or so, we've been researching a deep-sea specimen that has changed our understanding and comprehension of time. We've now found out that time is made of six discrete particles. One of the particles allows thoughts to be synchronized."

"So, you mean to tell me that this device will emit some kind of time particles that will align our thoughts in the operating room?" Matsumoto said, stammering a bit at the thought of it.

"Is it dangerous?" one of the nurses asked.

"Not that we know of," Fabienne answered.

"How does it work?" the nurse asked. "What will happen to my thoughts?"

"Well," Fabienne said, "the way we think it works is that when two or more people are performing a task, similar thoughts tend to align much more closely. But you'll still have free-flowing thoughts that are yours. Let's say you have to perform something to support the surgeons—you'll perform that procedure at the precise time the surgeon wishes you to perform it, without them having to ask you for it." Fabienne slowed her speech. "I know it's a lot to take in—you don't even know who we are, and we're sharing this astronomically absurd information."

"Well, the fact that it's so absurd makes me want to believe you," Matsumoto said, walking over to them. "Let's try it. Hell, if this works, maybe I can use this at home when my husband and I are making dinner. We keep bumping into each other."

* * *

SHILOH LOOKED LIKE a surgeon, complete with facemask, gloves, and a green gown. He walked inside the sterile operating room—there were two large workstations where the surgeons could view magnified images on their screens and use the hand devices to control the arms of the robot.

The Da Vinci robot was placed at the head of the surgery table. It had four arms, and they were all wrapped in sanitized blue plastic. The arms ended in sharp-looking scissors—it was like looking at a machine version of *Edward Scissorhands*. Dr.

Matsumoto and her partner took positions at their respective workstations. The third surgeon, who was going to perform an urgent radical mastectomy, had her monitor and instruments ready.

The anesthesiologist was also prepped, ready to make sure Minh didn't wake up or feel any pain during the procedures.

They wheeled her in on a surgical table.

Pham Kai, watching through the observation window, appeared strong—he had his usual thoughtful expression while staring through the glass, looking at the team working to save his wife. Sebastian and Fabienne stood to one side, giving him his privacy.

Fabienne walked over and explained to Pham Kai that when the *Divinio* particles were released, they wouldn't be able to see anything through the window. Pham Kai kept staring through the window, he was just glad his wife was getting the treatment he'd hoped she would get.

In the operating theater, Matsumoto turned to Shiloh and said, "Okay, we're all ready."

"When you notice an orange or rust mist in the room, you can start the procedures," he said, tapping the time warp icon.

In moments, the room filled up with luminescent orange particles. The nurses gazed wide-eyed at the mist.

Dr. Matsumoto observed the brilliance in the room as well, but was more concerned with gathering her focus for the surgery. She placed her head into the viewer that displayed Minh's shaved head, and began her work.

As the procedure progressed, Dr. Matsumoto couldn't believe how smoothly it was all going—they had reached the tumor with no difficulty, and had begun its removal, layer by layer. The pathologist stood by to provide instant results.

Halfway through the brain surgery, the surgeon performing the mastectomy informed them that her procedure was successful, and that she was now patching Minh up.

Dr. Matsumoto didn't respond to the announcement–she was staring through the viewfinder, preparing for the most dangerous portion of the operation.

The procedure called for a series of controlled transfers back and forth between the two surgeons, each controlling two of the four arms of the Da Vinci surgical robot. The delicate dance between the two required that one of them hold a blood vessel while the other removed the cancer cells, switching roles as they moved along its length. Both doctors had to know when to pass control to the other.

A nurse wiped the sweat from Dr. Matsumoto's brow. The doctor peered through the viewfinder, holding a blood vessel that if severed, would most certainly mean death. If she dropped it, it would sink deep into the brain tissue, and fishing it out would likely mean major motor failure of the arms and legs. But she had to release the blood vessel to get to the tumor tissue, and her partner had to keep it from falling.

Dr. Matsumoto could not explain why, but she knew it was time to let go of the vessel. As she did so, her partner's robotic arm inserted itself at the precise microsecond to catch it from falling. This passing to and fro of the blood vessel occurred several more times, and each time, they both knew when to act. They worked in silence as the entire operating team watched in awe. They couldn't believe the level of dexterity and synchronicity that was occurring in front of them–it was as if Dr. Matsumoto and her partner were one person.

"We're clear," the pathologist said in a hushed tone. "The last set of layers don't have any tumor cells. We're good."

Dr. Matsumoto let go of the controls and lifted her hands. All that remained was closing Minh back up, and her partner had that covered. She sat, looking through the viewfinder and making sure all went well.

Once completed, Shiloh and the operating team walked

out of the operating theater in silence, still in awe at what they had just done.

Three days later, in a dark room lit by the red, ambient light of LEDs, a soft voice said, “Pham Kai, I’m thirsty.”

CHAPTER TWENTY-SIX

Masters of the Broken Watches

SECRETARY OF DEFENSE Richard Richardson paced around the Oval Office. "Mr. President, your friend Cebrián is out of control. He commandeered a Swedish Gotland-class stealth submarine, complete with a full complement of crew, took them deep into the South China Sea, and fired on a sovereign Chinese destroyer. The Chinese government is up in arms, and they're looking for restitution."

The President raised his eyes from the full report already sent to him by Cebrián. "Dick, calm down. Cebrián saved the *USS Bainbridge* and her crew. Have you read these reports?"

"That's precisely my point, Mr. President," Dick said, raising his voice. "Cebrián has gone rogue! Did you know he also stole a Skjold-class stealth warship for his operations? I tell you, he has become too powerful. We need to arrest him."

"Dick, just listen to yourself," the President said, irritated. "You're calling him rogue, yet you're the one who authorized the use of force to retrieve the specimen without my approval."

"Mister President, you know I'm deeply loyal to you and our country," Dick said, lowering his voice out of respect. "My actions have only ever been meant to protect you and this great nation."

"Yes, but wrong actions taken for the right reason don't make them right," the President responded. "I know your heart is in the right place, Dick, but the world has changed. A discovery like this can't be contained. Cebrián is doing the right thing. He's already put in place a World Temporal Organization that's developing a manifesto of rules and regulations." The president paused. "Dick, I recommend you fall in line here and stop creating issues for Cebrián and his team."

"Respectfully, Mr. President, I don't agree with you on this one," Dick said. "My job is to protect this nation, and I *will* do my job. Cebrián has jeopardized the safety and success of the United States, and for that he is going to pay a heavy price." Dick stood up and leaned on the opposite side of the President's desk. "And until you fire me, I'll do what you appointed me to do."

The President leaned back in his chair. "Dick, I challenge you to stop him. He'll outsmart you at every turn. Call a congressional hearing to investigate his actions."

"Challenge accepted," Dick said. "You don't see it now, but Cebrián has already committed treason by sharing this discovery with the world."

"No, he hasn't," the President said, sighing. "You, on the other hand, have come dangerously close to committing the very crime. Now go, call the hearing and get out of my office."

Dick got up and left the Oval Office, mumbling under his breath.

* * *

"I CALL THIS session in order," Senator Edmond Price said after hitting the gavel twice on the table. "Each committee member will get five minutes to read his or her statement and ask a question. A committee member may yield their time to a fellow member. Doctor Cebrián, do you understand the meaning of this investigative hearing?"

"Yes sir, I do," Cebrián answered. He sat at a table with Sebastian. They both wore dark gray suits. The hearing was being televised as per the president's request. Both political parties had picked a team of nine senators and congressmen to head the investigation. The chair, Senator Edmond Price, was from the majority party, and Congresswoman Renee Parker was the ranking member of the minority party. Given the significance of the subject, all major U.S. networks were covering it live. Reporters and journalists from all over the world had converged for the hearing.

The audience in the room was packed with scientists and researchers from major universities. They were attending to support their partner, Cebrián.

Maria, Fabienne, Shiloh, Nidal, and Michelangelo sat right behind Cebrián and Sebastian. Maria was wearing a black fitted suit. Shiloh had his hair pulled back and was wearing a sports coat. Fabienne wore a white suit with a red shirt that accentuated her red hair. Nidal and Michelangelo were dressed in their formal Navy SEAL service uniforms–double-breasted jackets with six gold-colored buttons and a black necktie. On TV, the seven of them looked prepared and ready to engage. There was already a hashtag trending on Twitter called #WhoIsMaria.

"Do you also understand the seriousness of what we're investigating?" Senator Price asked.

"Yes, sir, I do," Cebrián answered.

"In that case, I would want both of you to stand up and raise your right hand," Senator Price said. "Do you solemnly swear or affirm that the testimony you're about to give before the committee will be the truth, the whole truth and nothing but the truth, so help you God?"

Cebrián and Sebastian both responded, "I do."

"Please be seated," Senator Price requested. "Doctor. Cebrián, the committee here has been assigned to determine if you, your team members, or your organization, have committed treason. Let me read it exactly how it's written in this document. 'An investigative hearing is conducted to determine when there's a suspicion of wrongdoing on the part of an official or private citizen whose actions now require the need for legislative action.'"

Senator Price was a man who looked and acted the part of an elder statesman. His white hair was combed back perfectly, and his nose supported silver-rimmed reading glasses. His job was to keep the hearing on track and maintain order. "These are very serious allegations, and they come from one of the highest offices of our nation, Secretary of Defense Richard Richardson. He believes that your actions have seriously jeopardized the safety of our country. He goes on to say that your actions have also hurt the growth and prosperity of our nation. That you have acted in a callous fashion with no regard to national security."

There was a shuffle and murmur in the audience. Ignoring the disturbance, he put the paper down and picked up another. "And here I have the report of your findings. It appears you and your team found a subterranean biological specimen that creates time nodules."

He paused, looking at both Cebrián and Sebastian, and then toward his committee members. "This specimen has a symbiotic relationship with certain marine life that lives inside the specimen and has learned to communicate with it. The marine life has also been able to add this time nodule to their anatomy through a biological opening. Using this time nodule, they're then able to release these time particles, giving them advantages in their daily lives." He cleared his throat and glanced at his committee members. "This sounds like science fiction. I feel like I'm reading a novel." A chuckle rippled throughout the room.

"These time nodules emit six different types of time

particles. One such marine life was accidentally caught by a Vietnamese fisherman that led you to this discovery." He shook his head in disbelief and continued. "In summary, and according to this report, our understanding of 'time' is now broken. Time as we all know, feel, and experience it, is never going to be the same. And one more thing, your team have collected over three hundred such nodules and distributed them to all the countries of the world." He looked up at the committee, Cebrián, and Sebastian.

He then consulted a third sheet of paper. "This is a report from Captain Francis Drake of the *USS Bainbridge*, explaining how your team used the time particles to save his men from drowning."

Cameras took a shot of Captain Drake and his XO John Paul Jones sitting two rows behind the Paramarines. Captain Drake had submitted his report against the wishes of the secretary of defense, but he didn't care.

The cameras continued to span the entire row. Next to Drake were three powerful men, guests of Dr. Cebrián–Rear Admiral Adalrik Karlsson of the Swedish Royal Navy, Fleet Admiral Alfred Burland III of the Royal Norwegian Navy, and Brigadier General Pete Montgomery of Andersen Air Force Base. The row was a massive display of brass. In addition to these men, the Chinese ambassador and the Vietnamese ambassador were there to provide any additional testimonials. The camera didn't catch him, but Basil Belen discreetly took a seat in the back.

Senator Price then turned around and lifted a foot-high stack of letters tied with a cord, placing it on the table. The thud was caught by his microphone, and the sound echoed throughout the hall. "These are letters from the heads of state of over three hundred countries and agencies, sending in their support for you and your Paramarines. This doesn't include the shipping container full of letters I've received from esteemed scientists, high school science teachers, college professors, astronauts, and medical doctors. Letters have come from all corners of the world, from the tiny island of Fiji to Australia. Even Israelis and Palestinians are united in their support of your work. I've received letters from celebrities and CEOs as well.

"So why, when there's such a tsunami of support from all over the world, from all walks of life, are we having this investigative hearing?" Senator Price paused and locked eyes with Cebrián. "It's because we wish to determine if any laws were broken. And now, I'll request my ranking committee member, Congresswoman Renee Parker from New York, to start the proceedings."

"Thank you, Senator Price," Congresswoman Parker said. "Distinguished committee members, Doctor Cebrián Alveraz, and Doctor Sebastian Miles—I've read all the reports, and I can't say that I fully understand the ramifications of this discovery. I do understand that this research is part of a bipartisan program funded by the U.S. government with..." She shuffled through some papers, "a budget of $300 million spanning ten years. And as I understand, your program is meant to find specimens that have special abilities and apply them through a process called biomimicry to help solve problems faced by humanity. Is that correct?"

"Yes, Congresswoman, that's an accurate statement," Cebrián answered.

"So, I have a basic question," the Congresswoman continued. "Why, when U.S. taxpayers are funding this research, are you sharing the outcome with the entire world?"

"Yes, this is what I'm talking about!" Dick shouted, watching the hearing in his office. "Great question, Renee! Show that bastard!"

Cebrián smiled and took a sip of his water. He pulled his microphone closer and said, "Congresswoman, you have answered your own question."

She looked baffled. "What do you mean?"

Cebrián continued to speak softly into the mic. "In your statement, you mention my proposal—to find specimens that have special abilities, and apply them through the process of biomimicry to help *humanity*. It's written in my proposal that my work will be used to help *humanity*. The definition of *humanity*, as by any dictionary, is humankind, mankind, man, woman, child, human beings, the humans, human race, mortals and Homo sapiens. The other definition is that humanity also means humanness, brotherly love, fraternity, sympathy, benevolence, and kindness. Where does it say humanity means only the citizens of United States of America?"

Applause broke out in the hall, and the chairman asked the audience to respect the Congresswoman's time.

"Thank you, Doctor Alveraz, for your answer. I have no more questions."

"Thank you, Congresswoman Parker," Senator Price said. "I'll now request Senator David Johnson from Maine to read his statement and ask his question."

Senator Johnson didn't care for niceties, jumping directly into his statement and question. "I, for one, don't agree with this view of brotherhood and apple pie. Let's all gather around the campfire and sing 'Kumbaya'. The world isn't that simple, Doctor Alveraz. What you have done has seriously endangered our country. Today, we have a failing infrastructure in America, homelessness is at its peak, and we're trillions of dollars in debt. We believe in capitalism, and this discovery would have given our nation much needed resources that would have been instrumental for its financial growth and prosperity." He paused. "Do you agree that you have seriously jeopardized the opportunity for a major financial windfall for the United States of America?"

Cebrián reached into his inside coat pocket and pulled out

a test tube. "What I have here is a test tube, with sand that I collected from the beach outside my office at Scripps." He opened the tube and emptied the contents on the table, creating a small mound. "I brought it here to prove a point."

Staring at Senator Johnson, Cebrián continued, "You see, this sand here, it's mostly made of silicon oxide, a material abundantly found everywhere in the world. In 1880, two scientists, who also happen to be brothers, Paul Curie and Pierre Curie, discovered that sand oscillates at a precise frequency—and one can predict the exact number of oscillations per second. It was a simple discovery. It took forty years for the first real oscillator to be developed, making it possible for the development of transistors, chips, and the current foundation of all our electronic devices.

"To answer your question directly—no, Senator, I absolutely did not jeopardize the financial well-being of our country by sharing this discovery. Capitalism isn't owning a resource and taking the whole world hostage for access to it. That, I believe, is called colonial mastery or imperialism. Capitalism is the existence of free market economy that allows for innovation, inventions, and development of amazing new technologies. If it weren't for companies like Intel, Motorola, Samsung, IBM, and others, we'd still be staring at this sand, not knowing what to do with it. The time nodules are like these sand particles you see on the table. By sharing this discovery with the world, it's like sharing the fact that sand oscillates at a precise frequency. It's science—and science represents fundamental laws of our universe that no one country will ever own."

Once again, applause broke out and the chairman had to settle everyone down. But this time, the clapping went on for a while, and the chairman had to keep asking for restraint and respect.

One by one, each committee member asked their

questions. Some yielded their time to their fellow members, and others asked almost the exact same questions. Cebrián stayed on point—not once did he appear flustered or out of control. He remained poised and polite, even when some members used strong language in expressing their opinions.

The President was also watching the hearing from his private dining room. He knew Cebrián would have no problem dealing with the investigative hearing. However, he didn't know that Cebrián would perform so well that he would end up winning the hearts and minds of the viewers.

The close of the hearing was soon at hand. "Congressman Damian Lucas from California has the final question," Senator Price intoned.

"Thank you, Chairman Price and ranking member Renee Parker, distinguished guests, and fellow members," Congressman Lucas began. "Doctor Cebrián, I, like all others on this committee, have been wowed by the discovery you and your team have found. Congratulations! I can say for myself that I'm blown away with all the possibilities the time particles will bring to our world. As you know, I come from a state that has developed some of the world's most amazing technologies."

He adjusted his glasses to read his notes. "I do, however, have one question. The reports state that you recruited a group of scientists from all over the world called the Honeycomb. All of the Honeycomb members constitute some of the world's top minds—and top hackers, two of whom hacked into the *USS Bainbridge* and the Chinese Luyang-I destroyer, creating all kinds of diversions to keep them from reaching their destinations. They also commandeered a Skjold-class stealth warship that your team used in their operations."

He placed his notes back on the table and stared, trying to read the expression on Cebrián's face, but there was nothing to read.

Congressman Lucas continued. "I also see you have an artificial intelligence supercomputer called Poseidon, which has the ability to break into the Pentagon and gain access to major satellites if the need arises. This artificial intelligence, as I understand, lives on a distributed network of computers all around the world, and is capable of encrypting any information that the finest international hackers couldn't gain access to. From these reports, I also see you have direct connections with the leaders of several countries, even their military leaders, a number of whom we can see seated in the audience today—Rear Admiral Adalrik Karlsson of the Swedish Navy, Fleet Admiral Alfred Burland III of the Royal Norwegian Navy, and Brigadier General Pete Montgomery of Andersen Air Force Base." Staring again at Cebrián he continued. "Phew, that is some firepower."

Congressman Lucas took a deep breath. "By the looks of all this, I feel you're running your program with complete autonomy. It appears you're not answerable to anyone—you have an amazingly large budget, with private planes and access to labs all over the world. You appear not to answer to any branch of the U.S. government. The President of the United States himself is a personal friend of yours—as are many of the world's most powerful leaders, for that matter."

Cebrián hearing the names of his friends turned and acknowledged them with a slight tilt and single nod of his head.

"So here is my question," Lucas said. "Shall we take this autonomy away from you and make it a controlled, monitored program?"

Lucas's question created a soft murmur in the room. Cebrián stared at the small mound of sand on the table. He remained quiet, to the point that his silence almost grew awkward.

"Great question, Congressman Lucas," he said. "I applaud you for asking me this very important, soul-searching inquiry.

Any answer I give will be an attempt to defend my actions. With your permission, I would like my partner Doctor Sebastian Miles to take the mic. Any explanation he provides will be satisfactory to me."

Sebastian, who had sat all day listening and taking notes, cleared his throat and took a sip of water to hide his surprise. He had no idea Cebrián would be passing him the baton.

He pulled the mic closer, adjusting its metallic neck to gain time and sort his thoughts. "Chairman, ranking members, distinguished members, guests, and friends. Thank you for giving us the opportunity to address your questions and concerns. It has been an eye-opening day for me.

"Over the years, while flipping through channels, I'd briefly pause on C-SPAN and catch the start of a hearing. It would hold my attention for about thirty seconds, and then I'd continue channel-surfing. I never paused to understand what was happening. Today, I've come to understand that these hearings we conduct are the epitome of democracy, where the government of the people, by the people, for the people can seek the truth. Chairman, with your permission, I'd like to stand."

The chairman glanced at his committee for any objections and gestured with his hand. "Please, feel free."

Sebastian stood up, picked up the wireless handheld mic from its rest, and walked out from behind the table. He stood facing the committee at eye-level. It had the effect of visually altering the balance of power, putting them on a more equal footing. Cameras were now following him, photographers scrambling out his way, moving to the side to take pictures.

"Thank you," Sebastian began. "The question asked by Congressman Lucas is the heart of this entire hearing. This hearing isn't about us sharing our discovery with the world, it's about the freedom and latitude with which we operate.

"Doctor Cebrián Alveraz's research program has

succeeded in recruiting dreamers, mavericks, and illogical non-conformists. We all joined because we knew that the only way to deal with the crises faced by humanity was to discover solutions on the edge of science—where, if I may say, no self-respecting scientist would ever go. Senator Lucas, we're not here because we want some kind of accolades and recognition. Your question suggests that we have a lot of autonomy, and you want to know if this autonomy would lead to arrogance and power that would corrupt us, correct?"

He paused and focused at the senator, who nervously cleared his throat. "You know why the leaders of the world support Doctor Cebrián Alveraz. It's because they know that the time for rhetoric, discussions, debates, and political nationalism is gone. Our world is facing an existential, catastrophic reality. We're facing problems that will most definitely wipe out the human race. We all thought it would be the nuclear holocaust, or a meteor, that would wipe us all out. Who knew that the mere act of living by the human race would cause its extinction?

"Logical, technical, and probable solutions won't work!" Sebastian said. "Senator Lucas, you ask about the autonomy by which Doctor Alveraz operates. It's this autonomy that will allow us to go to the deepest crevices of our earth, to scale the highest, most remote mountains, to go deep into jungles, sift through the sands of our deserts, and find the evolutionary specimens that will save our world.

"Whether it was by design or by accident, our leaders and politicians have done one thing right—they funded Doctor Alveraz's fantastical, almost impossible research, and gave him the autonomy to execute it.

"As a result, the first thing the research has given us is time. Time to save our world, time to find cures for deadly diseases, time to eradicate hunger, famine, malnutrition, and poverty. Time to travel the universe, and most importantly, time to expand our minds. So, Senator Lucas, I say to you, thank you. Thank you for giving us the autonomy we need to do our jobs!"

The room erupted with applause and cheering. The chairman didn't bother with the gavel. He just watched as the whole room broke into pandemonium. And that day, the world found out about Cebrián, Sebastian, and the Paramarines.

* * *

SHILOH'S FACE WAS larger than life on the big monitors. He was calling in from the robotics labs in Lawrenceville, Pittsburgh. He had just completed the technical development lab that would be used to create all kinds of devices using the time nodule.

On the other monitor was Fabienne, calling in from the village of Gloucester, near Boston. She was overseeing the design and development of the biological lab in the Marine Genomics Research Institute responsible for studying and cloning the time nodule.

Dr. Vu Ha was calling from his new office in Vietnam Maritime University. He had been made the head of his department.

Hamza, Talia, Dmitry, Josephine, Omar, and Kabir were beaming in from Bharati World Temporal Organization located in Antarctica.

Everything Cebrián had said in the submarine had come true. And after Sebastian's speech, Congress had cleared Cebrián and his team from any wrongdoing. He had been given complete autonomy to conduct his work.

Maria, Nidal, and Michelangelo stood in the middle of the POC in the basement of Vaughan Hall, building 8675. Poseidon's coral screen ran on one of the monitors.

The elevator doors opened and Maria's eyes lit up. Coming out of the elevator were two people who she and the team had developed a special fondness for—Pham Kai and Minh. Cebrián had flown them over from Okinawa, straight to San Diego. He had gotten special visas approved and invited them to join the Paramarines.

Behind Pham Kai and Minh were Adora and Charles, having flown in from Antarctica. Then, Sebastian and Cebrián stepped out.

They all met in the middle of the room, and among all the kisses, hugs, and handshakes, Shiloh and Fabienne voiced their jealousy. "Oh, my God, you guys are having a family reunion, this isn't fair!" Shiloh yelled. "FOMO! FOMO!"

They all moved into the conference room. The table lit up with all their faces, as well as Poseidon's deep blue colorful coral reef with a fish swimming from one end to the other. Sebastian traced the outline of the coral reef with his index finger It wasn't too long ago when he had first been in this room, where the adventure had started.

"Welcome," Cebrián said. Both Pham Kai and Minh wore wireless ear buds that translated what was being said in real time. "What can I say other than thank you, to all of you. When I had envisioned the charter of this research, I could never have imagined that our first biomimicry outcome would be of such a significant nature. I'm amazed how all of this has come together. From daring Vietnamese fisherman to linguists, adventurers and scientists, this team had to have this level of diversity to accomplish our goal. And most importantly—what I wish to share is that Charles, Adora, Pham Kai, and Minh have graciously agreed to join our team of Paramarines."

Everyone in the room started shaking hands and congratulating the four of them.

Charles interjected. He lifted his sleeves to show an elaborate tattoo on his right forearm. It was of the *Familia Sagrada*, the red Faberge egg, and the time nodule. The team all peered over the tattoo, smiling and feeling the significance of the moment.

Once the celebrations died down, Cebrián grew serious. "I strongly believe we haven't seen the end of Richard Richardson. I'm sure he'll be mounting a new attack on the legitimacy of our group. We know for a fact he has his team at the Pentagon monitoring us twenty-four-seven. He'll be waiting for us to make the slightest mistake that would justify a judicial clamping down of our work."

"What the hell is his problem?" Fabienne yelled.

"Fabienne, he feels he is doing the right thing. Our work and our principles are at direct odds with his philosophy and view of the world. For him, it's all about power and control. He genuinely believes that sharing the knowledge of the time nodule with the world has weakened the United States of America." Cebrián said. "I'm afraid now that the world knows about us and what we do, attacks like the one you guys faced at Anderson Air Force Base we all need to expect. Foreign governments, privately funded mercenaries, and militias will come after us. Our work provides the promise of amazing wealth, and that's where the danger starts for us. Which brings me to my main point." Cebrián grew serious, paused and out of habit rotated the outer bezel of his watch.

"Given the dangerous nature of our work, I'll understand if anyone wishes to depart from the team." Cebrián shared his thought.

They all looked around at each other, deciding who should speak. Sebastian was quiet—he wanted others to take the lead.

Adora spoke up. "Thank you, Cebrián. I, for one, am very concerned about the possible violent situations we'd land in, in our search for these specimens." She paused, looking at Charles affectionately. "On the other hand, I know how Charles and I are wired. We can't stand back and let you all discover the hidden animals without us."

Pham Kai and Minh were quiet. Knowing that they came

from a culture of deep respect, Sebastian understood that they wouldn't say anything until invited to speak. He asked Pham Kai to share his thoughts.

Pham Kai gently held Minh's hand and spoke in Vietnamese while Poseidon translated. "All my life, I have dreamt of being more than a fisherman. This adventure to save Minh has taught me one thing–I don't think I can go back to catching fish and selling them at the market. Even though it has been a good life for the two of us, I want to be part of something more." He kissed Minh's forehead. The room broke out in applause. He had summed it up for all of them.

"Pham Kai, I have something for you," Cebrián said. Pham Kai eyes grew larger, puzzled, but didn't say anything. Cebrián got up and pulled out a small box from his coat, and presented it to him with a bow.

Pham Kai, feeling embarrassed, looked at Minh. She nodded for him to go ahead. He opened the box, and tears started flowing down his face. It was his grandfather's wristwatch. Minh moved closer and held her husband's trembling hands.

"Okay, folks, I'll let you enjoy," Cebrián said, turning to the elevators. "I'm heading back to the office to read a new report Poseidon has submitted."

"What new report?" Sebastian asked.

Cebrián called for the elevator and then glanced at his Paramarines. Their eager faces said it all. He knew he would not be allowed to leave till he gave them some hint.

Stepping into the elevator he shared, "In the caves of Cappadocia, Turkey a new hidden animal may have been sighted. According to the locals this animal can change its shape to mimic other animals, and also appear in two different places at the same time."

As the elevator doors were closing he stuck out his hand and stopped them. The elevator complained by making a buzzing sound. He then shot off a final question, "Who would like to join me on this new adventure?"

Not waiting for an answer he removed his hand and the doors closed.

EPILOGUE

Cabrillo National Park – One week later

SEBASTIAN, YOU KNOW *something you're not telling us.* Maria's words kept playing in his mind. How did he end up communicating with the species? How did he know to follow the Rahpido tunnel wall that would get him to Sydney?

Sebastian stepped into the tidal pond. The usual surge of energy went through his body. He bent down and skimmed his fingers over the surface of the water. As soon as his fingers touched the water, the neural images came rushing back. But this time, they were different. The revelation shocked him, and shivers went through his entire body. All the mystery that had surrounded him throughout his life had now become clear.

He now knew where and when he had seen the red mist.

Sites to Visit

1. **Scripps Institution of Oceanography**: https://scripps.ucsd.edu

2. **Bocas del Toro Research Station**: https://stri.si.edu/facility/bocas-del-toro

3. **Ultimo Refugio**: http://www.ultimorefugio.com

4. **Darien and Cerro Tacarcuna**: https://lacgeo.com/darien-national-park-bioshere-reserve-panama

5. **Vietnam Maritime University**: http://daotao.vimaru.edu.vn

6. **Andersen Air Force Base**: https://www.andersen.af.mil

7. **Magellan Inn**: https://www.andersen.af.mil/News/Articles/Article/784284/andersen-opens-doors-to-renovated-dining-facility/

8. **Island Girl Coffee 'n' Quenchers**: https://www.islandgirlofguam.com

9. **Bombay Reef**: https://en.wikipedia.org/wiki/Bombay_Reef

10. **Bharati Antarctic Research Station**: http://www.ncaor.gov.in/antarcticas/display/377-bharati

11. **Gloucester - Marine Genomics Research Institute**: http://www.gmgi.org

ACKNOWLEDGEMENTS

These next paragraphs have been the hardest to write. How do you even begin, especially when armies of friends, family members, technical experts, scientists, and literary consultants have made this project a reality? How do you acknowledge them with your heart and say thank you?

The feeling of gratitude I have toward them is so strong that words on this page don't even come close to doing justice.

My daughter, Zoha, read the first ever manuscript and spent hours walking me through the areas that needed attention and rewrites. She went chapter by chapter highlighting my repetitions and inconsistencies. My wife, who had lost me for over four years while I was mentally and physically immersed in this project, gave me the support I needed to complete this book. And my daughter, Alina, who while accepting a new job, moving to a new city, selling her homes, taking care of an eighteen-month-old angel, still took the time to edit my first five chapters. My son-in-law Christian highlighted the fact that I needed to emphasize the main discovery of the protagonist.

My dear Farhad introduced me to his network of literary legends. My sweet Shaheen confirmed and edited all of the scientific lab equipment and recommended that I change Maria's gold bikini to a bronze bikini since gold was too cliché. My sister Roohi validated my recipes, especially when I only know how to make rice and omelets. My sister-in-law, Sobia, who reads two books a month, provided the positive and emotional support to get this book published. My brother, Arif, read the entire book on his phone. Being shortsighted he

ACKNOWLEDGEMENTS

would remove his glasses and hold the phone three inches from his left eye and read. And my sister-in-law, Kaukab, not a lover of science fiction still read the book and gave me her thoughts on the characters. My nephew, Kashif, who said "You are not a writer. You have not written a book, you have written a movie." My niece Hina highlighted the sentences that were her favorite and expressed her deep love for my characters.

Help also came from all walks of life, from my friends, Michael Kolbrenor, Ruth Netanel, Mellissa Salandro, Arnie Sholder, Leigh Bishop, Terry Reyes, Sandor Katz, Matthew De Reno, Andy Mecs, Shad Connelly, Keith Ferrazzi, Lynne Campeau Zapadka, Deborah Ledford, Maegan Beaumont, Elizabeth Law and Walker Kornfeld. You all made my work better and helped me get the story out of my mind.

Thank you!

ABOUT THE AUTHOR

RAZI IMAM is a Carnegie Science award-winning technology entrepreneur and the author of *Driven*, a John Wiley and Sons publication. His interest in creative writing began accidentally at the age of seventeen, when during the day he worked in the harsh dusty hot climate of Kuwait alongside some of the roughest blue collar workers who would spit and urinate on the side of the cargo ships, and then in the evening as a library clerk surrounded by literary professors, students and scientific books. He has an uncanny knack of creating stories that are a cross-section of global cultures, mysterious science, human ingenuity and hard-hitting action adventure.

His dream has always been to write books that would inspire readers to rise up and get involved in solving some of the greatest challenges faced by humanity such as hunger, poverty, illiteracy and disease.

He is also the CEO of the AI company 113 Industries, where his work in understanding human behavior acts as a catalyst for his stories.

For more information on Razi's new projects, please visit his author site: www.RazIimam.com

Made in the USA
Middletown, DE
22 May 2021

39510707R00213